In The Dark

Tessa Knox

Published by Tessa Knox, 2024.

This is a work of fiction. Similarities to real people, places, or events are entirely coincidental.

IN THE DARK

First edition. November 10, 2024.

Copyright © 2024 Tessa Knox.

ISBN: 979-8227474087

Written by Tessa Knox.

Chapter 1: The Fire's Embrace

The moment he set me down outside, I staggered, my knees too weak to hold me, and I wasn't sure if it was from the smoke or the sudden jolt of adrenaline that had twisted my insides. The cool night air sliced through the haze, but it did nothing to erase the heat that pulsed through my veins. It was as though the fire had branded itself onto my skin, and in some strange way, it had.

I drew in a ragged breath, my lungs still feeling like they were fighting the fire that had nearly consumed me. Aiden stood a few steps away, his gaze following me as though he could see right through the blanket of soot that clung to my skin, see the quiver in my hands, see the storm in my chest that I wasn't sure how to tame.

"You okay?" His voice was rough, like he'd been shouting through smoke and chaos, though his eyes were soft. Too soft. Too knowing.

I nodded sharply, the motion too quick, too forced. I wasn't okay. How could I be? The remnants of the fire were clinging to me—burnt wood, acrid smoke, and something darker. A shadow that lived in the space between us, one that neither of us wanted to acknowledge. But it was there, thick and heavy, just like the heat from the flames that had threatened to take everything I had.

"Yeah, just—" I looked at the wreckage behind me, the silhouette of my apartment building crumbling in the distance like a broken dream. "Just a little shaken up."

He didn't look convinced. His lips thinned, his brow furrowing as he stepped closer.

"Look, I know you're shaken up, but we need to get you checked out, alright?" Aiden's tone was the kind that brooked no argument, but I'd learned long ago that I didn't do well with authority.

I shook my head, a bit too violently this time. "I'm fine. I don't need a doctor. I just need a minute." I took a shaky step away from him, barely able to keep my balance. My mind was reeling. I didn't know what was more jarring—the fact that my life had just nearly gone up in smoke, or the inexplicable surge of awareness that had ignited between us the moment he touched me.

He didn't let me pull away for long.

"Then let me help you sit down," Aiden insisted, his voice soft but firm, like a man who wasn't used to hearing no. I wasn't sure if he was the type to always get his way, but the way he moved, the way he held his ground, suggested he did. And the fact that I was even considering letting him, made me question my own sanity.

I met his gaze, that stubborn determination in his eyes. I didn't know why it irked me so much, but it did. I didn't need saving. I didn't need anyone to tell me what to do. But the fire, the one that had been inside me long before the one that had nearly killed me, was fanning itself to life in his presence. That was dangerous. He was dangerous.

Still, I nodded, too tired to argue further. My legs felt like jelly, and my head was spinning in circles, caught somewhere between the urgency of the fire and the strange magnetism I couldn't seem to shake off.

Aiden led me to the curb, his arm around me just a fraction too tight. Or maybe I was just too aware of how it felt, the warmth of his skin seeping through the fabric of his uniform, the gentle press of muscle against mine. I blinked and looked away, trying to focus on the blackened street and the flashing red lights that painted the scene in a garish hue.

He crouched in front of me, his fingers brushing against my chin as he tilted my head up to meet his gaze. "You sure you're alright?" The question was softer now, less of an order and more of a plea. His brow was furrowed, worry etched into his features in a way that was startling, as though he had seen something deeper in me that I hadn't even realized existed.

"I'm fine," I insisted again, my voice stronger this time. I'd never been one to show weakness. I wasn't about to start now.

But Aiden didn't seem convinced. He searched my face for a moment longer, his eyes scanning every inch of me like he could see the fractures I was so desperately trying to keep hidden. I couldn't understand why he was looking at me like that—like he saw through the layers of deflection I had so carefully built over the years.

And then, with a sigh, he stood, his large frame looming over me like a guardian. Or maybe a jailer, I couldn't decide. "Alright," he said, his voice tinged with something that might have been regret. "But you'll need to answer some questions later. We're going to need to make sure you didn't inhale too much smoke."

"Fine," I muttered, feeling the strange pull between us deepening, twisting my stomach into knots. I wasn't used to men like Aiden. Bold, assertive, too sure of themselves, like they could fix everything with a flick of their wrist. But there was something in his voice, something in the way his gaze lingered on me that suggested he wasn't just here to check boxes and tick off protocol.

I shook my head again, trying to clear the fog. I wasn't ready to deal with whatever was going on between us. But, as I glanced back at him, I realized that I might not have a choice.

Because Aiden was a fire. And me? I was already burned.

The ambulance ride felt endless. The city lights passed by in a blur, streaking through the open windows in sharp, jarring flashes. I kept my eyes focused on the movement of the lights, avoiding Aiden's gaze, which lingered on me as though he could see straight through the fog of exhaustion and adrenaline that clouded my mind. His presence was like the heat of the fire itself—undeniable, oppressive, and a little too close for comfort.

I couldn't shake the feeling that something had changed between us, something I wasn't ready for, but Aiden was never one to leave things unsaid. His silence was a heavy thing, thick with unspoken words, but I wasn't sure how to navigate whatever was forming between us. Not yet.

"You sure you don't want me to stay with you?" His voice was a low murmur, almost drowned out by the hum of the engine and the soft beeping from the heart monitor they'd hooked me up to.

I turned my head just enough to catch the glint of concern in his eyes, the way his lips were pressed into a tight line, the way his posture was ever so slightly tense as though he were on the verge of breaking through whatever walls I'd already started to build.

"I'll be fine," I said, though the words felt hollow in my mouth. I wasn't sure if I was convincing him or myself. "I just need some space."

Aiden's jaw clenched, a flicker of something unreadable passing over his face before he looked away, staring out the window with such intensity that I almost wanted to apologize. For what, exactly? I wasn't sure. The whole situation felt like something spinning too fast for me to catch. The fire, the smoke, the way my heart beat too quickly when he touched me—too much of it was happening all at once.

When we arrived at the hospital, the chaos of the emergency room was like stepping into another world, one where everything moved fast, and nothing felt like it had any true meaning. The cold scent of antiseptic stung my nostrils, the harsh fluorescent lights above casting everything in an unflattering glare. Nurses moved past us in a blur of sterile white and hurried steps, while doctors barked orders, and the hum of machines filled the air.

Aiden stepped back as they wheeled me into the exam room, but not before his hand brushed against mine—light, quick, but it was enough. His fingers left an imprint on my skin, a reminder that he was there, that he hadn't just disappeared into the background of my life, like so many other fleeting figures. I wasn't sure whether to be relieved or irritated. Maybe both.

The nurse, a no-nonsense woman with short, graying hair, hooked me up to an IV with practiced ease. "Smoke inhalation's a tricky thing," she said, her voice brisk, yet strangely calming. "You'll be here for a while, but I don't see any immediate damage. We'll keep you overnight for observation. How are you feeling?"

"Fine," I repeated, a little too quickly. "Just... tired."

She raised an eyebrow at me, like she knew the game, like she'd seen this act a hundred times before. "We'll see about that. You rest, and I'll be back in a bit to check on you." With a nod, she left, and I was left in the sterile quiet of the room, alone with my thoughts.

But I wasn't alone for long.

A few minutes later, the door creaked open, and I didn't have to look up to know it was Aiden. His presence filled the space, and I could feel the weight of his gaze as it settled on me, like a physical thing. I forced myself to focus on the sterile white of the hospital sheets, tracing the faint pattern in the fabric as if it could somehow ground me, center me.

"How's your breathing?" Aiden's voice was softer now, less authoritative, more... uncertain. He shifted from foot to foot, the tension in his posture still there, but this time, it wasn't the tight, commanding sort. It was something else—something more vulnerable. He was worried, and it was clear as day.

"It's fine," I said, avoiding his eyes. "I'm fine. Really."

He exhaled a slow breath, and I could hear the frustration in it. "You keep saying that. But you don't look fine."

"Look, I don't need a babysitter," I snapped, before I could stop myself. "I'm not a charity case. You've done your part. Now go back to whatever it is you do and leave me to do mine."

I could feel the shift in the room, the air thickening as the tension between us crackled. For a moment, neither of us spoke. Aiden looked at me, his expression unreadable, and I realized I had overplayed my hand. My tone had been sharper than I meant, defensive—like I was pushing him away, even though a part of me didn't want to. I wanted to reach out, wanted to feel the comfort of his solid presence, but I was too stubborn to admit it. Too afraid of what that might mean.

"Okay." His voice was tight, but his gaze softened, his shoulders dropping slightly. "I'll go. But you know where to find me if you need anything."

I didn't respond. What was there to say? I wasn't sure what I wanted, or how to deal with the way he was making me feel. So, I stayed silent, and he didn't push. He just gave me one last lingering look before he walked out, the door clicking softly behind him.

And as the minutes stretched into hours, I couldn't shake the feeling that, despite all the walls I had built, he was still there. A shadow on the edge of my mind. A fire, waiting for me to let it in.

The day after the fire was a hazy blur, as if the world itself had been scorched in the same way I had. I woke up to the faint beeping of a heart monitor, the sterile smell of antiseptic mingling with the remnants of smoke that clung to my clothes, to my skin. The hospital room was quiet, almost too quiet, the hum of fluorescent lights above feeling like the only reminder that time still moved.

I rolled over carefully, testing the ache in my chest, the soreness that had taken root the night before. It wasn't just physical—no, the burn ran deeper than that, into places I wasn't sure I wanted to acknowledge. It wasn't just the fire I'd survived. It was the way Aiden's dark eyes had followed me after the chaos had settled. The way his presence still lingered like the smoke in the air, stubborn and inescapable.

I hadn't expected him to show up again. And yet, there he was, standing in the doorway as if he'd always belonged there. His uniform was gone, replaced with a dark t-shirt and jeans, his usual crisp, confident demeanor replaced with something softer, more subdued. He didn't look like the same man who had pulled me from the wreckage of my life only a few hours earlier. He looked human. Vulnerable.

"Hey," Aiden said, his voice low, tentative. The quiet intensity of it caught me off guard. "How're you feeling?"

I glanced at the IV still attached to my arm and then at the rhythmic beep of the heart monitor. "Better," I said, more out of habit than anything else. It was a lie, but one I told myself as much as I told him.

He didn't seem convinced. His eyes scanned me, lingering for just a beat too long on the small bruise that marred my cheek, a souvenir from the night's chaos. I hadn't noticed it until I'd woken up. Funny how the body could be so good at hiding pain.

"Are you sure?" Aiden's voice held a thread of concern, like a lifeline thrown into the murky water between us.

I sighed, pulling the blanket a little higher around my shoulders as if I could shield myself from the weight of his attention. "I'm fine. Just... a little tired."

His lips tightened, but he didn't argue. Instead, he stepped into the room fully, closing the door behind him with a soft click that felt louder than it should.

"You know, you don't have to keep pretending," Aiden said, taking a few steps closer. The space between us seemed to shrink with every word, every beat of my heart that drummed faster. "It's okay to admit when you need help."

I stared at him for a moment, that familiar prickling sensation creeping up my spine. "I don't need your help."

He raised an eyebrow, a small smirk tugging at the corner of his mouth. "Right. I forgot. You're tough as nails." He crossed his arms, his posture shifting, no longer the concerned savior but something else, something a little more playful, a little more dangerous.

I sat up straighter in the bed, meeting his gaze with a look that dared him to push. "I'm not some damsel in distress, Aiden."

"Funny," he replied, his tone light but edged with something else, something darker. "You sure look like one."

The comment hung between us, thick and heavy, and for a second, neither of us spoke. There was an undeniable spark between us, something I couldn't deny even if I wanted to. But what did that even mean? Was it just the trauma of the night? The adrenaline still buzzing in my system? Or was there something more? Something deeper that I wasn't ready to confront?

I looked away first, focusing on the small window to my right. The world outside was a pale morning, the sun struggling to break through the mist that hung low over the city. I could feel the weight of his presence, pressing down on me, waiting for something—anything—from me.

"I don't need saving," I finally said, quieter this time. "I can take care of myself."

Aiden didn't answer right away. Instead, he took another step toward me, his eyes still locked onto mine. There was a shift in the air, something almost magnetic, like the pull of the moon on the tide, slow and steady, impossible to ignore.

"I didn't save you because you couldn't take care of yourself," he said, his voice low, almost a whisper. "I did it because... I couldn't let you die."

The confession hung in the air, raw and unexpected. I blinked, caught off guard by the weight of it. He was standing so close now, I could feel the heat of his body radiating toward mine, an invisible thread that seemed to bind us together, even though I wanted to pull away.

"I'm not... I'm not the kind of person who needs saving," I said, struggling to find my footing. My pulse quickened again, the words coming out in a rush. "I'm not that... fragile."

Aiden's eyes softened, the intensity of his gaze shifting slightly, as if he was seeing me for the first time, really seeing me. "Maybe not. But that doesn't mean you don't deserve to be saved."

His words struck something inside me, something I wasn't ready to face. My chest tightened, and I had to fight to keep my breath steady. Why was this so hard? Why was it so hard to ignore the way he was looking at me, like I mattered more than just the woman who'd nearly died in a fire?

And before I could stop myself, before I could shut down the thoughts and feelings swirling inside me, I asked the question I hadn't meant to ask.

"Why did you come back?"

Aiden's eyes flickered, and for a moment, it felt like the world stood still. The sound of the machines, the quiet murmur of voices outside the door—all of it faded into the background as he took a step closer, his breath warm against my cheek.

"I told you," he said, his voice so quiet now, so earnest. "I couldn't let you die. Not like that."

I swallowed, my heart thundering in my chest, but before I could respond, the door swung open, cutting him off.

Aiden stepped back immediately, his jaw tightening, the moment broken. I felt the weight of his absence as he retreated to the corner of the room, but I couldn't stop the rush of disappointment that flooded me.

The nurse entered, her gaze flicking between us with a knowing look that made my stomach twist.

"I'm sorry to interrupt," she said, her tone polite but firm, "but we need to check your vitals."

As the nurse moved around the room, Aiden's presence faded into the background, but something in the air between us remained—something unresolved, something that would not be ignored. And I knew, in that moment, that I wasn't done with him. Not by a long shot.

But as the nurse turned to leave, I heard her mutter something under her breath, something that stopped me cold.

"I hope you're ready for what's coming next."

I turned toward her, my breath catching in my throat, but she was already gone.

And in that silence, I wondered—what was coming next?

Chapter 2: Scars and Sparks

The moment Aiden stepped into the apartment, the air seemed to shift. It wasn't the dust or the faint smell of mildew that clung to the walls, but something far more palpable. I could feel the space between us stretch, thick with history, filled with moments we hadn't spoken of, things we hadn't acknowledged, but could no longer ignore.

He didn't look at me, not at first. His gaze swept the room like a soldier scanning an unfamiliar battlefield—calculating, weighing risks, as though he could sense something just beyond the surface. The bare walls of my new home must have seemed like a reflection of me to him—stripped down, vulnerable, raw. Aiden was the kind of man who noticed everything, every shift in a person's stance, every subtle change in the air. And right now, it felt like the very air between us had thickened with unsaid words, waiting to be unleashed.

The quiet was almost unbearable. The apartment, with its half-empty shelves and mismatched furniture, looked nothing like the polished homes I once lived in. But it was mine, built piece by piece from the fragments of a life I wasn't entirely sure I recognized anymore. I wasn't the same woman I had been, not after everything had burned. I wasn't even sure if I could trust the woman standing in front of him, but Aiden had no problem trusting me once. He had thrown himself into the fire to pull me out, a hero in the truest sense. And now? Now, there was nothing heroic in his gaze. Only a wariness I hadn't expected.

Finally, he turned to face me. His eyes—dark and shadowed—locked onto mine, like they were pulling something from the depths of me that I wasn't ready to give. I wanted to speak, but the words wouldn't come. I wondered if he could see the fear that clung to me, the jagged edges of the woman I had become. The woman who had barely survived. But he had known me long before the fire. He had seen me in a way no one else had. And I wondered if he saw the same person now, or if the scars on my skin, both visible and invisible, were too much for him to bear.

"You're doing this," he finally spoke, his voice low and steady, but with an edge that made my skin prickle. It wasn't a question. It was an accusation wrapped in a simple statement. Like it was my fault, like I had chosen this path.

I tilted my chin, forcing myself to stand tall in front of him, even though I could feel my body trembling slightly beneath the weight of his scrutiny. "I didn't have much of a choice, Aiden. You know that."

The words felt sharp and bitter on my tongue, and I regretted them as soon as they left my mouth. But it was too late to take them back. I was done being apologetic. I wasn't the girl who had needed saving anymore. I had learned to stand on my own.

He didn't respond right away. Instead, he took a slow step forward, his boots silent against the hardwood floors. His gaze never wavered from mine, and I could feel the air between us charge, crackling with tension. It wasn't just the past between us, but the unspoken things—things neither of us were ready to say out loud. I felt the weight of his stare, heavy with something more than just curiosity or concern.

"You're not what you were," Aiden murmured, as if he was speaking to himself more than me. His voice was quiet but firm, and I didn't know whether to be insulted or relieved. It wasn't a judgment, not in the way I had feared. It was a statement of fact, one that somehow made my chest tighten.

"Neither are you," I replied, my voice barely above a whisper. It was true, wasn't it? He wasn't the man I remembered, either. The easy confidence, the playful smile—gone, replaced by a sharpness, a hardness that hadn't been there before. It wasn't just the way he carried himself; it was in the way his eyes studied everything, as if nothing and no one could be trusted. I wasn't sure if it was the fire that had changed him, or if it had always been there, lurking beneath the surface, waiting for the right moment to emerge.

"I'm not the same man you knew, Caroline," Aiden said, his voice a little rougher now, like he was fighting to keep control of something, something I wasn't sure I could understand.

I didn't respond right away, unsure of how to articulate what I was feeling. The truth was, I didn't recognize him at all. But at the same time, there was a pull between us, an undeniable gravity that neither of us seemed able to resist.

"I know," I said quietly, stepping back toward the small kitchen counter. My hands wrapped around the edge of it as if it were the only thing keeping me grounded. I felt suddenly exposed, as though every piece of my soul was laid bare in front of him, and I couldn't hide behind the walls I had spent so long building.

Aiden took another step forward, this time closer than I expected. He was too close now, his presence filling the room in a way that left me breathless. For a moment, we just stood there, inches apart, neither of us daring to make the next move.

"I'm not here to pick up the pieces, Caroline," he said softly, almost as if he was warning me. His voice was a low murmur, but it felt like a punch to the gut. "You need to fix this yourself."

The words stung, more than I was willing to admit. It was like he was rejecting the very thing I had come to him for all those months ago. But maybe he was right. Maybe I didn't need him to save me anymore. The thought made my heart ache in a way I couldn't explain.

"I don't need you to save me," I said, my voice steadier now, even as my stomach twisted. "I'm not asking you to."

For a long moment, there was only silence. The tension in the room seemed to thicken, like we were both holding our breath, waiting for something to crack.

And then, finally, Aiden nodded once, as if agreeing with an unspoken truth between us. He didn't say anything else, didn't try to change my mind. Instead, he stepped back, his gaze lingering on me for just a moment longer before he turned toward the door. I watched him go, and for the first time since he'd walked in, I felt the smallest flicker of something in my chest. Something like hope.

But it was fleeting, vanishing as quickly as it had come.

It wasn't the first time I'd found myself caught in the quiet tension that hung between us, but this time, there was something different—something sharper. I watched Aiden, his broad shoulders tensing as he ran a hand over the edge of the window, his fingers brushing the cracked wood like he was measuring the distance between the past and now. His face, so familiar yet impossibly distant, reflected a thousand emotions, each one sharper than the last. He was a puzzle I couldn't solve, even though I had spent far too many hours trying.

I swallowed hard, my throat dry despite the sudden flood of thoughts in my mind. He was standing there, so close, and yet so far. A part of me wanted to reach out, to close that distance, to undo whatever had happened between us. But the other part, the more cautious part, wanted to retreat, to hide the mess of my emotions that would only seem foolish in his presence. Aiden never did well with weakness, and right now, that was all I had to offer.

"I never imagined you'd be back in my life," I said, the words coming out before I could stop them. I almost regretted it the moment I spoke. I wasn't sure what kind of reaction I was expecting—something like sympathy, perhaps, or even anger. But Aiden's expression remained unchanged, an impenetrable mask.

He didn't answer right away. Instead, he took another slow, deliberate step toward the door, his boots tapping lightly against the floorboards, his gaze flicking back to the window as though checking for something. The silence between us stretched, a thin, taut wire that seemed to hum with unspoken words.

"I didn't come here to make things complicated," he said finally, his voice low but direct. "I came because you called me."

My heart skipped a beat at that, a small flutter of something—guilt, hope, confusion—settling deep in my chest. I had called him, hadn't I? The desperation of the moment, the feeling that I was teetering on the edge, had made me reach out to the one person I thought could help. But Aiden wasn't someone you called for comfort. He was the kind of man you called for answers, for solutions—nothing more, nothing less.

"I didn't mean for it to come out like that," I murmured, wishing I could take the words back. My lips felt dry again, and I took a slow step back, pushing myself further into the cramped kitchen. There, the walls were just as unforgiving, their peeling paint and chipped countertops a constant reminder of everything that had gone wrong.

Aiden's eyes followed me, and for a moment, I saw something flicker—something almost human, a softness that I hadn't seen in him in years. But it was gone just as quickly, replaced by the familiar mask of control. He leaned against the doorframe, crossing his arms over his chest, his eyes narrowing in that way he did when he was calculating.

"You don't have to explain yourself to me," he said, his voice softer now, though still laced with that familiar undercurrent of authority. "But you're still running from something."

The words hit me like a slap, but I didn't flinch. Instead, I stood taller, my back straightening as if to shield myself from the truth he had just revealed. It wasn't the first time someone had pointed out my tendency to escape, to keep moving instead of confronting the things that haunted me. But hearing it from him, from Aiden—someone who had once known me so completely—felt different. His words were a mirror, showing me what I tried so hard to ignore.

"I'm not running," I said quickly, though even I could hear the lie in my voice. I didn't know if I was trying to convince him or myself. "I'm... just living."

Aiden raised an eyebrow, and I couldn't help but laugh, though the sound came out more bitter than I intended. "Living? Is that what you're calling this? A new apartment in a building that's about to collapse around you? A life spent running on empty, pretending everything's fine?"

I didn't answer him right away, my mind scrambling for some retort, some defense. But he was right. I had built my life out of nothing but fragments, a house of cards that could collapse with a single gust of wind. The fire had done more than steal my family's wealth; it had torn apart every sense of security I had known. And now, all I had were these cracked walls and a life that never quite felt like my own.

"I'm doing the best I can," I finally muttered, more to myself than to him. I didn't want his pity, didn't want his concern. But it was hard not to feel it in the way he looked at me—like he knew every crack in my armor, every secret I kept buried deep inside.

He sighed, a long exhale that seemed to carry years of frustration. "You don't have to do this alone, you know."

I turned sharply, my heart tightening at his words. I hadn't expected him to say that, not after everything that had happened between us. Aiden wasn't the type to offer comfort, to reassure people when they were falling apart. He was always the one who fixed things, who put things back together, who protected those who couldn't protect themselves. But I wasn't the same girl who had needed saving.

"I'm fine," I said, the words catching in my throat. I wasn't fine, but I would be. I had to be.

Aiden didn't argue. He simply nodded, his gaze shifting back to the door. There was something in his eyes, a flicker of something I couldn't quite place. Maybe it was regret, or maybe it was something deeper, something more complex than either of us could understand. But whatever it was, it was gone before I could reach for it.

He took one last look around the room, his eyes lingering on the mess I had yet to clean up, the unspoken story of my life etched in every corner. Then, with a final, unreadable glance at me, he turned and walked out the door.

And just like that, he was gone again.

The door clicked shut behind Aiden, and I couldn't quite shake the echo of his presence lingering in the room. It was strange—how someone could leave, yet still fill every corner of your space. He had always been like that: larger than life, leaving an impression even when he wasn't trying to. I stood there for a moment, half expecting him to come back, to knock or call out to me as he had so many times before. But he didn't.

Instead, I let the silence settle in, the kind that makes you realize how much you've been avoiding. The quiet in this apartment, for all its imperfections, was far too close to the chaos I had spent years trying to outrun.

I crossed the room, my feet barely making a sound against the creaky floor, and sank onto the edge of the couch. The place was far from homey, with its mismatched furniture and unfinished repairs. It wasn't what I had imagined when I'd first signed the lease, but it was mine. It had to be enough.

I wasn't ready to call it a day just yet. There were still too many thoughts crowding my mind, too many questions that circled me like vultures. What was Aiden doing here, really? Why had he come back after all these years, after everything? And more importantly, why had I let him leave without even asking?

The sound of footsteps outside my door jolted me from my thoughts, and I immediately stood up, heart racing. It wasn't Aiden—his heavy, deliberate pace was unmistakable. This was lighter, quicker, more familiar.

I opened the door to find my neighbor, Ava, standing there with an eyebrow raised, her arms crossed loosely over her chest. She was a whirlwind in every sense of the word, constantly moving, always a few steps ahead of the rest of us. Her hair, a tangle of wild curls, was pulled into a messy bun that looked far too stylish for someone who had probably just rolled out of bed.

"You're still up?" she asked, her voice full of disbelief, as though she knew exactly how late it had gotten.

"Just trying to figure things out," I said, avoiding her gaze as I stepped aside to let her in. I had no intention of explaining the whole situation with Aiden. Not to her, not to anyone. She would only ask too many questions, and I wasn't in the mood for that.

Ava didn't seem particularly bothered by my reluctance to share, though. Instead, she walked straight into the kitchen, rifling through the cabinets as if she had every right to do so. I smiled despite myself.

"You know," she began, pulling out a half-empty bottle of wine, "you really ought to stop making yourself miserable in here all the time. Come out with me. Let's go somewhere and pretend we don't have lives to ruin."

I leaned against the doorway, watching her with a mix of amusement and frustration. Ava was the type of person who believed that nothing was ever truly as bad as it seemed, and if it was, a drink—or ten—could fix it. I envied her ability to escape so easily. I had tried, once, to push away everything that weighed me down. But it had never worked. It had always come back.

"Maybe later," I said, though I knew that was a lie. I wasn't about to walk away from this apartment just yet, not while there were so many things left unsaid between Aiden and me.

"Sure," Ava replied with a shrug, already pouring herself a generous glass. "Whenever you want to be pathetic, I'm your girl."

I laughed at that, despite my mood. She had a way of making me feel like I wasn't completely lost, like maybe I could still find some semblance of normal in this mess of a life I was living. But as I looked at her, something gnawed at the back of my mind. She wasn't the only one who noticed the tension in the air. It had been creeping in since the day I moved in—an unspoken awareness that something was wrong, that things weren't as simple as they seemed. The fire, the aftermath, Aiden. None of it was ever going to fit neatly into the life I was trying to rebuild.

"Well, if you're going to be pathetic," she said, her eyes narrowing in playful judgment, "you might as well do it with a drink in your hand."

I reached for the bottle she offered, but before I could take it, my phone buzzed. The vibration startled me, and I glanced at the screen, almost expecting it to be Aiden. But it wasn't. The name flashing across the screen made my stomach twist.

Oliver.

I hadn't heard from him in months. He was the kind of man who slid in and out of your life without any warning. Charming, manipulative, a master of knowing exactly what to say to make you feel like you were the only one who mattered. He was also the kind of man who could break your heart with a single look, and that was why I had stopped picking up his calls. That was why I had stopped hoping he might want something more than what we had.

"What's that about?" Ava asked, leaning over my shoulder to peer at the screen.

I quickly pressed the button to silence it, not wanting her to see the name any longer than necessary. "Just someone I used to know."

She didn't ask any more questions, thankfully. Instead, she took another swig from her glass, her eyes dancing with a mischievous glint that meant she was already plotting her next move.

I placed the phone face down on the counter, trying to push the lingering sense of unease aside. It didn't work. The screen had already burned that name into my memory, and I knew it wouldn't be long before Oliver came knocking again. He always did, and when he did, it was like the world shifted on its axis, leaving you uncertain whether you were falling or flying.

Ava wasn't paying attention, her focus entirely on the glass of wine in front of her. But as I caught sight of the flashing phone screen again, a familiar, ominous sensation curled in my gut. Something was coming, something I couldn't control—and Aiden's return might be the least of it.

Chapter 3: Igniting Confessions

The air smelled of scorched timber and smoke. A kind of heavy, damp, earth-bound smell that clung to your clothes and made your skin feel coated with the aftermath of something that had once been. I stood at the edge of the ruins, watching the firefighters and investigators move through the rubble with a kind of grim determination, their footsteps echoing in the hollow silence of the burned-out shell of the building. The place had once been a quaint little cafe, the kind with mismatched chairs and half-filled bookshelves where people went to talk over coffee, their words mingling with the clink of porcelain cups. Now, it was nothing but twisted metal and blackened beams, as though the flames had sucked every ounce of warmth and life from the place, leaving only the bare, cold skeleton behind.

It was impossible not to think about the fire that had claimed my father's estate. The way the flames had devoured everything in their path, consuming memories and promises, and how my heart had burned with loss right alongside the manor. I'd come to the site today, not out of some morbid fascination, but because it had felt too familiar, like the kind of loss you can't look away from, even if it pulls you deeper into its abyss. And then, as if the universe had decided I hadn't suffered enough, I saw him—Jonah Hale—moving with careful precision among the ashes, his face drawn in concentration, lips set in a hard line, as though he was piecing together some puzzle only he could see.

The moment I spotted him, something inside me tightened. Maybe it was the way the sun caught the dust swirling around him, giving him an almost otherworldly quality, or maybe it was the fact that I hadn't expected to see him again—not here, not under these circumstances. I thought I'd been free of the pulse of tension his presence had woven into my every nerve. Apparently, I was wrong.

Jonah paused, crouching down near a pile of singed debris, his gloved fingers brushing over the blackened edges of a broken window frame. He didn't notice me at first, too absorbed in the scene before him. I took a step closer, unable to tear my eyes away from the way he moved, his every action deliberate, like a man determined to hold together pieces of a fractured whole. There was something fiercely protective in the way he handled the remnants of the destruction, like the building itself was something precious he needed to protect—even in its ruined state.

The creak of my heel on the charred ground was enough to catch his attention. He straightened, eyes narrowing slightly as they swept over me, scanning me in that way he did—like he was weighing whether I posed a threat or if I was just another interruption in his day. When his gaze finally met mine, there was a flicker of recognition, followed by that familiar flash of irritation that seemed to hang between us like an unspoken challenge.

"I thought I told you to stay away from things like this," he said, his voice low but firm, carrying a note of authority that made me bristle.

I was no stranger to being told what I could and couldn't do, and it had never sat well with me. I'd spent my entire life being shaped by the expectations of others—first my father, then society, and now Jonah, it seemed. He was no exception. My lips curved into a wry smile, one that was meant to deflect, but it came out sharper than I intended.

"I'm not a child, Jonah. I can handle a little fire."

He straightened further, those intense eyes of his locking onto mine as if daring me to prove him wrong. "This isn't some innocent curiosity, Olivia. There's something going on here, something that's deeper than you think. It's not a game."

A jolt of something I couldn't quite name ran through me at his words. I knew he was trying to protect me—trying to keep me at arm's length from whatever dangerous situation this fire was hiding—but there was a sharpness to his tone that made me bristle, as though he didn't think I could handle it. It stung. A lot more than I was willing to admit.

"Don't tell me what I can and can't handle," I shot back, taking a step forward into the ashes, letting the smoke and the soot coat my shoes. "I've already lost too much to start letting people tell me what I can and can't do. If I want to understand why this happened, I will."

Jonah's jaw tightened, and for a moment, I thought he might retort. Instead, his expression softened just the slightest bit, and there was something in the way he looked at me—something like exhaustion, but also a strange vulnerability I hadn't expected to see in him. He didn't speak for a long while, the only sound between us the distant crackling of firemen working in the background.

Finally, in a voice that was almost too quiet to hear over the chaos, he said, "This isn't just about a fire, Olivia. It's... it's personal. I've seen this before. And it's a hell of a lot more dangerous than you think."

The words hung in the air like the smoke, swirling around us, heavy with the weight of things unspoken. For a moment, I saw something more in Jonah than the aloof, almost irritated man who had crossed my path before. I saw the scars beneath the surface, the parts of him that had been burned by something far more painful than fire, something that had left him just as fragile as the wreckage around us.

"I don't think you understand," he murmured, his eyes flicking briefly to the wreckage of the building, his shoulders tense. "Some things don't burn. They just... linger."

There was a quiet intensity in his words, an edge to his tone that made my chest tighten. The air between us thickened, charged with the kind of electricity that made me want to reach out and touch the space between us, to see if he was real or if he was just another illusion, like everything else in my life.

"Then tell me, Jonah," I said, my voice softer than I intended, "what's lingering?"

Jonah didn't answer me right away. Instead, his gaze flicked over the remains of the building as if he were calculating something in the quiet of his mind, measuring the destruction, adding up the pieces that only he could read. The air seemed to hold its breath, waiting, the tension stretching between us like a taut wire. There was a slight tremor in his hands as he turned back toward me, the weight of whatever he wasn't saying pressing on him like the heat of the fire itself.

When he finally spoke, it wasn't the harsh, commanding tone I'd come to expect from him. This time, his voice was softer, threaded with something raw and unguarded. "You want to know what's lingering?" His eyes locked on mine, the usual steel of his expression replaced by something much darker, something that cut deeper than any wound visible to the eye. "The last time I saw a fire like this... it wasn't an accident. Someone set it."

I blinked, the words not immediately sinking in. It wasn't just a fire. It wasn't the casual tragedy of someone being careless with a match or a forgotten cigarette. No. This was something deliberate. Someone had lit the fuse, and everything here—the charred earth beneath my boots, the hollowed remains of a building I could almost imagine bustling with life just weeks ago—was a consequence of a hidden malice. My stomach churned, the realization crawling up my spine like a creeping chill.

"You're telling me this is... intentional?" The words felt like lead in my mouth, as though speaking them would make it too real.

Jonah's jaw tightened. "I'm not telling you anything you don't already know. You've seen it. Look around, Olivia." His voice dropped even lower, barely a whisper now, as if he was afraid the very walls of the building might overhear him. "I've seen this pattern before, and it's not a random act. It's something personal. Someone is targeting places, people... making it look like accidents. But it's not. It never is."

His eyes were searching mine now, almost pleading for me to understand, as though what he was saying could be so much more than a warning. And as that realization sunk in, something inside me started to shift. I wasn't just an observer anymore, standing on the sidelines, waiting for life to decide my next move. I wasn't just some heiress playing at being useful. No, this was real. This was a game I hadn't chosen, but that didn't mean I wasn't already tangled up in it.

I shook my head, more to shake off the dread creeping into my thoughts than anything else. "So, what do you want me to do, Jonah? Stay out of it? Stay out of the way and pretend I'm just another victim of circumstance?"

He ran a hand through his dark hair, a gesture I'd come to recognize as a sign of frustration. "You don't get it. This isn't some little mystery you can unravel by walking through a few ruins with a notebook, hoping for clues to fall into your lap." His voice was firm, but beneath it, I caught the faintest trace of something else—something deeper, something that almost sounded like fear. "There are people out there who don't care about how many lives they burn to get what they want. And they're getting bolder."

"I'm not scared of a fire, Jonah. I'm not scared of whatever shadow you think is hanging over this place." I met his gaze, stubbornness rising within me like a protective wall. "But you? You're scared of something, and I think it's bigger than the flames. You've been holding something back, and it's eating you up inside."

His eyes darkened, his lips pressing into a thin line as though my words had struck a nerve. For a second, I thought he might walk away, might just turn his back on me and leave me standing there with nothing but the ashes to keep me company. But instead, he took a deep breath, one that seemed to deflate the tension in his shoulders just slightly. And then, he spoke again, but this time, his voice was rough, like gravel scraped over skin.

"Years ago, there was another fire. Same thing. People thought it was an accident, but I knew better." His voice faltered for the briefest of moments, and in that second, I saw something in him I hadn't expected: regret. "I wasn't there in time to stop it. By the time I got there... there were bodies."

My heart twisted. I hadn't known. I had never known.

Jonah's eyes locked with mine, and in them, I saw a storm of things unspoken, years of guilt and pain and loss all churned together, fighting for release. "I couldn't save them. And I've spent every day since wondering if I could have done something differently—if I could have been faster, more thorough, more... something. But I wasn't. And now, I'm trying to make sure that mistake doesn't happen again."

I could feel the weight of his words pressing into me, like the ashes of the fire itself were settling over my chest. This wasn't just a job for Jonah. This wasn't a case to be solved or a puzzle to put together. This was personal. And as much as I hated the idea of him carrying that burden alone, there was a part of me—one that I wasn't entirely proud of—that understood what it meant to hide pieces of yourself, to guard your heart from the wounds that came with exposing them.

I could see it in his eyes, the walls he'd built around himself. They were high and thick, far stronger than the ones around this building, and I knew then that my curiosity about the fire was nothing compared to the mystery of Jonah Hale. His secrets were tangled up in the same smoke that had burned through these buildings, and it wasn't just fire he was running from. He was running from the ghosts of the past, the ones that followed him even when he thought he could outrun them.

I swallowed the knot in my throat, trying to steady myself. "And you think this fire is connected? That someone is out there, playing a game with all of us?"

Jonah didn't answer immediately. Instead, he took a step back, his eyes distant now, looking at nothing and everything all at once. "I don't know, Olivia. But I do know one thing." He finally met my gaze, and there was an intensity in his eyes that made my heart skip. "This is just the beginning."

I should have walked away. I knew that the second those words left Jonah's mouth. I should have turned on my heel, ignored the gnawing curiosity clawing at me, and never looked back. But I didn't. Because in that moment, with the smoke curling up around us like some twisted phantom, I understood exactly what he was asking me to do. He wasn't just trying to keep me out of harm's way. He was trying to protect himself, too. He had already seen the horror of a life destroyed by the same kind of reckless fire that had claimed this place, and now he was trying to shield me from the very thing that had scarred him.

But it wasn't just about protection, was it? There was something else there—something unspoken. I could feel it hanging in the air, thick and suffocating, as though the distance between us was both a safety net and a trap. He wanted to push me away, yet there was a pull in the way his gaze lingered, in the way his jaw tightened every time he spoke. A part of him was still tangled in the mess of whatever past haunted him. But another part of him—the part that almost seemed to reach for me in those brief, vulnerable moments—was already caught up in this.

"I can't just walk away," I said quietly, the words falling between us like stones. "You think I don't see it? I'm not blind, Jonah. There's something wrong here. Something more than just a fire."

He was quiet for a moment, and I couldn't help but watch the way the muscles in his shoulders shifted, the way his gaze darted nervously, as if he was trying to decide whether to confess more or close himself off entirely. When he finally spoke, his voice was strained, like he was saying something he hadn't meant to say aloud.

"It's not that simple. You don't get to walk in and make sense of things like this. This... this isn't something you can just fix with a few clever questions or an afternoon stroll through the rubble." His words were clipped, but there was a strain in them that hinted at more—more than he was willing to reveal.

"I'm not trying to fix anything," I snapped, though my tone softened the moment I realized how harsh it sounded. "I'm trying to understand. And if you're not willing to let me do that, then fine. I'll leave you to your secrets. But don't think for a second that this is over."

For the first time, Jonah's eyes softened, and the protective shield he'd worn for so long seemed to crack, just a little. His lips parted as though he might say something, but then, just as quickly, they pressed back together in that familiar, tight line.

I stepped closer, not sure what I expected to happen but needing to close the distance between us. "You can't just shut me out, Jonah. Not anymore. Not after everything."

His gaze flickered to mine, and there was a moment where the weight of everything passed between us, unspoken but undeniable. He took a breath, like he was about to give in to whatever it was I had coaxed from him. But before he could open his mouth, there was a sharp crack from behind us, the sound of something large breaking. Both of us whipped around instinctively, the hairs on the back of my neck rising as I spotted a figure emerging from the shadows of the burned-out building.

The figure was tall, moving with an unnerving quietness, their silhouette framed by the orange haze of the dying firelight. My heart skipped a beat, panic flooding my chest. Who was this? And how long had they been standing there, watching us?

IN THE DARK

Jonah reacted faster than I did, his hand instinctively going to the side of his hip as though he was reaching for something that wasn't there. His body tensed, ready for confrontation. But then, his expression shifted. The defensive edge softened just a little, replaced by something else—something darker, more complicated.

"Who's there?" I asked, my voice firmer than I felt, the words coming out like a challenge.

The figure stepped forward, the shadows peeling back to reveal a face I didn't recognize—lean, sharp features, eyes narrowed beneath the brim of a dark cap. Their clothes were dark, almost blending into the night, and I could see the faint glint of something metallic on their belt. A badge, perhaps, or something more dangerous. My breath caught in my throat, and I took a cautious step back, the back of my heels brushing against the jagged remains of a broken chair.

"I should ask you the same thing," the figure said, their voice deep and gravelly, carrying a weight that seemed to push the air around us. They didn't move closer, but I could feel the presence of their eyes on me, sharp and calculating. "What are you doing here?"

Jonah stepped in front of me, blocking the view of my face as he positioned himself between me and the stranger. "This is none of your business," he said, his tone cold, the walls around him slamming back into place. "Move along. We're handling things here."

The stranger's lips twitched, but it wasn't a smile. It was something else. Something unsettling. "I'm afraid it's my business now," they said, their eyes flicking briefly to me before returning to Jonah. "Things are getting out of hand, and you've left too many loose ends. We need to talk."

Jonah's expression darkened, and I could see the muscles in his jaw twitching. "Not here," he bit out. "Not now."

But the stranger didn't seem to care about Jonah's dismissal. Instead, they took a step closer, and this time, I could see the glint of metal in their hand—some kind of sleek, black device that they held loosely at their side.

Jonah's whole posture shifted, tension rippling through his frame. I could see his mind racing, trying to figure out how to handle this new threat, but for the first time, he looked uncertain.

"You need to get out of here, Olivia," he muttered, his voice low enough that only I could hear.

I wanted to argue, to stay, to push for answers. But something in his voice, something in the way his eyes darted between the stranger and me, told me this was bigger than either of us could control.

Before I could say anything more, the stranger took another step forward, their eyes locking onto mine, and the air between us seemed to crackle with tension. And then, without another word, they raised the device in their hand, and everything went dark.

Chapter 4: Shadows and Secrets

The bar was quieter than usual when I walked in that evening, the hum of conversation dimmed by a thick, uneasy silence that hung like fog between the tables. The kind of silence that makes you feel like you've stumbled into a room of secrets, a room where nothing is as it seems. I shouldn't have come. I had a million things to do—papers to sort, emails to answer, a meeting with the landlord about the leaking pipes that had somehow been ignored for weeks. But I'd come anyway, and now I found myself standing at the counter, the polished wood cool beneath my fingers as I waited for a drink I hadn't ordered.

Aiden had arrived shortly before me, slipping into his usual corner booth, the same one where he always sat with his back to the wall, eyes scanning the room as if searching for something—or perhaps someone—he'd never find. There was a hardness to the way he held himself, a tension in his jaw that told me more than any of his words ever could. He wasn't here for idle chatter or to unwind after a long day. No, Aiden was a man with a purpose, even if that purpose had nothing to do with me.

And yet, I couldn't look away. The way he sat, the way he moved, like someone who had seen too much to ever be fully comfortable again. His dark hair was messy, like he hadn't bothered to run a comb through it in days, and the stubble on his jawline was rough enough to make me wonder how much time had passed since his last shave. His eyes, though—those eyes were the kind of blue that could swallow you whole if you weren't careful. Like oceans of cold water, but with a current just strong enough to drag you under.

I shouldn't have been here. Not now, not with him, not in a place that felt too familiar for comfort. But life had a way of pushing me in directions I never planned, and it wasn't like I had any better options.

So, I made my way across the room, slipping into the seat opposite him as though it were the most natural thing in the world.

"You always find your way here eventually, don't you?" he said, his voice low, but with that biting edge that made every word feel like an accusation.

I met his gaze with as much confidence as I could muster, even though my pulse was drumming in my ears, trying its best to betray me. "Guess I'm just drawn to the best drinks in town." I gave a casual shrug, but even I knew it sounded weak, like a half-hearted excuse for the way my stomach twisted just by being near him.

He leaned back, his eyes narrowing as he studied me, clearly waiting for me to crack. The thing about Aiden was that he could read me better than anyone else, and yet, I never knew if it was because he truly understood me, or because he was too good at pretending he didn't.

"So, what brings you here tonight?" he asked, his voice barely above a whisper. His words were too soft for anyone else to hear, but somehow they seemed loud enough for me. A challenge. A question I didn't want to answer.

"I'm looking for something," I said, finally giving in to the quiet that had settled between us. "But I'm not sure what it is yet."

There it was. The truth, veiled in the smallest of confessions. I didn't know why I had come here tonight, why I always found myself slipping into the same places when I felt like I was unraveling. Maybe it was the pull of the fire—the way it had marked me in ways I couldn't escape, the way it had defined the last year of my life. Maybe it was just Aiden himself, the complicated puzzle I couldn't solve no matter how hard I tried.

Aiden raised an eyebrow, clearly intrigued by my words, but he didn't press for more. That was the thing about him—he never forced me to reveal anything. He waited, patient as always, for me to give in and let him see the parts of me I thought I had buried.

"You know, you've got a habit of disappearing when things get messy," I said, my voice harsher than I intended. "Just when I think I've figured you out, you slip right out of reach again."

His lips twitched into a smile, but it wasn't a warm one. It was the kind of smile that held secrets, that made you wonder what was really going on behind the mask. "I never promised you anything," he said, leaning forward just slightly. "I never promised anyone anything."

And there it was again—his distance, the barrier he kept between us, unspoken but undeniable. Every time I thought I saw a crack in his armor, he closed it up tighter, leaving me standing there with nothing but my own frustrations. The part of me that wanted to reach across the table and shake him until he gave me answers was the same part that feared what I might find if I did. Because Aiden's secrets weren't just about him. They were tangled in the same mess I couldn't escape. The fire. The destruction. The truth about the things I was trying to outrun.

"I'm not asking for promises," I said quietly. "But sometimes, Aiden, I think you're the only one who has the answers. And I'm just trying to figure out how to stop running from whatever it is."

His expression softened for just a moment, the flicker of something that might have been regret before it was gone, replaced by that cold mask I had come to know so well. "Running isn't the problem," he said, his voice a little rougher now. "It's what you're running toward."

I didn't know how to respond to that. Because in some twisted way, I was starting to wonder if he was right. Maybe I wasn't just running from the past. Maybe I was running straight into the flames, chasing something I couldn't even define.

I wasn't sure when the moment happened, when the line between wanting to know and wanting to forget blurred into something more dangerous. One minute, I was sitting across from

Aiden, watching him through the haze of our shared silence, and the next, I found myself drawn into the mystery of his every move.

The fire was a twisted thing. It had left marks on both of us, etched in ways I couldn't fully explain—scars I couldn't scrub away, no matter how many times I tried. Aiden was no different. He wore his secrets like a second skin, and every time he walked into a room, the air shifted. It wasn't just his presence. It was something else, something buried beneath the surface, something that made my skin prickle with unease.

He was the kind of person you couldn't ignore, whether you wanted to or not. His energy filled the space between us, charged with a tension that could only be described as palpable. His gaze lingered on me for a fraction longer than necessary, those piercing blue eyes never missing a thing, studying every shift in my expression as though he were trying to solve a puzzle I didn't even know I was part of.

"Stop looking at me like that," I muttered, trying to mask the way his scrutiny made my chest tighten.

"Like what?" Aiden's voice was soft, yet there was an edge to it. A challenge, perhaps, or maybe just a frustration he kept tucked away. I couldn't tell, and that, more than anything, made my stomach churn. The mystery of him gnawed at me, like a dull ache that never quite went away.

"Like you're about to ask me to read your mind," I said, leaning back in my chair, crossing my arms tightly in a defensive gesture. "I don't do mind reading. It's not my thing."

His lips quirked upward in a half-smile, the kind that held no humor but hinted at something more complex, a quiet acknowledgment of the walls I'd built.

"Good thing I don't need you to," he replied, his voice a touch softer, like he had read the tension between us, the way I guarded myself with every word.

I bristled at his calm, like he had seen right through me and was letting it slip by unnoticed. "Then what do you need?" I asked, the words slipping out before I could stop them.

The flicker of something dark crossed his face, something too fleeting for me to grasp. He looked down at the table, his fingers absently tracing the rim of his glass, the movement giving away more than he intended. "I need you to stop asking questions," he said finally, but there was no malice in his voice, just a weariness I hadn't expected. "Not everything has an answer, and some answers... they aren't worth finding."

That gave me pause. It wasn't like him to admit defeat—or anything close to it. Aiden thrived on secrets, on silence, on keeping things close to the chest, as though the less people knew, the more power he held. But something about his words felt different this time. There was a fragility beneath the layers, something real, and it made my breath catch in my throat.

"Then why do you keep coming back?" I whispered before I could stop myself. "Why do you keep showing up when I'm starting to think I've figured you out?"

Aiden's gaze snapped to mine, his expression unreadable, but I could see the wheels turning in his mind. He wasn't ready to answer, I could tell, but the question hung between us, thick and heavy, pushing against the silence like a wall that refused to crumble.

"I don't know," he said finally, his voice quieter now. "Maybe it's because I'm not the only one with something to hide."

The words hit me harder than I expected. It wasn't an accusation. It wasn't even an observation. It was a truth, raw and unrefined, that settled between us like an unspoken promise. The thing was, I hadn't realized how much I had been hiding until he pointed it out. I'd convinced myself that the fire, the destruction, the people I had lost, had been enough to fill the space where my past had once been. But Aiden was right. I wasn't just running from the flames. I was running from the people I had once been, from the choices I'd made in the aftermath of everything that had burned away.

I took a long sip of my drink, needing something to focus on, something to hold onto. The glass was cold in my hand, the sharp burn of alcohol helping to numb the growing ache in my chest. "So, what do you want from me?" I asked, meeting his gaze once more, my voice low, almost tentative.

He leaned forward just slightly, eyes never leaving mine. "I want you to stop pretending you don't care," he said, his words deliberate, each one slicing through the tension between us like a knife. "I want you to stop running."

I wanted to laugh. The irony of it all was too much to handle. Here he was, the king of secrets, the master of distance, telling me to stop running. As if he hadn't been running his entire life.

"You're one to talk," I said, the words slipping out before I could stop them, sharp and cutting.

His lips tightened, the briefest flicker of something—regret, maybe, or understanding—crossing his face. But it was gone before I could read it. "Touché," he muttered under his breath.

The space between us was charged, the air thick with everything left unsaid. For a moment, we just sat there, the world outside the window moving in its usual, chaotic rhythm, while we remained suspended in our own little bubble of tension. It felt like we were standing on the edge of something, teetering between the past and the future, between truths that hadn't been spoken and lies that had been buried too deep to unearth.

"I don't know how to stop," I admitted, the words escaping before I could stop them. "How do you stop running from everything you've lost?"

Aiden's gaze softened, just for a moment, before he stood up, the movement so sudden it left me off balance, like I had just been yanked from the edge of a precipice. He didn't say anything as he

IN THE DARK 37

turned, walking away without a backward glance. But as he reached the door, he paused, his hand on the handle.

"You don't," he said without turning. "But maybe you can stop running toward the wrong things."

And with that, he was gone, leaving me to wonder if the flames I was running from had only just begun to catch up with me.

I spent the rest of the evening staring at my reflection in the glass of the bar, watching the hazy lights swirl in the depths of my drink, trying to make sense of the mess in my head. Aiden had left without another word, his parting leaving behind only the scent of his cologne and an unsettling weight in the air. My fingers drummed lightly against the edge of my glass, a soft rhythm to fill the silence that now hung too heavily around me.

The truth was, Aiden had left more than just a trail of unanswered questions behind him. He had left a part of himself in that moment, a piece of the puzzle I hadn't yet figured out. I didn't know what I was looking for—whether it was an explanation, an apology, or something more. But whatever it was, it was slipping through my fingers, every time I tried to reach for it. Maybe it was always meant to be this way, tangled up in secrets that neither of us could escape.

I was still trying to shake the thoughts of him when I stepped out into the cool night air. The streets were quiet, the usual hum of activity in the city muffled by the late hour. It wasn't like me to linger in places I didn't belong, but I couldn't help myself. There was something about this town, something about Aiden, that kept me here. The fire had burned everything I'd known to the ground, but there was still something in me that wanted to rebuild, even if it meant sifting through the ashes. And Aiden, whether I liked it or not, was part of that wreckage.

I had barely taken two steps before I heard it—the unmistakable sound of footsteps behind me. A quick, deliberate pace that matched mine, but I didn't have to turn around to know who it was. The familiar tension in my chest flared again, but this time, I didn't stop. I couldn't.

"Aiden," I said, not turning to face him, my voice sharp despite my best efforts to sound casual. "You're not done with me yet?"

His footsteps slowed, but he didn't stop. I felt his presence behind me, like a shadow that couldn't quite escape the light. "I told you I don't have answers," he said, his voice low but steady. "But you're wrong if you think this is over. Not for you. Not for me."

There it was again, that tension. The same charged energy between us, as if everything that had happened—the fire, the secrets, the years we'd spent circling each other—was building up to something neither of us was ready for.

"You're still trying to push me away," I said, stopping at the corner and finally turning to face him. "But I'm not the one you need to keep at arm's length. It's yourself."

Aiden didn't move, didn't blink. He just stood there, staring at me with those icy blue eyes that felt like they could pierce through everything I thought I understood about him. "You think you know me?"

I shook my head, the words coming out with more force than I intended. "I don't. But I know this much—there's something you're not telling me, something that's keeping you from being honest. You can hide all you want, Aiden, but eventually, you're going to have to face whatever it is that's burning you up from the inside."

He looked at me like he was measuring my words, weighing them against whatever truth he kept locked inside. For a moment, I thought he might just walk away again, disappear into the night like he always did. But then he stepped forward, closing the distance between us, and I felt the shift in the air around us, like the ground beneath us had cracked open.

"Maybe you're right," he said quietly, his breath just a whisper in the night. "Maybe there's something I need to face. But it's not something you're going to like."

I took a step back, a cold shiver running down my spine. This wasn't the Aiden I knew. He wasn't the one who offered up fragments of truth, only to reel them back in. There was a darkness to his words now, something I couldn't ignore.

"What are you talking about?" I asked, my voice barely more than a whisper, but desperate to understand.

He didn't answer at first. Instead, he glanced around, like he was scanning the street, ensuring we weren't being watched. And then, with a heavy sigh, he spoke again, his voice lower this time, almost as if confessing.

"Everything that's happened to you—the fire, the losses, the things you think you're running from—it's all connected. It's not just about you, Sarah. It's about me too."

I opened my mouth to respond, but the words died in my throat. I wasn't sure if I wanted to know the truth, or if I was better off staying in the dark. But I couldn't walk away from this—not now, not when I could feel the gravity of his words sinking in, twisting around the heart of everything I thought I knew.

Aiden's jaw clenched, his hands shoved into the pockets of his jacket as he stepped back, his eyes avoiding mine. "I'm not who you think I am," he said, his voice rough, like he was fighting something just beneath the surface. "And if you keep pushing for answers, you're going to regret it."

The warning hung between us, but it only made me want to dig deeper, to find the answers he was so desperate to keep hidden. I couldn't stop myself. I couldn't walk away from him again, not when I was this close.

Before I could respond, a car screeched around the corner, its headlights blinding us for a split second. Aiden stiffened, his eyes flicking toward the vehicle, and then back to me. I felt the tension in his body as he made the decision in an instant, the words unsaid but understood.

"Get in the car, now," he snapped, grabbing my wrist before I could protest. The urgency in his voice sent a jolt of fear through me, and without thinking, I followed him.

The door slammed shut behind me, the engine roaring to life as we sped away into the night. I didn't know what was happening. I didn't know where we were going. But I knew one thing for sure: whatever Aiden was hiding, whatever secrets he was trying to keep from me, they were far worse than I could have ever imagined.

And now, I was in deeper than I'd ever planned.

Chapter 5: The Push and Pull

The city always felt different at dusk—quieter, as though the world was holding its breath, waiting for the next move. The neon lights flickered to life like fragile promises, casting glows that didn't quite reach the shadows. I loved it here, this paradox of soft light and deepened darkness. I had been pacing around the apartment for what felt like hours, trying to summon the nerve to leave, to step out into the very thing I'd been avoiding: him. But how could I? It wasn't just the way he looked at me when we fought, or how his hands would clench as though he wanted to tear the world apart but never let it slip through his fingers. It wasn't even the way the tension between us made the air feel thinner, like we were both trying to breathe through something too thick, too sharp.

It was everything about him—his presence was a constant tug-of-war between wanting to stay as far away from the flame as possible and being drawn into its warmth, its danger. The problem was, I didn't trust myself around him anymore. Every time we were in the same room, the lines blurred, and I found myself playing this dangerous game of pulling away just to come closer again. Like now. Like tonight.

I leaned against the window, staring down at the city streets below. The glass was cool against my palm, and the faint hum of traffic beneath me felt like a heartbeat. I could have stayed there forever, but I didn't. I had a mission, one that was both reckless and necessary, as I had been reminded every time Aiden's voice crackled in my head. He'd told me to stay away, to stop asking questions that no one had answers to. And yet, here I was—about to cross the threshold, ready to challenge him once more.

The door opened just as I was about to grab my coat, the sound of it slicing through the stillness like a warning bell. Aiden's figure filled the doorway, his presence larger than the frame itself. He stood there, eyes narrowed, brow furrowed. The way he looked at me—like I was both the thing he wanted to destroy and the thing he wanted to protect—was both a curse and a temptation. He hadn't come here to talk. We both knew that. He'd come here to stop me.

"I told you to stay out of it," he said, his voice low, rough with something I couldn't quite place. Anger, frustration, maybe even fear. But there was a note of something else, something unspoken, something that kept the words from feeling final.

"And I told you I don't listen well." I pushed myself off the window, moving towards him with deliberate steps. I wasn't afraid. Not of him. Not of his anger. Maybe I should've been, but I wasn't. "You can't keep doing this, Aiden. You can't keep telling me to stay out of it and then expect me to just walk away. This—" I gestured between us, the space that always seemed to crackle with something more, something unsaid, "this isn't normal. Not for me. Not for you."

His jaw clenched. I saw the muscles tighten under his shirt, the subtle warning signs I had come to recognize. He was about to tell me something I didn't want to hear, something that would push me further into the unknown.

"You think this is some kind of game?" His eyes met mine, and there was no hiding the storm swirling in their depths. "You think I want you here? Want this... whatever it is we're doing? You have no idea what you're walking into. I'm trying to keep you safe."

"Safe?" The laugh that slipped from my lips was bitter, edged with something that felt dangerously close to despair. "From what, Aiden? From you? From yourself? You're not even giving me the chance to understand it."

His gaze softened, just slightly. "Some things are better left unknown."

"That's what you keep saying." I took a step closer, close enough to feel the heat radiating off him, close enough to almost touch the anger that still simmered between us. "But I can't live like that anymore. I can't just keep standing on the edge, waiting for you to decide when I get to know the truth. If you think I'm going to let you push me away, you're wrong. I'm not going anywhere."

I'd never seen him like this, so lost, so desperate to pull back, yet unwilling to let go entirely. The mask he wore, the one that always kept him so controlled, cracked just a little more with every word. I could see it now—the way his eyes flickered with something too raw to be hidden for long. Aiden didn't know how to let anyone close. That was his defense mechanism, his way of holding the world at arm's length. But I'd seen too much.

He reached for me, his hand hovering in the air between us, as though unsure whether to pull me in or push me away. I saw the moment of hesitation, the struggle inside him. It was brief but real, and it made something inside me ache. I knew this was it—the point of no return.

"Don't make me do this," he whispered, his voice tight with restraint.

I shook my head slowly, letting the space between us shrink with each heartbeat. "You're not doing anything, Aiden. You're just standing there, hoping I'll listen. But I'm not going to. Not this time."

His hand dropped to his side, and for a long moment, we just stood there, the silence louder than any argument we'd ever had.

The air in the apartment had thickened, a tangible weight settling between us. I could feel it pressing against my chest, making each breath a little more labored, a little more deliberate. He stood a few feet away, his back rigid, his fists clenched by his sides. It was as though he were bracing for impact, waiting for something—a confrontation, an apology, maybe even a breakdown. But I didn't know what he expected from me. I had already made it clear that I wasn't going anywhere. Not now. Not after everything.

Aiden was the kind of man who didn't leave room for softness, for vulnerability, and I hated that about him. He wore his wounds like armor, each one an excuse for his detachment, his silence. But there were cracks in that armor—cracks that I saw, even if he never acknowledged them. It wasn't that I wanted to fix him. I wasn't some misguided heroine with dreams of saving a man who didn't want to be saved. I didn't want to heal him. But I did want to understand him. There was something there beneath the surface, something I knew he wasn't ready to show. But I didn't want to wait. Not anymore.

"Tell me what's going on, Aiden," I said quietly, my voice a thread of patience, my tone that delicate balance of determination and hope. "Why are you doing this? Why are you pushing me away?"

He didn't answer at first. His eyes flicked to the door, then back to me, like he was trying to work out some invisible equation in his head. I could see him wrestling with the words, and I wondered if the answer he was looking for even existed.

"You wouldn't understand," he muttered, almost to himself, his gaze avoiding mine. "It's better this way."

"Better for who?" The question slipped from my lips before I could stop it. I wasn't sure if I wanted to know the answer, but I knew that he needed to hear the question. "You're not fooling anyone, Aiden. Least of all me. I know you don't want me to go anywhere, but you don't know how to let me stay."

His eyes flicked up to mine, and I saw something—something fleeting in the way his jaw tightened, the way his fingers flexed as if the words were trapped in his chest, fighting to get out.

"I'm trying to protect you," he said, his voice thick, almost hoarse. "You think you're helping, but you're not. You're making it worse. Every time you push me, every time you try to dig deeper, you're just putting yourself in danger. I can't... I can't let that happen."

Danger. The word hung in the air, heavy with something unsaid. I could feel the weight of it, and it made my pulse quicken, my heart stutter.

"You're not the only one who's capable of looking after themselves," I said, my voice sharp now, biting into the fragile thread of our tension. "And I'm not going to just walk away, Aiden. Not after everything. I deserve to know what's going on. What's so dangerous that you're willing to tear us apart over it?"

He flinched, the sharpness of my words striking him harder than any of our previous arguments. But it didn't stop him from stepping closer, his eyes narrowing as he moved into my personal space. His presence was a force, an undeniable thing that had a way of making my pulse race, of filling the air with a heat that had nothing to do with proximity. His voice dropped to a whisper, a dangerous rasp that made my breath catch.

"You think you're ready for the truth? You don't have the slightest idea what you're asking for." His fingers brushed the back of my hand, and I shivered involuntarily. "There are things I've done, things I've seen, that you wouldn't be able to live with. And yet, here you are, asking for more."

"Then make me understand." My words were quiet, but they felt like a challenge, an invitation to something neither of us knew how to handle. "You don't get to decide what I can handle. Not anymore."

The room seemed to shrink around us, the distance between us closing in like we were caught in some inevitable gravitational pull. He reached for me, and this time, I didn't step back. His hand cupped the side of my face, his touch hesitant, like he was unsure if I would let him. I should have pulled away. I should have kept my distance. But something inside me, something deeper and more instinctual than I cared to admit, urged me to stay.

For a moment, neither of us spoke. The silence was a different kind of tension, one that was no longer built on anger or frustration but on something far more dangerous—something that made my breath catch in my throat.

Aiden's eyes softened for the briefest second, his thumb brushing the edge of my jaw, and I could see the conflict in them. He wanted to pull me in. He wanted to keep me close, but the weight of whatever he was carrying held him back.

"I'm not good for you," he whispered, his voice low, filled with something that almost sounded like regret. "You don't want to get caught up in my world."

"I don't care about your world," I said, my voice barely above a breath. "I care about you."

The words hung between us, raw and unguarded, and I watched as the barriers he'd built around himself cracked just a little more. His grip on my face tightened, pulling me closer, until there was no space left between us, no way to deny the electricity that had been sparking between us from the moment we met.

And then, in the middle of the storm we'd been creating, something shifted. Something fragile and dangerous. But it was also something real. And it made everything that had come before feel like nothing more than a prelude to what we were about to face together.

The world outside had gone quiet, a sudden hush that seemed to hang over everything. No cars honked, no sirens blared—just the soft hum of the city, muted by the tension that had settled in this small apartment, a quiet pressure that neither of us had the words to dispel. His face, inches from mine, was drawn tight with something I couldn't name, but it didn't feel like anger anymore. It was something deeper, something far more complicated.

I felt the weight of his breath on my lips, the soft caress of it, and I swore I could hear the sound of his heartbeat syncing with mine. The space between us had evaporated, leaving behind a dangerous kind of stillness. For a moment, I thought that maybe, just maybe, he would kiss me. But then his fingers curled into a fist at his side, and he stepped back with a sharp exhale, like he was rejecting something that burned between us, something he couldn't allow to happen.

"You don't know what you're asking for," he said again, his voice rougher now, less certain.

"I know exactly what I'm asking for," I countered, taking a step toward him, keeping the distance small, intimate. I could see the way his chest rose and fell, the way his eyes flitted from mine, his guard still firmly in place. "I'm asking you to stop pretending like you don't want this. Like you don't want me here."

He shook his head, a bitter laugh escaping him. "It's not that simple, you don't get it." His voice cracked just a little, and I wondered if it was from frustration, or something else. I took another step toward him, suddenly so aware of the way the tension in the room seemed to pull us closer, as though we couldn't stay apart for much longer.

"But you can't keep me at arm's length forever," I whispered, the words slipping out before I could stop them. "I won't let you."

For the briefest second, I saw the flicker of doubt in his eyes, as if he were contemplating my words. And then the moment passed, and he turned away, his back to me as he rubbed a hand over his face. The frustration radiating off him was palpable, thick in the air like smoke.

"You're impossible," he muttered, more to himself than to me, but the words landed between us, sharp and pointed.

I wasn't sure what to say to that. Part of me wanted to argue, to force him to admit that there was something more to this, but another part of me understood the weight of what he was carrying, the unspoken burden that weighed him down. I wanted to be the one to help him share that load, but I knew he wouldn't let me. Not now, not yet.

"What happened to you, Aiden?" The question hung in the air, quiet but insistent. I didn't need an answer, not really. But I needed him to hear me say it. "You used to care about people. You used to be..." I trailed off, realizing how absurd it sounded. How little I knew of the man in front of me now.

"I'm not the person you think I am," he said, his voice a low growl, laced with something raw and vulnerable that he clearly wasn't ready to confront. He turned back to face me, and for the first time, I saw the conflict in his eyes. It wasn't anger anymore. It was regret. Pain.

"Maybe I don't know who you are," I admitted softly. "But I want to."

He took a step forward, the tension building once more, an invisible force pulling us together. "You don't," he said, his voice a whisper now. "You really don't. And you're better off not knowing."

It was a challenge, one that I couldn't ignore. And suddenly, I realized just how far we'd come, how much we had both invested in this delicate, dangerous dance. His words were walls, but I was ready to tear them down, even if it meant I might break myself in the process.

I didn't respond immediately. Instead, I watched him, studying the way he moved, the way he tried to hide the vulnerability that crept into his expression, the way his hands clenched at his sides. He was so afraid of this—of us, of whatever this connection was between us—that it made my heart ache. But I wasn't afraid. I was sure now. I had to push, even if it meant risking everything.

"You don't get to decide what I can handle," I said again, a little sharper this time, a little more certain. "You don't get to decide what's too much for me. I'm already in this, Aiden. Whether you want me here or not, I'm already involved. And I'm not going anywhere."

The silence stretched between us, thick and suffocating, until he took another step back, running a hand through his hair in frustration. "You're not listening," he said, the words almost strangled. "I don't want you to get hurt. You don't get it—this isn't a game."

I could feel the distance between us growing once again, the emotional chasm widening in the space he had put between us. It wasn't just physical distance anymore; it was something deeper. Something that neither of us was willing to bridge just yet.

"I'm not afraid of the danger," I said, taking another step forward, refusing to let him retreat any further. "I'm afraid of losing you."

His eyes met mine, raw and vulnerable, and for a split second, I saw him—really saw him—more than just the tough exterior, more than the man who pushed me away every chance he got. He was breaking. He was just trying to keep me from breaking with him.

Before I could say anything more, his phone rang, the sound breaking through the fragile moment between us. He glanced at the screen, his face instantly hardening as he stepped away, as if the weight of whatever he saw on the display was enough to snap the connection between us like a brittle thread.

"Don't," he warned, holding up a hand as if to silence any further words. His expression was unreadable now, a mask once again in place. "I have to take this."

I stood there, frozen, as he answered the call, his voice low and clipped. But even as he spoke, I could feel something changing, something shifting in the air between us. And for the first time in a long while, I wondered if I'd made a terrible mistake.

Because in that moment, I realized we were both already in over our heads. And neither of us knew how deep the water really was.

Chapter 6: Beneath the Mask

The fire had long since been smothered, its orange embers now nothing more than dull, ashen ghosts beneath the dark sky. Aiden's truck was parked at the edge of the lot, the only sound the steady hum of the engine as it cooled. My boots scraped against the gravel as I made my way toward it, the familiar weight of the day pressing on my shoulders. The moment I slid into the passenger seat, I could see that Aiden hadn't spoken a word since we left the scene, his hands tight on the steering wheel, his jaw clenched.

The air in the truck was thick, heavy with a silence that seemed to close in around us. I didn't mind it—sometimes silence was better than words. But tonight, something felt different. It was as if the space between us had grown, thickened, and it begged to be filled with something, anything.

I shifted in my seat, the leather creaking beneath me. "You okay?" I asked, my voice soft, hesitant.

He didn't answer at first, eyes straight ahead, his face illuminated by the dim glow of the dashboard. The muscles in his neck tensed, and I wondered if I had asked the wrong question. Maybe it was a question he didn't have an answer to. Or maybe it was a question he didn't want to answer. But before I could think of something else to say, his voice broke the silence, low and rough.

"It's not the fire that gets to you. Not really." He sighed, the sound weary, like he'd been carrying something heavy for far too long. "It's the people you can't save. The ones who don't make it out."

I turned my head to face him fully, the weight of his words hanging in the air. The pain in his voice was unmistakable, raw and jagged, like the kind of wound that never quite heals, no matter how much time passes.

"Aiden..." I started, but he held up a hand to stop me.

"I wasn't always this guy," he said, his voice thick with an emotion I couldn't quite place. "This... firefighter, I mean. I wasn't always the one running into the flames. I used to be the one running away from everything."

The confession hit me harder than I expected. I knew Aiden had demons—everyone had their demons—but I hadn't known it was this. I hadn't known how deep they ran.

"Why?" I asked before I could stop myself, the word slipping out like a breath I didn't realize I was holding.

Aiden's eyes flickered to me for a moment, a quick glance that I could feel like a spark against my skin, before he focused on the road again. He exhaled a long, slow breath, the kind that seemed to pull the weight of years with it.

"I didn't choose this life," he said, his voice quieter now, almost like a confession. "I didn't choose to become a hero, if that's what you want to call it. I didn't choose to run toward danger, to put my life on the line for strangers."

I swallowed, unsure if I was supposed to say something or just wait for him to continue. He didn't look at me as he spoke, his words coming slower now, like he was piecing together a memory long buried.

"I used to be a mechanic," he said, a bitter laugh escaping his throat. "A good one. I worked on trucks, cars, whatever needed fixing. That's what I thought I was good at. I didn't think I was meant to be... this. But one night, there was a fire. A big one. I was on my way home from a late shift when I saw the flames. I didn't know what to do, but something inside me—maybe it was fear or maybe it was just... instinct, I don't know—I ran toward it. I couldn't stop myself. I had to help."

His hands tightened on the wheel again, and I could feel the tension radiating off him. I stayed quiet, letting him speak, knowing that whatever he was about to say next was going to change everything.

"When I got there, there was a woman inside," he continued, his voice barely above a whisper. "She was trapped. I tried to get to her, but the fire was too much. The smoke, the heat. I couldn't get close enough. I had to watch her burn alive, and there was nothing I could do. Nothing."

I felt the air leave my lungs, the weight of his words crushing the breath from me. I didn't know what to say. How could anyone know what to say in the face of such pain? I reached out, my hand hovering for a moment before I placed it gently on his arm. It wasn't much, but it was something.

He turned his face to me then, his eyes dark, haunted, the memory still alive in them. "That moment... it changed me. I couldn't just walk away from it. I couldn't pretend it never happened. I had to do something to make up for it. I had to become someone who could save people, even if it meant risking my own life every day."

The words hung between us, thick with the unspoken weight of guilt and regret. Aiden had been running from that night for so long, trying to outrun the image of that woman's face, the memory of her screams. And in trying to save others, he was trying to save himself from the haunting guilt he carried with him every time he suited up.

The silence stretched on, but this time, it felt different. It wasn't heavy with the weight of unspoken words; it was a quiet kind of understanding. I didn't know if I could fix what had broken him, or if anyone could. But in that moment, I knew that whatever we had between us, whatever it might become, it was real. Because, for once, Aiden wasn't hiding behind the mask. And neither was I.

I didn't know when it happened, when the space between us had shifted from something distant and professional to something else entirely. Maybe it had been that night—when he finally let the mask slip, just enough for me to see the cracks beneath. Or maybe it had been longer than that, creeping up on me in quiet moments when I found myself looking at him in a way I hadn't before. Either way, I couldn't ignore it now. Whatever this was between us—this unspoken bond, this shared vulnerability—it was real.

The truck pulled to a stop in front of my building, the engine shutting off with a soft growl. We sat there for a beat, neither of us in a hurry to get out. His hand rested on the gearshift, fingers flexing and unflexing as if they were still trying to find a rhythm. I wondered if he was thinking about the fire we'd just walked away from or about the woman he couldn't save. I couldn't be sure. I wasn't sure about anything when it came to Aiden.

"Do you want to come up?" I asked, the words tumbling out before I could stop them. It wasn't an invitation I had planned to offer. It just... felt right, like it was the next logical step in this strange, uncharted territory we had wandered into together.

His gaze shifted to me, a flash of something unreadable in his eyes. "Up?" he asked, his voice low, teasing in that way he sometimes did when he was trying to mask what was going on inside.

"I mean... unless you have somewhere else to be," I said, a slight edge of sarcasm slipping in. I couldn't help it. The tension in the air was thick enough to cut with a knife, and I wasn't sure if I was relieved or terrified to be standing on the edge of something new with him.

He glanced out the windshield, then back at me. I could almost hear the wheels turning in his head as he weighed the options. Finally, he nodded. "Yeah. Okay."

We both climbed out of the truck, and I led the way up the stairs to my apartment. The hallway was dimly lit, the faded yellow lights casting shadows on the walls. I unlocked the door and stepped inside, the familiar scent of coffee and cinnamon wrapping around me like a blanket. Aiden lingered behind me, his presence a quiet weight that seemed to fill every corner of the small space.

I moved toward the kitchen, suddenly feeling self-conscious. I wasn't sure why—Aiden had seen me at my worst. He had seen me drenched in sweat, covered in soot, and stumbling out of a burning building. And yet, here I was, fussing with a coffee pot as if I was trying to impress him with my domestic skills.

"So," I said, trying to sound casual as I grabbed a couple of mugs from the cupboard. "You don't have to stay long. But if you want coffee, I can make some."

He didn't respond right away. Instead, he looked around the room, taking in the mismatched furniture and the pile of books that had started to take over one corner of the living room. There were no decorations, no pretensions. Just me, in my chaotic little world. Aiden seemed to take it all in, his eyes softening as they moved over the space.

"You have a lot of books," he said finally, his voice warm with something like approval.

"I read a lot," I replied, a smile tugging at the corner of my lips. "It's either books or whiskey. And while I'm partial to a good bourbon, I tend to think books are less destructive in the long run."

Aiden chuckled, the sound a little rough, but there was a flicker of something behind it—something close to genuine amusement. "I'll take your word for it."

I turned back to the coffee maker, trying not to focus too much on how his gaze lingered on me. It wasn't a creepy, invasive kind of stare, but more like he was trying to figure me out, piece by piece, the same way I had been trying to figure him out for weeks now.

"What about you?" I asked, trying to redirect the conversation. "What do you do when you're not saving people from burning buildings?"

Aiden was quiet for a moment, the shift in his demeanor subtle, but I felt it. It was like he was pulling away, just a little bit, retreating back into that space where he was a little untouchable. But it didn't last long. He tilted his head, considering the question for a moment before answering.

"I fish," he said. "Not as much as I'd like, but when I can, I go out. Just me, a rod, and some water."

I raised an eyebrow, genuinely intrigued. "You fish?"

He shrugged, the casual motion belying the depth of the thought behind it. "It's peaceful. I can think. I can be... alone."

I could tell there was more to that statement, but I didn't press him. It was rare enough to see him open up as much as he already had. I didn't want to scare him away by digging too deep, too soon.

Instead, I poured the coffee and handed him a mug. He took it with a quiet nod, and for a moment, we stood there in silence, sipping our drinks, both of us trying to navigate the sudden shift in the air between us.

"I guess it's your turn now," he said, a playful glint in his eye as he looked at me over the rim of his mug. "What about you? You always seem to have something you're hiding, too."

I blinked, taken aback by the question. I wasn't used to being the one on the spot. But there it was, that challenge in his voice, daring me to let the mask slip.

For a moment, I considered playing it safe, giving him some carefully crafted answer about work or my so-called 'perfectly normal' life. But that wouldn't be the truth, not really. And in this moment, when the night had stretched longer than expected and the weight of our shared silence hung heavy in the room, I knew I owed him something more.

"Maybe I'll tell you someday," I said instead, a small, teasing smile dancing on my lips. And for the first time, I didn't feel the need to hide. Not from him. Not anymore.

The night stretched on in quiet conversation, our words weaving around us like a delicate thread, binding us in a way I hadn't anticipated. Every so often, the silence would fall between us, thick and palpable, but it wasn't uncomfortable—not anymore. It was as if we were both letting the weight of the world rest on the edges of the space, just a little bit lighter than it had been before.

"I should probably go," Aiden said after a long pause, the words carrying a heaviness that didn't quite match the casual way he said them. He set his empty mug down on the kitchen counter, his fingers lingering on the ceramic like he was holding onto something.

I nodded, the ache of his departure suddenly creeping up on me, uninvited but impossible to ignore. "Yeah, probably." But the words tasted wrong on my tongue, too quick, too sharp. What did I want? To hold him here, to unravel him further? To find out what else lay beneath that armor of his? Was I getting too attached, too quickly?

I didn't have an answer. Not yet.

I stood with him as he walked toward the door, the weight of his presence filling the room, even as he moved toward the exit. I couldn't stop the sudden impulse from pushing through me, this overwhelming urge to ask him to stay.

"Aiden..." I said, my voice barely above a whisper, the word feeling foreign as it crossed my lips.

He stopped, one hand on the doorknob, his back to me. There was a tension in his posture, a hesitation that told me he wasn't ready to leave either—not entirely.

"Yeah?" He didn't turn around, but I could hear the softness in his voice, the way it carried with the same vulnerability that he'd shown me earlier.

"Are we really doing this?" I asked, the question simple, but laden with more meaning than I knew how to put into words. "Are we pretending we're just colleagues, just two people who share a job and nothing more? Because I can't keep doing that. Not after tonight."

His hand tightened on the doorknob, but he still didn't move. I could see his reflection in the glass, his jaw clenched tight, as if he were weighing something heavy in his mind.

"I don't know what you want from me," he said, his voice low, strained. "I've never done this—been this open, been this... vulnerable." He let out a soft, bitter laugh. "You think I don't want to take that mask off, to stop pretending? But I can't. Not yet. Not with you."

The words hit me harder than I expected, stirring something deep inside me that I didn't have a name for. Something between us had changed, and I wasn't sure if that change was a good thing or something far more complicated.

"I don't want you to pretend," I said, my voice firmer than I felt. "I just want to know you. The real you. Not the guy who walks into burning buildings or saves people from disaster. The man behind the mask, Aiden. Who are you when there's no one around to see?"

He finally turned, his eyes locking onto mine, and for a moment, I thought I saw something—an opening, a crack in the impenetrable wall he'd spent years building around himself. But just as quickly, it disappeared, replaced with that same guarded look I had come to know so well.

"I don't think you want to know that," he replied, his words a quiet warning, as if he were afraid I might get too close, too deep.

"I think I do," I said, my voice soft but steady. "I think I deserve to know it."

Aiden's gaze softened, the fight fading from his eyes. But then, just as quickly, his face hardened again, a look of resolve settling in. "It's not that simple," he said, his voice steady now, like he had made up his mind.

I stepped toward him, reaching out, but I wasn't sure what I wanted to do—whether I wanted to pull him in or give him the space he so clearly needed. But something inside me pushed forward, urging me to close the distance between us. "I'm not asking for your story, Aiden. I'm asking for... you. Whatever that looks like. I can't keep pretending that we're just a fire investigation team, that we're not... something more."

He was quiet for a long moment, his expression unreadable. I could see the conflict in his eyes, the struggle between wanting to hold me at arm's length and wanting to reach out, to let someone in. But then, in a move that caught me completely off guard, he stepped closer. Too close, and yet it felt like the most natural thing in the world.

"I'm not a good guy, Lucy," he said, his voice low, almost a whisper. "I've made mistakes. Big ones. And I'm still paying for them every damn day."

"I don't want perfect," I replied, my heart pounding in my chest, every word feeling like a gamble. "I just want you."

For a long, long moment, neither of us moved. There was an electricity in the air, a charged silence that hummed between us, threatening to boil over at any second. And then, just as I thought he might say something else, something that would either bring us closer or push us apart forever, a sudden sound sliced through the tension—the sharp, insistent ring of my phone.

I pulled away, irritation flaring before I even glanced at the screen. "I swear, if it's another fire...," I muttered under my breath, reaching for the phone. But when I saw the name on the caller ID, my stomach dropped, and I felt the world shift beneath my feet.

"Aiden, it's... it's the department," I said, my voice suddenly thick with dread. "There's been another fire. They need us."

His eyes met mine, and in them, I saw the same recognition—the same fear that this was the thing that would pull us apart, that we couldn't hold onto what we had, not with everything else we had to face. Not now.

He took a step back, his expression hardening again. "We'll talk about this later," he said, his tone final, but the flicker of something else still there, just beneath the surface.

"Yeah," I whispered, feeling the weight of the moment settle on my shoulders like a storm cloud. "Later."

But I had a feeling that later was a long way off. And as I grabbed my gear and headed for the door, I couldn't shake the feeling that everything had just changed.

Chapter 7: Forbidden Flames

The evening was thick with the scent of rain that hadn't quite arrived but threatened to. It lingered in the air, cloying, and as I walked along the cobblestone streets, I could almost taste it, sharp and metallic on my tongue. My heels clicked against the uneven stones, a sound that echoed too loudly in the quiet of the evening, my pulse thumping in sync with each step. The city was a maze of faded facades and shuttered windows, yet I knew the twists and turns of it better than I knew myself.

I had learned, the hard way, to walk through this place without being seen, without drawing attention. But tonight felt different. Maybe it was the weight of the sky above me, or the way the shadows stretched impossibly long, but I felt the eyes of the world on my back. And somewhere, within the folds of the air, I knew I wasn't alone.

It was impossible not to notice him. He was standing beneath the flickering streetlamp, his figure a silhouette against the dull glow, his features obscured by the faint mist that had begun to creep in from the bay. But there was something about the way he held himself—uncompromising, unwavering—that pulled me in. My breath caught in my chest, the world narrowing down to just the space between us. I could feel the familiar, dangerous pull in my gut, the magnetic force that had begun to make itself known from the very first time we'd crossed paths.

Even in the dim light, his presence filled the space around him. He was all sharp angles, strong lines—his jaw, set with determination, the slight curl of his lips that betrayed a wry amusement at some private joke I hadn't been privy to. He hadn't moved an inch since I first spotted him, but I could sense him studying me, his gaze not so much on my body, but on my soul. As if he were trying to read the depths of me, strip me bare without so much as a touch.

"You've been avoiding me," his voice broke the silence, low and smooth, like velvet wrapped around an unspoken threat.

I stopped in my tracks, my heart skipping in spite of the calm I tried to project. "I didn't realize you were keeping track."

His laugh was soft, but it carried the weight of something heavier, something unspoken. "I always keep track. Of everything. Especially you."

I wanted to say something, anything, to push him back, to keep him at a distance. But the words felt foreign, tangled in the hollow of my chest, and for once, I didn't know what to do with the silence between us.

He took a step closer, his presence now a tangible thing, pressing into the space between us with a force I could not resist. "You think this is easy for me?" The question was more of a statement, his eyes dark, the storm clouds reflecting in them as they held mine with an intensity that made the earth beneath me seem to tilt. "You think I want to feel this? Want to be here, in this mess?"

I swallowed hard, the weight of his words settling heavy on my chest. The truth was, I couldn't understand him—not fully. But I wanted to. I wanted to peel back the layers of him the way a child might peel an orange, to feel the sting of the pulp, the mess of it, to dive deeper until I could unravel what had made him this way.

"You don't have to do this, you know," I said quietly, taking a tentative step back, trying to create distance between us even as my body betrayed me. "I don't know why you keep pushing me, why you keep coming back—"

"Because you're here," he interrupted, and this time, there was no mocking edge, no amused inflection in his voice. Just the raw truth of it, stripped bare. "You're here, and I'm not going anywhere."

The words slid between us like a promise, one that felt both comforting and terrifying. I wanted to tell him to leave, to walk away. But my lips refused to obey the thought, as if they too had decided to surrender to the inevitable pull of him.

Before I could make up my mind on what to do with the panic rising in my chest, he was right in front of me, too close, the heat of his body burning into mine. His hand reached out, brushing the strands of hair that had fallen in front of my face, his fingers lingering just a moment too long.

My breath hitched, and I felt it—this strange, undeniable force between us, as if the universe had folded itself around our connection, twisting it into something neither of us could ignore. I should have pulled away, should have screamed, or slapped him, or done something—anything—to push him out of my world for good. But instead, I stood frozen, my heart hammering in my chest, caught between the rush of longing and the quiet, persistent voice that warned me to walk away.

His fingers drifted down my arm, the contact light, a whisper of a touch that sent a shiver racing across my skin. "You can't keep running from this," he murmured, the words settling in my bones. "We both know that."

The world shifted, the air between us thick with unspoken tension, and I realized then that this—whatever it was—was never meant to be simple. We weren't meant to make sense of each other, not in the ways we wanted. What we were chasing was as dangerous as it was irresistible, and it would destroy us both before it ever had a chance to burn itself out.

But I couldn't bring myself to walk away.

I didn't leave. I didn't walk away, even when every instinct screamed for me to turn and run. It was as if the ground beneath me had been replaced with quicksand, and the harder I struggled, the deeper I sank into him. Into this.

His eyes—those stormy, dangerous eyes—held me in place, each glance a thread weaving us closer, binding us in a way I couldn't escape, no matter how hard I tried. The space between us crackled, charged, a tension that made the air thick and heavy, suffocating.

"What are we doing, Lila?" His voice, raw and unsteady, broke through the haze of my thoughts. It wasn't a question, not really. More like a plea, though I couldn't tell if it was for me or for himself.

I swallowed, my throat tight, words stuck somewhere between my chest and my mouth. "I don't know," I said, my voice betraying me with its unsteady edge. I didn't know. How could I? The way he looked at me, the way he made me feel—unseen and yet fully known—made everything else seem irrelevant. There was only him. And the undeniable pull that kept me tethered to him, despite the warnings, the history, the dangers I was all too aware of.

He exhaled sharply, his breath a low, tortured sound. "We can't do this." His words were firm, but they trembled, as if he, too, were fighting the pull. Fighting the inevitable. "You know that. It's too dangerous."

"Dangerous," I repeated, the word hanging in the air like smoke, curling around us. The word was too familiar. Too tied to the parts of me I didn't want to remember. The parts I had spent years trying to bury. "It doesn't feel dangerous. It feels like I'm breathing for the first time."

He stiffened, his jaw working as if he were forcing back the words he really wanted to say. His hand, which had been so gently grazing my arm, jerked back like I'd burned him. But the heat between us didn't dissipate; if anything, it grew.

"You don't get it," he muttered under his breath. "This is more than just us, Lila. There are things... things I can't protect you from. Things that—"

"Things you don't want me to know about?" I cut in, the edge to my voice sharper than I intended. A harsh laugh escaped me. "I'm not some delicate flower that needs to be protected, okay? I'm not going to break just because you say I will."

He flinched, the flicker of something almost pained crossing his face before it was masked again by that impenetrable wall he'd built around himself. I wanted to tear it down, wanted to see the truth in him, even if it terrified me. Even if it meant seeing the worst parts of both of us.

"I didn't ask for this," he said quietly, his voice breaking as if the words hurt him. "I didn't ask to care about you, to want you, to feel... this." He gestured between us, his eyes searching my face as if he were trying to find the words to explain something he didn't fully understand himself.

And there it was again—his vulnerability, raw and exposed for just a second, before he closed it off and hid it behind that cold façade of his. My stomach twisted, a knot of both frustration and yearning.

"I didn't ask for it either," I replied softly. "But here we are. And I'm not going anywhere."

He shook his head, looking away, his fists clenching at his sides. "You don't know what you're getting into," he muttered, more to himself than to me. "This... this is bigger than you and me, Lila. You think you want this, but you don't. You have no idea what I've done. The things I've seen. The people I've pissed off."

"Then tell me," I demanded, stepping closer, my chest tight with the sudden rush of desperation. "Tell me what I'm walking into. Tell me what's so bad about me wanting to be with you."

His eyes flicked to mine, dark and stormy, searching. "You think you can handle it?" he asked quietly, his voice steady now, but there was an edge to it, a sharpness that made my pulse race. "You think you can handle the truth about me?"

"I've handled worse," I said before I could stop myself, the words slipping out with more conviction than I felt. "I've been through hell and back, and I'm still standing. I don't break, not anymore."

His eyes softened for the briefest of moments, and I saw something in them—something broken, something fierce. He was trying to protect me, I knew that much. But the way he looked at me now, with such intensity, made it clear that there was no protecting me from what was coming.

"You're not like the others," he whispered, his voice thick with emotion. "You don't deserve this. You don't deserve the mess that comes with me."

"I don't care about your mess," I said, my voice barely a whisper. "I care about you."

He let out a short, bitter laugh. "You have no idea what you're saying."

I took another step toward him, close enough now that I could feel the heat radiating off of him, could smell the dark, intoxicating mix of his cologne and something deeper, something untamed and raw. "Maybe I don't. But I want to. I want to understand. I want you to stop running from me."

He took a breath, his gaze drifting over my face like he was memorizing every inch of me. Then, with a deep exhale, he took a step back. "I can't promise you anything," he said, his voice rough, "but I'm not walking away. Not yet."

That was all he gave me. But for the first time, I thought maybe it was enough.

The night seemed to hold its breath as I watched him walk away, each step deliberate, as though he were leaving behind something precious but too dangerous to keep. I couldn't look away, even though I knew the further he got, the harder it would be to reach him. And yet, part of me had to know—had to test whether he meant what he'd said. Whether, deep down, he truly believed there was nothing left between us but smoke and ash.

I stood frozen, the air thick with something unsaid, something I couldn't touch. The silence was oppressive, suffocating, and as I forced myself to exhale, I felt a rush of frustration claw at my insides. I had never felt so powerless. So vulnerable.

"Lila," his voice broke through the haze, a whisper carried on the wind, as sharp as it was soft. He hadn't gone far, not far enough for me to lose him yet. He stopped, standing at the edge of the street, his silhouette barely visible in the dim streetlight. "Don't you see? This—" He gestured toward the empty space between us. "This can't happen. Not like this."

I wanted to argue, wanted to yell at him for being so damned noble and stupid at the same time, but all that came out was a soft, almost desperate sigh. "Why not?" My voice cracked despite my attempt to keep it steady. "What is it about us that's so damn broken?"

He turned around slowly, as if the effort was too much. His eyes met mine, burning with something that could have been regret—or was it something darker? "You don't understand. I don't want to hurt you. But if we keep going—if we keep doing this—everything you care about will burn."

The word "burn" hit me like a punch to the chest. He was right, I knew that much. But the part of me that refused to back down, the stubborn piece of me that had been forged in the fire of my own demons, wouldn't let him push me away.

"And if I can't let you go?" I took a step toward him, my heart pounding, the distance between us narrowing with each beat.

For a moment, there was nothing but the rush of blood in my ears and the crackle of tension in the air. He didn't speak, didn't move. But I could see it in his eyes—he was torn. Torn between wanting to pull me into his arms and wanting to shove me away for my own good.

"I won't be the one to destroy you, Lila," he said finally, his voice low but steady. "You have no idea what's at stake here. People—dangerous people—don't let things like this happen. And they don't forgive."

I paused, the weight of his words sinking in. I had a thousand questions, a thousand fears I couldn't even begin to voice. I thought I had known pain before, thought I understood loss and grief. But the truth of what he was saying—the implication of what I could lose if I kept pushing him—gnawed at me.

"What are you so afraid of?" I whispered, the words more fragile than I wanted them to be. "What is it that's haunting you?"

His expression shifted, an unreadable mask falling over his features. "If you knew the answer to that," he said, his voice tinged with bitterness, "you'd run in the opposite direction so fast, your feet wouldn't even touch the ground."

And for a moment, I believed him. The look in his eyes was enough to send a shiver down my spine, a chill that had nothing to do with the night air. It was as if there was something lurking beneath the surface, something dark and dangerous, that could pull me under without warning.

But I wasn't ready to run—not yet. Not while I still had the taste of him on my lips, the imprint of his touch still burning through my skin. I wasn't ready to walk away from the one thing that had made me feel alive in a world that had long since forgotten how to breathe.

"I'm not afraid," I said, surprising myself with the steadiness of my own voice. "You don't get to make that decision for me. Not now. Not anymore."

His lips twisted into a wry smile, a bitter, broken thing that made my chest ache. "You think you're strong enough for this? You think you're strong enough to survive what's coming?"

The question hung in the air like a blade, suspended above us, sharp and unforgiving. I swallowed, my throat dry, but I couldn't back down. Not now, when I could feel the heat of him still surrounding me, his presence seeping into my bones like some sort of curse.

"I don't know what's coming," I admitted, my voice a little softer now, but still firm. "But I know I can't let you go. I won't."

He exhaled sharply, a sound like frustration, like defeat. For a moment, I thought he might give in, might pull me toward him, kiss me until we both forgot how impossible this all was. But instead, he turned, his back to me once again, as though walking away were the only thing left for him to do.

I felt my heart sink, a hollow ache settling in my chest, but I refused to let him see it. Refused to let him think he had the power to destroy me with a few well-chosen words.

But then, just as I was about to turn away myself, I heard the unmistakable sound of a car approaching. The sharp hiss of tires against the wet asphalt. I looked up just in time to see the sleek black sedan skid to a halt beside him.

The door opened, and a figure emerged, someone I didn't recognize, but the way he moved—so fluid, so sure—made my stomach drop. This was no ordinary stranger. This was someone who had come for him.

And suddenly, I wasn't so sure anymore. Whatever this was, whatever we were about to face, was about to become a whole lot bigger than either of us had imagined.

Chapter 8: Whispers in the Ashes

The wind howled outside, tugging at the edges of the old curtains in the living room, as if trying to whisper its secrets to the walls. The fire crackled in the hearth, a defiant dance of flame that painted the room in shades of gold and orange, casting long shadows that stretched like ghosts on the polished floor. I watched them for a moment, those shadows, fascinated by how they moved and swayed, always just beyond reach. It was as though they knew something I didn't.

Aiden leaned against the doorframe, watching me with an intensity that made my pulse quicken, though I wasn't sure if it was from the fire or from the way his eyes seemed to flicker with a hidden fire of their own. His hands were shoved into the pockets of his worn leather jacket, the one he always wore when we were about to go somewhere serious. He had this look, that edge of danger, a sharpness to his posture that made everything inside me flare with something dangerous and raw.

"I don't think you're going to like what I found," he said, his voice low, the words laced with a quiet certainty.

I swallowed, a knot forming in my stomach. We had both been searching, sifting through the ashes of my family's history, hoping to uncover some sliver of truth about the fires that had destroyed so many lives. About the fires that seemed to follow Aiden wherever he went. There was no denying it anymore; the pattern was undeniable. Every step closer to the truth seemed to burn everything else to the ground.

"What did you find?" I asked, my voice almost a whisper, as though saying the words aloud might break something between us that was already fragile enough.

He stepped closer, just enough so that I could feel the heat of his presence, but not so much that it felt too overwhelming. His scent, something earthy and woodsy, wrapped itself around me like an invisible cloak, drawing me in.

"Your family's name, it's been mentioned more times than I care to count," he said, his voice steady, though I could see the tension in the way his jaw clenched. "But not in the way you think."

I took a step back, my breath catching. The name that had haunted me for as long as I could remember. The name I had tried to bury. My family had always been at the center of so many rumors, so many whispers, but I had always hoped they were just that—rumors. Nothing more. But now, with every piece of the puzzle falling into place, I was beginning to wonder if they were more than just idle gossip.

"Go on," I urged, my heart pounding in my chest.

Aiden's eyes flickered with something unreadable. He hesitated, as though weighing how much to say. For a moment, the only sound in the room was the crackle of the fire and the rhythm of my heartbeat, both threatening to drown out everything else. Then, slowly, deliberately, Aiden spoke.

"They've been connected to the fires, Evelyn. Not just the ones that started after we met, but long before. Your family... there's a pattern. One that doesn't just involve your bloodline, but something darker. Something deeper."

His words struck me like a blow to the gut. The room seemed to spin, and I gripped the back of the armchair for support, suddenly feeling very small in the face of something much larger than I had ever imagined. I had spent my entire life trying to outrun the legacy of my family's past, only to find that it had always been waiting for me in the shadows, lurking just beneath the surface.

"I don't understand," I said, my voice trembling, despite my best efforts to steady it.

Aiden's gaze softened, and he took a step closer, his hand brushing mine for the briefest of moments, the contact sending a jolt of warmth through me. It was a comfort, even as the storm raged inside my chest.

"You don't have to. Not yet," he said, his voice low and soothing. "But what we're dealing with... it's bigger than us. Than you, than me. There are forces at play here that neither of us can control."

I wanted to argue, to tell him that we could handle this together. That we always had. But I knew, deep down, that he was right. This wasn't just about us anymore. It was about something much older, something that had been pulling strings long before we ever crossed paths.

"I don't know if I can do this," I whispered, the words slipping out before I could stop them. "I don't know if I can keep going, knowing what I might be a part of. The things my family has done, the things they might still be doing."

Aiden reached for me then, his fingers threading through mine, firm and steady. His touch anchored me, gave me something solid to hold onto in the face of all the uncertainty swirling around us.

"You don't have to face it alone," he said, his voice fierce. "I won't let you."

But even as the words left his mouth, I felt the cold weight of doubt settle over me. We had both been so sure, so certain that we could survive whatever came our way, but now? Now I wasn't so sure. The shadows, the whispers, they were all closing in around us, and I was starting to wonder if loving him—loving us—was worth the danger that seemed to follow us at every turn.

"Do you ever wonder if we're in over our heads?" I asked, the question slipping out before I could stop it.

Aiden's expression faltered for a split second, the faintest trace of uncertainty crossing his face. But then, just as quickly, it was gone, replaced by that same resolve that had always drawn me to him.

"Every damn day," he muttered, pulling me closer, his lips brushing against my forehead. "But that doesn't mean we stop. Not yet."

Aiden's words echoed in my head like the warning of an approaching storm. We were standing on the edge, each whisper of truth threatening to send us plummeting into something we were both terrified to understand. Still, I couldn't look away. Despite the fear gnawing at my insides, I found myself caught between a reluctant desire to uncover more and a growing need to run far from the mess we'd waded into.

"Evelyn," he said softly, his voice steady even as the world around us felt like it was beginning to buckle. He stood at the edge of the hearth, one hand resting on the mantle, the other raking through his hair in that frustrated, restless way he always did when his thoughts were miles away. "There's more, but I don't want you to get lost in it."

I caught the subtle way he hesitated, his eyes flickering to the door as though he half-expected someone to burst in, as if danger lurked just beyond our four walls. Maybe it did. Maybe we were too far in already to turn back. His hand dropped from his hair, and his gaze snapped back to mine, intense as ever. There was something about him that still pulled at me—something that made me wonder if we could really find a way through the darkness together.

But his tone had shifted, becoming quieter, more measured, as though he was trying to spare me from something even darker than the truth he'd already shared. The way he was looking at me, his brow furrowed as though he were trying to decipher me as much as I was trying to figure him out, made me pause. There was no easy answer anymore.

"I'm listening," I said, my voice betraying none of the turmoil inside me. I wasn't sure if I wanted to hear what came next, but the unspoken promise between us—the way his breath caught when I spoke, the way his chest tightened when he met my gaze—made it impossible not to ask for more.

Aiden sighed and glanced around the room again, then took a step closer, his boots clicking softly against the hardwood floor. The space between us seemed small, but the distance had never felt wider. The soft flicker of the fire reflected in his eyes, lighting up the harsh lines of his face, casting him in a sort of shadowed light.

"The fires," he began, his voice dropping even lower. "They weren't random. Whoever started them... they were methodical. And they weren't just after the buildings, the destruction. It's... it's bigger than that."

He paused, clearly wrestling with something, his eyes darting to the floor as if searching for the right words. I waited, breath held, my chest tight with anticipation.

"My family," he continued slowly, the words hanging between us, thick with implication. "They didn't just watch the fire take down the town. They fed it. Encouraged it. This... this was no accident. And it's connected to your family in ways I'm not sure either of us are ready to understand."

I took a step back, almost stumbling, as if the ground beneath me had shifted. The air felt suddenly too thick, too heavy to breathe. Aiden's family? He couldn't possibly be talking about his father—the man whose name was whispered in every corner of town like some kind of boogeyman, the one who'd disappeared without a trace years ago. But Aiden had always avoided speaking of him, always skirted around the subject like it was some sort of unspoken rule. And now here he was, throwing that name into the fire. It felt like betrayal, but even more than that, it felt like the ground beneath my feet had fractured into a million tiny pieces, each one pulling me deeper into the dark.

"Wait," I said, my voice sharper than I intended, my pulse racing. "You're saying your family was involved? That they... they had a hand in this?"

Aiden's eyes flickered, but he didn't back away. "Not just a hand," he said quietly, his voice now edged with something I couldn't quite place. "They were part of it. And I think your family knew. Hell, they may have even helped."

My stomach twisted, a mixture of disbelief and something darker I couldn't quite identify. The idea that my own bloodline could be involved in something so sinister sent a shiver down my spine. And the way Aiden said it—so matter-of-factly, as though he had already accepted the truth—it made me question everything I'd ever known. I'd always heard the rumors, the whispers of my family's involvement in the fires of the past, but I'd always dismissed them as gossip. This was different. This was something worse, something that held the weight of history and danger behind it.

"You can't seriously believe that," I whispered, though a part of me knew that he did. And the cold, jagged edge of the truth he was presenting hit me harder than I was ready for.

Aiden's eyes softened, and he reached for me, his hand warm against my cool skin. His thumb brushed over my knuckles, a silent apology, but it didn't ease the ache in my chest.

"I don't know what to believe anymore," he said, his voice hoarse. "But I do know one thing, Evelyn. Whatever happened, whoever did this... it's not over. It's still out there. And I don't know if we're just pieces in some game that's been played for far too long."

His words hit me with the force of a freight train. The realization that we weren't just entangled in some personal vendetta, that we weren't merely victims of a series of unfortunate events, was like a punch to the gut. We were part of something much larger than either of us had imagined. And the danger? It wasn't in the past. It was still very much alive, lurking in the shadows, waiting for the right moment to strike.

I looked up at him, the weight of his words sinking in. "What now?" I asked, my voice barely more than a breath.

Aiden didn't answer right away. He only pulled me closer, his arms wrapping around me as if he were trying to protect me from the storm that was brewing just outside our door. And for a moment, I let him. I let myself lean into him, my head resting on his chest, listening to the steady beat of his heart beneath the chaos that was threatening to engulf us.

But even as I closed my eyes, I couldn't shake the feeling that we were teetering on the edge of something far worse than either of us could imagine.

I woke up to the sound of rain. It wasn't the comforting patter against the windows, but the relentless beating that seemed to echo through the walls, as though the world was drowning in its own secrets. The storm had arrived, and with it, the gnawing suspicion that we had only just begun to scratch the surface.

Aiden was already gone. His side of the bed was cold, the sheets slightly rumpled, but he wasn't there. The moment I opened my eyes, I felt the absence of him, more tangible than the space between us had ever been. He hadn't left a note, no words of reassurance or explanation. But the silence spoke volumes. It was the kind of silence that settled like a fog, heavy with things left unsaid.

I pulled myself out of bed, the weight of the night pressing on my shoulders, dragging me down as if it had conspired to steal my energy while I slept. The house, once so familiar, now felt like an unfamiliar maze. Each room whispered warnings, and every shadow seemed to hide something sinister. Even the kitchen felt colder than usual as I moved through it, filling the kettle with water, my hands shaking ever so slightly.

But it wasn't just the house that felt off. It was everything. It was the town we lived in, the people we'd trusted, and the creeping feeling that we were being watched. The closer I came to the truth, the more tangled I became in the web of lies, secrets, and betrayal. And as much as I wanted to believe in the story Aiden and I had started to weave, I was starting to wonder if it was one written by someone else altogether.

I turned the corner into the living room, my feet cold against the wooden floors, and my gaze immediately flicked to the table where Aiden had left his jacket, a small leather notebook tucked into the back pocket. I had seen it before, the way he would pull it out when he thought no one was looking, scribbling things down with an intensity that suggested he was keeping secrets even from me. His shadows were as deep as mine, but somehow I never thought to ask what was hidden in them.

I reached for it now, the leather soft under my fingers, the familiar weight comforting and ominous at the same time. I flipped it open, and the first page caught my attention. There, scrawled in jagged ink, was my family's name. Beneath it, a string of dates, events, names I recognized and others I didn't. But it wasn't just random notes. It was a timeline. A timeline of fires. Of destruction. Of things that Aiden had already known but hadn't shared. And my blood ran cold as I realized the depth of his involvement.

I slammed the book shut before my thoughts could spiral further, trying to steady my racing pulse. But it wasn't enough. I needed answers. I needed to understand what this meant. Why was he keeping this from me? What had he uncovered that I wasn't ready to see?

Before I could gather myself, the sound of a car pulling into the driveway broke through my thoughts. I froze, heart skipping a beat. I hadn't expected him back so soon. The rain was coming down harder now, pounding against the windows, muffling everything outside.

But I could tell—it was him. His truck, unmistakable in the foggy morning light, was parked just outside.

I moved to the window, trying to make sense of what I saw. He stepped out, his silhouette a shadow against the storm, and I caught the way he glanced around, his movements cautious, deliberate. Something was off. This wasn't the same Aiden I'd woken up with. This was someone different. The storm outside mirrored the one building inside me, and I couldn't help but wonder if it was finally time to confront the truth.

He opened the front door without knocking, and my pulse quickened as I turned to face him, the quiet tension in the room thickening like the air before a lightning strike. Aiden's gaze flickered over me, not quite meeting my eyes, his jaw tight with something unspoken. And when he finally spoke, it wasn't what I expected.

"I need you to stay inside today," he said, his voice clipped, sharp. "Lock the doors. Don't open them for anyone."

"Why?" I asked, my voice steady despite the fluttering unease in my chest.

Aiden's eyes darted to the window, to the streets beyond, as though expecting someone to appear from the mist. He shook his head, running a hand through his rain-soaked hair, frustration etched in every line of his face. "Because they know we're getting close. And I don't want you caught in the crossfire."

Crossfire? My mind whirled. Who was he talking about? What did he mean? I took a step toward him, not sure if I was angry or terrified, but not about to stand idly by. "You can't just drop that on me and expect me to—"

A sudden noise cut me off. A sharp knock at the door. We both froze. Aiden's eyes went wide, the color draining from his face as he jerked his head toward the back door.

"Go," he hissed, the command leaving no room for argument.

I didn't wait for him to tell me twice. I rushed to the door, heart pounding, but before I could get more than a few steps, I heard another knock. Closer this time. And then another. Faster. More insistent.

I didn't move. Not because I didn't want to, but because something in the air had shifted, a crackle of energy I couldn't explain. I felt the weight of every decision we'd made until now bearing down on me, suffocating me with its inevitability. The truth we'd been running from had finally caught up to us.

The door swung open. And standing there, drenched from head to toe, was someone I never expected to see.

Chapter 9: A Taste of Betrayal

The sun was low in the sky, casting a warm amber glow over the quiet town, but all I could see was the distance growing between Aiden and me. His back was turned, his broad shoulders hunched slightly as he looked out toward the horizon, his hands shoved deep into the pockets of his worn leather jacket. His profile was shadowed, but I knew him well enough now to recognize the tension in his jaw, the sharp line of his lips that no longer curved in that easy, mischievous smile.

I should have left him alone. The conversation we'd had just minutes earlier, in the small café we frequented, had been filled with awkward pauses, half-finished sentences, and a strange undercurrent of discomfort that seemed to settle between us. I tried to brush it off, convinced it was just a passing moment, some stress from his work or maybe the weight of the world outside his control. But as I stood there, the taste of unease lingering in my mouth like something sour, I realized I had been lying to myself.

"You okay?" I asked, my voice trembling slightly, though I did my best to keep it steady, to pretend that everything was fine. That we were fine.

He didn't answer immediately. Instead, he shifted slightly, as though weighing the words, or perhaps dodging them altogether. Then he finally spoke, his voice a little too controlled, a little too guarded. "Yeah, just... tired."

That didn't sound right. Aiden wasn't the type to shy away from sharing what was on his mind, even if it was something as trivial as how his day had gone. So why did I feel like there was something he wasn't telling me? Something crucial. Something that had the potential to break the fragile peace we'd managed to carve out in this otherwise unpredictable life we were trying to build together.

I took a step closer, my fingers brushing the cool metal of the railing that ran alongside the dock. "Are you sure? You've been acting strange since we got here."

His eyes flicked to mine, a quick, darting glance that didn't quite meet my gaze. That should have been my first red flag.

"I'm fine," he repeated, more firmly this time. "It's nothing."

"Nothing doesn't make you act like you're being chased by your own thoughts," I said, a little sharper than I intended, but the words came out before I could stop them. It wasn't like me to push, to prod, but something inside me was demanding answers, even if I didn't want to hear them.

He exhaled slowly, his chest rising and falling in a deep sigh, as though the weight of the world rested on his shoulders. He turned to face me then, his eyes searching mine for something—maybe for the reassurance that I would let it go, that I would give him the space he clearly craved. But instead, I stood firm, meeting him with all the resolve I could muster.

"I'm not going to drop it, Aiden," I said, my voice low but unwavering. "Not this time. You've been pulling away from me for days now, and I need to know why."

He stiffened at the words, the muscle in his jaw tightening. For a long moment, he said nothing, his silence louder than any protest. Then, almost reluctantly, he spoke, his voice betraying the crack in his composure.

"You don't know everything about me, Mags."

I froze, my breath catching in my throat. The weight of his words hung between us, heavy with the unspoken implications. What did he mean by that? What was I missing?

"I know you, Aiden," I replied, my voice trembling now, though I refused to let it falter. "I know you more than I ever thought possible. I know the way your eyes light up when you talk about your past, about your family, about the things that matter to you." I stepped closer, needing to be nearer to him, to feel the connection that had always been between us. "But I need to know all of you. I need to understand what's going on, even if it's not pretty."

Aiden closed his eyes for a moment, as though battling some internal war. When he finally opened them again, there was something darker there—something that made the hair on the back of my neck stand on end.

"It's not what you think. It's not what you want to hear."

The words hung in the air, unsettling in their ambiguity. I waited, but he remained silent, his gaze shifting to the water below, where the darkening waves lapped gently against the shore.

"I'm not the man you think I am," he finally admitted, his voice barely above a whisper.

My heart skipped a beat. "What does that mean?"

But before he could answer, a car pulled into the parking lot behind us, its headlights cutting through the dimming twilight like a sudden jolt of electricity. Aiden stiffened, his eyes narrowing as he turned toward the sound of the engine.

"Don't," I said, my voice tight with a sudden sense of foreboding. But it was too late.

A figure stepped out from the car—a woman. Tall, with dark hair and a confident stride, she was dressed in sleek black, her presence commanding even in the distance. I had never seen her before, but something about the way she moved made me feel like I had stumbled into a moment I wasn't meant to witness. Aiden's expression had gone cold, the vulnerability I had seen moments earlier replaced by a guarded, almost hostile air.

"Who is she?" I asked, my stomach twisting as the feeling of betrayal began to sink in.

Aiden didn't answer right away. Instead, he stepped toward the woman, his steps brisk, his posture stiff. I stood there, frozen, the weight of his silence pressing down on me like a leaden cloud. And in that moment, I realized—whatever secrets Aiden had been hiding, they were more dangerous than I could ever have imagined.

I wanted to scream at him, to demand the truth right there, but something in me—the part that still loved him more than I could admit, even to myself—held me back. Maybe it was fear, or maybe it was because I still wanted to believe that Aiden wasn't the man I was beginning to suspect he might be. But as the woman approached him with that predatory grace, something inside me cracked.

She was too poised, too confident, to be anyone less than important. She wasn't the kind of woman who waited for an invitation; she was the kind who simply took what she wanted, who stepped into your world with the assurance of a seasoned player. Aiden's reaction confirmed everything I needed to know. The way he stiffened at the sight of her, the barely perceptible tension in his shoulders—it was as if he were facing a ghost from a past he'd never wanted me to meet.

I took a tentative step forward, my pulse quickening. "Who is she, Aiden?" I asked again, my voice sharp, though I tried to keep the panic from overtaking my words.

Aiden didn't immediately answer. Instead, his eyes flickered from me to the woman and back again, and I saw the briefest flash of something in his expression—regret, maybe, or something far darker. It was gone so quickly, replaced by the usual cool indifference that had become his armor. He cleared his throat, as though gathering his thoughts, or perhaps trying to find a way to explain something that had no easy explanation.

"Her name is Leah," he finally said, his voice tight, strained in a way I hadn't heard before. "She's... an old acquaintance."

"Acquaintance?" The word sounded hollow coming from him, like it wasn't enough to explain the way he'd stiffened the moment her car had rolled up. There was more to it, so much more, and my insides twisted as the realization began to settle. "You don't look like you're exactly thrilled to see her."

"I'm not," Aiden admitted quietly, though he quickly masked the vulnerability with a shrug. "But it's complicated."

Complicated. Of course it was. Nothing with Aiden was ever simple, was it? My mind raced, connecting dots I wasn't sure I wanted to connect. Could this woman have something to do with whatever it was that had been eating at him these past few days? Was she the reason he'd been pulling away from me, the reason his words were always clipped, his eyes distant? I wasn't sure I was ready to know, but the nagging sense of betrayal in my chest made it impossible to ignore.

Leah stopped a few feet away from us, her heels clicking sharply on the pavement. She wore a smile that felt rehearsed, practiced, the kind of smile that didn't reach the eyes. She was sizing me up, I could tell. It didn't take a detective to figure out she wasn't just a passerby—she was someone who had come to stake a claim.

Aiden's jaw clenched as Leah gave me a quick once-over, her eyes narrowing slightly before she offered me a nod that didn't quite resemble a greeting.

"Mags, this is Leah," Aiden said, his voice tight. "Leah, this is Mags. My... girlfriend."

Girlfriend. The word felt foreign on his tongue, as if he wasn't quite used to saying it, like it was something he was trying on for size but didn't quite fit. The tension between us deepened, and I resisted the urge to turn away, to run, to find some corner where I could breathe without feeling this suffocating sense of betrayal wrapping around me.

Leah's lips twitched into something close to a smirk. "Nice to meet you," she said, her tone smooth but carrying an edge, like she wasn't sure whether to be polite or outright dismissive. "I've heard so much about you."

I wasn't sure whether she was mocking me or trying to assert some dominance over the situation. Either way, it didn't matter. She was already here, and my place in Aiden's world felt smaller than ever.

"I didn't realize you were coming," Aiden said, his voice strained, though he forced a smile. "Is everything alright?"

Leah's gaze flickered to me again, but this time it lingered just a second too long, like she was evaluating me, sizing me up in a way that made my skin crawl. Then, without missing a beat, she turned her attention back to Aiden.

"I'm fine," she said curtly, her voice cool. "But I need to talk to you. It's important."

The words were loaded, carrying some heavy weight that neither of them seemed willing to acknowledge. I couldn't help but feel like I was being left out of a conversation that had already been written long before I ever walked into the room. My pulse quickened as I fought to maintain my composure, but I could feel the walls closing in around me, squeezing the breath out of my lungs.

Aiden turned to me, his face unreadable. "Mags, maybe we should—"

"No," I interrupted, the words coming out more sharply than I intended. "No, we're not doing this. If you need to talk, then talk. But I'm not standing here like a fool while you've got your secrets hidden in plain sight."

Aiden flinched at my words, his eyes flickering with a mixture of frustration and something else, something that looked an awful lot like regret. But it wasn't enough to stop him. It never had been.

"Let me handle this," he said softly, his gaze still holding mine, though there was a distance in it now—a barrier that hadn't been there before. "Please."

I didn't know what to say. Part of me wanted to argue, to demand answers, to rip the truth out of him whether he was ready to face it or not. But the other part of me—the part that had fallen in love with him despite all his flaws, despite the ghosts he carried—knew that if he wasn't ready to share it, there was nothing I could do to change that.

So, instead, I nodded stiffly. "I'll be around." My voice felt cold, even to me. "But when you're done pretending nothing's wrong, you can come find me."

With that, I turned and walked away, each step heavier than the last, as the weight of his secrets crushed the space between us. I had no idea how we'd come back from this—or if we even could. But the taste of betrayal was already lingering on my tongue, and I couldn't shake the feeling that the truth was far more dangerous than I ever expected it to be.

I barely heard the click of the door behind me as I walked away, my pulse pounding in my ears. Every step felt like I was marching deeper into a fog, the air thick with uncertainty, each breath more suffocating than the last. I hadn't planned to leave—hadn't planned to storm off with nothing but a cold, searing knot in my stomach. But something in the way Aiden had looked at me, something in his eyes, had ignited a fire I wasn't prepared for. I needed space. Space to breathe. Space to think.

I hadn't realized how far I'd walked until I found myself by the water, the lake shimmering under the moonlight, stretching out like an endless sheet of glass. The soft ripple of the waves was the only sound breaking the stillness, but even that felt like an intrusion against the buzz of tension still clinging to my skin. I sat on the edge of the dock, dangling my legs over the side, trying to shake off the unease that had settled in my chest. It wasn't working. Nothing was working.

What had I been thinking?

The question lingered in the air like a bad joke. What had I been thinking, believing that Aiden was as simple as the man he let me see? The charming, handsome, reckless guy who always seemed to know exactly what to say to make me laugh, to make me feel like the world wasn't such a bad place. How naive I had been to think that he could be that version of himself and nothing else.

But this—this secretive, guarded version of him? This man who would look me in the eyes and say nothing was wrong when every instinct screamed that something was? I didn't know him anymore.

I sucked in a breath, willing the tears that threatened to spill to stay where they belonged—locked behind the walls I'd built. I wouldn't let him see me break. Not when I didn't know what he was hiding. Not when I had no idea how deep this went.

The soft crunch of gravel underfoot pulled me from my spiraling thoughts, and I glanced over my shoulder to see Aiden walking toward me, his hands in his pockets, his steps slow but deliberate. His face was unreadable, though there was something there—something dark and raw—lurking behind his calm exterior.

"Mags," he said my name like a prayer, a plea, as though it could somehow erase the distance that had opened between us in the last few minutes. "Can we talk?"

I wanted to say no, to turn away and keep walking until I was miles from him, far enough to breathe without the suffocating weight of his secrets pressing down on me. But I couldn't do it. Not when his voice sounded like that—so soft, so desperate. It was the Aiden I knew, the one who had always been willing to fight for what mattered.

So I stayed silent, my gaze focused on the ripples in the water as he came to stand next to me, close enough that I could feel the warmth of his presence but not close enough that it felt comforting.

"You should have told me about her," I finally said, my voice quiet but firm. "About Leah. You should have told me what she meant to you."

Aiden didn't flinch, though I saw the subtle shift in his posture. He was still holding something back, but this time I wasn't going to let him get away with it.

"I wasn't hiding it from you," he said, his voice gruff, as if he were forcing the words out. "I didn't think it mattered. I thought... I thought it was in the past."

I gave a short laugh, bitter and dry. "The past doesn't just disappear, Aiden. It never does. Not for people who really matter."

He stood still for a moment, the silence thick between us. I could almost feel the weight of his thoughts pressing down on him, and I knew that whatever he was thinking, whatever he was struggling to say, he was scared. Scared of losing me. Scared of whatever it was he was hiding.

"I didn't want you to know about her because I knew it would change things," he said, his voice tight, like the words were a confession. "I knew it would make you question everything. But I never meant to hurt you."

The ache in my chest deepened at his words, but I didn't turn to him. If I did, I was afraid I might crumble. "You should have trusted me enough to let me decide for myself whether I could handle the truth."

"I do trust you," he said quickly, taking a step toward me. "More than anyone else. But sometimes... sometimes the truth isn't something you can just say, Mags. Sometimes it's dangerous."

I scoffed, the sound sharp in the quiet night air. "Dangerous? What, you think I can't handle it? That I'm some fragile thing who'll fall apart if I know the truth?"

He exhaled sharply, his breath heavy in the night. "No, that's not what I meant. But there are things in my past that—things I thought I left behind. I didn't want them to come back, not when I've finally started to have something real with you."

"Real?" I said, my voice rising, the bitterness seeping in again. "How real can it be when you're keeping secrets from me? When you're still hiding parts of yourself like I'm not even worth the truth?"

He didn't answer at first. Instead, he stood there, his hands trembling slightly at his sides, his eyes cast down toward the water. When he finally spoke, his voice was rough, almost broken.

"I never wanted you to find out about Leah. She's not just an ex, Mags. She's... complicated. She was involved in things that I've been trying to outrun for years."

The revelation hit me like a slap, my mind scrambling to process the implications of his words. "What kind of things?" I demanded, my heart in my throat.

Aiden's lips tightened, and he looked at me, really looked at me for the first time in days, and there was something in his gaze—something darker than anything I had ever seen in him before.

"I can't tell you that," he whispered, his voice barely audible over the lapping of the water. "Not yet."

Before I could reply, before I could even begin to ask him what the hell that meant, I heard it. The unmistakable sound of tires screeching, of an engine revving. It wasn't just any car—it was a sound I knew all too well, a sound I'd been dreading. And before I could turn, before I could ask him what was happening, Aiden's face went pale.

"Mags," he said, his voice hoarse, full of a fear I'd never heard in him before. "Get down. Now."

It was too late.

The headlights of a black SUV appeared, blinding, roaring up the path behind us. And as the car skidded to a halt just a few feet away, I realized—with a sickening twist—that the truth I'd been searching for was about to come crashing down on us both.

Chapter 10: Crossroads of the Heart

The kitchen smelled like cinnamon and something else—something sharp, like the bite of freshly cracked pepper. I couldn't tell if it was the cloying scent of the apples baking in the oven or just the leftover tension from last night's argument that hung in the air. Aiden had stormed out, and I had slammed the door behind him, but the thing that stung wasn't the coldness of the door against my palm; it was the emptiness that followed in his wake.

I turned away from the window, staring at the steaming coffee mug in my hands. The steam curled upward, teasing the air in delicate wisps, but all I could think about was the storm inside me. It was the same storm he carried—dark and tumultuous, with flashes of brilliance, but one that always threatened to overwhelm us both.

Footsteps echoed on the stairs, and I stiffened, gripping the mug a little tighter. I knew that walk, that heavy, slow pace. Aiden. The man who could make my heart race with a single look, yet shatter it with a single word.

The door creaked open, and there he was, standing in the threshold. His hair was still damp from the shower, his face drawn, but there was something about him that made my chest tighten. Something unreadable, like he was holding a secret in the lines of his face, and the world was waiting for him to finally let it slip.

"I don't know what I'm supposed to say," he said, his voice low and rough, as if he'd been up all night trying to figure it out too.

I lifted the coffee mug to my lips, not because I wanted it but because I didn't know what else to do with my hands. "You don't have to say anything, Aiden. You've already said it all. Or at least, that's what I thought last night."

His gaze flickered to the coffee, then back to my eyes. "I wasn't thinking clearly. I don't—" He paused, running a hand through his damp hair. The motion was so familiar it nearly broke me. "I don't want to lose you."

The words hung between us, and for a long moment, neither of us moved. But it wasn't just the space between us that was wide and uncertain. It was the distance between everything we had built and everything we had torn down. The walls, the barriers, the things unsaid—they were all just as real as the air we breathed.

"You can't keep doing this, Aiden. This push and pull. I'm not some prize you can win, or something you can just drop whenever it's convenient." The bitterness in my voice surprised me, but it was there, hot and sharp, and it made his eyes narrow with something like pain.

"I never wanted it to feel like that," he said, stepping closer, but there was still that invisible barrier between us, like we were both afraid to touch the other first. "I just—I don't know how to let people in without screwing it up."

I set my mug down on the counter, the clink of ceramic sharp in the otherwise quiet room. "That's the problem, Aiden. You've built your whole life around not letting people in. But you can't have a relationship based on walls. Not with me."

His jaw clenched, and for a moment, I thought he might leave again, might say something that would drive me further away. But instead, he sighed, the sound escaping him like a long-held breath.

"I know. And I hate that I've pushed you to this point. I hate that I've made you feel like you have to choose."

"Because that's exactly what I'm doing." I stared at him, the weight of it all sinking in like a stone in my chest. "I'm standing at a crossroads, and I don't know which way to turn. I love you, Aiden. But love doesn't erase fear. It doesn't erase the scars we carry. And every time you shut me out, you make it harder to believe that we can survive this."

He flinched, like I'd struck him with those words, and for a fleeting moment, I regretted saying them. But then I remembered how many times I had swallowed my own doubts, how many times I had tucked my heart away just to keep it safe. And I couldn't do that anymore. Not with him.

"I know," he whispered. "And I don't deserve you. But I'm asking you to take a chance on me. Take a chance on us."

There it was. The plea that always came with the weight of his past, the darkness that hovered around the edges of everything he was. He wore it like a second skin, and even though I loved him, even though I saw the man underneath the scars, there were moments when I couldn't help but wonder if loving him would mean losing myself in the process.

"You say that, but how do I know this time will be different?" I took a step back, trying to keep my emotions in check. "How do I know that when things get tough, you won't shut down again? How do I know you'll stay?"

His expression faltered for just a moment, the crack in his armor visible but fleeting. But then, in a voice that seemed so small and vulnerable, he said, "Because I can't live without you."

There it was, the truth that lay beneath the tough exterior—the thing I had always known, even when he tried to push me away. And for a moment, I believed him. But belief wasn't enough to erase the doubts, the fears that whispered in the back of my mind.

I reached for him, the move instinctual, and he stepped forward, his hands trembling as they cupped my face. His touch was gentle, almost hesitant, as if he were afraid I might break beneath it. But it was what I needed—a quiet promise that, even if we didn't have all the answers, we still had a chance.

I closed my eyes, inhaling the warmth of him, and for the first time in what felt like forever, I allowed myself to hope.

His hand was still warm against my face, his thumb brushing lightly over my skin, sending a trail of heat through me. But his touch wasn't enough to quiet the buzzing in my mind. I could feel the storm stirring beneath my ribs, a tightness I couldn't ignore. Aiden, his presence like a magnet pulling me closer even when I knew better, still felt like a riddle I couldn't solve.

"I need more, Aiden," I whispered, my voice barely a breath, as though saying it aloud might make it too real. "I need you to stop running."

He froze. I could hear his breath catch, just the tiniest hitch. His fingers tightened against my jaw as though he were holding himself together by sheer force of will. "I'm not running," he murmured, his voice thick with emotion. "I just don't know how to make you understand how much you mean to me without breaking everything else in my life."

I pulled back slightly, studying him with cautious eyes. There it was again—the edge in his words. The way he kept himself tethered to the shadows, refusing to step fully into the light. I wanted to scream at him to let go, to let me in, to let himself be seen in all his fractured glory, but it was like trying to shake the walls of a house that had been built for too long. I didn't know if it was possible to tear it all down.

"Then what do you want from me, Aiden?" The words stung, more than I had expected. I wasn't trying to be cruel, but the weight of everything between us was suffocating. "You keep me here, on the edge, like a bookmark in a book you're not quite ready to finish, and I—"

"I'm not trying to keep you on the edge," he interrupted, the rawness of his voice stopping me mid-sentence. "I'm trying to protect you."

I blinked, the sudden sharpness in his tone sending a jolt through me. "Protect me?" The laugh that bubbled up wasn't one of amusement—it was hollow, bitter. "From what, Aiden? From you? From us?"

He winced, as if my words were a blow he hadn't expected. He let out a slow breath, his gaze drifting to the floor as he struggled to find his next words. "From my mess. From my mistakes. From me."

There it was—the thing he never said, the thing that lurked in every corner of the house, in every glance, every conversation. He was afraid of ruining me with his past. I could see it, feel it, all of it, right there in his eyes. He wanted me but didn't know how to trust that I could handle the wreckage he carried.

"You don't get to decide that for me," I said, my voice trembling with the weight of everything unsaid. "I'm not made of glass, Aiden. You don't have to protect me from your past. I'm here. I'm with you. But I can't be the person you want me to be if you keep holding everything back like it's some dirty secret."

He looked at me then, really looked, and for the first time in what felt like forever, the mask slipped. I saw him—the real him. The man who was broken but trying so damn hard not to break anyone else in the process.

"I'm not trying to hide anything from you," he said, his voice quiet but firm. "I'm trying to keep you safe from my demons."

I stepped forward, closing the gap between us. "You're not the only one with demons, Aiden. You don't get to carry this weight alone anymore. You never did."

His eyes darkened, his lips pressing together in a line of frustration. "You think it's that easy? That you can just walk into my life and make it better? It's not a fairy tale, Charlie. It's real. And real is messy."

"I don't need a fairy tale," I shot back. "I need you. The real you. And I need you to let me help you carry this." I swallowed, the words coming out shakier than I'd intended. "I need you to stop running from us."

For a long moment, neither of us spoke. The silence stretched between us like a fragile thread, pulling taut with everything we hadn't said, everything we hadn't allowed ourselves to feel.

Finally, Aiden spoke again, his voice so low I almost didn't catch it. "I'm scared, Charlie."

I had expected anger, frustration, even guilt, but not fear. And yet, here it was—raw and unguarded, a crack in the armor he wore so well.

I took a step closer, my heart pounding in my chest. "Me too," I admitted, the words coming out before I could stop them. "I'm terrified. Terrified that I'm too much for you. That I'll fall in love with a man who won't let me in."

He closed his eyes at that, and when he opened them again, the weight in his gaze made my breath catch. "I won't push you away anymore," he whispered, his voice hoarse. "But I need you to understand that it's not because I don't want to. It's because I don't know how to do this. Not with all the pieces of me that are broken."

I reached for him then, my hand trembling as I touched his chest, feeling the steady thump of his heart beneath my fingertips. "Then let's fix it together," I said softly. "One piece at a time."

His hand found mine, his grip firm, but there was still that hesitance—still the fear that clung to him like a second skin. "I don't know if I can give you what you need," he said, the vulnerability in his words threatening to unravel me.

"You already have," I replied, my voice barely above a whisper. "But you have to let me have all of you, Aiden. Or we'll never have anything at all."

His eyes searched mine, uncertainty still flickering in his gaze. But slowly, almost imperceptibly, he nodded. And in that quiet gesture, I knew we were standing on the edge of something new. Something uncertain, something terrifying. But it was ours, and for the first time, that felt like enough.

The quiet between us stretched, pulling tighter and tighter until I thought I might choke on it. His hand, still gently gripping mine, seemed to hum with the weight of his thoughts. It wasn't anger anymore that clouded his eyes, but something else—something deeper, more unsettling. I could see it in the way his chest rose and fell, like he was trying to steady himself, but every breath he took was filled with uncertainty.

"Don't you ever get tired?" I asked, the words escaping before I could stop them. "Tired of carrying all of it alone?"

Aiden didn't answer at first, and the silence weighed heavily between us again, like a wall I wasn't sure how to break down. He ran a hand through his hair, the movement so familiar it almost made my heart ache. "I don't know any other way," he said, his voice barely above a whisper. "Maybe it's because I'm too broken to let anyone else in."

I shook my head, feeling a flare of frustration burn in my chest. "You keep saying that like it's some sort of permanent condition. But you're not broken, Aiden. You're just... you're just afraid."

He gave a low, bitter laugh, but there was no humor in it. "You think fear is what's holding me back?" He looked at me, his eyes dark and tired. "Fear of letting you down? Fear of not being enough? Or maybe..." He paused, and for the first time, his gaze flickered with something sharper, something almost accusatory. "Maybe I'm afraid of how much I need you. Because needing someone like that—letting them in too far—could be more dangerous than any demon I've ever faced."

I took a step closer, my heart pounding as the words spilled from me without thinking. "And you think I can't handle it? That I'm just some fragile thing that will shatter if you show me who you really are?"

"No." His voice dropped an octave, softer this time, like he was ashamed. "I think I'll shatter first."

I didn't know how to respond to that. The weight of his vulnerability hung in the air like a storm cloud, threatening to break, but not yet. Not until he was ready to let it go.

"Well, then maybe we're both screwed," I said, trying to lighten the tension with a half-smile. "Because it's pretty clear I'm already in too deep."

Aiden didn't smile back, but I saw the flicker of something in his eyes—a mix of relief and something else, something unreadable. He stepped toward me, just a fraction, closing the distance until the tips of his shoes brushed mine. His breath was warm against my skin, his presence filling every corner of the room.

"I don't want to ruin this," he said, almost pleading. "I don't want to ruin you."

"You're not ruining me," I shot back, the frustration bubbling up once again. "You're just... you're just not letting me be part of this. Part of you. And I don't know how much longer I can keep waiting for you to figure it out."

Aiden opened his mouth, but the words never came. Instead, he closed the gap between us, his hands coming up to cradle my face as he kissed me, soft and tentative at first, as though testing the waters, trying to gauge if I would pull away.

I didn't. I couldn't. I kissed him back, letting everything I had been holding inside pour into that one, quiet moment. All the fear, all the hope, all the love. It was all there, and it was all real. For once, neither of us hesitated. There was no pushing and pulling, no walls between us. Just a raw, unspoken connection that felt like a promise.

When we finally broke apart, I was breathless, my chest rising and falling with the effort of holding it together. Aiden rested his forehead against mine, his hands still tangled in my hair, as though afraid that if he let go, I would slip away from him forever.

"I'm sorry," he whispered, his voice thick with emotion. "I'm so sorry for everything."

I shook my head, the words stuck in my throat. How could I be angry when all I wanted was for him to believe in us, in me? But the truth was, I couldn't just pretend everything would be okay. I couldn't ignore the fact that something deeper was still holding us apart—something neither of us had the courage to face.

"We're not okay," I said, my voice quiet but firm. "Not yet. But maybe we could be."

Aiden closed his eyes, his jaw tightening as if he were preparing for something he wasn't sure he was ready for. When he opened them again, there was a kind of resolution there, a faint glimmer of hope that was both terrifying and beautiful.

"I don't know if I'm ready for this," he confessed, his hands dropping to his sides. "But I'm willing to try. For you. For us."

My heart skipped a beat. The vulnerability in his voice, the way he was standing there, bare and open, made something inside me shift. Maybe, just maybe, we could make this work. Or at least, we could try.

I took a deep breath, forcing myself to meet his gaze, to show him the quiet strength I had been hiding all this time. "We'll figure it out," I said, my voice steady even though my hands were shaking. "Together."

There was a flicker of something between us—something both fragile and powerful—and for a moment, I thought maybe, just maybe, we were on the brink of something new. Something real.

And then, just as I was about to say something more, a loud knock shattered the moment.

I froze, my heart skipping a beat as Aiden's face went rigid. We both turned toward the door, the weight of the interruption hanging heavily in the air.

The knock came again, louder this time. A sharp, insistent sound that made the hair on the back of my neck stand up.

Aiden's gaze flicked to mine, and I saw the same fear I had seen earlier—only this time, it was darker, more urgent. "Stay here," he said, his voice low, his eyes never leaving mine. "Don't open that door."

Before I could respond, he was already moving toward the door, his body tense, like he was preparing for something he wasn't ready to face.

And in that moment, I realized that whatever was on the other side of that door was something we weren't prepared for.

Something that could change everything.

Chapter 11: A Heart's Reckoning

I should have known. The whispers had been there all along, hidden in the spaces between our conversations, in the subtle shifts of his gaze when the past came up, in the way his voice faltered just a little when I asked too many questions. Aiden was never fully mine to begin with. But somehow, that realization felt like a slow-moving train, one I saw coming but was too caught in the wreckage to escape. I had thought I knew him—really knew him—but as the words tumbled out of his mouth, I realized just how little I understood.

The rain hadn't stopped for days, a relentless curtain of gray that stretched across the sky like a heavy woolen blanket. It hung low over the town, pressing in on everything. Even the air felt thick with it, the scent of wet earth and pine sharp against my senses. I stood in the doorway of his cabin, staring at Aiden as he leaned against the rough-hewn beams, looking somehow smaller, more lost, than I had ever seen him before.

"I'm sorry," he whispered, his voice barely audible over the soft patter of rain on the roof. His eyes were haunted, distant, as though he wasn't sure how to look at me anymore. And in that moment, I couldn't decide if I wanted to slap him or pull him into my arms and promise everything would be okay.

But everything wouldn't be okay. I had learned that the hard way.

"You should have told me," I said, my voice cracking like the dry wood beneath my feet. I wanted to be angry, to scream at him for hiding this from me, for weaving this tangled web of lies. But instead, the anger fizzled out, replaced by something cold, something that felt a little too much like regret.

He didn't answer, just stared at me, his jaw clenched so tightly I thought it might crack. There was a long silence between us, thick with unspoken words, until I couldn't bear it anymore.

"How long?" I asked, my voice barely a whisper.

Aiden hesitated, running a hand through his dark hair, as though searching for the right words. When he finally spoke, his voice was rough, the words jagged. "Since your brother died."

I felt the air rush out of me like I'd been punched in the stomach. "What?" The word came out a strangled gasp, like it had lodged itself in my throat, unwilling to leave.

He took a step forward, his eyes searching mine with a vulnerability that almost made my knees buckle. "I didn't know then. Not at first. I didn't know it was him. But it was. Your brother... I... I was the one who—"

"No." I shook my head violently, trying to make sense of what he was saying. "No, you're lying. You can't—"

"I didn't know," he repeated, his voice so raw it was almost a plea. "I swear to God, I didn't know it was him. But when I found out..." He trailed off, his hands trembling as he shoved them into his pockets.

I didn't know how to process this. The man I had trusted, the man I had fallen for, had been involved in my brother's death in some way I couldn't yet understand. How could I reconcile the love I felt for him with the horror that was now twisting inside me?

"You're telling me... that all this time, you've known?" I asked, my voice cracking under the weight of the question.

He nodded slowly, his face pale, guilt washing over him like a wave too powerful to fight.

"I should have told you," he admitted, his voice shaking. "But I couldn't. I couldn't bear to see the way you would look at me. I thought... if I kept quiet, if I kept my distance, I could protect you. But I didn't. I'm sorry. I should have been honest with you from the start."

The words should have been a balm, but they stung like salt on an open wound. I should have walked away right then. Should have turned my back on him, on everything he represented. But

I couldn't. Part of me wanted to, but another part of me—some darker, more desperate part—still clung to the connection we shared.

"You're sorry," I repeated, the words tasting foreign on my tongue. "You're sorry... but my brother's dead, Aiden. And I have to live with that. I don't get a do-over. I don't get to pretend it never happened."

He winced at my words, his face crumpling like a paper left out in the rain. "I know. I know you don't. And I know I don't deserve your forgiveness. But please... don't hate me."

Hate him? How could I hate him when every instinct in me told me to hold him close, to tell him that everything would be okay, even when I knew deep down it couldn't be? The love I had for him still lingered, stubborn and insistent, like the scent of his cologne that lingered on my pillow long after he was gone.

"You should have told me the truth," I whispered, the words heavy with the weight of everything we had been through. "From the beginning."

"I know," he said, his voice strained, like each word was being dragged out against his will. "I was weak. I was scared. But I never meant for this to happen. I never meant for things to get so... twisted."

The rain outside was starting to let up, but the storm inside me raged on. I didn't know what to do with the fragments of my heart that were still inexplicably drawn to him, still reaching for the man who had broken me.

The storm outside had quieted, but the air between us still crackled with a tension that was hard to ignore. I should have walked out, should have slammed the door behind me and never looked back. But the truth—bitter and raw—kept me rooted to the spot, forcing me to face something I wasn't ready to confront.

Aiden stepped closer, hesitant, as if waiting for me to signal whether he should approach or stay away. The distance between us seemed insurmountable, despite the fact that only a few steps separated us. He had always been the type to act first and think later, but now? Now, he looked like a man who had been stripped of everything he knew, a man who wasn't sure if he was worthy of even a glance from me.

I tried to steady my breath, but it felt like a futile attempt. "How?" The question slipped out before I could stop it. "How could you let it get this far?"

His shoulders hunched, as though the weight of my words had physically struck him. "I never planned for any of this, you know. It wasn't supposed to be like this. When I first met you, when we first... started this—whatever this was—I never thought it would get so... complicated."

"Complicated?" I laughed bitterly, the sound sharp and unnatural. "That's one way to put it."

Aiden's hand rose, as though to reach for me, but he stopped mid-motion, his fingers curling into a fist at his side. I didn't know what he was waiting for—permission, forgiveness, or maybe just the truth. It didn't matter. I didn't know what I needed either.

"Do you remember the night I told you about my brother?" he asked, his voice quieter now, the raw edges of guilt lacing each word. "The one who was a soldier, the one I said died?"

I nodded, my throat tightening at the memory. Aiden had spoken of his brother in passing, in the way someone might mention a fleeting thought. But the look in his eyes then had been far from casual. It had been loaded, too heavy for something so trivial as a casual mention. I never imagined it might tie to my brother. Or worse, that Aiden might have known him long before he knew me.

"What if I told you he wasn't just some soldier? What if I told you he was a part of a mission—one that I never should have been involved in?"

The pit in my stomach deepened. The truth was coming, slow and deliberate, like a dark storm cloud rolling toward us. I could feel the ground shifting beneath my feet, and yet I couldn't tear myself away from his words. I had to hear it. I had to know.

"Aiden—"

"It wasn't supposed to happen like this," he continued, his voice hoarse. "The mission—what we were doing—it went sideways. Fast. And in the middle of all of it, in the middle of the chaos, your brother—"

"My brother?" I interrupted, my heart skittering in my chest.

Aiden closed his eyes as if steeling himself for what was to come. "Your brother wasn't just in the wrong place at the wrong time. He was—he was part of it. But not how you think. It wasn't supposed to go down the way it did."

I shook my head, my mind swirling with confusion and disbelief. "Wait. Are you telling me that my brother—"

"He didn't have a choice," Aiden cut me off, his voice sharp, desperate. "He was undercover. He was working with us. He was supposed to be helping us bring down a... a larger network, but... but everything went wrong."

The room spun. I grabbed the back of a chair to steady myself, my fingers gripping the wood so hard that my knuckles turned white. "Are you telling me my brother was involved in something illegal? That he was part of your... your operation?"

"It wasn't like that," he said quickly, taking a step forward. "He was a good guy. He had to do what he did to protect—" His words faltered, and he cursed under his breath, running his hand over his face. "God, I don't even know how to explain it. But he was never supposed to die. He never should have been there that night. I should have protected him."

I shook my head, the pieces of the puzzle still too far apart to fit together. "Why didn't you tell me this? Why didn't you tell me the truth?"

"I didn't know how," Aiden confessed, his voice a soft confession, barely a breath between us. "The guilt... the weight of it. It's been eating at me since it happened. I've been living with it, hiding from it, hoping I could find a way to make things right without you ever knowing the full extent of what happened."

"I've been living with it too," I shot back, my voice cold and brittle. "But I had no idea you were involved. No idea that my brother's death was more than just an accident. You knew him. You knew what happened. And you didn't tell me."

His face crumpled in pain. "I should have. But I didn't know how to explain it. I didn't know how to tell you that I was involved, that the man you... the man you loved was tied up in all of this."

The words hit me like a slap, but it wasn't the words themselves that stung—it was the rawness in his eyes, the brutal honesty that poured out of him now that it was too late. Aiden had never been this vulnerable before, and for a moment, it almost felt like he was unraveling in front of me. But I wasn't sure I could untangle the mess he had made.

"Tell me everything," I demanded, the weight of the past pressing down on me. "No more secrets. No more lies."

Aiden nodded, his expression hardening. "I will. But you need to understand. This is bigger than just us. What happened—what's still happening—it's not something we can walk away from. Not anymore."

And as his words echoed in the silence between us, I realized I wasn't just caught in a tangled web of lies. I was standing at the precipice of something far darker than I could have ever imagined.

I don't know why I stayed. Maybe it was the look in his eyes, the rawness of the pain I could see there, or maybe it was the fact that, despite everything, the pull between us had never really gone away. I wanted to hate him—I really did—but every time I looked at Aiden, all I could see was the man who had shared his fears, his dreams, and yes, even his regrets with me. How could I hate him when all I wanted to do was help him carry the weight of it all?

"You're telling me there's more?" I asked, my voice steadier than I felt. "That whatever you're involved in… it's still going on?"

Aiden nodded, his eyes flickering with something darker. It was a look I had seen before—when he thought I wouldn't notice, when he thought he could hide just how deep the shadows ran. But I noticed. I always noticed.

"I didn't want this for you, Lyla," he said, his voice thick with regret. "You shouldn't have been dragged into this mess. But it's not over. Not yet. The people I was working for—they've got more on their agenda, and it's not just about a mission anymore. It's bigger than that. There are things, things I can't even begin to explain without putting you in more danger."

"I'm already in danger, Aiden," I shot back, my frustration rising. "You think I don't get it? You think I don't understand that? My brother is dead, and I—" I paused, biting down on the words that threatened to break free. "I've spent so long burying this pain, pretending like I can just keep moving forward, but now you're telling me that everything—everything—is connected, that none of it was an accident?"

His gaze softened, but the anguish in it only made everything worse. "It wasn't supposed to be like this. I never wanted to drag you into this world. But the more I tried to pull away from it, the more it pulled me back in. It's not just about my past—it's about what's coming next."

I shook my head, the storm inside me growing more chaotic with each word he spoke. "What's coming next, Aiden? What are you saying?"

He swallowed hard, stepping back like he needed space to breathe. I knew he didn't want to say it, didn't want to burden me with the truth. But it was already here, hanging in the air between us like an unbearable weight. And I had a sinking feeling it wasn't going to go away.

"It's not just about me," he finally said, his voice tight. "There are people, powerful people, who will stop at nothing to get what they want. And I'm the one standing between them and what they need. If they think I've betrayed them—"

"You're not going to betray them," I interrupted, though even as the words left my lips, I wasn't sure I believed them. "You're not that man, Aiden. You never were."

His gaze was unreadable as he looked at me, the faintest hint of a smile tugging at the corners of his lips, though it didn't quite reach his eyes. "You don't know what I'm capable of."

"That's where you're wrong," I said, my voice trembling with a mix of anger and desperation. "I know exactly who you are. And maybe that's the problem."

He didn't flinch at my words, though I saw the faintest trace of something—guilt, maybe—pass over his features. "You shouldn't be here. Not now. Not after everything that's happened."

"Then why did you come back?" I demanded. "Why did you come back to me, if you knew it would only drag me deeper into this mess?"

He stepped forward, his eyes hardening, and for a second, I thought he might reach out to me. But then he stopped, fists clenched at his sides, as though the act of touching me was something that might break him.

"Because I don't have a choice," he said, his voice low, almost desperate. "I'm already too deep in. If I walk away, it could mean the end of everything. But if I stay... if I stay with you, it could mean the end of you. I can't protect you from this, Lyla. Not the way you deserve."

"I'm already in this," I said softly, my own voice barely above a whisper. "I've been in this from the moment I found out my brother was involved. And I can't just walk away now. I can't pretend none of this matters."

"You're wrong," he said fiercely, his gaze locking with mine. "It does matter. You matter. More than anything. But that's why you need to stay away from me. If they come for me, they'll come for you too. You have no idea how dangerous this is."

I opened my mouth to argue, but before I could speak, the sound of footsteps in the hallway interrupted. My heart leaped into my throat as the door creaked open. And then I heard it—the sharp click of a gun being cocked.

Aiden was already moving, his body a blur as he placed himself between me and the door, his eyes scanning the room like a soldier preparing for battle. "Get down," he ordered, his voice low and steady.

The sound of footsteps grew louder, closer now, and I froze. I could feel the cold knot of fear twisting in my gut as I realized just how far this had gone. Just how much danger I was in.

I didn't have a chance to react before the door flew open, and the dark silhouette of a man stepped into the room. His face was hidden in shadow, but the gun he held was unmistakable, gleaming in the dim light.

"Aiden," the man said, his voice smooth but with an edge of malice. "I think it's time we had a conversation."

The room went deathly still. And in that moment, I realized that this wasn't just about Aiden's past. It was about mine, too. A tangled web that had ensnared us both. And there was no getting out.

Chapter 12: Bound by Fire

The air was thick with smoke, the sharp tang of burning wood and acrid metal stinging my nose. I could barely see a foot in front of me as I stumbled through the charred remains of what had once been my family's estate. The fire had consumed everything, leaving only a hollowed-out shell where memories had once lived. Each step felt heavier than the last, the weight of the world pressing down on me.

I wanted to run, to escape the hell that had become my reality. But there was nowhere to go. Not now. Not when he was standing there, his figure barely discernible in the haze, waiting for me. Aiden. The one person who both terrified and exhilarated me all at once. The man who had set my life on fire in more ways than one.

The heat from the flames licked at my skin as I drew closer, the weight of his gaze locking onto me like a magnet pulling at my very soul. It was an intoxicating, suffocating sensation—one I had never been prepared for. Not in my wildest dreams, or nightmares, could I have imagined the pull he had on me. The way his presence made everything else seem irrelevant, as though nothing existed in the world except for the two of us.

"You're a fool for coming back here," his voice was low, but it cut through the noise of the fire like a knife. It was a familiar tone, one I had grown accustomed to—part amusement, part challenge. But now there was something else in it, something I couldn't place. "I told you to stay away."

I wasn't sure if it was the smoke or the shock of the situation, but I felt my pulse quicken. Every word he spoke seemed to draw me in deeper, like I was caught in an undertow I couldn't escape. "You didn't leave me much of a choice, did you?"

Aiden didn't respond at first, his eyes scanning the wreckage around us. His jaw was clenched, and the muscle in his cheek twitched, a sign I had come to recognize when he was struggling to keep his emotions in check. He was always the strong one, the stoic protector who never let anyone see his weakness. But right then, with the smoke curling around us, the flames casting eerie shadows, I saw something in him I hadn't before. It wasn't fear—he didn't fear anything—but it was... vulnerability. A crack in his armor that I wasn't sure I could repair.

"Maybe I didn't want you to have a choice," he finally said, stepping closer, his hand brushing mine in a gesture so brief it might've been a figment of my imagination. But it sent a jolt of electricity through me nonetheless.

The heat was unbearable now, the fire roaring behind us like an animal on the hunt. I couldn't tell if it was the danger or Aiden's proximity that made my heart beat faster. Maybe it was both. "You've always had a way of taking things from me," I murmured, my voice catching in my throat. "Even the things I thought I could keep."

He took another step forward, his shadow swallowing mine. "I've never taken anything that wasn't already yours, Lila. You just didn't realize it until now."

His words settled into my chest like a weight I couldn't shake. I swallowed, fighting the tightness in my throat, but I couldn't help it. "Is that what you tell yourself? That it was always meant to be? That you were always supposed to be a part of my life?"

There was a pause, and then a humorless laugh slipped from his lips. "You think I don't question it? Every damn day I wonder why I didn't stay away from you. But you don't get to choose who you love, Lila. Not really. Not when everything else is falling apart around you."

I felt the sting of his words, even if I didn't want to admit it. There was truth there—painful, raw truth. The kind of truth that twisted deep inside me, making me question everything I thought I knew about us, about him, about myself. "You always think you know what's best for me," I shot back, bitterness flooding my veins. "But you've never been the one to clean up the mess."

The fire crackled in the background, as though it had a life of its own, hungry and relentless. Neither of us moved, standing face-to-face amidst the destruction we had both caused in our own ways. "This mess," he said, his tone softening, "it's ours. All of it. You're not alone in this."

I wanted to believe him. I wanted to believe that the wreckage of my life could be salvaged, that somehow, in the middle of all the lies and betrayal, there was still something worth saving. But the doubt lingered, hanging in the air between us like the smoke. Could I trust him again? Could I trust myself?

Aiden's hand reached out, and this time, I didn't pull away. His fingers brushed against mine, sending a spark of warmth through my cold skin. There were no words for this moment, no explanations. Just the connection that tied us together, even if neither of us fully understood it. Even if we didn't know if it was enough to survive the flames that had consumed everything else.

I closed my eyes for a moment, feeling the heat radiating off him, feeling the pulse of energy between us, a wild, uncontainable force. "What happens now?" I whispered, not sure if I was asking him or myself.

His lips brushed my ear, a whisper of breath against my skin. "We find out."

The flames licked the edges of my consciousness, each crackling spark a reminder that everything around us—everything I thought I knew—was crumbling. But Aiden, impossibly close now, was the anchor I couldn't seem to loosen myself from. His fingers brushed my wrist again, this time lingering, as though he, too, felt the gravity of what we'd become to one another. I could taste the heat of the fire in the air, but all I could focus on was the feeling of him, a current surging between us that seemed stronger than the chaos around us.

"You shouldn't be here," Aiden's voice broke through my thoughts, low and jagged like a shattered stone, but the words didn't feel like they belonged to the man who had always kept me at arm's length. There was something softer now—something desperate—wrapped in the lines of his voice.

"You've said that already," I replied, my breath coming a little quicker than I wanted it to. "Doesn't seem to stop me."

"Maybe I don't want it to," he murmured, so softly that I almost didn't catch the words, but they landed with the weight of a confession. He was too close—too close to let my heart remain calm. But then again, I wasn't sure I wanted it to be calm anymore. There was something in his touch, in the tension between us, that made it feel as though the earth itself might crack open, leaving nothing but us.

"You're not afraid, are you?" I asked, daring to challenge him. I knew what he was capable of—what we both were—but even in this madness, I wondered if he could feel it, too—the creeping fear that maybe this was it. The end of us.

"No," he answered, almost too quickly. A bit too loudly, as though convincing both me and himself. He was a man who wore certainty like armor. And I was beginning to wonder if that certainty was a lie, as much to him as it was to me.

The fire continued to rage behind us, its guttural roar drowning out anything else. We stood there, surrounded by the crackling, the heat, and the ever-growing cloud of smoke, as though the world was imploding around us. But there, in the middle of it all, was Aiden—his presence a flickering flame I couldn't escape. His hands, once so distant, were now tracing patterns across my skin, almost as though he was trying to memorize me. I wasn't sure if it was a comfort or an interrogation, but I didn't stop him.

I didn't stop him when he cupped my face, the familiar warmth of his palms both reassuring and electric. He leaned in, the intensity of his eyes a searing force I couldn't look away from.

"Why do you do this to me?" he whispered, as if he, too, were caught in a snare of his own making.

"Do what?" I breathed out, my voice almost lost in the crackling inferno.

"Push me," he said, his fingers brushing against my jaw with such tenderness that it felt like a betrayal. "Make me want things I know I shouldn't. You don't think I know it's dangerous? All of this…you."

I wanted to pull away, to stand on my own, but I didn't. The pull between us was undeniable, a force far stronger than either of us. I wanted to feel indignant, to lash out at the man who had become both my prison and my salvation. But instead, I found myself whispering, "What are we supposed to do now?"

His gaze faltered for a split second, before he leaned closer, his lips brushing my ear. "We survive. Together."

There it was. The word I had always feared. Together. As if it were simple. As if it didn't mean everything. His hand slid to the back of my neck, pulling me closer still. The fire roared behind us, and for a brief moment, I forgot about the destruction. I forgot about the lies. I forgot about the world around us that was slipping into chaos. All I could feel was him—his heartbeat, his breath, the tension in his body that mirrored my own. And it made me wonder…could I really do this? Could I throw myself into this storm, knowing that we were both torn apart by forces far beyond our control?

"Are you sure?" I asked, the question slipping out before I could stop it. "Are you sure we can survive this?"

For the first time, I saw something—raw and unguarded—flash in his eyes. It was a flicker of doubt, of vulnerability that almost made me falter. I had always seen Aiden as a man with the answers, a man who knew exactly what he was doing at all times. But in that moment, as the fire surged and the world seemed to spin faster, I realized that maybe, just maybe, he was as lost as I was.

"I don't know," he whispered, his lips brushing against my forehead. "But I'm not giving up on us."

The words hung in the air between us, charged with something that could either be our salvation or our undoing. I had heard promises before. I had watched them crumble into dust. But this? This felt different. It felt real. And yet, the fear—the fear that it could all be nothing but ashes in the end—clung to me like the smoke that stung my eyes.

We stood in the midst of it all, this hell of our making, and for the first time in what felt like a lifetime, I didn't feel the urge to run.

The heat from the fire pressed against me, but Aiden's embrace was warmer still, holding me in place, tethering me to him. I could hear his heart, steady and strong, beneath the chaos. I could feel his breath, shallow and ragged, against my skin. We were standing at the edge of everything, and for once, it didn't seem so terrifying.

"Together," I whispered, tasting the word on my lips, trying it on for size. I still wasn't sure if I believed it, but in that moment, I wanted to. I wanted to believe that it could be enough.

Aiden nodded slowly, his forehead resting against mine. "Together," he echoed, and the promise, fragile as it was, wrapped itself around me like a lifeline.

And just like that, the world seemed to tilt in a new direction.

The fire was relentless. The kind of force that consumed everything in its path, leaving nothing but ashes. But here, in the midst of the inferno, Aiden and I stood, clinging to each other as though we were the only two things left that mattered in the world. The heat from the flames curled around us like a lover's whisper, trying to pull us apart, but somehow, we held on.

I could feel his heartbeat against my chest, steady and strong, while mine seemed to stumble, unsure if it was supposed to follow the rhythm of the world around us or create its own chaotic beat. Aiden's hands moved to the small of my back, drawing me closer, and in that moment, with the fire crackling behind us, I couldn't tell where the flames ended and we began.

"You're not going to walk away from this, are you?" Aiden's voice was low, like a secret meant only for me, but the edge of uncertainty was there, sharp and unmistakable.

"No," I whispered, my lips brushing against his ear. "Not anymore."

The truth hung between us like a fragile thread, barely tethered to anything solid. It wasn't just the fire that threatened to consume us—it was everything we'd built on lies, on half-truths and moments of weakness. Yet even as I said the words, something inside me shifted. There was no longer any hesitation, no doubt. This was it. We were in this, together, for better or worse.

I pulled back just enough to meet his gaze, to look into those dark eyes that always seemed to hold a thousand secrets. They flickered with something I couldn't quite name—longing, yes, but also something else. Desperation. And I wasn't sure if it was the fire blurring my vision or the rawness of this moment, but I saw him more clearly than I ever had before.

"Aiden," I said his name, and it felt like the first time I'd ever truly spoken it. Like it had weight, like it had meaning.

He ran a hand through his hair, a gesture so familiar that it made my chest tighten. But when his fingers met his forehead, I noticed something else. His hand trembled, ever so slightly. Just enough to tell me that beneath the layers of confidence and control, there was a man who had just as many cracks as I did. It was both reassuring and terrifying.

"I don't know how to fix this, Lila," he confessed, his voice barely audible over the roar of the fire. "I don't even know if it can be fixed."

A part of me wanted to pull away, to shield myself from the raw vulnerability he was offering. But that part of me was quiet, smaller than it had ever been before. I took a breath, steadying myself as I closed the gap between us. "Maybe it doesn't need to be fixed," I said softly, placing my hand on his chest. "Maybe it just needs to be... understood."

He looked down at me, his brow furrowed in confusion, but there was something else in his eyes. Recognition. A flicker of understanding, as if he realized that this—whatever this was—wasn't about saving the pieces of our broken past, but rather surviving what was coming. And what was coming, in all its terrifying inevitability, had nothing to do with what had happened before.

The ground beneath our feet trembled, a subtle warning that we weren't safe, that the world was still burning, still shifting. I felt the rumble of it through my bones, but Aiden didn't flinch. Instead, he stepped closer, his face inches from mine, his breath hot against my skin.

"We don't have to survive it alone," he said, the words a promise, but one laced with fear.

I didn't want to hear the fear in his voice. I didn't want to acknowledge the reality that maybe, just maybe, we were both in over our heads. But as I looked up at him, my fingers still pressed against his chest, I realized that there was no running from this anymore. The flames had already burned away everything that could have kept us apart. We were standing in the ruins of everything we knew, and it was too late to turn back.

"I'm not going anywhere," I said, my voice steady and sure, though my heart raced in my chest. "I'm not going to let you burn alone."

His lips hovered just above mine, the space between us thick with tension and unspoken promises. But before he could speak, before either of us could say the words that seemed to hang in the air like smoke, a sharp crack sounded from behind us.

I turned just in time to see the structure of the estate—what was left of it—shift, the weight of the fire pulling it down in one swift, terrible motion.

"No!" I shouted, but it was too late. The roof caved in with a deafening crash, sending a massive plume of smoke and debris into the air.

Aiden grabbed my arm, yanking me away from the falling wreckage just as a piece of the structure crumbled and sent shards of stone flying. We barely made it to safety, the force of the explosion knocking us both to the ground. My heart pounded in my chest, my hands shaking as I looked up, eyes wide in shock.

The fire had claimed the house. But it was far from over.

Aiden was already moving, pulling me to my feet, his grip tight and determined. "We need to go," he said, urgency in his voice. His gaze flicked to the horizon, and for the first time, I saw a glimmer of something else in his eyes—fear. Real fear.

"What's happening?" I asked, my throat tight.

"We're not alone."

Before I could process his words, the sound of footsteps echoed from the shadows, growing louder with each passing second.

And then I saw them. Figures emerging from the smoke, their faces obscured but their presence unmistakable.

We were no longer the only ones in the fire.

Chapter 13: Embers of Redemption

I stared at the remains of the house—the charred beams, the scorched earth where my mother's rose garden had once flourished with the delicate scent of jasmine and wildflower. The fire had claimed everything, but it hadn't claimed the memories. They lingered in the smoke that still curled lazily into the rising sun, in the places where my childhood had been formed, twisted, and, ultimately, betrayed.

Aiden didn't move as he stood a few paces away, his boots planted in the darkened earth, eyes tracing the edges of the devastation. His posture screamed restraint, but I could see it—his hands flexing at his sides, his knuckles tight enough to go pale. The man was a puzzle, and every time I thought I had him figured out, he shifted just enough to leave me grasping at shadows. His silence today didn't help matters. I needed answers, but for the first time since we'd met, I wasn't sure if I should push him for them. Maybe it wasn't his truth I should be after, but my own.

"Aiden," I said, the word coming out as more of a sigh than an inquiry. It was strange how we had become these two strangers bound by a past neither of us fully understood. My gaze moved over to him, trying to gauge his reaction. "Is this what you came for? The wreckage?"

He didn't flinch. If anything, his shoulders tightened even more, if that was possible. The man was made of steel wrapped in shadows, a presence that stood tall despite the carnage around us. It should've been comforting, knowing he had my back, but today, it felt more like a cage I couldn't escape.

"I didn't come for this." His voice was rough, gravel sliding through it, like he hadn't used it in days. Maybe he hadn't. "But I'll stay until it's sorted."

"Sorted?" I scoffed, crossing my arms tightly over my chest, half in defiance and half to hold myself together. I knew the routine by now—pretend like nothing was affecting me, feign strength when all I wanted was to collapse into him. "There's no sorting this, Aiden. Nothing left to fix."

He met my gaze then, his eyes too intense, too searching. I could feel the weight of it, like he was trying to read me, pull my thoughts out one by one. I hated how easy it was to let him. How often had I wanted him to see inside me, to understand the parts of me no one ever had?

"You don't get to decide that," he said, his words low but firm. It wasn't a threat—just a statement, an undeniable truth he was laying down between us like a line that shouldn't be crossed. But there it was—another reminder that I couldn't ignore the past. The fire wasn't just the end of a chapter. It was a beginning I wasn't ready for.

I took a step forward, my boots crunching over the ground as I approached the edge of what was once the heart of my family's home. There was something hypnotic about the remnants, the dark outline of the foundation still visible beneath the ashes. I could almost hear my mother's laugh in the distance, could almost see the way her hands had moved over the old oak table while she'd worked, folding laundry, making breakfast, living her quiet, unassuming life. She had been a presence—a force of nature in her own way. And now all that was left were these fractured memories that refused to let me go.

"Aiden, do you remember the night of the fire?" I asked, my voice barely a whisper, even though the question needed no softness. It was raw, unfiltered, and it spilled from me like a confession. A crack in the dam I'd spent years building.

His eyes flickered, a shadow passing over them, but he didn't answer immediately. I could see it in his face—the reluctance, the struggle. His hands were clenched at his sides, but they didn't tremble. "I remember enough," he said finally, and I didn't need to hear more to know that the "enough" was all he was willing to give. That was the problem with Aiden. He was always holding something back. And while it made him a damn good ally when things were easy, now it felt like a betrayal.

I wasn't sure whether to press him further or to let the silence drag on. But my gaze, drawn by some unseen pull, turned to the horizon where the last of the night's shadows still clung to the far side of the valley. The sun was rising higher now, painting the sky in streaks of purple and gold, as though even the heavens were trying to erase what had happened here.

But I knew better. Nothing could be undone. Not this time.

"My mother used to tell me stories about how the past always finds a way to catch up with you," I said, more to myself than to him. The words felt foreign on my tongue. It had been years since I'd thought about her advice, years since I'd let those words anchor me. "I didn't believe her then. But now..."

"Now you see it for what it is," Aiden finished for me. His voice was softer now, not so much a statement as an understanding. He knew the weight of what I was carrying, even if he didn't know all the pieces. And it struck me then—there was no way out of this, no escape. We were both trapped in the same twisted web of history, no matter how far we tried to run from it.

The wind picked up, swirling the ash around us, and for a brief moment, I wondered if it was the wind or my own heart that felt like it might break into a thousand pieces.

I turned my back to the wreckage, feeling the weight of Aiden's eyes on me, the unspoken tension hanging between us like a fine thread, fragile and taut. The last of the night's shadows had all but disappeared, replaced by the orange light of dawn, its warmth touching my skin in a way that almost felt too gentle for what lay ahead. But nothing could soften the truths I was starting to grasp, those jagged pieces of my past that had been hidden in plain sight, scattered just beneath the surface. I couldn't escape them now, not with Aiden standing there, quietly demanding answers with nothing but his presence.

"Why did you come back?" I asked, not turning around. It was a simple question, but it carried weight, the kind of weight that made the air feel thick, like it was too heavy to breathe in properly. "You could've stayed away. This is none of your business anymore."

I could feel the heat of him behind me, his every movement quiet, deliberate. I didn't want to ask, didn't want to care, but there it was—a strange, twisting need to understand why someone who had already walked away was now lingering at the edges of my world once more. There was something almost cruel about it, like he was both my past and my future, yet offering nothing but silence in return.

"I came back because you're here," Aiden's voice came low, careful, almost guarded. "And because you need more than this." He gestured toward the ruins behind me, his arm cutting through the air like a physical barrier between the world we once knew and the one we now inhabited.

I couldn't help it—my chest tightened, a strange mix of relief and frustration threatening to swallow me whole. Part of me wanted to believe him, to latch onto that idea that maybe he had returned for me, for us, but another part recoiled at the thought. Nothing was ever that simple. No one was as innocent as they seemed, and Aiden… well, he wasn't someone who played by the rules.

I finally turned to face him, our eyes locking for the briefest moment before he looked away, his gaze drifting to the horizon as if it could offer him some sort of salvation. I saw the pull in his expression—the strain of a man fighting against something, maybe even himself. He'd always been like that—running from something he couldn't name. And I'd been right there, just far enough to watch him stumble, but never close enough to catch him.

"You're right," I said, taking a step closer. "I need more than this. But I need to know the truth. All of it."

His jaw tightened, and I saw it then—his walls, solid and impenetrable, rising back up between us. It was as though he had built them himself, stone by stone, and now I was left standing in the rubble, waiting for him to make a move. But I wasn't going to beg for answers. Not anymore.

"I'm not here to give you answers, Lex," he said, the words slicing through the stillness between us. "I'm here to make sure you don't make things worse."

The sting of those words caught me off guard, and I flinched, a sharp intake of breath that I quickly masked with a forced laugh. "Oh, of course. Keep me from making a mess of my own life, right? You've done such a great job of that already."

Aiden's eyes flashed at the sarcasm in my voice, but he didn't respond, only shifted his weight from one foot to the other, like he was waiting for me to calm down, to give him the chance to explain himself. But I wasn't in the mood to wait for him to parse his thoughts. Not after everything we'd been through.

"You think you know what's best for me, don't you?" I took another step toward him, the distance between us closing, the tension rising with each passing second. "You think that showing up here, standing by my side, means something. But you don't get it. I don't need you to save me. I never did."

Aiden's eyes darkened, the familiar flash of frustration there, but his voice remained steady, even when I knew his words could cut through stone. "This isn't about saving you, Lex. It's about understanding why you're doing this. Why you're digging into things that might bury you."

"You don't know what's buried." I crossed my arms over my chest, determined not to let him see how much his words had affected me. "You don't know what's been hidden from me all this time."

He took a deep breath, his chest expanding with the effort, as though he was trying to hold himself back. "And you're willing to risk everything just to uncover it? You're willing to burn down the world to find the truth, even if it's something you might not want to hear?"

I stopped, a harsh laugh bubbling up from my throat, but it didn't feel like humor. It felt like a bitter release. "Burn it all down? The world's already gone up in flames, Aiden. What's left to burn?"

His gaze softened then, the edges of his anger smoothing into something else—something I couldn't name, something too complicated to understand in that moment. But whatever it was, it unsettled me, like the first sign of a storm on the horizon, the pressure building in the air.

"You're not the only one with secrets, Lex," he said quietly, his voice threaded with something raw, something vulnerable that I wasn't used to hearing from him. "I came back because I couldn't stand the thought of you going through this alone."

I opened my mouth to respond, to tell him that I didn't need his pity, but the words lodged in my throat. For a second, I felt the weight of everything—every choice I'd made, every betrayal I'd endured—and it struck me that maybe, just maybe, he wasn't as far away as I'd always believed. Maybe he wasn't the only one running.

The wind kicked up again, stirring the dirt and ash into little whirls of motion that scattered as quickly as they came. It wasn't a relief. It was just another reminder that things didn't settle, didn't calm, not here, not now. I didn't know if Aiden felt it too—the weight of unfinished business that lingered in the air like smoke—but I suspected he did. And I hated that we were both trapped in the same suffocating space, pretending to move forward when everything was still on fire beneath us.

"Do you think the truth will make it better?" Aiden asked, his voice breaking through the tension like a jagged stone cutting through water. He didn't meet my eyes, his stare fixed on the horizon, but I could hear the edge in his tone. "You think you'll find some neat little ending to all this?"

"Neat?" I laughed, but the sound was dry, brittle, like the air between us. "If I wanted neat, I would've stopped looking years ago. I've never wanted neat." My words, sharp and raw, hung in the air, daring him to argue. But Aiden didn't bite. Instead, he stood there, silently watching, as though waiting for something. Something I couldn't quite name.

"Then why bother?" His gaze flicked to me, then quickly back to the horizon. The question hung in the air, heavy with the frustration of years, of choices we had both made but hadn't spoken aloud. "Why dig up all these old bones?"

I wanted to snap at him, to tell him that it was because I needed to know, needed to understand what had driven us all into this mess. But instead, the words stuck, like they always did with him. "Because some things can't be buried forever, Aiden. No matter how deep you try to dig."

The silence that stretched between us was charged, as though it were a living thing, pulsating with tension. It was then that I realized—this wasn't just about me, or my family, or even the fire. This was about us, the two of us standing here in the wreckage of everything we'd known. Maybe we hadn't been in control of what had happened, but now, we were standing at a crossroads.

The kind of crossroads where one wrong turn could change everything.

"You think this is easy for me?" His voice came out rough, almost like a growl, and I found myself taking a step back, caught off guard by the vulnerability in it. "You think I haven't spent every damn day since that night trying to figure out how to fix this? How to fix what I did?"

His words landed like a blow, unexpected and jarring. I blinked, trying to steady myself, trying to process the quiet admission that I hadn't expected. But before I could respond, he turned his back on me, running a hand through his hair in frustration. "You don't know what it's like to carry that kind of guilt."

I could feel the pull in my chest, the rush of emotions that were suddenly too much to contain. Part of me wanted to rush to him, wanted to put my hand on his arm and tell him that I understood, that I wasn't some stranger to carrying weight. But I didn't. I couldn't. Because I wasn't sure anymore if I even wanted to understand him. Not when every time we spoke, every time we got close, he pushed me away again.

"You think I don't know about guilt?" I said, my voice rising, not out of anger but out of something else. Something I couldn't quite control. "You think I haven't spent every damn night wondering how the hell I ended up here? How the hell I ended up with you standing in front of me, making promises you can't keep, and telling me things that only make it worse?"

The air between us seemed to crackle with the energy of everything we'd left unsaid. The tension was suffocating, and yet, I couldn't bring myself to move, to break the spell that had us both frozen in place.

Aiden didn't respond right away, and for a moment, I thought maybe he wouldn't. Maybe he'd walk away, like he always did. But then, without warning, he turned back toward me, his gaze fierce and unreadable.

"I didn't come back to fix anything," he said, his voice steady but thick with emotion. "I came back because I couldn't stand the thought of you getting caught in this alone."

I almost laughed, but it wasn't funny. It wasn't funny that here we were, standing in the remains of everything we'd known, and the man who'd walked away so many times was still trying to convince me that he was here for me now.

"You don't get it," I said, the words catching in my throat as I struggled to keep them together. "I've always been alone. Always."

Aiden's face softened, his lips tightening into something close to a frown. "Then why the hell do you keep pushing me away?"

I opened my mouth to answer, but before I could, a sharp sound split the air, followed by the unmistakable scent of smoke—thick, acrid, and far too close for comfort.

My heart stopped. I turned toward the sound, my pulse spiking, and the first thing that caught my eye was a faint glow on the horizon. But this wasn't the soft light of dawn. It was fire. The kind of fire that hadn't been here moments ago. A fire that had appeared out of nowhere, like a dark omen, and it was headed straight toward us.

"Lex..." Aiden's voice was strained, his expression now hard and alert. He was already moving, his hand outstretched, grabbing my wrist. "We need to move. Now."

Before I could even process his words, before I could react, I felt the first heat of the flames licking at my back, and the world around me shifted from stillness to chaos.

Chapter 14: A Dance in the Dark

The music hummed softly around us, as if it were a pulse of its own, steady and unrelenting. The crystal chandeliers overhead cast fractured light that danced across the polished floors, flickering like restless flames. I could feel the weight of the night pressing in, thick with unspoken words and the kind of tension that stung my skin, making each breath sharp, each movement deliberate. His hand rested just below my ribs, the warmth of it traveling through the delicate fabric of my dress, sending strange shivers down my spine. His touch was oddly possessive, and though it was gentle, it left no room for retreat. And I had to admit, in that moment, I didn't want to retreat.

His presence loomed larger than life. It was impossible to ignore him, as if he were not just a man in a room full of faces, but something other—something that had the power to tilt the axis of my world with a mere glance. The way his eyes held mine, intense and unblinking, sent tendrils of unease creeping into my chest. I should have been afraid, perhaps even terrified, of being caught in the orbit of someone like him. But there was something in the way he moved with me, the way his grip tightened when I faltered, that made me forget the dark corners of the ballroom, the secrets he was hiding, and my own instinct to flee.

"Don't look at me like that," I said softly, my voice barely rising above the cadence of the violins. I wasn't sure whether I meant it as a warning or a plea. I certainly wasn't asking for him to stop looking at me, but the weight of his gaze bore down on me as if it could see right through to places I hadn't even discovered in myself.

He didn't respond immediately. His lips curved slightly, the smallest hint of amusement dancing in the corners of his mouth. But his eyes—they never wavered. There was something cruel in them, something that suggested he knew exactly what I was thinking, what

I was hiding. The thought made my pulse spike, and for a moment, I forgot to breathe.

"I never said I was looking at you," he replied, his voice a low rumble against the air between us, so close I could feel the words as much as hear them. "Perhaps you're just looking for something in me."

I nearly stumbled, and it had nothing to do with my steps, nor the slip of my heel on the polished floor. No, it was the sudden, overwhelming wave of his words crashing over me, making me wonder if he knew more than he let on.

"You're reading too much into it," I muttered, forcing my attention back to the rhythm, to the music, to the swirling notes that seemed to mirror the whirling thoughts in my head. It was absurd. I couldn't let myself be swept up in whatever game he was playing. I wasn't some naïve girl, lost in the mysteries of a stranger's charm. I had learned long ago that people were only as trustworthy as their secrets, and his were buried too deep for me to uncover.

But as I tried to pull away, as I shifted my focus to the far side of the room, to the clusters of glittering guests and the artfully arranged tables, he tightened his hold. The gesture was subtle, imperceptible to anyone watching, but I felt it all the same—a tightening of his fingers, a subtle but undeniable pull. He was not letting me go.

"You've been running for so long," he murmured, his words softer this time, almost a lullaby. "Tell me, how long do you think you can keep it up? Running from the truth. From me."

His breath lingered against my ear, as if he could already feel the pulse beneath my skin, the tension building in my chest. I fought the urge to shiver, to recoil, but there was no escaping the proximity of him, the way his presence wrapped around me like a second skin, warm and suffocating. And the truth, whatever it was, remained just out of reach. The questions hung in the air between us, heavy and thick, as if they could shatter the fragile thread that connected us to the world outside the dance.

I forced myself to meet his gaze, steady, unwavering. "You don't know anything about me," I said, though my voice trembled despite my best effort.

"Don't I?" He leaned in, his lips brushing against my temple as he spoke. The feeling was electric, and I could feel the heat of him, seeping into my bones. "I know that you're terrified. And I know you think running is the answer. But you can't outrun the things that are already inside you."

His words left a sting in their wake, a prickling sensation that made me want to pull away. But I didn't. I stayed, held in place by the weight of his voice, the magnetic force of his presence.

"You're wrong," I said, my voice low, more to convince myself than to convince him. "I'm not running from anything."

He smiled then, slow and knowing. "We all are, in some way," he said softly. "The question is, how long can you run before the past catches up with you?"

The music surged, and the delicate strain of the violins lifted into a crescendo, carrying me away. But as I swirled in his arms, spinning in that impossible dance, the shadows that clung to him clung to me too, and I couldn't help but wonder if they would always be there, even when the lights dimmed and the last note faded.

The music swelled, swirling around us like smoke, enveloping everything. It hummed in the space between us, thick and full of unspoken promises. His grip tightened, just slightly, on the small of my back, as though he were grounding both of us in this strange world where the boundaries of reality had blurred. I didn't need to look up to feel the weight of his presence, heavy and all-consuming, pressing against me from all sides. It was a feeling I had never quite known, this mixture of fear and intrigue, of warmth and coldness in the same breath.

I wanted to speak, to demand answers, but the words caught in my throat. It was as if the space between us was a bubble—fragile and perfect, but destined to burst the moment I let myself slip into it. His breath was warm against my ear again, and I shivered, unsure if it was from the heat of his proximity or the chill of his words.

"Do you always dance like this?" I finally found the courage to ask, though I wasn't entirely sure what I meant. I wasn't talking about the steps, the movement of our feet across the floor. No, it was something deeper than that. The rhythm of our bodies, the strange way we seemed to be moving as one, though neither of us had spoken a word of understanding.

"Only with the right partner," he replied smoothly, his voice dripping with something far too assured for my liking. "But then, you've always been the right partner, haven't you?"

I couldn't bring myself to look at him, though I felt his eyes boring into me with the intensity of a storm waiting to break. He was playing some game, no doubt about it. But there was a danger in his words, in the calculated way he chose them. It was as if he knew something I didn't, something crucial that was hidden just beneath the surface of everything I had believed about my life.

The crowd around us had begun to blur, their faces merging with the ornate architecture and gilded chandeliers, as though they were simply figments of my imagination. They were all ghosts to me now, existing only in the periphery, their voices a distant hum that barely registered. My entire world had narrowed down to this moment, to this man, this dance, this unrelenting pull that I couldn't explain but couldn't seem to resist.

I caught a flash of movement from the corner of my eye—another figure in the crowd, watching us intently. It wasn't enough to draw my attention away from him completely, but it was enough to leave a flicker of unease in my chest. Who were they? Why were they looking at us like that?

I couldn't focus on them for long. The figure faded into the shadows just as quickly as it had appeared, and I was once again drawn back to the steady, unyielding presence beside me. His grip was unshakable, as though he were afraid I might slip away, that I might disappear if he let go. The thought should have unsettled me more than it did, but instead, there was a part of me that felt tethered, rooted to the ground by him.

"I'm not the woman you think I am," I said abruptly, though I wasn't entirely sure why. I could feel the weight of the words hanging between us like a confession, though I didn't quite know what I was confessing. But I had to say something. Anything. I needed to regain some semblance of control in this strange dance.

He didn't answer right away, his gaze momentarily flickering over my face, studying me with that same unsettling intensity. I could feel his eyes on me even when I tried to look away, as though he were dissecting my every movement, my every breath.

"Maybe I don't need to know everything," he said, his voice smooth, but there was a hidden edge to it now, a sharpness that made my pulse race. "Maybe I just need to know that you're here, now. That you're with me."

His words landed between us with the weight of a promise, one I wasn't sure I was ready to accept. And yet, I didn't pull away. Instead, I found myself leaning into him slightly, allowing the music, the dance, and the strange force of his presence to envelop me completely.

"But what about the truth?" I asked, though my voice faltered. "The things we're running from? What happens when they catch up with us?"

The shift in his expression was subtle, but it didn't escape me. His jaw tightened just a fraction, his gaze hardening for the briefest of moments. "You're still running," he said softly, as though it was a confession of his own. "But we both know the truth is already here. It's been here all along."

I didn't understand what he meant, but I didn't ask. Some questions, I realized, were better left unspoken, at least for now. There was a power in silence between us, a current of something neither of us had named, but both knew existed.

We danced in time with the music, my heart racing in rhythm with the soft violins. The world outside the ballroom had all but disappeared, and for a fleeting moment, I thought—no, I hoped—that this was how it was always meant to be. That somehow, I was meant to be here with him, caught in this unspoken bond that neither of us could escape.

But then, as if to pull me back into the world, the music faltered—just for a beat—and in that silence, I heard it: the sound of footsteps, sharp and deliberate, approaching us through the crowd. I didn't turn to look, but the hairs on the back of my neck stood at attention. Someone was coming. And I couldn't shake the feeling that they weren't just walking to join the party.

The next moment, his grip on me shifted, not in a comforting way, but in a way that suggested we were no longer dancing for the sake of it. He was positioning me, moving me as though preparing for something. What, exactly, I wasn't sure. But the weight of his touch—the power in his movements—spoke volumes. Something was about to happen. And I wasn't ready for it.

His hand, firm and unyielding against my back, kept me close, anchored in a way that was both comforting and unsettling. Every step we took on the polished floor seemed to carry us deeper into the heart of the night, deeper into something I wasn't sure I wanted to understand. The music wrapped around us, a constant, pulsing reminder of the strange, almost dreamlike quality of the moment. It was a slow dance, but there was nothing languid about it—every movement was charged, every shift of weight felt like it could lead to something explosive.

"I'm not afraid of you," I said, though I wasn't sure if it was entirely true. But then again, I wasn't sure what I was afraid of. It was impossible to tell where the danger lay anymore. With him? Or with the secrets that seemed to swirl just out of my reach, teasing me with their proximity?

His lips curled into a smile that could have been a warning, but I wasn't sure if it was meant for me or for himself. "No?" he asked, a single brow arched in challenge. "Then why are you still holding your breath?"

I hadn't realized it, but I was. My chest felt tight, constricted in a way that had nothing to do with the closeness of our bodies. It was as if the air around us had thickened, pressing down on me, forcing me to acknowledge the unspoken things between us.

I didn't respond, not because I didn't have an answer, but because I wasn't sure I wanted to admit it. The truth was, there was something magnetic about him, something that had me completely off balance. I had spent so long running from everything I didn't understand, and now here I was, caught in the pull of something I couldn't escape.

The faint murmur of voices rose in the background as other dancers moved through the space, their laughter, their conversations, a soft hum that felt distant, irrelevant. All I could hear, all I could feel, was the heat of his hand on my back, the way his fingers seemed to brush against my skin with every step, like he was claiming me with every moment.

"I told you," he murmured, almost too low for anyone to hear, "you can't outrun the past. Not forever."

His words seemed to hang in the air like a cloud, heavy with meaning. The past. My past. What was he hinting at? Was he talking about the lies I had buried, the pieces of myself I had hidden away so carefully? Or was it something else, something more? I could feel the tightness in my throat, the unmistakable rush of fear, but it wasn't the kind of fear I had known before. It wasn't about physical danger, not exactly. It was the kind of fear that whispered of things left undone, of truths that had yet to be spoken.

"I don't know what you want from me," I said, my voice shaking ever so slightly, betraying the calm I was desperately trying to maintain.

He tilted his head, studying me like a puzzle he was determined to solve. "I don't want anything from you," he replied, his voice low, almost tender. "Not yet."

That 'not yet' lingered between us like a thread, pulling me closer, making my heartbeat accelerate in a way that felt entirely out of my control. But I couldn't back away, not while he was looking at me like that, like he could see every part of me—every flaw, every hesitation—and still want more.

The violins rose again, the soft, sweet notes filling the space between us, and for a moment, I let myself get lost in the rhythm, let myself forget. The soft sway of his body, the warmth of his hand, the way we seemed to move as one—it was intoxicating, and I wanted to stay in this moment forever. But there was a sharp edge to it now, something darker that I couldn't ignore.

As the music swirled, the pressure of his hand on my back changed, shifting subtly but unmistakably. It was like he was guiding me, pushing me toward something I wasn't ready for. The warmth of his palm seemed to burn through my dress, and for the first time, I realized how much control he had over this situation, over me.

I opened my mouth to speak, but the words caught in my throat. It wasn't just him anymore. The feeling was there—something else was coming, something I couldn't explain.

I felt it before I saw it. The change in the air. A shift, a subtle but undeniable chill creeping through the room, replacing the warmth that had surrounded us. I looked around instinctively, my heart suddenly racing. The dancers seemed oblivious, lost in their own worlds, but I knew something had changed. There was a tension, a prickling sense of danger that swept through the room like an electric charge.

And then, through the crowd, I saw him.

The figure that had been lurking at the edge of the ballroom, the one who had been watching us with quiet intensity, was now making his way toward us. His movements were slow, deliberate, as if he knew exactly what he was doing. The crowd parted for him without a second thought, as though they were parting for royalty, for someone too powerful to be ignored.

I tried to pull away from him, to retreat, but his grip was unyielding. He wasn't letting me go—not now, not when the man was almost upon us. I could feel the weight of his presence before he even spoke. The air around us seemed to hum with an energy I couldn't place, an unfamiliar charge that made the hairs on the back of my neck stand on end.

The man stopped just a few feet away, and I could feel his gaze like a physical presence, a weight that pressed down on me with the force of something ancient, something unforgiving.

"Well," he said, his voice rich with authority, "it looks like the game is about to change."

The words hung in the air, suffocating, and before I could say anything—before I could make sense of the situation—he stepped closer, the smile on his lips nothing but trouble.

And then everything went black.

Chapter 15: The Flame of Betrayal

I had always thought that love was a thing you could hold in your hands, like a fragile bird with a soft, warm belly that would trust you if you held it gently enough. That's what I believed, anyway, when Aiden first walked into my life. He had that aura of mystery, that quiet strength that everyone noticed but couldn't quite explain. We were opposites in every way. I was a loud storm of words and ambition, and he... well, he was the calm before the storm. A breath of silence in a world that never stopped spinning. The kind of man you thought you could rely on, because nothing about him seemed to crack or shift. But I was wrong. And in that wrongness, everything I thought I knew about myself—about trust, love, and family—fractured.

The night I found the letter, tucked in the back of the antique bookcase that had been in my family for generations, everything changed. It was hidden beneath layers of dust, the paper yellowed and curled at the edges as if it had been waiting for me. At first, I thought it was just another piece of forgotten history—old family business that I had no real desire to delve into. But as I unfolded the crinkled parchment, my eyes scanned the words. My heart stuttered, and my breath hitched.

Aiden's name.

And next to it, a signature I recognized all too well.

My father's.

I read it again, the ink blurring as the weight of the words settled over me like a thick fog. Aiden and my father had a connection I couldn't have imagined in a thousand years. There, in the careful strokes of my father's pen, was a deal—a pact—that tied my family's fortune to Aiden in a way I could not untangle. I wasn't just seeing betrayal in the ink on the page; I was feeling it, deep in my bones. My father had made promises to Aiden's family long before I even knew him. Promises that spoke of trust, of shared secrets, of alliances that would change the very course of our futures.

I ran my fingers over the faded script, but it didn't give me any answers. It only deepened the confusion I had already been nursing since that first encounter with Aiden's past. Aiden's silence when I asked him about it haunted me more than any lie could. He didn't deny it. He didn't protest. His hands, usually so steady, trembled slightly when he reached for the letter, his eyes clouded with an emotion I couldn't place—guilt? Regret? Fear?

"Why didn't you tell me?" I asked, the words feeling like acid as they passed my lips.

He swallowed hard, his voice lower than I had ever heard it. "I didn't know how to explain it," he said, the words almost inaudible, but they cut through me like glass. "I never wanted you to find out this way."

"Then how did you want me to find out, Aiden?" I nearly shouted, my voice trembling as I tried to control the surge of anger that was bubbling up inside me. "When would have been a better time? When we were married? When I was carrying your child?" The words came out sharper than I meant them to, each one a sword I thrust into the heart of something I once believed was invincible.

He looked at me, his dark eyes searching mine as if trying to find the right thing to say. His gaze was haunted. I hated him for it. Hated him for putting me in this position. I had trusted him with everything—my heart, my family's trust, my future—and now I stood here, shattered, watching it all crumble into dust at my feet.

"I'm sorry," he whispered, his voice thick with emotion, but I couldn't hear it anymore. The apology wasn't enough. I needed the truth. I needed to understand how my father's secrets had bled into the present like poison in my veins.

"You're sorry? Sorry doesn't cut it, Aiden!" The words erupted from me before I could stop them, and I turned, storming towards the door, the weight of betrayal hanging around me like a suffocating cloud.

He called out to me, his voice raw and desperate. "Please, just listen—"

But I couldn't. I didn't want to listen anymore. I didn't want to hear the explanations or the excuses. Not when I had spent years trusting him, not when everything I thought I knew about him had turned out to be a carefully constructed illusion. I slammed the door behind me, but even then, I could hear his voice, still pleading, still calling my name from the other side.

I didn't stop. Not until I was far away, standing on the balcony of my apartment with the city sprawling below me, the cold air biting my skin as if it were trying to wake me from this nightmare. The lights flickered in the distance, and for the first time in ages, I felt utterly alone. A silence deeper than anything I had known settled in my chest, suffocating me. I didn't know what to believe anymore. My family's past. Aiden's lies. Everything I had thought was solid was now shaking under my feet, and I couldn't find anything to hold on to.

In the stillness of that moment, I realized something that scared me more than anything else. I didn't know who I was without all these tangled connections. Without Aiden, without the legacy of my family, without the lies I had been living with, who was I really?

The question echoed through me, and for the first time, I wasn't sure I wanted to find the answer.

I couldn't stay in the apartment. It felt like the walls were closing in, trapping me with the echo of Aiden's voice, of his desperate attempts to explain the unexplainable. The rawness of it, the depth of the lie that had been woven between us, was too much to bear. The air itself seemed to conspire against me, thick with the memory of his touch, the tenderness in his eyes when I had believed he was the one I could trust above all else.

So, I did what I always did when life became too much to handle: I ran. Not physically, not anywhere that would make sense, but to the only place I could still find a semblance of peace—my grandmother's cabin by the lake. It had been hers before she passed away, and I had never thought to let it go. The wooden structure stood nestled among pines like a forgotten secret, untouched by the rest of the world. It was where I went when everything felt too big, too loud, too much. Out here, surrounded by the quiet hum of nature, I could almost convince myself that everything hadn't unraveled.

I arrived at the cabin just as the sun was beginning to dip beneath the horizon, casting the sky in shades of violet and rose. The air had a bite to it, but it wasn't unwelcoming. I pulled my jacket tighter around my shoulders as I made my way inside, the familiar scent of pine and wood smoke settling over me like a warm blanket. There was comfort in the stillness here, in the soft creak of the floorboards beneath my feet.

But as I stepped into the living room, a flicker of something—an old memory, maybe—swept over me. The room was just as it had always been: a stone fireplace, deep armchairs, a collection of mismatched bookshelves that seemed to have been assembled over decades rather than years. But the absence of her—the warmth of my grandmother's presence—lingered like a shadow. I sat on the couch, staring out the window at the lake that shimmered beneath the moonlight, wondering how much longer I could keep pretending to be whole.

I tried to focus on the peaceful scene outside. The moon glistened off the water, sending shards of silver across the surface. But my mind kept wandering back to the letter, to the discovery that had rocked me to my core. The legacy that had been passed down to me wasn't just a family heirloom or a prized possession. It was a shackle, a chain tied around my wrist that I couldn't escape from, no matter how far I ran.

And Aiden. His silence still haunted me. His face when I'd walked away, his eyes filled with something that seemed too much like regret—regret for what? That he hadn't told me sooner? Or was it because he never thought I'd find out at all?

I leaned forward, elbows on my knees, and buried my face in my hands. I wasn't sure if I was crying. It felt more like something inside me had cracked open and was bleeding out slowly, like a wound I couldn't see but could feel deep inside my chest. The truth had a weight I wasn't ready for. It was heavier than I could lift, and now it threatened to crush everything I had thought I knew about my life, about who I was. My father had known about this connection with Aiden, but he'd never mentioned it. He'd never even hinted at it. How had he kept this from me? And why did Aiden stay silent when he could've told me the truth, when he could've saved me from this despair?

I reached for the cup of tea that had been sitting on the small table beside me, my fingers trembling as I wrapped them around the warm porcelain. I took a sip, savoring the comfort it offered, but it did little to settle the storm raging inside me. The quiet of the cabin only amplified the chaos in my head.

It wasn't until late into the night, when the house had settled into an almost unnatural stillness, that I heard it—a faint knock at the door. At first, I thought it was just the wind, but then it came again, a soft tap that echoed in the otherwise silent night. My heart jumped into my throat, and I stood, frozen.

I wasn't expecting anyone. No one knew I was here, not unless they had tracked me down somehow, and I wasn't ready to face anyone, let alone the one person whose name had been tearing me apart.

The knock came again, louder this time, followed by the sound of a familiar voice.

"Emery. Please, open the door."

It was Aiden.

I felt a strange twist in my stomach, a mixture of anger and something far more complicated—something that threatened to unravel me all over again. The soft, pleading tone in his voice tugged at something inside me that I was desperately trying to ignore.

I didn't move at first. I couldn't. I wasn't ready to face him. Not yet.

"Emery, I can't leave until we talk. Please."

His voice cracked, and it was like a blade to my chest. He was breaking, and that only made my anger flare hotter. How dare he show up here? How dare he try to reach me after everything? But still, something in me pulled me towards the door. Despite myself, despite the hurt, I wanted to hear what he had to say, even though I knew that hearing him might destroy the last pieces of me that still clung to some semblance of hope.

I crossed the room slowly, my feet heavy against the wooden floor, and opened the door.

There he was, standing in the dim light from the cabin, his face drawn, his hair falling across his forehead in that way I had always found endearing. But now, that same face was filled with something far more troubling—guilt, regret, and an emotion I couldn't name.

"You shouldn't have come," I said, my voice softer than I intended.

"I know," he whispered, stepping closer, his eyes pleading with me. "But I need you to understand. I didn't want this. I never wanted you to be caught in the middle of this."

"Then why didn't you tell me, Aiden?" I demanded, my voice rising again. "Why didn't you trust me enough to tell me the truth?"

The silence between us stretched, an unbearable gap that felt like a vast ocean, wide enough to drown any remaining hope. Aiden was standing in front of me, eyes shadowed and face weary, but the distance between us was not just physical. It was everything I hadn't known about him, everything I now realized he'd kept from me. The betrayal was an old wound—his, mine, and my father's—and I had only just discovered it had festered right beneath my skin.

I took a slow step back, my heart pounding in my chest like a war drum. Every breath felt like a battle. "I don't understand." The words left my mouth before I could stop them, thin and broken, as if speaking them aloud would make it all make sense.

His hands flexed at his sides, the raw tension in his shoulders betraying his own battle with something I couldn't fathom. "You don't have to," he said quietly, the depth of regret in his voice settling around us like fog. "You just need to know that I never meant to hurt you. You were never part of this... this mess."

I could feel the tension building within me, my fists clenching. "Then why didn't you tell me?" The question tumbled out before I could reconsider. "Why didn't you let me in on the truth from the beginning? If you cared about me—"

"I do care!" His voice cut through mine, louder now, desperate. He stepped closer, but I took a sharp step back, raising my hands in defense.

"You can't just say that, Aiden," I whispered, a shaky laugh escaping me. "You can't just say you care and expect everything to be okay. You've known what this means all along. And I—" My voice broke, a strange ache tightening around my throat. "I thought I was the one you were trying to protect. But I'm the last thing you were worried about, weren't I?"

He stilled, like the words had hit him harder than he'd expected. There was a flicker of something in his gaze—something that I hadn't seen before. Regret? Fear? His jaw tightened as if he were trying to hold back a torrent of words, of explanations that I wasn't sure I wanted to hear.

The night air was heavy now, the only sound between us the quiet rustle of the trees, the soft sigh of the wind pressing against the cabin walls. My heart was hammering in my chest, the silence between us suffocating, the weight of it pressing against my ribs.

"I never wanted you to be caught in the middle," he said finally, his voice rough. "You have to believe me."

"I don't know what to believe anymore," I murmured, my breath coming in short, uneven bursts. Every word out of his mouth only seemed to deepen the confusion. How could I trust someone who had kept this from me? How could I trust someone who had knowingly let me fall deeper into a lie?

Aiden stepped forward again, and this time I didn't retreat. But his approach wasn't full of the calm certainty I had once known. There was a hesitance to his movements, a wariness in his eyes that made him look more vulnerable than I had ever seen him. "Emery," he began, his voice strained. "You have to understand. There are things, connections, that you don't know about. Things that go back... much further than either of us. My family—your family... it's all tangled in ways I didn't know how to explain."

I crossed my arms tightly over my chest, clenching the fabric of my jacket as if it were the only thing keeping me grounded. "Then why didn't you tell me? Why keep it a secret?"

"I didn't want to lose you." His voice cracked, the words falling out as though they were the last thing he had left to hold on to.

And in that moment, something inside me shifted. I saw it in him, the raw honesty, the desperation, and yet... it wasn't enough. It wasn't enough for me to simply forgive him, to let this all go because of the pain in his eyes. No, something deeper had been broken, something I wasn't sure we could ever repair.

"I'm not the one you've lost yet," I said, the words slipping from my mouth before I could even stop to think. The sharpness of it caught even me off guard. It felt like I was daring him to prove me wrong, to give me something that would bring us back from the edge.

Aiden's eyes flickered, his expression unreadable for a moment before something like frustration flashed across his face. He ran a hand through his hair, clearly struggling with something, with a decision, or perhaps with the weight of his own actions. "I never wanted this for you, Emery. I never wanted to drag you into my family's mess, my... my past. But now that it's come to this, I can't walk away. I can't just let you go without telling you everything."

I swallowed hard, the lump in my throat thick and stubborn. I wanted to believe him, to reach out and take whatever explanation he was offering, to hold on to the Aiden I had once known. But the words lodged in my chest like a splinter, refusing to dislodge, refusing to let me feel anything but the weight of betrayal.

"You should have told me sooner," I said softly, stepping back toward the door, the cool night air rushing in. "I don't know if I can hear what you have to say now, Aiden."

He was silent for a long time, his eyes never leaving mine, searching me, pleading with me in a way that made my resolve waver. But I couldn't do this. I couldn't keep looking at him with the same trust that had once been there, because trust wasn't something you could just give back once it had been shattered.

And then, before I could react, before I could say another word, a loud crash echoed from the woods behind the cabin, followed by a voice I didn't recognize. "Emery, get away from him!"

Chapter 16: The Ashes of Yesterday

I had never been one to keep things tidy. As a child, my room had been a chaotic nest of books, tangled jewelry, and notebooks filled with half-finished thoughts. The kind of place where things weren't lost but rather waiting for the right moment to be rediscovered. Now, years later, that same sense of organized chaos had found its way into my study, the one room in the house that I could truly claim as mine. The rest of the old house, with its peeling wallpaper and sagging floors, had always belonged to my mother, then my grandmother. But the study, the one room where the light always felt a little too harsh, where the shadows seemed to linger longer than they should, was mine.

On a small table, an open box lay surrounded by piles of photographs and brittle, yellowed papers. I could smell the faint trace of dust and old ink, a combination that should have been unsettling but instead felt oddly comforting. As I carefully picked through the remnants of forgotten lives, each letter, each photograph felt like an invitation, a whisper from the past. I wasn't ready to hear them yet, not completely, but I couldn't stop myself. I couldn't resist the pull of their secrets.

I unfolded another letter, its creases sharp and deliberate, as though someone had read it and tucked it away, hoping no one would see. The handwriting was elegant, almost too perfect, and the words spoke of things I hadn't yet understood. Love. Betrayal. Choices made in silence, under cover of night, hidden in the fragile safety of a world that no longer existed.

And then there was a photograph. A picture of a man and a woman, arms entwined, their faces caught in an expression of shared intimacy that felt too real, too vivid for a moment that had long since passed. The woman, her hair dark and wild like the stormy sea, looked almost familiar. I could see traces of myself in the curve of her jaw, the tilt of her head. But the man? He was a stranger, his features sharp, almost dangerous. Something about the way he held her made my heart stutter, a quiet dread creeping in at the edges.

I couldn't stop staring at them. There was something about the photograph that gnawed at me. It wasn't the simplicity of the image—it was too quiet, too full of things unsaid. A moment captured, yes, but I could feel the weight of the things that had come before and after that smile, that soft look in their eyes.

I set it down carefully, trying to steady the feeling of unease that curled around my chest. My fingers traced the edges of the paper, the same paper that had borne these secrets for decades. My family's legacy, the stuff of half-remembered whispers, stories that I had never been privy to. Until now. But even as the truth began to unfurl like a ribbon in front of me, I couldn't shake the feeling that I was being drawn into something much darker than I'd ever anticipated.

It wasn't just Aiden I had been lying to. I had been lying to myself. This was more than curiosity. It was something deeper, something instinctual. A need to understand the roots of the family that had shaped me, for better or worse. To piece together the broken fragments of history and see if they could ever be made whole again.

And yet, the more I uncovered, the more I realized just how little I knew about the people whose blood ran through my veins. My grandmother, the woman who had raised me, had always been a fortress. She didn't speak of the past—not the real past, not the stories that had shaped her. She spoke of love, of sacrifice, of hardship, but never of the moments that had scarred her. The letters, the photographs—they were the first glimpse I'd had of the woman she had been before the one who raised me, before she'd wrapped herself in silence and grief like a protective cloak.

I unfolded another letter, this one written in the same delicate script but with a more urgent tone. The words were rushed, desperate, pleading. And at the end, there was a name—Aiden. The name that had haunted me, the one that had somehow wound its way into my life, despite my best efforts to forget it. The name I hadn't wanted to see, hadn't wanted to acknowledge.

The realization hit me like a slap, and for a moment, I couldn't breathe. My world tilted, spun. Aiden was here, in these letters, in these secrets. But it wasn't just him. It was my family. The same blood, the same twisted threads that bound us all together. Aiden wasn't just a man I had loved—he was part of something bigger, a piece of a puzzle that I hadn't even begun to understand.

I could feel the weight of the truth pressing down on me, suffocating me with its implications. I wasn't sure what I was supposed to do with it, how to make sense of it all. But I knew one thing for certain: the answers I'd been searching for had always been here, buried in the ashes of the past. All I had to do was reach for them.

The walls of the study had started to feel suffocating, their peeling paint pressing in like an oppressive weight. I had become too accustomed to the scent of old wood and forgotten things. The edges of the letters were starting to curl beneath my fingers, the ink fading in places, but the message was still there, still sharp. I had to read between the lines, not just in the letters but in the spaces they left behind. The answers were in the things that weren't said, in the silences that held more weight than the words themselves.

I glanced at the clock on the wall, its hands creeping toward the late hours of the night. The house was quiet now, the kind of silence that settled deep into the bones, the kind that could drive a person mad if they let it. I wasn't sure what I was hoping for, but I knew I couldn't stop. Each letter felt like a breadcrumb leading me deeper into a forest I wasn't sure I could escape. My fingers trembled as I reached for the next one, a crumpled sheet of paper, its edges torn, as though someone had ripped it in frustration and then shoved it back into the envelope.

I unfolded it slowly, the rough texture of the paper scratching against my fingertips. The words were jagged, as though written in haste, the ink smeared in places. But it was the name at the bottom that caught my eye: Aiden. Again, his name, like a thread woven through everything, binding me to this story I didn't want to be part of but couldn't escape.

The letter was a confession of sorts, though it wasn't quite the apology I had expected. There was no remorse, no self-pity. Just a cold acknowledgment of mistakes made—decisions that had been justified at the time but now felt hollow. "I did it for us," the letter said, the words so simple yet loaded with meaning I wasn't sure I could fully unpack. The rest of the letter blurred together as I scanned the lines, each sentence pressing against me like a weight I couldn't push off. The past, it seemed, wasn't as far behind me as I had hoped. It was creeping forward, crawling toward me in the dark.

But what struck me most was the way the letter ended. It wasn't just a final plea or an empty promise. There was something almost urgent in the way the words spilled out at the end, a desperate appeal for forgiveness that carried the weight of a hundred years of secrets. I set the letter down, my heart pounding in my chest, the familiar ache of betrayal settling deep in my gut. What did I even expect to find? Did I think that uncovering these truths would somehow make everything better?

I ran a hand through my hair, the motion almost involuntary, as I stared at the pages spread across the table. The weight of history, of bloodlines that stretched back further than I could see, was beginning to suffocate me. I wasn't just reading letters anymore. I was reading lives. Lives that had been twisted and torn apart by choices made long before I was born. Choices that, in their own way, had led me here, to this very room, on this very night.

I could hear the creak of floorboards upstairs, the sound of my grandmother's slippers scraping softly against the hardwood as she made her way to bed. It had become a nightly ritual: the sound of her movements, slow and deliberate, marking the end of another day. It was comforting in a way, this rhythm of life. But tonight, it only served to remind me that I was alone in this. The pieces of this puzzle, these fragile fragments of the past, belonged to me now. I had inherited the weight of them, whether I wanted it or not.

I turned my attention back to the photograph I had found earlier, the one with the man and woman whose faces had haunted me all evening. I couldn't shake the feeling that I knew them, even though I was certain I hadn't. There was something in their eyes, a shared look of understanding that felt too intimate, too familiar. But it wasn't until I held the photo up to the light that I noticed something I had missed before. The woman's face, the one that had seemed so familiar, wasn't just a reflection of me. It was a reflection of someone else—someone I couldn't quite place but whose presence had been lingering at the edges of my memories.

My heart skipped a beat as I realized the truth, the horrifying realization slowly settling into my chest like cold stone. The woman in the photograph wasn't just related to me. She was my grandmother's sister, someone I had only heard whispers of, a name spoken only in passing, with no real details. And the man—he was someone I had been told nothing about, someone who had apparently been an integral part of a story that no one had ever dared to tell.

I sank into the chair, the room suddenly feeling smaller, more suffocating. I had always known there were things my grandmother wasn't telling me, things she had kept hidden behind her closed lips and carefully curated smile. But this—this was more than I had ever imagined. This was the family secret that no one had ever dared speak aloud, the one buried so deep in the past that it had almost become a myth, a ghost story parents told to their children to keep them in line.

IN THE DARK

But now, it was real. And I was trapped in the middle of it, a reluctant participant in a story that had been years in the making. I wasn't sure what I was supposed to do with this knowledge, what I was supposed to do with the man in the photograph, the woman whose face mirrored my own. But there was one thing I knew for certain: I was no longer just a spectator. I had stepped into the heart of the past, and there was no turning back.

I took a deep breath and set the photograph down on the table, the weight of it pulling my shoulders lower as I studied the delicate features of the woman who shared my blood. My grandmother's sister, a figure wrapped in silence, a woman who had clearly played a role in some dark chapter that had never been shared with me. I didn't know what I expected—perhaps that the mystery would somehow soften with the knowledge, that it would make sense in the way that puzzles often do when you finally snap the last piece into place. But the more I uncovered, the more the pieces seemed to shift and rearrange themselves, pulling away from any tidy conclusions.

I leaned forward, the weight of the room pressing in on me like the thick fog outside, muffling every sound. The clock ticked on, oblivious to the turmoil in my chest. The letters, the photographs—they were pieces of a larger narrative, a narrative I wasn't prepared to face, yet somehow couldn't look away from. I thought about the years I had spent in the safe, placid world my grandmother had built for me, a world constructed of half-truths and carefully curated stories. Every person I loved had been part of that tapestry, woven together by a thread of love and lies, stitched so neatly that I hadn't questioned a single moment until now.

I turned my attention back to the crumpled letter, the one that had sent my pulse racing just a few minutes ago. I read it again, letting the words settle into the empty spaces in my mind, searching for meaning. The letter was short, the ink faded in some places, as though time had slowly eaten away at it. But the words at the bottom hadn't diminished. They stood clear and sharp, the last line cutting into me as though they had been written only yesterday.

"I loved you then, and I love you now. No matter what comes."

I could hear the words in my mind as if they were spoken aloud, the voice so vivid that I could almost reach out and touch it. It wasn't Aiden's voice—it was something older, more distant. It belonged to the man in the photograph, the one with the sharp features and the dangerous glint in his eyes. I had no idea who he was, yet there he was, a ghost from my past, haunting me at every turn.

I stood up abruptly, needing to move, needing to get out of that room where the walls seemed to close in around me with every second I spent there. I took the photograph and letter with me, clutching them in my hands as I left the study behind. The hallway stretched before me, dimly lit by the flickering light from a single lamp at the end. I wasn't sure where I was going—just that I needed to get away from the past, if only for a moment, if only to breathe.

I reached the front door, my fingers trembling as I gripped the handle. It was late, the house dark and silent, but I couldn't bear to stay inside anymore. I needed air, space, something to steady the frantic rhythm of my heartbeat. The wind outside had picked up, rustling the trees that lined the property, their branches swaying in a dance with the gusts of wind. The world felt more alive out here, in the cold, with the scent of wet earth and distant rain.

I closed the door behind me and stepped into the night, the crunch of gravel beneath my boots a small comfort in the otherwise quiet world. The night stretched endlessly before me, but I didn't know where to go or what to do with the chaos in my mind. I could still see the photograph, still hear the words of the letter echoing in my head.

The past was calling to me, dragging me back toward a truth I wasn't ready to confront.

IN THE DARK

It wasn't long before I heard the sound of footsteps behind me. I turned quickly, my heart in my throat. The air felt colder now, the chill of the night biting into my skin as I saw a figure emerge from the darkness.

"Aiden," I whispered, though I wasn't sure if it was him at all.

He stepped closer, the familiar shadow of his tall frame emerging from the night, his presence as tangible as the weight of the secrets I was holding. His eyes met mine, that same intensity that had always been there, the quiet storm I couldn't ever seem to escape.

"What are you doing out here?" he asked, his voice steady, but there was something in it that made my chest tighten. He wasn't asking because he didn't know—I could feel the tension hanging between us, the unspoken questions that neither of us had dared to voice.

"I—" My words faltered. "I need to know the truth. Everything. I'm tired of hiding from it."

His gaze softened just for a moment, but it was gone as quickly as it had appeared. He stepped closer, his hands sliding into the pockets of his coat. "You're not ready for this, Mara."

"Maybe not," I said, my voice steady despite the roiling uncertainty inside me. "But I'm going to find out whether I'm ready or not. And I think you know that."

There was a long pause between us, the kind of silence that drips with too many words left unsaid. He looked at me, his jaw tense, eyes unreadable.

"You're playing with fire," he said, his tone barely a whisper in the cold air.

"I've been playing with fire my whole life," I replied. "But I'm done running from it."

And just as I thought the conversation might shift, the ground beneath us trembled. At first, I thought it was the wind, but then I heard it—a faint hum, like an engine, distant but growing nearer. A vehicle. But who? I hadn't expected anyone. The sound grew louder, and I instinctively took a step back, my pulse spiking. The figure behind me stepped forward, his posture rigid.

Then, out of the darkness, headlights pierced the night, and my world tilted on its axis.

Chapter 17: A Flicker of Hope

The sunlight sliced through the canopy of leaves above, casting dappled shadows across the quiet street. There was a soft, steady hum in the air—distant traffic, birds arguing over territory, the lazy whir of a lawnmower struggling against the overgrowth. But none of it reached me, not really. The world felt muffled, like I was submerged beneath the surface of everything, and no matter how hard I tried, I couldn't bring myself to the surface.

I was supposed to be done with him. I had convinced myself—over and over—that I was finished with Aiden. After everything, how could I still care? But then I saw him, standing there, leaning against the side of my car like he had every right to be. He was wearing that old, worn leather jacket that I used to love, and I had to fight the impulse to walk up to him and rest my hand against the cool material like it could somehow erase the distance that had come between us.

He straightened when he saw me, his face pinched with what looked like both hesitation and determination. And for a moment, I thought maybe I was imagining it—his eyes, the way they followed me, the deep furrow in his brow that hadn't been there before. But then he opened his mouth, and I heard it—the rasp, the sincerity that I wasn't sure I was ready for.

"I owe you an explanation," Aiden said, his voice softer than I remembered, almost tentative. He ran a hand through his dark hair, his gaze shifting nervously. "I've been thinking about this... about you, and what happened. And I know, I know that I don't deserve a chance, but if you can give me a moment..." He trailed off, looking as if the words were stuck, just out of his reach.

I crossed my arms tightly, suddenly very aware of how much space there was between us. I had spent too long convincing myself that this was it—no more, no more games, no more late-night texts that never said anything but everything. But the apology in his voice was like a thread, pulling at me, tugging at the parts of me that still wanted to believe in something good.

I took a step back, enough to put distance between us, but not so much that I couldn't see the regret swimming in his eyes. "You want to explain?" I echoed, the words barely leaving my mouth before I felt the sting of them. It wasn't like me to give him an inch, but something—something about the way he was standing there, like he was waiting for me to take a breath before he did—made me hesitate.

Aiden swallowed hard, his throat bobbing. His eyes flicked to the ground, as if searching for the right words in the cracks of the pavement. When he looked up again, the weight of his gaze felt different, heavier in a way that made my pulse thrum faster. "I should've fought harder," he said quietly, almost to himself. "For us. For you. I made decisions that hurt you, and I can't change that, but I need you to know... meeting you? It was the best thing that ever happened to me."

The words hit like a punch to the gut, but I didn't flinch. Instead, I let the weight of them settle in my chest, simmering beneath the surface. "Aiden, you left," I said, my voice low, controlled. It was the simplest way to sum it up—the most painful, the most truthful. "You walked away without a word. No explanation, no reason."

His lips pressed into a thin line, and I could see the frustration in the way his hands clenched by his sides, like he wanted to reach for me, but didn't know how. "I didn't know how to fix it," he confessed, his voice barely above a whisper. "I didn't know how to fix us, so I thought the best thing was to disappear. But it wasn't. God, it wasn't."

I exhaled, steadying myself against the surge of emotion that I didn't want to acknowledge. I wanted to hate him for the hurt, for the betrayal, but somehow, it all seemed to slip through my fingers, like sand in the wind. His words, however flawed, seemed real—too real to ignore. And I hated myself for it.

"You think I don't know that?" I snapped before I could stop myself. "You think I don't know what it's like to want someone and still push them away, to watch them walk out and not be able to do a damn thing about it?"

Aiden's face softened, like he understood the sting behind my words, the bitterness that I'd tried so hard to keep buried. "I never meant to hurt you," he said, his voice steady now. "I thought I was doing the right thing by leaving, by letting you go so you could live your life without me screwing it up. But all I did was make everything worse. You deserved better than that."

The warmth of the afternoon sun didn't seem to touch me anymore. The air felt thick, like a storm was coming, and the distance between us was suddenly unbearable. I should've walked away, should've turned around and kept moving. But instead, I found myself stepping forward, closing the gap between us.

"You can't undo the past, Aiden," I said, my voice barely above a whisper. "You can't just—" But I trailed off, my words slipping away when his hand reached for mine, tentative but desperate.

"I know," he said, his thumb brushing over my knuckles, sending a jolt of warmth through me. "But I want to try. If you'll let me."

The offer hung there between us, suspended in the quiet air, and for the first time in months, I didn't feel the sting of anger or betrayal. I felt... a flicker. A spark that, despite everything, was still there.

I didn't know what to do with the emotions swirling inside me. They were messy, uninvited, and, frankly, inconvenient. Aiden's words hung in the air like smoke, thick and confusing, and I couldn't seem to escape them no matter how much I tried. The frustration of wanting to be angry, to yell at him for everything he'd done, collided with the faintest thread of hope that I'd buried a long time ago. That thread, now painfully visible, seemed to be stretching and pulling at my insides.

His hand was still hovering near mine, close enough that I could feel the heat radiating from his fingertips, but not close enough to make contact. It was like he was testing the waters, waiting for me to either run or pull him in. And all I could do was stand there, stuck in the middle of it all, caught between the woman I used to be—strong, determined, unwavering—and the one I was becoming, the one who wanted to forgive him, who still wanted to trust him despite the wreckage.

"I don't want your pity," I said, the words falling out before I had a chance to process them. My voice was quieter than I intended, but the sharpness of the accusation in it still stung. "And I don't need you to fix anything."

Aiden blinked, the shock on his face quick but fleeting. It was replaced with something softer, something almost… understanding. "I'm not here to fix you," he said, his words deliberate, like he was carefully placing each one in front of me, making sure they wouldn't fall apart. "I'm here because I need to at least try and fix… us."

The softness in his voice, the vulnerability I never thought I'd see in him, made my stomach twist. Was this an act? Or had he really changed? I couldn't tell. Maybe it didn't matter. Maybe I didn't want it to matter.

I let out a breath, staring at the ground for a moment, trying to keep my cool. "What do you think you can do?" I asked, unable to stop the disbelief from creeping into my voice. "After everything?"

His gaze never left me, unwavering, even though I could see the faintest flicker of frustration in his eyes. "I don't know," he admitted. "I just know that I've never felt this… I've never wanted something this much. I made a lot of mistakes. But you? You weren't one of them."

IN THE DARK

I could have sworn I saw the corner of his mouth twitch into a smile, like he knew the exact effect his words were having on me. And it pissed me off. He was so confident in his ability to charm me, to twist my insides into knots with a few carefully chosen words. I hated it. But the truth was, it was working.

"What do you expect me to do with that?" I asked, my voice rising. My heart was pounding now, and I didn't know if it was from the anger or the fact that I felt so alive, so much, in his presence. And I didn't want to feel alive. Not with him. "You expect me to forgive you just because you suddenly decided you didn't screw things up? That's not how this works, Aiden."

He didn't look away, didn't back down. Instead, he stepped closer, the space between us shrinking to something almost unbearable. "I don't expect you to forgive me. Not yet. Hell, maybe you never will. But I do expect you to let me try. To give me a chance to show you that I can be better than the guy who walked away without a word."

My chest tightened. I hadn't realized how badly I needed to hear that until now—until I felt it in the pit of my stomach, that strange longing for something I didn't think I could have anymore. My mind was telling me to walk away, to keep going, to get out of this mess before it all fell apart again. But my heart? My heart was already racing ahead, wanting to give him that second chance, wanting to believe in something I wasn't sure was real.

"I don't need you to be perfect," I said, almost as a whisper, but the words were like a confession I didn't want to make. "I just need you to show up. To stop disappearing when things get hard."

For a moment, the world seemed to stand still, and the only thing that existed was the space between us. Aiden's eyes softened, and there was something so raw in his expression that it knocked the breath out of me. He reached out, slowly this time, his fingers brushing the back of my hand. The touch was warm, gentle, and for a moment, I let myself believe that maybe—just maybe—he was telling the truth.

"I'm here now," he said, his voice steady, but I could hear the underlying tension in it. "And I'm not going anywhere."

The words hung between us, thick and charged. I wanted to pull away, to tell him that it was too late, that I couldn't keep living in this limbo of hope and disappointment. But something about the way he was standing there—so much more grounded than I remembered—made me think that maybe, just maybe, this could be different.

"Why now?" I asked, my voice barely above a whisper. "Why after everything?"

He exhaled sharply, as if he'd been holding his breath for far too long. "Because I can't keep running from the best thing that ever happened to me," he said, his words heavy with meaning. "I've spent too much time making excuses, thinking I was doing the right thing. But the only thing I did was lose you. And I can't do that anymore."

The air between us was thick now, the weight of his confession pressing down on me like a physical thing. My mind screamed at me to pull back, to protect myself, but my heart? My heart was dangerously close to giving in.

I should have walked away. I should have turned on my heel and pretended like none of this—none of him—mattered. But standing there, in the fading light of an autumn afternoon, with him so close, I could feel his words curl around me like smoke, suffocating and intoxicating all at once. The tension between us was palpable, humming in the air, as if the world itself was waiting for me to make a choice.

But I couldn't—couldn't just let go of everything. Not yet.

"Why do you keep doing this to me?" I finally whispered, my voice shaking more than I intended. Aiden's eyes flicked to mine, that mixture of regret and determination still etched on his face. He opened his mouth to speak, but I wasn't done. "Do you know how many times I've been angry with you, Aiden? How many nights I've spent fighting the urge to call you, to yell at you, to—"

"Stop." The word came out sharp, like it pained him to hear it. His hand, trembling slightly, reached up to touch the side of his head, a gesture that I knew meant he was lost in thought. He wasn't ready to hear the truth—certainly not the way I was about to say it. But there it was, spilling out of me anyway. "I've been angry with you because I trusted you. And you just... left. Like I was nothing."

The words stung. The second they left my lips, I regretted them, but they had already been said, and they hung between us, making the space feel smaller, tighter. Aiden took a step back, his face darkening as if the truth had hit him harder than I ever could. For a moment, there was a crack in the armor he'd built around himself, and I wondered if maybe, just maybe, there was something in him that still cared.

"I never meant for you to feel like that." His voice was raw, the kind of rawness you only hear when someone's been carrying something heavy for far too long. "But I didn't know how to fix it. I didn't know how to make it right."

I swallowed hard, pushing the lump in my throat down as best I could. "You don't get to just come back and expect everything to be fine. That's not how this works. You can't just walk away, and then when it's convenient for you, come back and expect to pick up where we left off."

The hurt in my chest was a constant ache now, a dull throb that refused to fade, and no amount of apologies would heal it. But as he stood there, watching me, looking almost as broken as I felt, I couldn't help but wonder if there was something worth salvaging. Something I wasn't ready to admit yet.

Aiden's jaw tightened, his hands clenching at his sides as if he were restraining himself from doing something rash. "I'm not asking you to forget, or to forgive me right away. I'm asking you to let me show you that I can be the man you deserve."

His words hung in the air, waiting for my response, but the thing was, I wasn't sure if I was ready to hear it. I wasn't sure if I wanted to risk opening myself up to the possibility of being hurt again. And yet, despite all of that—despite the bitterness, despite the doubts—I still wanted to believe him.

"Show me?" I laughed bitterly, shaking my head. "How do you show someone that you care after you've already broken them? After you've already proved that you can't be trusted?"

Aiden stepped forward, closer now, until I could feel the heat of his body warming the space around us. "I don't know how to fix it, but I'm damn sure going to try," he said, his voice low, like the weight of his words carried more than just meaning—it carried the weight of everything that had gone wrong, everything that had been lost.

I was fighting against myself now, every instinct in me telling me to walk away, to protect myself from this mess of emotions he was dredging up. But there was a tiny part of me—the part that had spent so long loving him, the part that had been aching for something real—that wanted to let him try. Wanted to let him prove he wasn't the same person who had left without a word.

"You don't owe me anything, Aiden," I whispered, more to myself than to him. "But don't make promises you can't keep."

For a moment, I thought he might argue, but instead, he nodded, his expression softening. "I won't," he said quietly. "I won't promise you anything I can't keep. But I'll be here. And I'll show you, day by day, that I can be what you need."

His words hit me harder than I was prepared for. I wasn't sure what I was supposed to do with them. I wasn't sure if I wanted to do anything with them at all. But something about the sincerity in his eyes made me wonder if maybe I was being too harsh. Maybe—just maybe—he wasn't the only one who needed to change.

I turned away, needing space to breathe, to clear my head. But as I took a step back, the ground beneath me shifted, and suddenly, my foot caught on a loose stone. I stumbled, hands flailing to find something to steady myself. And just like that, Aiden was there, his arm wrapping around me before I could hit the ground.

I hadn't expected him to catch me. I hadn't expected him to care enough to reach out. But there he was, holding me steady, the warmth of his body pressing against mine, the faintest trace of his cologne—spicy, warm, familiar—filling my senses.

For a moment, I forgot how to breathe. I forgot everything except the feel of him.

His voice was barely above a whisper when he spoke again, his words lingering between us like an unspoken promise. "I'm not letting go this time."

And for the first time in a long while, I wondered if maybe—just maybe—I was willing to let him keep that promise.

The soft rustle of leaves above us was the only sound, but in that silence, I heard something else—a warning, perhaps, or maybe a signal. I wasn't sure. But before I could process it, before I could make sense of the flood of emotions rising in me, I felt the unmistakable presence of someone else—someone watching us.

My heart stopped.

Chapter 18: Bound by Shadows

The café smelled like burnt caramel and fresh rain, a paradox I couldn't quite place. It was the kind of smell that lingered in your clothes, settling deep into your bones until you could no longer remember the scent of anything else. I breathed it in, letting it ground me, and tried to focus on the files in front of me. The soft click of a laptop closing behind me brought me back to the present. I glanced up and found him there, leaning against the doorframe with his arms crossed, that smug look still lingering on his face like he knew exactly what I was thinking. He probably did.

"I hate it when you do that," I muttered, though I couldn't help the faint smile that tugged at the corner of my lips. It was a fight I'd given up long ago—the fight against his ability to read me like a book.

"I don't know what you mean." His voice, low and rich, carried the same easy confidence it always did, though there was something new beneath it now. It was darker, tinged with something I couldn't quite identify.

I shook my head, flipping through the papers on the table. They were all pieces of a puzzle, a puzzle I was determined to solve. The names, the dates, the connections—there was something bigger here. I could feel it tightening around me like a noose, but every time I thought I had a hold on it, something slipped through my fingers. And he—well, he was always right there beside me, close enough to catch me when I stumbled but far enough to keep me guessing.

We'd spent the last week buried in paperwork and coffee, attempting to piece together the shards of a mystery that, at first glance, seemed ordinary enough. A string of fires. Arson, no less. But something didn't sit right with me. Too clean. Too precise. Too much of it didn't add up. And there was the nagging feeling, the one that had been there from the beginning, that there was someone pulling strings from behind the scenes, someone who knew exactly how to manipulate the situation to their advantage.

"You still think it's connected to the corporation?" I asked, not looking up as I sifted through yet another stack of papers.

He pushed himself off the doorframe, his steps purposeful and measured as he moved across the room to where I sat. I couldn't help but notice how the weight of his presence seemed to fill the space between us, drawing the air tighter, heavier. I glanced up briefly, catching the glint of something in his eyes—something that wasn't there before. Maybe it was the exhaustion, or maybe it was something else entirely. It didn't matter. Not yet.

"I know it is," he said, his voice almost too calm. "The pattern's there. All the signs point to it. We just need the right piece to confirm it."

I didn't argue, though the skepticism still curled in my gut. I wanted to trust him. I wanted to believe that he wasn't just stringing me along like the others had done. But the closer we got to the heart of this, the more the lines between ally and enemy blurred.

I turned my attention back to the papers, but he didn't move away. I could feel his gaze on me, intense and steady. "We make a good team, don't we?" he asked, and I could hear the humor in his tone, like it was a game. Or a challenge.

"Don't get cocky," I muttered, though the words lost their sting when I found myself meeting his eyes. There was an unspoken understanding there, a recognition of something neither of us was willing to voice aloud. This—whatever this was—wasn't just business anymore. It was personal. It had crossed that line the moment we agreed to put aside everything else and work together.

His smile was small but it reached his eyes, dark and knowing. "You're not as tough as you pretend to be."

"And you're not as smart as you think," I shot back, though the words didn't feel as sharp as they should have.

The silence stretched between us, comfortable in its own way. I had no idea how we got here, to this place where trust felt like something we could almost touch but never quite hold. He was right about one thing. We made a good team. But that didn't mean I was going to stop being cautious. Especially not with someone like him.

When I stood, the chair scraped against the floor with an irritating squeal. I grabbed my coat, the motion sharp, but my fingers brushed his as I passed. The contact was electric—nothing new there, but it still sent a jolt through me. We both froze for a moment, locked in that space where a touch could mean anything or nothing at all.

"I'm going to head out," I said, my voice steadier than I felt. "You coming?"

He paused, as if he were weighing something in his mind. "I'll catch up with you later."

I nodded, stepping out into the chill of the night air. The city was alive around me, a thousand little lights flickering in the distance, but all I could focus on was the feeling that had settled in my chest—something that couldn't be ignored. That nagging sense that we were dancing around a much larger picture, a picture I wasn't sure I was ready to see.

I walked away from the café, my breath forming little clouds in the cold air, but it wasn't the cold that made me shiver. It was the quiet, the anticipation, the knowledge that whatever we'd stirred up between us was far from over. And the shadows? They were closing in faster than either of us could have predicted.

The morning light was harsh as it filtered through the blinds, casting long shadows across the room. It made everything look sterile, distant, as though the world beyond those narrow slats didn't exist at all. But I couldn't escape it. Not now. Not with the case weighing on me like a heavy, unyielding cloak. I grabbed my coffee, the steam rising in slow curls, but it barely registered. Instead, I found my eyes drifting back to the map on the wall. Pins, strings, and post-its—each one representing a piece of the puzzle, a piece that I thought I had a handle on. But the longer I looked at it, the more it seemed like a cruel joke, mocking my every attempt to make sense of it.

A knock at the door broke my concentration, and I didn't have to turn to know who it was. The tension between us had built up over the last few days, and it was only a matter of time before we'd have to face whatever was simmering beneath the surface. It was too dangerous to pretend it wasn't there.

"Come in," I called, trying to sound casual, but my voice came out tight, almost brittle. There was no escaping this now. We were in this together, for better or worse.

The door opened with a familiar creak, and his presence filled the doorway before he did. "You look like you've been up all night," he remarked, his voice laced with that same mix of sarcasm and genuine concern that he seemed to reserve only for me.

"Sleep's overrated," I said, offering him a tight smile that didn't reach my eyes. I hadn't slept in days, not properly. The fire, the connections, the feeling that we were on the brink of something much larger than either of us had imagined—it kept me awake, kept me moving. Kept me wondering just how much of it was a coincidence and how much was deliberate.

He leaned against the desk, eyeing the map with a kind of weary curiosity. "Have you figured it out yet?" he asked, his fingers drumming lightly on the surface of the wood, sending a shiver of awareness up my spine.

"No," I said flatly. "But I will."

A brief silence stretched between us, thick and pregnant with unspoken words. There was always a tension when he was around, like we were both afraid to step too close for fear of what might spark between us. I didn't want to deal with the consequences of crossing that line, but I was already standing at the edge, looking down.

"You know," he said after a beat, his voice dropping lower, "it's not just about the arson anymore. There's more to this. More than we're seeing."

I turned my gaze back to the map, suddenly aware of how much we were missing. "I know," I muttered, my fingers tracing the edges of the map, following a route I hadn't considered before. "It's almost like someone wants us to follow the trail, but just far enough to lead us astray."

His gaze narrowed. "You think we're being played?"

"Could be," I replied, but the words tasted like ash. The thought that we might be pawns in some larger game made my skin crawl. But the idea that we were being manipulated meant that someone, somewhere, knew exactly how much we'd figured out.

He straightened up and moved closer, his boots clicking on the hardwood floor. "We need to get ahead of this. We can't wait for someone to make the first move."

There was a fire in his eyes now, something urgent that made me want to believe him, to trust that we could actually do this together. But I was too well-versed in betrayal to throw myself into something I didn't fully understand. Still, there was something magnetic about him, something that tugged at me, made my heart skip when he looked at me just right.

"You're right," I said finally, breaking the silence. "But we can't rush into this. Not yet. We need more information."

The words hung between us like a challenge. He met my gaze, his jaw tight, the air around us suddenly charged with something new—something that wasn't just about the case anymore. We both felt it, that strange, magnetic pull that had been there from the beginning, but neither of us was ready to admit it aloud.

"Then what's the plan?" he asked, his voice soft but insistent, like he was daring me to let go of my reservations, to stop hiding behind the safety of caution.

I didn't answer immediately, unsure of where this conversation was going, or where it would lead us. I turned back to the map, mentally retracing the steps we'd taken, piecing together the fragments we had. "We dig deeper. We go to the source. But we do it carefully."

"Carefully," he repeated, a smirk tugging at the corner of his lips. "That's not your style."

"Maybe it should be," I shot back, not fully meaning it. The truth was, I didn't know if we could afford to play this carefully anymore. But I wasn't going to tell him that.

He took a step back, his hands slipping into his pockets, eyes never leaving me. "I'm with you. But you don't get to play it safe anymore. Not when we're this close."

I knew he was right. Every instinct screamed at me to dig deeper, to throw caution to the wind, but I wasn't ready to lose myself in this. Not yet. Not until I knew exactly what we were up against.

"You're not the only one who's in this," I said, my voice low and steady. "And I don't need you to remind me."

He raised an eyebrow but didn't press. Instead, he gave me a nod, a silent acknowledgment that whatever this was—this alliance, this tension—it was becoming something we both couldn't ignore anymore.

I sighed, running a hand through my hair, the weight of everything pressing down on me. "We'll need to move quickly, but not recklessly. You get that, right?"

"Right," he said, the word a promise. It wasn't enough to settle the storm inside me, but it was something. And that was more than I'd had before.

We were both in this now, bound by something darker than the case. And I had no idea how we'd make it out, but one thing was certain: it was going to change everything.

The city's pulse was a steady hum beneath my skin as I moved through the streets, my steps quick and purposeful but not rushed. I could almost hear the echoes of my thoughts crashing against each other, too loud, too urgent. The closer we got to the truth, the more the weight of it pressed down on me. I had known from the start this wasn't going to be easy, but I hadn't anticipated just how tangled the threads were, how tightly they wound around everything I thought I knew.

It had been days since the last meeting, since the tension in that room had felt almost unbearable. The case was slipping from our grasp with every passing moment, but the more I tried to pull the pieces together, the more elusive they became. The deeper we dug, the darker it got. I'd grown accustomed to danger, to risk, but this was different. It was personal.

I had hoped that stepping away, taking a breath, would help clear my head. But of course, that never worked. I could still feel his presence lingering, an uninvited shadow at the edge of my thoughts. It was impossible to ignore him when every time we spoke, every word he said, seemed to add a new layer to the mystery. The stakes had become too high to keep pretending that the lines between us weren't blurring. The more time I spent with him, the more I realized just how hard it was to distinguish what I wanted from what I needed. And right now, I needed answers.

I pushed through the door of the small office building, the musty air hitting me like a slap in the face. It wasn't much—just a cramped room stacked with file cabinets and cluttered desks—but it was ours. For now, at least. There was a comfort in the disarray, a quiet reassurance that we weren't in danger of being watched or listened to. At least not here.

IN THE DARK

He was already there, sitting at one of the desks, his face lit by the harsh fluorescent light above him. His brow furrowed in concentration, but when I walked in, his gaze snapped up, meeting mine with that familiar intensity. I hadn't expected the way my heart skipped a beat, the sudden rush of warmth that shot through me. This wasn't supposed to be happening. Not now, not with everything else on the line.

"I was wondering when you'd show up," he said, his voice low, a touch of amusement lingering in the words. "Did you miss me?"

The question was casual, but there was an undercurrent to it, something I couldn't ignore. I met his eyes and forced my tone to stay steady. "I didn't realize I was supposed to show up at all."

His smile was sharp, too knowing. "You always show up when it counts. Don't act like you've got anywhere else to go."

There was something about the way he said that—so sure of himself, so sure of me—that sent a flicker of unease through me. I was supposed to keep my distance. I was supposed to keep this professional. But the more we worked together, the more I found myself second-guessing everything I'd told myself.

"Don't start," I muttered, walking over to the table, where the files were spread out in chaotic disarray. I focused on them, trying to shut out the noise in my head, trying to ignore the pull between us that was growing stronger with each passing day.

But he didn't stop. "I'm just saying, you can't keep pretending like this doesn't matter." His voice softened, a hint of something else in it. Something that was neither gentle nor mocking, but something deeper. More real.

I didn't look up, even though I could feel the weight of his gaze on me. "What matters is finding out who's behind all this. We're not exactly playing in the safety zone anymore."

He leaned back in his chair, folding his arms across his chest. "I know. And we're getting closer to the edge. You can feel it, can't you?"

I didn't answer immediately, but I could feel the truth of his words settle in my gut. Yes, I could feel it. The walls were closing in, the danger creeping closer with each step we took. And yet, every time I thought about stopping, about pulling back, I couldn't. There was something else driving me, something I couldn't quite name.

I looked up at him then, my breath catching for just a moment. He was watching me, his expression unreadable. But there was something there. A flicker of something that I couldn't place. "We can't stop," I said, more to myself than to him.

"I know," he replied softly, his gaze never leaving mine. "But we need to be careful. Someone doesn't want us to find out what we're looking for."

I felt a chill run through me at his words. It was one thing to suspect it, to feel it in the pit of my stomach. But it was something entirely different to hear him say it out loud.

"That's why we have to move fast," I said, my voice firm, even though I didn't entirely believe it myself. "Before they realize we're onto them."

He nodded, but there was something guarded in the way he moved, as if he was weighing something carefully. "Agreed. But we need more. We can't just go in blind anymore."

I turned back to the files, but my mind was elsewhere. We were too deep into this now to turn back. But I had no idea how much deeper it was going to get. And that terrified me more than anything.

"Let's get to work then," I said, swallowing down the growing sense of dread in my chest.

The hours stretched on, our conversation dwindling as we focused on the files in front of us. But as the clock ticked, I couldn't shake the feeling that something was shifting, something beneath the surface that we weren't seeing. I looked up, ready to ask him what was bothering him, when the shrill sound of my phone buzzing broke through the tension in the room.

I picked it up, only to freeze at the name on the screen. It was a number I hadn't expected to hear from again.

Before I could answer, I heard the unmistakable sound of footsteps in the hallway. Someone was coming.

And just like that, everything I thought I knew shifted once again.

Chapter 19: A Heart Rekindled

The garden, a secluded patch tucked away between crumbling stone walls and thick clusters of ivy, was a sanctuary forged from years of neglect. The ground beneath my feet was damp with dew, the air rich with the earthy scent of overgrown moss and wildflowers. It felt like time had forgotten this place, as if it existed outside the reach of the world. The weight of the day—its disappointments, its sharp edges—began to dissolve, leaving behind only the soft, persistent hum of nature, like a lullaby that soothed the soul. A small fountain, its stone basin weathered and cracked, murmured in the corner, its water cascading in a gentle rhythm that matched the steady pulse in my own chest.

Aiden stood beside me, his silhouette a quiet contrast against the wildness that surrounded us. The way he was looking at me, with an intensity that felt both familiar and new, stirred something deep within. It had been years since I'd seen that look in his eyes, a mixture of longing and vulnerability, like he had forgotten how to hope until now. The years between us had not been kind, and yet here we were, standing in the fragile space between past regrets and the uncertain promise of the future.

I could feel the weight of his presence in a way that made me both uneasy and deeply connected. His hand brushed against mine, tentative at first, as if he were testing the waters. The brush of his skin against mine sent a rush of warmth through me, a spark that reignited memories I had long tried to bury. His hand encircled mine, his fingers firm but gentle, and in that touch, I felt an old ache, a pull I couldn't deny.

"Is this real?" I asked before I could stop myself, my voice barely above a whisper. The question hung between us, fragile and uncertain. I had to be sure, because I couldn't bear another heartbreak, another cruel twist of fate.

His gaze softened, his thumb brushing the back of my hand in a soothing motion, as though trying to erase the doubts that lingered like smoke in my mind. "I don't know what it is, but it's real enough for me."

I swallowed, the lump in my throat sharp. His words were simple, but they carried weight, like a promise wrapped in the rawness of something true. And for the first time in a long while, I let myself believe it.

There was no sound but the soft rustling of leaves, the faint hum of the world outside the garden's walls. For a moment, I allowed myself to close my eyes, to breathe in the air that felt so different here—fresher, almost like it was meant for something new. A chance.

When I opened them again, Aiden was leaning closer, his gaze still locked on mine. There was a hesitation in his movements, a quiet conflict warring in the depths of his eyes. It was as if he, too, was trying to figure out whether this was the right moment, the right choice. But I didn't need to think about it anymore. My heart had already made its decision, and it had been a long time since I'd felt that kind of certainty.

The world around us seemed to hold its breath as I stepped toward him, my heart pounding in my chest. Every inch of space between us disappeared with a single movement, and then his lips were on mine, tentative and careful at first, as if he were waiting for me to pull away. But I didn't. I couldn't. The kiss deepened, the years of distance and silence between us breaking away with every press of his lips. It was like waking from a long, cold sleep, the warmth spreading through me like wildfire.

I could taste the salt of his skin, feel the slight tremor in his hands as they slid to my waist, pulling me closer. It was everything I had forgotten I needed, everything I had never allowed myself to want. There was no rush, no urgency. Only the soft connection of two people finding their way back to each other, against the odds, despite the scars that still marked our hearts.

When we finally pulled away, both of us breathing heavily, our foreheads rested together. I closed my eyes, not wanting to face the truth just yet, afraid that if I did, this moment would vanish like smoke in the wind.

But Aiden's voice was soft, his breath warm against my skin. "I've missed you."

The words were simple, but they were everything. They shattered the walls I had built around myself, the ones I'd used to protect my heart from him, from the world. I hadn't realized until that moment how much I had needed to hear those words, how much I had been holding on to the hope that he might still care.

I didn't trust myself to speak at first. The emotions that surged within me were too overwhelming, too raw. Instead, I closed my eyes again and let the moment stretch out, wrapping around us like the garden's vines—tangled, uncertain, but also full of life. We had both changed, been broken, and yet here we were, standing in a place that felt like the beginning of something new.

The soft murmur of the fountain was the only sound now, its steady rhythm grounding us, reminding me that some things, like love, could still flourish even after the storm.

The quiet of the garden held us in its embrace, its wildness acting as a shield against everything that had come before. Aiden's hand was still around mine, his thumb tracing slow, deliberate circles over my skin. It was a tender touch, but there was something more—a silent reassurance, as though we were both trying to convince ourselves that this wasn't just a fleeting illusion. The weight of years apart pressed on me, the memory of the years when our lives had taken separate paths. It was hard not to feel the sharp edges of those losses, the unanswered questions, the words that had never been spoken. But in the way his hand held mine, there was something deeper—a shared understanding that perhaps we could rebuild what had been broken.

"You're still here," I said softly, the words slipping out before I could catch them. I almost regretted it as soon as I said it, because the truth in it felt too raw, too vulnerable to put into words.

Aiden let out a quiet laugh, low and almost rueful, like he knew exactly what I meant, and yet still couldn't completely process it. "And where else would I be?" he asked, his voice tinged with a kind of humor that felt like a lifeline.

I opened my mouth to respond, but no words came. What could I say? That I had spent the last several years trying to forget him, trying to push away the memories that clung to me like a second skin? That his sudden reappearance felt like a twist of fate, both cruel and kind? That seeing him again made me question everything I had built in the years without him?

Instead, I squeezed his hand, feeling the familiar warmth of him, the way he had always been my constant even when I hadn't wanted him to be. He was the one who had always known me, even when I was doing my best to forget myself.

"So, what now?" I asked, the question coming out quieter than I'd intended, as though speaking it too loudly might shatter the fragile peace we had found. "Is this... real? Or is this just a moment, something temporary?"

Aiden's gaze held mine, steady and unflinching. "I don't know," he admitted. "But it's all I've wanted, all I've needed." His voice was thick with emotion, his words more meaningful than any promise he could have made.

I felt a lump form in my throat, the weight of those words heavy, more than I had been prepared for. "And what if this is just us clinging to the past?" I asked, my voice trembling despite my best efforts to remain calm. "What if we're just chasing ghosts?"

He reached up, his hand brushing against my cheek, the touch sending a shiver down my spine. "I don't think we are," he said quietly, his voice low and earnest. "I think we're finding something new, something worth fighting for."

The tenderness in his touch, in his words, unraveled me, and for the first time in years, I let myself believe him. Maybe it wasn't about what had been, about trying to recreate the past or undo the mistakes we'd made. Maybe it was about what could be—what we could build, together, from this moment.

But that didn't mean the past was easily forgotten. There were still shadows lingering in the corners, things unsaid, things unresolved.

"What happened to us, Aiden?" I asked, my voice barely a whisper. It wasn't a question I'd ever wanted to ask, but now it seemed impossible not to.

Aiden's expression tightened, a flicker of regret passing over his face before he took a deep breath. "I don't know," he said quietly. "It's a long story, one I don't think we have the time to get into right now."

I nodded, understanding that. There were things we couldn't go back and fix, no matter how much we wished we could. The time to make those decisions had long passed. But that didn't mean it didn't still sting, didn't still hang over us like a storm cloud waiting to break.

"So we just... pretend everything is fine?" I asked, my tone sharp, betraying the uncertainty I felt bubbling inside. I wasn't sure I was ready to let go of all the hurt, the anger, the unanswered questions.

Aiden sighed, the sound filled with a weary kind of understanding. "I'm not asking you to pretend anything. I just don't want us to keep hurting each other. There's enough of that already. Maybe it's time we stop focusing on the past, on what went wrong. Maybe it's time to see if we can start again, just this once."

I swallowed hard, trying to make sense of his words, trying to make sense of all of it. Could we? Could we really find a way back to each other after everything that had happened? I wasn't sure, but I couldn't deny the flicker of hope that had sparked in my chest, a spark that grew with every word he said, every look he gave me.

"I don't know," I said, my voice soft, honest. "I wish I did."

Aiden leaned in, his lips brushing against my forehead, a soft, lingering kiss that made my heart skip a beat. "It's okay not to know," he murmured. "I don't know either. But I do know that I want to find out with you."

In that moment, everything else faded away—the doubts, the fears, the walls I had built around myself. All that was left was him, his warmth, his steady presence beside me, and the undeniable truth that for the first time in years, I wasn't alone.

The world outside the garden could wait. Here, in the quiet, in the softness of the moment, we had all the time we needed.

The garden, once untouched, had become a world unto itself, where the noise of the outside world couldn't penetrate. Even the wind seemed to soften as it passed through the thick branches overhead. I stood there, with Aiden beside me, feeling the weight of the moment—heavy, but not in a way that suffocated. It was a weight that spoke of something grounding, a tether to reality I hadn't realized I'd been missing until now.

Aiden's presence next to me was like a warm blanket, cocooning me in a space that felt simultaneously safe and charged. It was as though we were the only two people left in the universe. I could hear the soft rustle of leaves and the distant hum of insects, but everything else faded into nothingness. The past was somewhere far behind, and for the first time, I could see the future—uncertain, yes, but filled with a possibility that hadn't been there before.

"So, what now?" I asked again, this time the words more playful, as though I were testing the waters of something new, something unspoken.

Aiden gave me a sideways glance, his lips curling into the smallest of smiles. "You keep asking me that, like I have all the answers. Are you sure you want to know?"

I tilted my head, raising an eyebrow. "What's the alternative? That we stand here forever, like statues?"

He chuckled, the sound light and easy, but there was something underlying it, something that told me he was just as uncertain as I was. "I'm not sure about forever," he said, "but I'd like to think we've earned more than just a moment." He paused, looking out over the wild expanse of flowers that had sprung up around us. "You've changed."

I felt the sting of his words before I even had a chance to consider them. "I'm not the same person I was, if that's what you mean," I said quickly, almost defensively. "People don't stay static. They grow."

"I didn't mean it like that," Aiden said, his tone gentler now. "I just... I don't know. It's not bad. It's just different. You feel different."

I couldn't help the little flicker of guilt that stirred in me. Of course, I had changed. We both had. Life had a way of forcing you to do that. The years apart, the heartbreaks, the choices—none of them had been easy. But I hadn't realized how much they'd molded me, twisted me, until now.

"Well," I said, taking a deep breath, "if we're being honest, I don't know who I am anymore either." The words slipped out before I could stop them, and I regretted them instantly. It felt like too much to admit, too vulnerable a thing to say aloud.

Aiden was quiet for a moment, and when he spoke again, his voice was soft. "We've all got our masks, haven't we? Worn them long enough that we forget how to take them off." He looked at me then, really looked at me, his eyes searching. "But maybe this is a place where we can try. Maybe it's time to take them off."

I didn't answer him right away. The idea was tempting, more tempting than anything I'd felt in years. The thought of letting go of the walls I'd so carefully built around myself was terrifying, but I could see something in his eyes—a plea for honesty, a chance for something different. I'd never been good at letting people in, not after everything we'd been through. But there was something about Aiden that made me want to try.

The moment lingered, suspended in the air between us, a fragile truce. Then, from the corner of my eye, I caught a flicker of movement at the edge of the garden. It was almost too swift to catch, but my heart jolted in my chest nonetheless. I blinked, convinced that I had imagined it, but then the movement came again—a shadow, darting between the trees.

"What was that?" I whispered, my voice suddenly tight with unease.

Aiden's gaze shifted in the same direction, his posture tensing ever so slightly. "I don't know. Stay here."

Before I could respond, he was already moving toward the edge of the garden, his footsteps quick but quiet. I stood frozen for a moment, my mind racing. This was a place of peace, a sanctuary. Nothing should have been able to disturb it. But the air had changed, becoming thick with a strange tension, as though the world outside had come crashing in to remind us that nothing, not even our stolen moments, was ever truly safe.

I hesitated, a war waging inside me. Part of me wanted to stay put, to hold on to the fragile peace we had created. But the other part—an insistent, gnawing part—urged me to follow, to find out what was lurking in the shadows. With a final glance at Aiden, I stepped forward, my heart pounding in my chest.

The ground beneath me was soft, damp from the morning dew, but my feet seemed to find their way without hesitation. I moved quickly but quietly, stepping carefully to avoid any noise that might give us away. The air smelled different now—cooler, heavier, like the calm before a storm.

I caught up to Aiden just as he reached the edge of the garden, his body taut and ready for whatever came next. "Do you see anything?" I asked, my voice low.

He shook his head, but his eyes were scanning the area with sharp focus. "Nothing yet. But I don't like the way it feels."

Before I could respond, there was a sudden rustling from the underbrush, a soft crack of a branch snapping underfoot. I turned, my breath catching in my throat as a figure stepped into view—a person, tall and cloaked in shadows, their face hidden.

My heart skipped, every instinct screaming that something was terribly wrong. But before I could react, a voice broke the silence—low, menacing, and familiar.

"Looking for something?"

Chapter 20: Secrets in the Smoke

The smoke always has a way of lingering, doesn't it? It clings to your skin, drifts through your hair, and settles in the pit of your stomach like something that shouldn't be there—like a secret you're not quite ready to hear but already know. I stepped back into the charred remains of my family's old property, the remnants of the fire licking at the edges of the past I thought I'd buried. The air was thick, heavy with the acrid scent of burnt wood and something else, something metallic. It made my heart pound a little faster, like a warning from the universe. The charred remains of my childhood home sat in front of me, a jagged silhouette against a sky that seemed a little too gray, a little too heavy.

It wasn't the first fire. It wasn't even the second. But this one, this one felt different, as though the flames had come not just to destroy but to remind. Remind me of what? I wasn't sure. But I had a sinking feeling that the truth was about to unfold in ways I wasn't ready for. The ground beneath my boots was soft, the grass a faint green that looked almost unreal against the scorched earth around it. It was like the world had paused, holding its breath, waiting for something to happen. But nothing happened—at least, nothing that I could see.

And then he was there, standing in the doorway of the remains of what had once been my father's study. Elias. His figure was as stark and sharp as the broken edges of the house, his dark eyes scanning the area, missing nothing. His jaw was clenched, lips pressed tight like he was keeping some kind of secret, and when he looked at me, his expression softened just enough to make my heart skip. But I wasn't fooled. Neither of us were here for anything simple anymore.

"Found anything useful?" I asked, my voice thick with the smoke that had begun to settle in my lungs.

Elias didn't answer right away. Instead, he crouched down by the burnt-out remains of an old oak shelf, his fingers tracing the edges of what had once been a stack of leather-bound books. There were no books left now, just ash and the scent of something too bitter to ignore.

"Nothing," he said, standing up slowly. His eyes were sharp, alert, and I could see the storm in his mind. The same storm that had been brewing in mine since I'd first walked into this nightmare.

"I don't believe you," I said, crossing my arms, eyes narrowing. "You've got that look—the one you get when you're about to break some bad news."

Elias glanced at me, the corner of his mouth tugging upward in something that could have been a smile if it weren't so cold. "Maybe I'm just tired of repeating myself."

"Well, it's a good thing you're not the only one here," I replied, eyes scanning the wreckage once again. "So, what exactly are we looking for, then? A clue? A reason? Or just an excuse to make sense of all this chaos?" I gestured to the ruins around us, my voice rising.

Elias didn't respond immediately. He let my frustration hang in the air like the smoke, suffocating and all-encompassing. Finally, he spoke, his voice low, but the words hit me harder than I was expecting.

"This wasn't just a random fire," he said, his eyes locking onto mine with a seriousness that made my skin tingle. "Someone did this on purpose. They're sending us a message."

I took a step back, suddenly aware of just how quiet the world around us had become. The usual noises of the city felt distant, muted, like we were standing on the edge of something far bigger than we could ever understand. I had a choice now: turn away, walk out of the ruins and pretend I hadn't heard it, or lean into the storm and find out what really lay hidden in the ashes.

I wasn't going anywhere.

"Do you think it has to do with my father?" I asked, my voice trembling slightly despite my best efforts to hold it steady. "The fire that took him... the one that took everything from us?"

Elias didn't flinch, didn't look away. "I think it has everything to do with him."

I exhaled sharply, the weight of his words sinking in. "You think someone's trying to punish me for things that happened before I was even born, don't you?" I said it like I was daring him to disagree. But Elias didn't argue, not this time.

We were both standing on the edge of something we couldn't control. And for all the walls I'd built up between us, for all the things I had told myself over the years to keep my distance, there was one thing I couldn't deny: Elias had become as much a part of this mystery as I had. Maybe even more so.

I took a deep breath and moved toward the ruins of the study. "So, what now?" I asked, my voice steadier now, my resolve firming with each step I took.

Elias followed me, his presence a steady weight at my back. "Now, we find out who wants us to remember. And why." His words were a promise, not a suggestion, and I knew there was no turning back. Whatever this was, it wasn't just a fire anymore. It was a reckoning, and it was coming for us, whether we were ready or not.

We didn't speak as we walked back from the remains of the house, the charred ruins fading into the distance as the city stretched before us—vast, indifferent, and a little too quiet. Elias's footsteps echoed beside mine, steady but heavy with something unspoken, and I couldn't shake the feeling that we were being watched. It wasn't the first time I'd had that sense, but this time it felt different. More intense. As though the city itself was holding its breath, waiting for the next step, the next move in some elaborate game.

"Do you ever wonder if we're playing into their hands?" I asked, breaking the silence at last. My voice was barely above a whisper, but it felt like it cut through the thick air between us, charged and expectant.

Elias didn't respond at first, but I felt his gaze on me, sharp, searching, like he was trying to read me in the spaces where words fell short. "I think we've already lost," he said finally, his voice low. "The moment you stepped into that fire, we both did."

I stopped walking, the weight of his words settling over me like the smoke from the blaze. My eyes were fixed on the streets ahead, watching the city pulse with life—people going about their business, oblivious to the firestorm that was about to erupt beneath their feet. A firestorm that we were both caught in.

"So, what now?" I asked, turning to him, the question more pointed than I meant it to be.

Elias's lips twisted into something that could have been a smile but wasn't. "Now? We find out who's behind this. And why."

I nodded, the answer too simple, too clear. And yet, it didn't bring the comfort I was hoping for. The truth never did.

We parted ways on the corner of Harrow Street, the air between us crackling with tension. Elias had his methods of getting things done, his connections, his network of informants, but I wasn't interested in waiting for him to work through the shadows. I needed something concrete, something I could touch and hold onto. And the only place I knew to start was my family's estate. The one place I should have never returned to.

The car ride felt like a lifetime, the city passing in blurry streaks of neon and asphalt. My thoughts were a mess—fragments of memories, half-formed suspicions, and a creeping sense of dread. When I finally arrived, the gates of the estate loomed in front of me like an impenetrable wall. The iron bars creaked as they opened, the familiar sound doing nothing to quell the storm in my chest. I hadn't been here in years, and even the house, now worn and weathered, seemed to be watching me, waiting. It knew something I didn't. It always had.

The front door swung open with a quiet protest, and the scent of old wood and stale air greeted me as I stepped inside. The house was unchanged, as though it had been frozen in time, preserving all the memories I thought I had forgotten. Every step I took on the grand staircase seemed to echo, reminding me of the history that lived in these walls. History I wasn't sure I was ready to confront.

"Hello?" My voice was a whisper, but it felt like I had screamed. The house was empty, its silence pressing in around me.

I wasn't sure what I expected to find—perhaps the remains of the life that had been, the traces of a family broken apart by tragedy. But instead, I found something else entirely. A letter, neatly folded, left on the marble foyer table. The envelope was simple, the handwriting elegant and precise, and yet there was something about it that made my pulse quicken.

I ripped the envelope open, my fingers trembling slightly as I unfolded the paper inside. The words on the page were clear, concise, but they sent a chill crawling up my spine.

You think you know the truth, but you haven't seen the whole picture. The fire was only the beginning. If you want to understand, you'll need to look deeper. All will be revealed when the final spark ignites.

I read it twice, each time the words becoming more twisted in my mind. A warning. A promise. But most of all, a challenge. Whoever had written this wasn't playing games. They were trying to force my hand, trying to push me into something that I wasn't ready for.

Before I could process the letter, the sound of a door creaking open upstairs caught my attention. My breath caught in my throat. I wasn't alone.

I moved quickly, my heart racing, and stepped toward the grand staircase, my mind running wild with possibilities. Was it Elias? Had he followed me here, somehow knowing what I would find? Or was it someone else—someone connected to the fires, someone whose face I hadn't seen yet?

I reached the top of the stairs and turned down the hallway toward the study. The door was ajar, and inside, the dim light from the window spilled across the room, casting long shadows that seemed to move with a life of their own.

I paused just outside the door, my breath coming in short, sharp bursts. Whoever was in there hadn't heard me, or maybe they simply didn't care. With a deep breath, I pushed the door open.

What I saw inside stopped me in my tracks. The figure in the room, hunched over a desk, scribbling something furiously on a piece of paper, didn't look up. But I knew who it was.

"Looking for something?" Elias's voice rang out, sharp and cutting, as though he had been waiting for me all along.

I swallowed hard, the realization sinking in like a stone in my stomach. "You've been here the whole time, haven't you?"

Elias finally looked up, a flicker of something I couldn't quite place in his eyes. "You're not the only one with questions."

The silence in the study was suffocating, a weight pressing in on my chest as I stood frozen in the doorway. Elias wasn't the type to look over his shoulder, not unless he wanted to. And now, with his dark gaze finally meeting mine, there was no more pretense. No more games. I was caught, and so was he.

"You've been keeping secrets," I said, the words slipping from my mouth with a sharpness I hadn't expected. It was strange how quickly everything had unraveled, how suddenly this man, who had been my ally, had transformed into something else. I didn't know if it was betrayal that stung or something worse—something harder to define, like the feeling of being on the wrong side of history, of a story that was no longer just mine.

Elias raised an eyebrow, his lips curving slightly into that trademark smirk of his. "Secrets?" he repeated, his voice deceptively calm. "I'm merely working with the facts I have. Just like you."

I took a step into the room, the floorboards creaking under my boots. I was done being cautious. I wasn't about to let him off the hook. "You think you're being clever," I snapped. "But you're not. Not anymore. I've seen enough to know you've known more than you've let on."

He leaned back in the chair, folding his arms across his chest, his expression turning unreadable. "I never said I wasn't keeping things from you," he replied softly, the words careful, measured. "But secrets, as you call them, are sometimes necessary. Sometimes, they keep people alive."

I wasn't sure whether his answer was meant to calm me or stir me up, but it did the latter. Every word he spoke seemed more like an admission, an invitation to dig deeper into the very thing I was afraid of finding.

"You're not making any sense," I said, my voice low but laced with frustration. "Alive? You're telling me you've been keeping things from me to protect me?"

"Not just you," he replied, his eyes darkening with something I couldn't quite place. "Everyone."

I was about to retort, but a sudden movement behind him caught my eye—a flash of something silver, quick and deliberate. Before I could react, Elias was out of his chair, his hand gripping my wrist with surprising force, pulling me away from the desk.

"Get down!" he hissed, just as a sharp crack rang out, followed by the unmistakable sound of something heavy crashing into the walls behind us. My heart slammed against my ribcage as I instinctively ducked, pressing against the floor as Elias shielded me with his body.

The world seemed to hold its breath for a moment, the air thick and still, only to be shattered by the deafening roar of something—gunfire, glass shattering, a force too powerful to ignore.

"What the hell?" I gasped, barely able to hear myself over the pounding in my ears.

"Stay down," Elias growled, his grip never loosening from my wrist as he tugged me toward the back of the room, away from the window where the shot had come from. His body was tense, every muscle coiled like a predator on the verge of pouncing.

"Who the hell was that?" I demanded, struggling to keep my voice steady. My heart was still racing, and I could feel the blood pulsing in my fingertips, but this was different now. This was no longer about figuring out arson or family secrets. Someone had just tried to kill us.

"Someone who doesn't want us to find the truth," Elias said, his words clipped. He pulled me behind a massive bookshelf, a safe haven in the middle of the chaos. "Stay here. Don't move."

I watched as he moved with purpose, his every action swift and precise, as if he had done this before. I wanted to argue, to tell him I wasn't a child, but something in his eyes told me it wasn't a suggestion. It was a command.

I didn't argue.

Seconds later, the sound of footsteps outside the room sent a chill through my spine. Elias was already crouched low, his eyes trained on the door as if he could will it to stay shut. I held my breath, willing myself to be as silent as possible, to not even make a sound, though my pulse screamed at me to run.

"I thought we were done with the games," a voice called from the hallway—deep, rich, and entirely too familiar.

My stomach dropped.

It was him.

I knew that voice, but I hadn't heard it in years, not since... not since everything had fallen apart.

I dared a glance at Elias, who had gone as still as stone. His eyes locked onto mine, and in that brief moment, I saw something I had never seen before—fear. He wasn't the type to be afraid. But in the low light of the room, there was a flicker of something darker, something that told me we weren't just dealing with a dangerous enemy. We were dealing with someone who knew us both. Someone who knew everything.

I heard the footsteps growing closer, slow and deliberate. The hairs on the back of my neck stood up.

"Move," Elias whispered urgently, his hand gripping my arm as he pulled me to my feet. We were both pressed against the bookshelf now, hearts pounding in our chests, ears straining for the next sound. The door handle rattled, the sound of it turning, and in the next moment, the door swung open.

I wasn't prepared for what I saw.

Standing in the doorway, a tall figure framed by the dim light from the hallway, was someone I never thought I'd see again. Someone I had all but erased from my memory, someone I had thought was long gone. But there he was, eyes cold, lips curling into that familiar smirk.

"Did you really think you could run from this?" he asked, his voice laced with amusement. "Because it's far too late for that."

And just like that, I realized I hadn't been prepared for any of it. The past, the present, the future—they were all tangled together in a way I couldn't escape.

And the worst part? I didn't know who to trust anymore.

Chapter 21: The Betrayal Unseen

I hadn't expected the air in the room to feel so dense, as if the walls were closing in around me with every breath I took. My hand gripped the edge of the desk, knuckles white, as the weight of what I'd just uncovered settled like a stone in my stomach. I stared at the papers scattered across the surface, evidence of a betrayal I hadn't been prepared to confront. And yet, here it was, glaring at me with a brutal clarity that made my heart stutter in my chest.

The letters were hastily written, their smudged ink a testament to the desperation of the one who had written them. They weren't meant for my eyes, of course. If they had been, they would have been far more careful. But the moment I found them—stuck in the back of a drawer, hidden beneath an assortment of old files and forgotten trinkets—I knew. I knew that nothing was as it seemed. Nothing had ever been.

I turned my head slowly, my gaze scanning the room. The quiet hum of the air conditioner was the only sound, a backdrop to the tumult in my mind. My fingers trembled, but I couldn't look away from the paper in front of me. Aiden's name had appeared in the text. That, in itself, was enough to send a sharp pang of unease through my veins. But it was the other name, the one I hadn't expected, the one that had no right to be involved, that cut me deeper than I ever imagined possible.

I didn't want to believe it. I didn't want to see what was so plainly laid out before me, yet I couldn't tear my eyes away. The betrayal wasn't about secrets whispered in the dark or promises broken in the heat of a moment. No, this was something worse, something more calculated. It was a quiet manipulation, a slow, deliberate push that had been building for months, maybe even years. And it was all leading back to me.

I leaned back in the chair, my gaze flickering to the window as I tried to steady my breathing. The late afternoon sun spilled through the glass, casting long shadows across the room. It should have been comforting. Instead, it felt suffocating, as if the very light had conspired to reveal things I wasn't ready to see.

My mind raced, but the clarity of it all only made it harder to swallow. I could feel the sting of betrayal in my chest, as if someone had taken a knife and twisted it, slicing through all the trust I had built. For so long, I had believed in the people closest to me. I had let my guard down, let myself believe in something that now felt foolish, naive.

But the hardest part wasn't the betrayal itself. No, it was the person behind it. The one I hadn't suspected. The one I thought I could count on. And as much as I wanted to hurl the papers across the room, I knew I couldn't. Because the truth had been placed in front of me for a reason. It was there to be understood, to be acted upon. And if I didn't confront it, if I didn't figure out what to do next, I'd never be able to move on.

I heard the door creak open, and instinctively, I shoved the papers aside, smoothing my hands over them as if to erase any evidence of what I had just discovered. Aiden's voice called out to me from the threshold, warm and steady, as always.

"You alright?" he asked, his footsteps cautious, as though sensing the change in the air.

I glanced up at him, forcing a smile that didn't quite reach my eyes. The sight of him, so familiar, so comfortable, made my stomach twist in a way that left me breathless. I wanted to tell him. I wanted to throw everything at him, to demand answers, to make him see what I'd uncovered. But I couldn't. Not yet.

"I'm fine," I lied, my voice coming out a little too sharp.

He raised an eyebrow, a small frown forming on his lips as he stepped further into the room. He always knew when something was wrong, always had an uncanny ability to read me like an open book. But this—this was different. This was something I couldn't share with him. Not without knowing the full extent of it. Not without knowing how deep the rot went.

"You sure?" he pressed, his gaze searching mine. "You look... tense."

I couldn't hold his gaze for long, the weight of my discovery too much to bear. I turned away, pretending to focus on the cluttered desk in front of me. Anything to avoid the warmth of his concern.

"I just... have a lot on my mind," I murmured.

He didn't buy it, I could tell. But he didn't push, either. Instead, he let out a quiet sigh and moved to stand beside me, his hand resting briefly on my shoulder in that way he did when he was trying to comfort me without words. It almost felt like a lifeline, but in that moment, I couldn't shake the feeling that I was sinking under the weight of everything I hadn't told him.

"I'll give you space," he said, his voice softer now, more understanding. "But if you need anything, you know where to find me."

I nodded, too afraid to look at him again, afraid that the mask I wore might slip, exposing the jagged edges of the truth I was so desperate to keep hidden. As he left, I stayed in the room, the silence closing in around me like a suffocating fog. The betrayal, now fully realized, hung in the air like a storm waiting to break.

And I was the only one who knew.

For now.

I spent the next few days in a fog, as if I were walking through the motions of life without truly inhabiting it. The betrayal hung over me like a storm cloud, casting a shadow over everything I touched. It made the sun feel less warm, the air less breathable. Each time Aiden looked at me with that quiet, knowing affection, I felt like a stranger.

IN THE DARK

I wanted to push him away, but I couldn't. Not yet. Not when the truth was still too raw, too jagged to share.

I had to confront it, but I wasn't ready. The pieces of the puzzle were too scattered, too incomplete, and if I moved too quickly, if I made a misstep, I might lose everything. So, I did what I always did when things felt like they were slipping through my fingers—I buried myself in work. In the world that was familiar, in the tasks I could control. And when I wasn't working, I found solace in the quiet of my apartment, where no one could find me, no one could ask questions I wasn't ready to answer.

I spent hours in the evenings hunched over the desk, staring at the papers, tracing the names and dates with my fingertips, willing them to make sense. The ink seemed to swim in front of my eyes, shifting and blurring as my thoughts spun in endless circles. I couldn't make sense of it—not fully—but I knew enough to understand the weight of what I'd discovered. The person responsible for the chaos, for the manipulation, had been hiding in plain sight. The person I thought I could trust, the person who had seemed so innocent, so loyal, had been playing a game all along. And I was the last to know.

It was maddening. How could I have missed it? How could I have been so blind?

I wasn't stupid. I had seen the signs, felt the subtle shifts in the air, but I had convinced myself that I was imagining things, that the little moments of doubt were nothing more than the tricks my mind played when it was tired or overwhelmed. But the letters told a different story, one that I couldn't ignore.

And then, there was the matter of the phone call. I hadn't been expecting it, not after everything that had happened. The number on the screen was unfamiliar, but there was something about it that made my pulse quicken. A fleeting thought told me not to answer. But I ignored it, as I had ignored so many warnings before.

"Hello?" I answered, my voice cautious, unsure of what I was about to face.

"Is this... Claire?" The voice on the other end was unfamiliar, sharp, with a kind of detached professionalism that made the hairs on the back of my neck stand up.

"Yes," I replied, my grip tightening around the phone. "Who's this?"

There was a pause on the other end, as if the person was considering whether or not to speak. Finally, they spoke again, this time with a slight edge to their voice. "I think we need to talk."

My stomach dropped, a cold sweat breaking out across my forehead. "About what?"

The voice chuckled, but it wasn't a pleasant sound. It was the kind of laugh that made you feel like you were being toyed with. "About your little discovery. The one you're trying so hard to ignore."

My pulse stuttered, my heart pounding in my chest as the words hit me like a freight train. It wasn't just the betrayal I had uncovered. It was the fact that someone—someone who knew what I knew—was out there, waiting, watching. They were as tangled in this mess as I was, and they weren't about to let me walk away unscathed.

"Who is this?" I asked, my voice shaking now, betraying the fear I was trying so desperately to suppress.

The voice on the other end laughed again, this time louder, as if they found my confusion amusing. "You know who I am. The question is—do you really want to find out what happens next?"

The line went dead before I could respond, leaving me standing there, phone pressed to my ear, heart racing. I stared at the screen, half-expecting the call to come through again, to hear that voice taunting me with more cryptic threats. But it didn't.

What was I supposed to do now? Who else was involved in this? How far did this web of deceit stretch? And more importantly, who else had been keeping secrets from me?

I set the phone down with trembling hands, feeling the cold seep into my bones as if I had just stepped into a storm. I wasn't safe—not anymore. This person, whoever they were, had the upper hand. They knew something I didn't. And I had no idea how deep this rabbit hole went.

The next morning, I stood in front of the mirror, trying to steady my breathing. The bags under my eyes, the pale skin—none of it seemed to matter. I couldn't let it show. I couldn't let anyone know what I was carrying. Not yet. Not until I had answers.

Aiden was already gone by the time I stepped into the kitchen. He had left me a note—something sweet, something to remind me that he cared. I should have found comfort in it, but all I could do was stand there, reading the words over and over, trying to convince myself that everything was fine. But everything wasn't fine. And I wasn't sure it ever would be again.

I made my coffee, the warmth of the cup offering the only semblance of normalcy I could cling to, and tried to breathe through the tension that had settled like a knot in my stomach. I needed to find out more. I needed to confront this head-on, no matter what the consequences were.

But as the door creaked open and I heard Aiden's footsteps in the hallway, I realized with sudden clarity that I was no longer sure who I could trust. Even the ones I loved most had been hiding their own truths from me. And now, as much as I wanted to lean on him, to tell him everything, I knew I couldn't.

Not yet.

The morning after the phone call, I sat in the same spot by the window, waiting for something to change. For the light to shift in a way that would make everything feel less heavy. But the sun stayed stubbornly high, casting everything in the same sharp-edged clarity. If anything, it only seemed to highlight how little I knew, how far I'd fallen into this labyrinth of lies without even realizing I'd been led there.

Aiden hadn't come home last night. That wasn't unusual—he was always staying late at the office or meeting with clients—but today, the absence felt like an anchor dragging me deeper. I should've reached out, should've called him. But I couldn't. Not with everything swirling inside me. Not when I didn't know who to trust, not even him.

I grabbed my purse and made my way out the door, forcing myself into the world outside. The weight of the betrayal wasn't something I could carry alone in this apartment any longer. I needed space, air, a different perspective. I needed to remind myself that the world was still spinning, that I wasn't stuck in this strange, suffocating limbo where nothing felt real.

The streets were busy with their usual hustle—cars honking, people darting around on the sidewalks, the sounds of life carrying in the breeze. It should've been comforting, the pulse of the city surrounding me. But instead, I felt like I was standing on the edge of something, looking down into a vast, empty chasm. I took in a shaky breath, trying to steady myself, to remember how to breathe.

It wasn't until I reached the café down the street, a little hole-in-the-wall place I'd frequented when I needed to think, that something unexpected happened. As I approached the door, I saw him. Kevin. My brother. The last person I wanted to see right now, but somehow, the one I most needed. He was sitting by the window, his back to me, his usual easy posture a striking contrast to the tight knot in my chest. I hadn't spoken to him in days, not since the argument we'd had about... well, about everything. There had been a time, not long ago, when I could tell him anything. But now, that connection felt like it had been severed in a way that left me wondering whether I'd ever be able to get it back.

I almost turned away. I could've walked out and pretended I hadn't seen him. But instead, I found myself stepping through the door, the bell chiming softly above my head. Kevin didn't notice me at first, too engrossed in the newspaper spread out in front of him. It gave me a moment to collect myself, to remind my pulse that there was still something solid in the world. Something worth holding on to.

When he finally glanced up, his eyes widened for just a moment before he slid the paper to the side, a slow, deliberate movement. "Claire," he said, his voice both warm and guarded. The tension in his tone was immediate, like a taut wire stretching between us, ready to snap.

I didn't sit. I couldn't. Instead, I leaned against the counter, crossing my arms over my chest. The sudden need to avoid looking at him, to put some kind of barrier between us, surged up from nowhere.

"Hi," I said, my voice too sharp. Too brittle.

"Everything okay?" he asked, and for a split second, I thought I saw something flicker in his eyes—a hesitation, a flash of guilt that he quickly masked with a forced casualness. He was better at hiding things than I'd realized.

I swallowed. "I don't know."

Kevin studied me for a long moment, and just when I thought he might press further, when I thought he might dig deeper into whatever hole I was trying to bury myself in, he nodded and leaned back in his chair. "What's going on, Claire?" His voice softened, the edges of his usual sarcasm gone.

It was then that I realized: he knew. He had to. There was no way he hadn't picked up on the tension, the things left unsaid between us. He knew something was wrong, and he wasn't going to let me bury it anymore. I could feel the walls between us crumbling with each second that passed, but I wasn't ready to tear them down. Not yet.

"I'm not sure you're the right person to ask," I muttered, my voice breaking as the words came out. "It's... complicated."

"You know I can help, right?" He leaned forward, his gaze intense now, steady. "Whatever it is, we can fix it together."

Fix it? My mind immediately raced to the only thing I could think of—the betrayal, the secrets, the lies that had been tangled around me like a noose. But how could I drag him into this? How could I involve him in something so... dangerous? He had his own life, his own problems. I wasn't about to drag him down into the mess I had created.

"I'm not sure anyone can fix this," I said quietly. "I don't even know if I can."

His expression shifted, becoming more guarded, more distant. But before he could respond, the door to the café opened, and a familiar face walked in. I didn't need to see who it was to feel the sudden shift in the air.

It was Aiden.

My heart stuttered in my chest. What was he doing here? The weight of his presence was like a physical force, a palpable thing that pressed against the walls of the small space. And as he made his way toward us, his gaze locking with mine, I couldn't shake the feeling that everything was about to change.

I opened my mouth to say something, anything, but before I could, Kevin stood up. The change in him was immediate, a cool mask falling over his features. He nodded at Aiden, his voice casual but clipped. "Didn't expect you here, man."

Aiden's gaze flicked to me, a small, unreadable smile tugging at the corners of his lips. He stepped forward, his voice low. "I could say the same thing."

The tension between us grew thick, a living thing, crackling in the air as I stood frozen, caught between two worlds I wasn't sure I could ever reconcile.

And just when I thought I might finally break the silence, Aiden's phone rang. The ringtone was familiar—a song I'd heard him play countless times—and my stomach dropped.

He didn't check the caller ID. He just answered, his voice dropping to a whisper as he stepped away from us, moving toward the corner of the room.

And I watched, feeling the walls close in once again, as the words from the other side of the line seeped into the quiet of the café.

"Everything's in motion. It's too late to stop it now."

Chapter 22: Dangerous Alliances

The night air was thick with uncertainty, carrying the scent of rain that hadn't yet fallen but hovered over the city like a promise—or a threat. The streetlights flickered in a rhythm that seemed almost deliberate, casting long, dancing shadows over the cracked pavement. I tucked my hands into the pockets of my jacket, the fabric worn thin from too many months of too many nights just like this one, all spent in the pursuit of answers I couldn't seem to grasp. I should have felt more afraid, considering what I was about to do. After all, the man I was meeting wasn't the sort you trusted. But then, trust had become a foreign concept to me, something I hadn't held in so long that I wasn't sure I knew what it even looked like anymore.

Aiden had been furious when he found out about the meeting. I could practically hear his gritted teeth over the phone, his words harsh and clipped, urging me not to go. "This is reckless," he'd said, and it had taken all my willpower not to hang up on him then and there. The thing was, though, Aiden's fury had a way of pushing me away, even when his concern bled through, as if everything we'd been through together was bound in some unspoken thread that pulled taut every time we came too close to the truth.

He had warned me—more times than I could count—that alliances like this never ended well. And maybe he was right. I wasn't naïve enough to believe I was making the smart choice, but desperation has a funny way of quieting that voice in your head that tells you to be cautious. It dulls everything, replaces careful calculations with impulse. So I let the cold air bite at my skin, my breath coming in little white puffs as I walked toward the back alley where he said he'd meet me.

I hadn't told Aiden about the terms of our arrangement. He didn't need to know that I'd offered secrets of my own in exchange for the information I needed. It was stupid. It was dangerous. It was exactly the kind of thing I'd have warned anyone else against doing. But I didn't have anyone else. Not really.

I had no idea what this man looked like, but I wasn't concerned with that. I'd been told only one thing: he'll find you.

The clink of distant traffic, the occasional mutter of a passing car, faded as I stepped deeper into the shadows, the coolness of the night wrapping around me like an embrace. The alley was narrow, and the walls seemed to close in as I walked further in. My footsteps echoed too loudly, betraying me in a place where silence should have been my ally.

Then, I saw him.

He didn't look like much at first glance—just a silhouette leaning against the brick wall, hands tucked into the pockets of his jacket, his face half-hidden beneath the brim of a cap. But there was something about the way he held himself—an ease, a certainty that suggested he knew far more than he was letting on.

The tension between us thickened the moment I stepped closer. I could feel his gaze before I saw it, sharp and assessing, as if he was sizing me up to see if I was worth his time. He didn't speak right away. His silence was deliberate, a challenge. I stood still, meeting his gaze with my own, refusing to be the one to break first.

"I was beginning to think you weren't going to show," he said, his voice a low murmur that seemed to stir the air around us, laced with something both mocking and dangerous.

"I'm here," I replied, my voice steady, though my heartbeat was an insistent thrum in my ears.

His lips curled slightly, a smile that didn't quite reach his eyes. "I expected someone with a little more fire."

I tilted my head, a smirk tugging at the corners of my mouth. "I've got more than enough for you, if you're interested in getting to the point."

He stepped closer, just enough to make me shift my stance, but not enough to make me feel threatened. Not yet. "I think you and I both know that trust is a luxury neither of us can afford. But here we are, making an arrangement that could destroy both of us."

I felt a sharp, cold truth slice through me at the words. He was right. We were walking a fine line, and the fall on either side wasn't something I wanted to contemplate. "So let's get it over with then," I said, my voice laced with a bite I hadn't intended.

He reached into the pocket of his coat and pulled out a small, folded piece of paper. Without a word, he handed it to me, his fingers brushing mine just for a moment. A jolt of heat ran through me, and I caught my breath before I looked down at the paper.

A name. A place. A time.

"That's all I need," I said, crumpling the paper in my hand, my pulse quickening.

He didn't move. Instead, he just studied me, his expression unreadable, like he was measuring the weight of the moment. "It won't be easy," he warned. "But nothing worth having is."

I didn't answer. I didn't need to.

The rain had started now, soft and steady, falling like a curtain between us. It soaked through my jacket, chilled my skin, but I barely felt it. The deal was done. The stakes had been set. And I was no longer the one on the edge of control—I had it now, in my hands, even if it was only for a brief, fleeting moment.

The next move was mine.

The rain had picked up by the time I turned to leave, the sound of it pattering against the pavement almost drowned out the chaotic mess of thoughts inside my head. The small piece of paper—the one that had felt so significant in my hand moments ago—was now crumpled in my fist, soggy and cold from the misty downpour. I should have been trembling, should have felt a rush of panic course through me as I realized what I'd just done. But I didn't.

Instead, there was an unfamiliar sensation settling in my chest, one that thrummed with something between anticipation and dread. I could barely make sense of it. Perhaps it was the absence of fear, or the peculiar clarity I now had in knowing that I was in control. For once, I wasn't just floating through life, reacting to the tide of whatever came my way. No, now I was the one pulling the strings, even if I wasn't entirely sure where those strings led.

The city felt different as I walked away, the streets darker now, each shadow cast by the flickering streetlights seemingly more ominous than before. I couldn't stop thinking about what I'd just agreed to. Every instinct told me to turn around, to burn the paper and walk away. I could go back to Aiden, admit I had been wrong, let him take the reins. But something in me rebelled at the thought. I had spent too many years in the backseat, too many years letting someone else make the decisions for me.

I glanced at the paper again, held it in the palm of my hand as I turned the corner, my fingers brushing over the wet edges. Aiden had warned me against this. He had warned me not to trust anyone, especially not someone like him. And yet, here I was—walking a razor-thin line between madness and clarity, between freedom and destruction.

I didn't know who this man really was. I didn't know if he would hold up his end of the bargain or if I would be left with nothing but regrets and a trail of wreckage. But I did know one thing: he had information that could change everything. And that information was worth any price.

The thought of Aiden sent a small pang through me. His frustration had been palpable when he found out I was meeting with the stranger. His voice—sharp and worried—had crackled over the phone, every syllable cutting into me with the same force. "You can't trust him. Don't do it."

I hadn't listened. And now I was left to wonder if I'd made a grave mistake or if I had just taken the first step in turning the tables for good.

The next few days blurred together. It wasn't until I found myself sitting in my apartment, the rain still drumming steadily on the window, that I realized how quiet it had gotten. I couldn't help but replay every moment of that meeting in my mind, piecing together his cryptic words and trying to understand his motives. He'd said so little, yet I felt as though I had already given him far too much.

I wasn't stupid enough to believe the man had no agenda of his own. He had made his price clear, after all. Information for secrets. But what struck me, what unsettled me, was the way he'd looked at me. There had been something almost familiar in his gaze, like he knew exactly who I was, exactly what I'd done, and exactly what I was capable of. Maybe he didn't have all the answers, but I didn't think he needed them. Not yet.

A knock at the door snapped me out of my thoughts, and I jumped. It was so unexpected that my heart skipped a beat. The apartment was silent otherwise, a quiet refuge from the storm outside. My first instinct was to ignore it. But then I heard the familiar voice—rough, concerned, but tinged with something like exhaustion.

"Aiden."

I hesitated, my fingers brushing the edge of the door. Part of me wanted to open it, wanted to let him in and explain myself, to tell him everything. But then another part of me fought back—telling me I didn't owe him anything, that I had made my own choices, and this was my fight, not his.

But in the end, the door creaked open, just a crack, and his face appeared in the space between the hinges. He didn't say anything at first—just stood there, looking at me with those familiar, dark eyes that I had come to both trust and fear. He looked like a man who hadn't slept in days, a man who had seen too much and still couldn't make sense of any of it.

"You did it," he said, his voice low, heavy with disappointment. "You met with him."

I didn't answer right away. I should have. I should have explained. But instead, I just stared at him, at the way his brow furrowed, the way his lips pressed together as if he were trying to hold back everything he wanted to say.

"You're playing a dangerous game," he continued, his tone sharp. "This isn't just about you anymore. It never was. And yet you keep pushing, keep making these decisions like they don't affect—" He stopped himself, a breath escaping through his nose, and for a moment, I saw the flicker of something else in his eyes. Something soft, something vulnerable. But it was gone almost as quickly as it had appeared, replaced by that familiar mask of frustration.

I leaned against the door, crossing my arms. "I didn't ask for your opinion. I didn't ask for your permission." The words came out before I could stop them, biting and sharp. "I did what I had to do."

Aiden exhaled slowly, his expression unreadable. "What you had to do... or what you wanted to do?"

I opened my mouth to answer, but the words got caught in my throat. There it was. The truth I wasn't ready to face: I hadn't just made a decision. I had chosen this. Chosen to take a risk. Chosen to stake everything on the possibility that I could control the outcome.

"I did it because it's my fight too," I said, my voice quieter now. The words seemed to settle between us, heavy with meaning.

Aiden didn't respond at first. His eyes stayed on me, and for the first time, I wasn't sure what he was thinking.

The silence between us stretched taut, like the thin line I was walking. Aiden stood in the doorway, his posture rigid, his jaw clenched so tightly that I half expected him to break something. He was furious, I could see that, and yet there was something deeper in his eyes—something more than just anger. Maybe it was fear, or maybe guilt. It was hard to tell with Aiden; he had a way of hiding things, burying emotions beneath layers of sharp wit and calculated indifference.

I didn't want to admit it, but I felt a pang of regret. I didn't regret the decision I'd made, not exactly. But I did regret that it had pushed him away, forced him into this corner where he had to watch me make choices that—no matter how necessary—felt like a betrayal. He had warned me. God, how many times had he warned me? Yet here we were, and I was the one standing with my foot already in the fire.

"You're not hearing me," Aiden said, his voice low and controlled, a dangerous calm that made my chest tighten. "This isn't just about you or me. You think you can handle him, but you have no idea what you're getting into."

I pushed myself off the doorframe, stepping closer to him, trying to steady the ground beneath my feet. My heart hammered against my ribs, but I wasn't about to let him see that. "I can handle it. I can handle him," I said, the words tasting like acid on my tongue. Even as I spoke, I wasn't sure if I was trying to convince him or myself.

Aiden's gaze flickered over my face, like he was searching for the cracks, the lies beneath my bravado. But I wasn't going to give him the satisfaction of seeing my uncertainty. I had made my choice, and I needed him to understand that, no matter how much he hated it.

"Don't," he said suddenly, his voice sharp enough to slice through the tension. "Don't act like this is something you can control. He's dangerous, Olivia. You don't get to just walk in, shake his hand, and come out with whatever it is you think you want. It doesn't work like that."

"I know how it works," I shot back, almost too quickly. "I'm not the one who's naïve here."

His eyes darkened, a flash of something darker than frustration. "Then why are you pushing me away? Why keep doing this alone?"

I didn't have an answer for that. Or maybe I did, but I couldn't say it out loud. Maybe it was because I was alone—really alone—and the idea of depending on someone else, anyone else, had started to feel more like a weakness than a strength. Even Aiden, despite all the years we'd spent together, had his own motives. His own secrets. He was not an open book, not in the way I wanted him to be.

I could feel the distance between us stretching like an invisible thread, taut and ready to snap. But I didn't know how to fix it. I didn't know how to make him see that I had no choice. That this was the only way.

"I have to do this," I said finally, the words hanging heavy between us. "I can't keep running from things. I need answers, and I'm not going to get them by sitting here waiting for someone to hand them to me. I'm going to do whatever it takes."

Aiden looked like he wanted to say more, his mouth opening and closing as though the words were caught somewhere deep inside of him. But instead, he just nodded, the tightness in his jaw betraying the frustration that he was trying to hold back.

"Just be careful," he muttered, his voice softer now, almost resigned. "I can't protect you from everything."

I didn't respond. What could I say? He was right. He couldn't protect me from this. No one could.

He turned to leave, but before he reached the door, he paused, his hand resting on the frame. "You're not alone in this, Olivia. Don't forget that."

The door clicked shut behind him, and the silence that followed felt like a weight pressing down on my chest. I stared at the door for a long time, the words he'd left hanging in the air still swirling in my mind. I wasn't sure if he meant them as a warning or as something more.

But the fact remained: I had a meeting with the man who held the answers I so desperately needed. And I had no idea how deep this game really went.

I didn't have time to second-guess myself. The clock was ticking, and the world wasn't going to wait for me to figure out what came next.

I grabbed my jacket and headed for the door, forcing myself to ignore the tightness in my chest. The night was still young, and I had no intention of letting it slip away. The rain had stopped, but the sky was still overcast, a heavy darkness that matched the storm brewing inside me.

The address he had given me was only a few blocks away. It should've been a simple walk. But the closer I got, the more my instincts screamed that something was wrong. I couldn't put my finger on it. The streetlights overhead flickered in strange patterns, casting shadows that seemed to move of their own accord. I paused for a moment, scanning the surroundings, but nothing seemed out of place.

When I finally reached the building, a worn-down brick structure that looked like it had been forgotten by time, I hesitated before entering. The door was already ajar, as though waiting for me. I stepped inside, my breath catching in my throat as I tried to adjust to the dim, musty air.

The sound of footsteps echoed through the hallway, sharp and quick—too quick. I wasn't alone.

A voice broke the silence, low and menacing, its tone sending a chill crawling up my spine. "I thought I told you to stay away."

I froze, every muscle in my body locking into place. There was no mistaking that voice. It wasn't the man I'd agreed to meet. It was him.

Chapter 23: The Heart's Descent

I had never known silence like this. It wasn't the peaceful kind that came from a solitary afternoon, the quiet hum of a world left to its own devices. No, this was the kind of silence that clung to the air, thick and suffocating, as if the earth itself was holding its breath. Aiden and I sat across from each other in the small kitchen, the only sound the faint clink of his coffee cup against the saucer, a delicate rhythm that neither of us could quite escape.

I was beginning to understand why people often described love as something that could break you. Love, it seemed, was never as simple as they made it out to be. We were tangled in something darker now, something I had never anticipated when I first laid eyes on him—when I had thought that perhaps, just perhaps, he could be the one to hold my heart and shield it from the cruelty of the world. But there was no shield, not now. No armor. Only the raw, bleeding edges of truth that sliced through us like a jagged knife.

The air between us was charged, but not in the way it used to be. Once, it had been electric, full of a dangerous sort of thrill. Now, it felt like we were teetering on the edge of a cliff, staring down into an abyss that promised nothing but emptiness. I wanted to reach across the table and grab his hand, but I couldn't. Something was stopping me, something too deep for words. And I was afraid that if I spoke, everything would come crashing down. So instead, I sipped my tea, trying to ignore the tightness in my chest, the sense that I was losing him even though he was still right there, his eyes watching me with an intensity I could hardly bear.

"What's wrong?" he finally asked, his voice low and rough, like gravel sliding down a hill. "You've been quiet all morning."

I met his gaze, feeling the weight of his scrutiny like a thousand tiny needles against my skin. "Nothing's wrong," I lied, forcing the words past my lips with the ease of someone who had long since grown accustomed to dishonesty. The thing was, I wasn't just lying to him. I was lying to myself too.

Aiden didn't buy it. He never did. Not when it mattered. He set his cup down with a soft clink, his eyes narrowing ever so slightly. "You've been acting different lately," he said. "More distant. I can feel it, Marlowe. Something's changed."

My heart skipped, and for the briefest of moments, I thought about telling him the truth—the whole, ugly truth. But I couldn't. I couldn't because it would destroy him. And worse, it would destroy us. The web I had woven around us was too intricate, too tangled to escape from now. I had made my choices, and those choices had set us on a path that couldn't be undone.

"It's nothing," I said, and even I knew it was a hollow attempt to brush off the heavy conversation.

Aiden's face softened, but the shadows in his eyes remained. He didn't believe me, but he was willing to let it go—for now. I didn't deserve that kind of patience, not when I had been so unworthy of it for so long. But he was the kind of person who gave second chances without hesitation, as though believing in the best of people was worth the risk of being let down. And maybe that's what I loved most about him, the thing that drew me in like a moth to a flame. But in that same breath, it was also the thing that terrified me most. Because now, as much as I wanted to protect him from the truth, I was afraid that the truth would tear him apart—and it would tear me apart with him.

The tension in the room grew thick, suffocating, and just as I thought I couldn't stand it anymore, the doorbell rang. Aiden's eyes flicked toward the front door, and then back to me, his expression unreadable. "I'll get it," he said, his tone a little too stiff, as if he too needed a distraction from the silence that had settled over us like a heavy fog.

I nodded, grateful for the momentary reprieve. My hands trembled as I set my teacup down, fighting the urge to reach for something—anything—to calm the frantic beating of my heart. I wasn't ready for whatever was waiting on the other side of that door. Not today. Not when I could barely keep my own secrets straight, let alone handle whatever storm was about to descend.

Aiden stood up and walked to the door with his usual fluid grace. He opened it, and I caught the faintest shift in his posture, as if the very act of answering the door had braced him for something he wasn't expecting.

He stepped aside, and a woman walked into the room. Her presence was immediate, undeniable—a force of nature wrapped in a black leather jacket and sharp, knowing eyes. I hadn't seen her in years, but I knew her face, the way she moved, the way she carried herself like a predator on the hunt.

I froze.

"Hello, Marlowe," she said, her voice as smooth as honey but laced with something darker. "I see you've been busy."

My breath caught in my throat, the world around me suddenly spinning. How could she be here? How could she have found me?

"You shouldn't be here," I muttered, even as my mind raced to calculate the damage her appearance could cause. I had buried the past, buried it so deep that I had almost forgotten the weight of the secrets it carried.

But here she was, standing in my kitchen like a ghost from a life I had desperately tried to leave behind.

Aiden's eyes flicked between us, confused and wary, but not yet understanding the magnitude of the storm that had just walked into our lives. And I knew—deep down—that this was it. The moment that would unravel everything.

The woman standing in my kitchen—Charlotte—was no stranger, though I had spent years pretending she was. Her very presence was a breach, an intrusion into a world I had painstakingly built and convinced myself was solid. She was a reminder that no matter how far I ran, how tightly I locked away the doors of my past, there were always cracks. Cracks that people like Charlotte had a way of finding and exploiting.

Aiden, still standing by the door, stared at her with furrowed brows, the silence between them thick with unasked questions. He was too polite to let his confusion show on his face, but it wasn't hard to read the tension in his stiff shoulders and the sharpness in his eyes. "Do you two know each other?" he asked, his voice careful, almost too careful.

I opened my mouth to speak, to explain, to say anything that might lessen the blow, but the words got caught in my throat. How did you explain a ghost from the past? How did you tell someone that a woman like Charlotte wasn't just part of my history but a part of me, a part that I had fought tooth and nail to forget?

Charlotte's eyes never left mine as she crossed the room slowly, deliberately, with the kind of grace that made every move look purposeful. Her gaze was piercing, like she was looking straight through me, to places I wasn't ready to revisit. "Oh, we know each other, alright," she said, her voice a smooth, almost velvety drawl. "Though I suppose you've forgotten. That's the thing with you, Marlowe. You forget things. And people."

I felt the color drain from my face, but I couldn't tear my gaze away from her. There was an edge to her words, a bitter undertone that made my pulse race. I had tried so hard to bury everything connected to her, to leave behind that chapter of my life that had been wrapped in secrets and shadows. But there she was, back in my life, pulling me back into the mess I thought I had outrun.

Aiden's confusion deepened, his eyes darting between us. He wasn't the type to miss details, but this was too much, too fast for anyone to process. "Marlowe?" he said, turning to me now, his voice laced with a thread of concern. "What's going on?"

I opened my mouth to respond, but the words failed me. How could I explain? How could I explain the tangled web I had woven with Charlotte at the center of it all? The lies, the betrayals, the mistakes I couldn't take back. And yet, there she stood, an unwilling witness to everything I had tried so hard to leave behind. She had always been a reminder of the parts of me I hated most.

Charlotte turned back to Aiden, giving him a cool smile, the kind that said she wasn't interested in explaining herself. "Let's just say Marlowe and I have a... history," she said, her eyes flicking back to me, as if daring me to disagree. "A complicated history."

Aiden didn't like the sound of that. I could see it in the way his lips pressed into a tight line. His protective instincts flared, and for the briefest moment, I wondered if he would ask her to leave, if he would defend me against whatever dangerous thing she represented. But instead, he looked back at me, waiting for an answer, for any explanation I might be able to give.

The silence stretched, thick and uncomfortable. Charlotte, as if sensing the tension, slid herself onto one of the kitchen chairs, as if she were perfectly at home in my space. She rested her elbows on the table and stared at me with that same unsettling calm, as though she were waiting for me to crack.

I could feel Aiden's gaze on me, could feel the weight of his expectations and his fear. "Marlowe," he said again, his voice soft but insistent, "you need to tell me what's going on."

The walls I had built around myself, the ones I thought were sturdy enough to withstand anything, started to crumble. Slowly at first, then faster, until I couldn't hold it back anymore. "Charlotte," I said, my voice barely above a whisper. "She's part of... my past. The kind of past I was trying to leave behind."

Aiden's brows furrowed deeper, and I could see the gears turning in his mind. He was trying to make sense of it, but I could see he was struggling. I didn't blame him. How could he understand the depths of the mess I had created for myself?

Charlotte smiled, a small, knowing curve of her lips. "You should tell him, Marlowe. After all, he's already in the middle of it, whether he knows it or not."

I tensed, the hairs on the back of my neck rising. There was something in her tone, something that wasn't just a statement, but a threat. "What are you talking about?" I asked, the words almost choking me.

She tilted her head, studying me as if I were some puzzle she was enjoying unraveling. "You've made a lot of decisions, haven't you?" she said, her voice smooth, like she knew exactly what buttons to push to get a rise out of me. "Aiden might not be the only one who's in danger. You've been dancing on the edge of something much bigger than both of you. But don't worry," she added, her smile wide and cold, "I'm sure you'll figure it out. You always do."

The words hit me like a slap, sharp and painful. My heart raced in my chest as I struggled to make sense of what she was implying. What danger? What had I done?

Aiden's voice cut through the air, tense and strained. "What are you talking about, Charlotte?"

She leaned back in her chair, her fingers idly tapping the edge of the table. "It's not for me to say," she said with a shrug, as if the game had already shifted into something she controlled. "But it's coming, Marlowe. You won't be able to stop it."

I stood frozen, my mind a whirl of questions I couldn't answer, my breath shallow. She wasn't just here for a casual visit. No, this was something far more dangerous. Something I had known, deep down, would eventually find its way to me. And now, it had.

Charlotte's presence in my kitchen had transformed the air into something dense and choking. I couldn't remember the last time I'd felt this exposed, as if every secret I'd tucked away in the recesses of my mind was now being pried open and displayed for the world to see. She leaned back in her chair, casual, almost too comfortable, as though she had every right to be here. And, in some twisted way, maybe she did. Maybe I had paved the way for this moment, even though it felt like a betrayal to admit it.

Aiden had shifted closer to me, standing just a few feet away, as if by proximity he could offer some kind of protection, though I suspected he was equally afraid of what Charlotte would reveal. The quiet tension between us was thick enough to suffocate, and I could almost hear the wheels turning in his head, trying to piece together the puzzle I'd left unsolved for so long. He didn't trust her, not yet. But he was starting to see the way things worked in my life, the way my history bled into the present in messy, unexpected ways.

"Enough with the cryptic games," Aiden finally said, his voice low but firm. "Either you tell me what the hell is going on, or I'm walking out that door."

Charlotte chuckled softly, the sound smooth and almost too knowing. "You think it's that simple?" She let her gaze linger on him, an unreadable smile tugging at her lips. "You think you can walk away from this? From her?"

The words stung, even though they shouldn't have. But I wasn't ready to face the truth, not yet. I wasn't ready to have all the layers peeled away so quickly. Aiden was already too close to seeing everything I had worked so hard to hide, and the thought of losing him, of having him see me for the mess I truly was, made my stomach twist.

"I've made mistakes," I said, the words coming out in a rush. "Big ones. And I—"

"Stop," Aiden cut me off, his voice harder now. "I don't need you to apologize. I need to know what she's talking about. I need to understand why you're acting like someone else. This... this isn't you, Marlowe. And I can't keep pretending it is."

Charlotte was enjoying the show. I could tell by the way her eyes sparkled, the amusement flickering just beneath her polished exterior. "You're not so different from her," Charlotte said, almost wistfully. "You think you're immune to the mess she's made of her life, but you're wrong. You've been tangled up in it all along, even if you don't realize it."

The words made no sense, but they rattled me. How much did Charlotte know? How much had I unknowingly dragged Aiden into?

I felt Aiden's gaze shift back to me, his patience thinning. "What does she mean?" he asked, his tone now tinged with an edge I didn't want to hear. "What's she talking about?"

I couldn't answer. My throat had closed up, and I felt that familiar rush of panic settle in my chest. I wanted to scream at Charlotte, to tell her to leave, to make her take her threats and her cryptic words with her. But I couldn't. Because I knew that as much as I hated the truth, as much as I wanted to deny it, it was coming—whether I was ready or not.

"Tell him," Charlotte said softly, her voice like a velvet blade. "Tell him everything, Marlowe. It's the only way to fix this."

My pulse was hammering in my ears, and for the first time in a long time, I felt the weight of my choices pressing down on me. The lies I had told, the ones I had told myself... all of them were standing in front of me now, in the form of a woman who knew too much.

Aiden was still waiting, his eyes never leaving mine. He was patient, yes, but the line in his jaw was taut, his brows furrowed with frustration and something else—hurt, maybe? I wasn't sure. But I couldn't let him see that. Not like this. Not when I had no answers to give him.

"I can't—" I started, my voice breaking as I struggled to find the words.

Charlotte's gaze flicked from me to Aiden, then back again. "She can't, because she's afraid. Afraid that you'll leave her. Afraid you'll see the person she's been hiding for so long."

Aiden flinched, just slightly, but enough for me to notice. It felt like a slap. "I'm not going anywhere," he said, though his voice wavered just enough to make me question whether that was true. "But you need to start being honest with me, Marlowe. I can't do this—whatever this is—if you keep shutting me out."

The words landed with the force of a punch. It was like all the air in the room had been sucked out in one sharp, brutal inhale. I wanted to tell him, I did. But the truth was a weight I wasn't sure I could carry, let alone pass on to him.

Charlotte was watching, her expression still unreadable, but I could see the faint satisfaction lurking behind her eyes. She was enjoying this. Enjoying the power she had over me, over us.

"I've seen this before," she said quietly, almost to herself. "The slow descent into chaos. It's never pretty, but it's inevitable. You'll see, Marlowe. You'll see soon enough."

The room seemed to close in around me, the walls pressing in like they were getting smaller by the second. I could feel the heat of Aiden's gaze, still waiting for the truth, and yet all I could think about was the last thing Charlotte had said. The descent.

I swallowed hard, the words thick in my throat. I had to say something. Something.

But before I could, the phone rang.

Aiden's eyes flicked toward the noise, and for a brief, fragile second, the tension broke. He looked at me again, his eyes softening with something close to apology. "I don't want to push you, Marlowe. But you're going to have to tell me sooner or later."

I couldn't answer. I couldn't breathe. The phone rang again, its shrill sound cutting through the thick, suffocating silence.

And then, with one final, sharp glance, Charlotte stood and walked toward the door, her footsteps almost silent. "I'm leaving," she said, her voice low but edged with something dangerous. "But trust me, Marlowe. This isn't over. Not by a long shot."

As the door clicked shut behind her, I stared at the phone, my hand frozen in midair, the weight of the decision pressing down harder than I had ever felt before.

The screen lit up, a name flashing across it. A name I hadn't seen in years.

And my heart stopped.

Chapter 24: Inferno of the Heart

The heat hit me first. It was a suffocating, oppressive wall, a force that had no place in a world that wasn't meant to burn. My skin prickled, a warning shot fired by instinct as I stood at the edge of what had once been a sanctuary. Now, it was just a ruin, the wreckage of memories and promises crumbling beneath the weight of everything we had ever feared.

I barely felt Aiden's hand on my arm, a quiet reminder that we were still tethered to the world we hadn't yet abandoned. It wasn't a comforting gesture. More like a lifeline, a way to keep from being swept into the chaos around us. We didn't speak; there was no need. His eyes said everything, sharp and focused, narrowing slightly as he studied the horizon where the smoke seemed to rise from every direction. The world was burning, and we were standing in the center of it.

"I didn't think it would come to this," I murmured, almost to myself, the sound lost beneath the roar of the flames that were now licking the sky, eager to devour anything and everything in their path.

Aiden didn't answer immediately. I could feel his breath, warm and steady against my cheek, as he shifted slightly, aligning himself with my side. His silence was his way of saying that words weren't enough anymore. I understood that. We'd gone past the point of easy conversation, past the point where anything could be undone with a few well-placed syllables. It was too late for that.

The first crack of the ground beneath us shattered the stillness, a warning. I glanced at Aiden, the tightness in his jaw the only indication that he'd noticed too. Every footstep we took was heavy now, burdened by the weight of the choices we'd made. We couldn't go back. There was no going back.

"You sure you're ready?" His voice was low, but there was no doubt in it. Only resolve.

I didn't hesitate. "You think I'm going to back down now?"

His lips twisted into a grin, though it was tinged with something darker, something more desperate. "Wouldn't blame you if you did."

I gave him a sidelong glance. "You always did underestimate me."

Before he could respond, there was a movement ahead—too swift, too calculated—and then the figure emerged from the haze of smoke. My heart seized in my chest. The last person I ever expected to see again. He was a ghost, a specter from the past, one I thought I had buried long ago. But there he was, tall and imposing, the familiar cruel glint in his eyes as he regarded us.

"Did you really think you could outrun your destiny?" It was him. Nathaniel. The man who had been the architect of everything that had shattered my world. His voice was smooth, too smooth, like syrup, coating everything in a thin layer of venom. His smile didn't reach his eyes; they were cold, empty.

I swallowed the knot in my throat, anger coiling tight in my chest. This was it—the moment I'd feared, the confrontation I had never fully prepared for. Nathaniel was here, standing before me, and I was supposed to find the strength to end it all. But how? How could I do that when everything he'd ever done was still reverberating in my bones? When every breath I took was still shadowed by the destruction he'd wrought?

"You should have stayed away," I said, my voice steadier than I felt. There was no fear now, only a kind of clarity I hadn't known I had in me. "This ends tonight."

His laugh was sharp, mocking, the sound of someone who had never known the meaning of remorse. "Is that so? You think you've won, don't you? You think this is the end, that somehow you and your little toy soldier," he glanced at Aiden with derision, "are going to walk away from this?"

I didn't answer him. There was nothing to say. Words were useless. This wasn't about talking anymore. This was about survival.

Aiden's hand found mine, squeezing once in silent solidarity, his grip as firm as it had always been. There was no room for doubt now, no time for second-guessing. The flames were closing in, and Nathaniel was standing in front of us like some twisted harbinger of everything we'd fought against.

I took a step forward, the crunch of debris beneath my boots louder than the roar of the fire. My voice was steady, though it felt like every word was forged in the furnace of my own fury. "You can't control everything, Nathaniel. Not anymore."

His smirk faltered, just for a second, but it was enough. A flicker of unease passed through his eyes, too quick to be fully recognized but impossible to ignore. And that was when I understood—he was afraid. Not of the flames, not of the destruction surrounding us, but of me. Of what I had become, of what I was willing to do to stop him.

The air around us grew thicker with each passing second, the smoke swirling as though it had a life of its own, the fire drawing nearer. But the heat, the suffocating heat—it didn't matter. I could feel nothing but the pulse of adrenaline that surged through my veins, drowning out the rest of the world.

"I'm not afraid of you," I said, the words coming easier now. It was the truth, and the truth had never been more powerful. "You're just a man. And men, no matter how many lives they ruin, are always vulnerable."

Aiden shifted beside me, his stance widening as he prepared for whatever came next. His voice was quieter, more lethal than I'd ever heard it. "You're done, Nathaniel. Your game is over."

The ground trembled underfoot, a deep, gnawing vibration that seemed to crawl its way into my bones. Aiden's grip tightened around my hand, a steady anchor amidst the chaos, but there was no mistaking the tension that was creeping up his arm, no mistaking the flicker of uncertainty that had slipped into his expression. He didn't speak, but the clench of his jaw, the narrowing of his eyes, told me everything I needed to know. He was ready for this. Ready to put an end to everything Nathaniel had done.

Nathaniel, for his part, didn't seem moved by the rising fury of the world around us. He stood there, like a man who had long ago made peace with the storm, watching us with a calculated air. His eyes, cold and empty, flicked between Aiden and me, calculating, always calculating.

"You're so sure of yourselves," he said, his voice low, a taunting sing-song. "But the fire? It's already here, isn't it? You can't outrun it, you can't control it. All you can do is watch."

I forced a breath in, steadying myself against the impending rush of panic that threatened to swallow me whole. He was right. The flames were everywhere. It wasn't just the fire surrounding us, either. It was everything we'd fought against, all the pain and betrayal, all the lies, now closing in like a great consuming wave. How could we stop something that had been burning so long?

But Aiden was beside me. His hand was still in mine, and it was warm. And as I looked at him, the certainty in his eyes pushed away the shadows in mine. He wasn't scared. He wasn't running. Neither was I.

"I don't know who you think you are, Nathaniel," Aiden said, his voice quiet, deliberate, "but you've underestimated me from the start."

Nathaniel's smile was slow, almost too slow. There was something dark and venomous in it, like he was savoring a twisted secret he didn't want to share. "I don't underestimate anything," he murmured, the words wrapping around me like a noose. "But I do know what it feels like to burn. And you're about to find out just how hot it gets."

The sky above us seemed to crack open, lightning flashing, and for a moment, I wondered if the world itself was preparing to end.

But the lightning didn't touch the earth. It only danced above us like some kind of divine spectator, watching the destruction unfold.

"You talk a lot for someone who's lost," I said, my voice suddenly louder than I intended, a touch of defiance that bubbled up from the deep place inside me where fear had been trying to take hold. "Isn't it exhausting, Nathaniel? Trying to control everything? Pretending like you're untouchable?"

He stepped closer, the air between us crackling with something charged. "You think I'm untouchable?" His eyes narrowed, a dangerous glint flickering in their depths. "I'm not untouchable. I'm simply prepared to win."

Aiden's hand squeezed mine tighter, a warning. And then the air shifted, a subtle change that made my skin prickle. Nathaniel wasn't just talking. He was playing. And we were the pieces on his board.

Without a word, Aiden moved first, a quick, fluid motion as he stepped into Nathaniel's space, forcing him to back up a step. My heart thundered in my chest, but it wasn't fear. It was something else—something primal that surged through me, urging me forward, urging me to act.

I followed, moving with purpose, not waiting for Aiden's next move. We were together in this—no separation, no hesitation. And it felt right. It felt like the only way forward.

Nathaniel stumbled, caught off guard by the sudden shift in power, but it didn't take long for him to recover. He was quicker than I expected, more dangerous than I wanted to admit. He lunged, his hand grabbing at Aiden's shoulder, but Aiden was already moving, ducking low and turning, throwing Nathaniel off balance. I could feel the shift in the air, the intensity of the moment pressing down on us as the fire raged on, encircling us like a beast ready to consume.

Nathaniel stumbled, his feet slipping on the cracked earth, and before I could even register what was happening, Aiden was there, his arm outstretched, a flash of something sharp in his hand. A knife, gleaming in the firelight. He didn't hesitate. He didn't need to.

The blade cut through the air with a swift, almost graceful arc, and Nathaniel staggered back, a gash appearing across his cheek, the blood slick and dark in the flickering light. But there was no pain in Nathaniel's eyes. There was only rage.

"Is that all?" he sneered, wiping the blood from his cheek with a single swipe. "How predictable."

I barely had a moment to react before Nathaniel lunged at Aiden, fists flying. I didn't think. I just moved. My own hand found the sharp edge of a broken piece of metal, a jagged shard from one of the crumbled walls. Without hesitation, I ran toward him, my heart in my throat, my breath shallow and ragged.

"You won't win," I spat, swinging the shard at him. He blocked it, but I didn't stop. There was no stopping. Not now.

The fight had taken on a rhythm of its own, a cruel dance we'd been forced into by fate. But as Nathaniel stumbled again, something inside me clicked. This wasn't just about winning. It wasn't just about survival. It was about reclaiming the world we'd almost lost. About ending the nightmare he had created for us.

I wasn't going to be consumed by the flames. And neither was Aiden.

Not today.

The world was a blur of motion, heat, and desperation. Nathaniel's face twisted with rage, a mask of fury that only seemed to grow darker with each passing moment. His every movement was sharp and deliberate, calculating, and for a split second, I wondered if he truly believed he could win. Could he really think he had the upper hand after everything?

Aiden moved beside me, his presence like an anchor, the kind that pulled me back from the edge, the kind that made me breathe when my lungs seemed full of nothing but smoke. I looked at him, and I saw the same determination in his eyes, the same refusal to back down. There was no room for fear here. Not anymore.

"Are you done, Nathaniel?" Aiden's voice cut through the chaos, calm but steady. "Because I think we've had enough of your games."

Nathaniel sneered, the kind of grin that only a man who knew he'd lost, but didn't know how to admit it, could wear. "You think this is over?" he spat, his words like acid. "This is just the beginning. You may have put me in a corner, but I always have one last card to play."

Aiden's hand tightened around the knife, his jaw set in that dangerous line I knew so well. "Then play it. We're not going anywhere."

The words were barely out of his mouth when Nathaniel's entire demeanor shifted. He moved faster than I expected, like a striking cobra, slashing toward Aiden, his body twisting in a way that was almost inhuman. Aiden barely had time to react, blocking the blow, but it was the sudden shift in Nathaniel's tactics that made me freeze.

There was something different about him now. Something deeper. The fire didn't seem to affect him in the same way. In fact, it almost seemed to fuel him, like the smoke and ash swirling around us only made him stronger, more dangerous.

I could feel the burn of the flames on my skin, but I didn't look away. I couldn't. Not now. Not with everything that had led us here, with every choice, every sacrifice. We had come too far to turn back. And then it hit me. Nathaniel wasn't just fighting for power. He wasn't just fighting to win. He was fighting for something more—something darker. His eyes glinted with the knowledge of something we hadn't yet seen, and I felt a chill creep up my spine.

"Why?" I demanded, my voice sharp, slicing through the tension. "Why do all this? What do you really want?"

Nathaniel's laugh was low, guttural, and filled with something cold and ancient. He didn't answer immediately, as if savoring the moment, letting the suspense stretch out like a taut wire ready to snap.

"You'll find out soon enough," he murmured, just loud enough for us to hear.

Aiden took a step toward him, his expression a perfect mask of concentration. I could see the muscles in his shoulders flex as he readied himself for another strike, but there was something in his eyes now. Something he wasn't saying. He was waiting for something.

That's when I saw it.

A shadow—no, a figure—lurking just behind Nathaniel, hidden in the smoke, blending into the flames like a predator. My heart skipped, and instinct took over. I lunged forward, pulling Aiden's arm with me just as the figure emerged from the haze.

It wasn't just a person. It was her.

"Mom?" The word came out before I could stop it. But I couldn't mistake her face, the way she moved. My mother was standing there, looking as though she'd never left.

But that wasn't possible. She had died. She'd been lost to the world years ago. I remembered the final goodbye, the hollow feeling of standing at her grave, knowing I would never see her again.

Except here she was.

I tried to take a step toward her, but Aiden's grip tightened on my arm, pulling me back.

"Don't," he warned, his voice tight with a mixture of confusion and concern. "It's not her."

But how could it not be her? Her eyes, that familiar glimmer of mischief, the way she tilted her head—there was no mistake.

Nathaniel's voice broke through my disorienting thoughts, the sound cold and smug. "What's the matter? Surprised? You thought you were done with me? With everything? There's no escaping the past, not when it's waiting for you."

I didn't know what to feel, what to think. The smoke was thick around me, the fire relentless in its quest to consume everything, and yet all I could focus on was the woman standing before me.

Her lips parted, and a soft, breathless laugh escaped her. "I told you this would be a family affair, didn't I?"

My pulse raced, and my knees felt weak beneath me. I couldn't breathe. This couldn't be real. This wasn't her. She had been dead, gone, buried. The weight of it pressed against my chest until I felt like I might suffocate.

"Mom," I whispered, reaching out again, but this time Aiden held me back with an iron grip. His face was a study of disbelief, but there was something else there too. Something darker.

"You're not her," Aiden said slowly, his voice a razor's edge. "You can't be."

But the woman, the thing in front of me, tilted her head again and smiled, that same smile that had haunted my childhood, that smile that had always held a secret.

"Don't be so sure," she said softly, almost too quietly for me to hear over the roar of the fire, before she vanished into the smoke.

The ground beneath us shook again, harder this time. The fire raged higher, closer, and I realized, too late, that I had no idea where she had gone—or what Nathaniel was truly capable of.

And then, through the smoke, I saw him. Nathaniel wasn't alone anymore. Behind him, there were more shadows—more figures stepping from the edges of the flames. The world around me seemed to slow, the very air pressing in as a new terror swept over me.

And it hit me then, with a brutal clarity.

We weren't just fighting for our lives.

We were fighting for something much worse.

Chapter 25: Edge of Ruin

The charred remnants of what had once been a sprawling garden lay in front of us, a field of blackened stems and the bitter scent of ash thick in the air. A few stubborn sparks smoldered in the dirt, but the worst was over—at least, that's what we kept telling ourselves. I could feel Aiden beside me, the weight of his presence pressing against the rawness of my thoughts. It wasn't just the fire that had left a mark on me—it was him. Always him.

I flexed my fingers, the knuckles stiff from clenching, and tried to push back the surge of emotion threatening to boil over. Later, I told myself. Deal with it later.

But later never seemed to come, not when we were constantly pulled into this web of tension, not when everything between us was never quite settled, just hanging by threads too delicate to trust. He hadn't said a word since we arrived at the scene, and I wondered if his silence was the same as mine—an unspoken acknowledgment that the fire had been the least of our problems.

The sun was low in the sky, a blood-orange ball sinking behind the wreckage, casting long, eerie shadows that made the whole place feel haunted. I hated how much it reminded me of us—half-burned, still smoldering, but pretending we were fine. I kept my gaze fixed on the horizon, the wind carrying the faint sound of sirens in the distance, an annoying reminder of the things I couldn't control.

"You know," Aiden's voice finally broke the silence, low and rough, like he'd been holding it back for far too long, "this place... it used to be beautiful."

I nodded, but I couldn't bring myself to look at him. If I did, I might start noticing the things I wanted to ignore—the slight slump of his shoulders, the way his jaw tightened every time the wind shifted, the unsaid things that clung to him like smoke.

"It could be again," I said, keeping my tone casual. "Once it's cleared, once we rebuild. There's nothing here we can't fix."

That wasn't entirely true. Some things couldn't be fixed, no matter how much effort you put into it. Some things, once broken, stayed that way, no matter how hard you tried to piece them back together. And we, both of us, were living proof of that.

"I don't think that's what you meant," he said after a beat, turning his head to look at me. The heat of his gaze burned through the air between us, but I refused to meet it.

"What are you talking about?" I asked, even though I knew exactly what he meant. I wasn't some naive fool.

"You can't hide from it forever, you know." His voice dropped a fraction, and it felt like the earth beneath my feet had shifted. I'd spent so much time telling myself that the damage was done, that there was no going back, but I'd never been quite so good at convincing myself as I was others.

"Hide from what?" My voice was sharper than I intended, but it didn't matter. I was tired. Tired of pretending, tired of everything. "This is exactly what I mean, Aiden. This—" I gestured to the devastation around us, "—this is what happens when you don't take care of the things that matter. This is what happens when you forget about the small things."

He opened his mouth, then closed it again, as if weighing his words. "I didn't forget about you, Annalise. Don't ever think I did." His eyes softened for a second, and I could see it—the regret, the weight of the things he hadn't said. But that wasn't enough anymore. Regret didn't fix things. It only made them more complicated.

"I'm not talking about that," I said, stepping back, my chest tightening. I needed to put distance between us before my emotions turned into something I couldn't control. "I'm talking about everything we've avoided, all the things we haven't said. The things we've pretended are okay because we don't want to deal with them."

He didn't answer, just stared at me like he was trying to figure out what I wanted from him. Like maybe he thought he could fix it with the same careful, steady patience he used when he rebuilt old cars—bit by bit, part by part. But this wasn't a car. This wasn't something that could be fixed with just a few turns of a wrench and a little elbow grease. This was us. And I didn't know how to make him see that.

"You're wrong," he said finally, his voice strained. "I never wanted to hurt you."

"I know you didn't," I whispered, the words escaping before I could stop them. "But you did. And so did I."

The confession hung in the air between us, thick and suffocating. I hadn't wanted to admit it, but I couldn't keep pretending it wasn't true. I wasn't innocent in this. I'd hurt him too—maybe not in the same way, maybe not in ways he could see, but I had.

"I don't know how to fix this, Annalise." His voice cracked slightly, and the vulnerability in it nearly broke me. Almost.

I wanted to tell him that it didn't matter, that maybe we weren't supposed to be fixed. That maybe the best we could do was find a way to live with the mess. But I couldn't. I was too tired, too worn down by the weight of everything we were ignoring.

"I don't either," I admitted, finally meeting his gaze, and the look in his eyes was enough to break my resolve.

We stood there for a long time, the silence stretching between us, heavy with everything we weren't saying, everything we couldn't say. The fire was gone, but the wreckage remained. And I didn't know if we'd ever have the courage to rebuild.

I forced my hands to stop trembling as I wiped the ash from my cheek, a futile gesture considering the thick layer of soot that coated everything in sight. My skin felt foreign, rough against the air. Aiden's presence behind me was like a shadow, his stillness too perfect, too complete. I didn't want to turn around; I didn't want to look at him, because every time I did, I found myself feeling more exposed, like he could see right through all my defenses.

I sighed and began walking toward what was left of the house. The foundations were still standing, but the walls that had once held warmth and laughter were nothing but crumbling charcoal. The sight of it, the ruin of it all, should have made me angry, but it didn't. Instead, it filled me with a sick sense of resignation. It was all too familiar, the constant rebuilding. First the house, now us.

Behind me, Aiden shifted his weight, finally speaking again. "We'll rebuild," he said, his voice quieter this time, softer, like he was trying to convince both of us. But I knew better than to listen to the false comfort in his tone.

"I don't think we can," I muttered, more to myself than to him. My words echoed against the hollow shell of what used to be home, reminding me of the last time I had stood here—before the fire, before the months of silence and unspoken apologies. Before I'd let myself believe we could make it through the storm.

"Annalise." His voice was sharp now, as if he was trying to wake me up from the trance I'd slipped into. "Don't do this. You know we can."

I turned to face him then, my arms crossed tightly across my chest. He stood there, still dressed in the remnants of his firefighting gear, his hair mussed and face smudged with soot. His eyes, those damn eyes, still held the same intensity that made me feel like the center of the universe when they focused on me. I hated how much power he had over me. How easily he could turn my carefully constructed walls into rubble with just a glance.

"I don't know if I can do this anymore, Aiden," I whispered, though the words felt like stones in my mouth. "I don't know if I can keep pretending everything's okay when it isn't."

His face softened, and I saw the flicker of something—guilt, maybe, or maybe just the simple recognition of my exhaustion. He took a step forward, and I didn't move back. My heart was thudding in my chest, but I refused to let it show. I wasn't ready for this. Not yet. Not after everything.

"I'm not asking you to pretend, Annalise." His voice was low, almost tender, and for a second, I almost believed him. I almost believed that he understood. "But we're in this together. I want to rebuild with you. I can't do this alone."

The sincerity in his eyes was enough to make my chest ache, but I couldn't let myself be swayed by it. I couldn't allow myself to fall into the trap of hope again, only to have it ripped away when the next inevitable disaster struck.

"Maybe you're right," I said, turning away from him, my voice barely a whisper. "Maybe we can rebuild. But not today. Not now."

His silence stretched behind me, and I could almost feel the weight of his disappointment settling around us. But this time, it didn't feel like it was about him. It felt like it was about me—about the fact that I had finally come to the painful realization that maybe we weren't meant to rebuild. Maybe we had already broken too many times to ever make it work again.

"You think I'm giving up on us?" Aiden's voice was tight, a trace of frustration creeping in, but I didn't turn to face him. I couldn't.

"I think we've both given up on us," I said, my words cutting through the air between us. "I think we've been standing in the ashes of what we used to be for too long. And I'm tired, Aiden. I'm tired of trying to fix something that might be beyond saving."

There was a pause, a long, heavy moment where I wondered if he would finally walk away. If he would do what I had been too scared to do. But then I heard the soft sound of his boots crunching on the ground behind me, and I turned, expecting to see him leaving.

Instead, he was kneeling in front of me, his eyes level with mine, his hands hovering at his sides as if he was unsure of how to touch me. His posture was desperate, vulnerable—so unlike the confident man I had known, and it tore at me in ways I couldn't explain.

"Annalise," he said, his voice low but clear, "I never stopped fighting for us. Maybe I didn't know how to fight the right way, but I never gave up on you. On us."

I swallowed, fighting back the sting of tears that I knew would break the fragile control I had left. He was so close now, I could feel the heat of his body, smell the faint scent of smoke that still clung to him. It wasn't just the fire we'd survived—it was everything we had been through together, everything that had tried to tear us apart, and yet here he was, still reaching for me.

"I don't know how to trust you anymore, Aiden," I said, the words tasting like ash in my mouth. "Not after everything that's happened. I'm not sure I can trust myself."

He didn't speak for a long time, and I almost thought he might finally walk away. But then his hand moved, and before I could react, his fingers brushed against my cheek, a soft, careful touch that sent a shiver down my spine.

"You don't have to trust me right now," he said, his voice barely a whisper. "But I'm here. And I'm not going anywhere."

I wanted to pull away, to run from the weight of his words, but something inside me—a flicker of the woman I used to be—didn't want to. It wanted to reach for him, to believe him, just for a moment.

But believing him meant breaking all the walls I'd spent so long building around my heart, and I wasn't sure I was ready for that yet.

The tension crackled between us, thick and unnerving, like the stillness before a storm. Aiden's hand remained just inches from my cheek, his fingers hovering like he was waiting for me to make the first move. I should have pulled away, should have told him that I didn't need his comfort, didn't want it. But the truth was, in that moment, I wasn't sure what I needed. I wasn't sure what I wanted.

"I should go," I murmured, more to myself than to him, because saying it aloud made it sound like a command rather than a plea. The thought of leaving, of walking away from the wreckage of my past, felt like an impossibility.

Aiden's gaze flickered to my mouth, then back to my eyes, his brow furrowed with an expression that was part frustration, part desperation. "No. Not like this."

I swallowed hard, forcing my breath to steady as if my pulse didn't seem to recognize the difference between a moment of quiet reflection and an impending disaster. His voice, the soft, broken edge of it, gnawed at my resolve. "You can't keep running from this, Annalise. From us."

I let out a bitter laugh, but it was empty, hollow, as if I had forgotten how to do anything but fall apart. "And what would you have me do, Aiden? Stay?" The word felt like acid on my tongue. "You don't get it. There's nothing left to stay for. This—" I waved a hand to encompass the destruction around us, "—this is all that's left."

His face softened, his eyes unreadable for the briefest moment before a sharp edge crept back in. "This is not all that's left. Not unless you want it to be."

I shook my head, the sting of his words pushing me back a step, making the air around me feel impossibly thin. "I'm not sure I know how to not make it that way anymore."

He didn't reply right away. Instead, he stepped closer, his presence overwhelming. There was a charged silence between us, the kind that felt like it was teetering on the brink of something I wasn't sure I was ready for.

"I'm not asking you to fix this overnight," he said, his voice raw. "I'm not asking for promises, Annalise. But I am asking you to stop pretending like there's no way forward. Because if we don't even try—if we don't even look—we'll lose what's left before we have the chance to fix it."

I wanted to scream, to shout at him that it wasn't that simple. But the truth was, his words stung because I knew he was right. I knew that somewhere, deep down, I had already made up my mind. And yet, I stood there, frozen in place, battling against the knowledge that walking away from him meant walking away from a part of myself I wasn't sure I could afford to lose.

"I'm tired," I said, the words slipping out, barely a whisper.

The fight drained out of him then, and for the first time in what felt like years, I saw something else in his eyes. Something softer. "I know you are. So am I."

The air between us felt different in that moment, as if the walls I'd built had finally cracked just enough for the light to break through. But it wasn't enough. Not yet. Not by a long shot. Because no matter how much I wanted to let go, no matter how much I wanted to surrender to whatever this was between us, there was still too much history weighing us down.

I couldn't do it. I couldn't just let go and pretend like everything would magically fall into place.

Without thinking, I took a step back, my heels scraping against the gravel, a quiet sound that seemed far too loud in the thick silence between us.

"I need time," I said, my voice shaking more than I wanted it to.

He didn't try to follow me. He didn't reach out. He just stood there, watching me, his chest rising and falling with each breath, and I felt a pang in my chest at the loss of the warmth that had always been so effortlessly there when we were together. I didn't want to turn away from him, but I knew I had to. I had to.

"I'll give you time," he said quietly, almost too quietly, like he didn't know whether or not I'd still be there when he came back.

I started to walk, each step feeling heavier than the last, as if the weight of my own indecision was pulling me down. The ruins of the garden stretched out behind me, the blackened remains of what was once full of life now a barren wasteland. It mirrored the mess in my chest—the confusion, the longing, the hurt. The raw, painful truth that no matter what I said, no matter how many walls I put up, I could still feel him. He was still there, an echo I couldn't escape.

I was halfway across the yard when the sound of approaching footsteps made me freeze.

"Aiden?" I said, not turning around, my voice more fragile than I intended.

But the footsteps didn't stop.

My pulse quickened. I wasn't ready for this—not yet.

The sound of boots on gravel came closer. I heard the sharp inhale before I heard the voice. "Annalise, don't—"

I spun around, but it wasn't Aiden.

Standing in front of me, silhouetted against the fading light, was someone I hadn't seen in years.

A face I thought I'd buried long ago.

"Surprised to see me?" the voice drawled.

And suddenly, the earth beneath me seemed to shift.

Chapter 26: A Line in the Sand

The morning light spilled through the curtains, soft and insistent, as if it too were trying to wake me up, shake me out of the fog that had settled around my mind. I hated mornings. Not because of the light or the promise of a new day, but because they always felt like the beginning of something I couldn't control. The quiet in the house was unsettling. Aiden had already left. His absence was like a weight pressing down on my chest, making it hard to breathe.

I pulled myself from the bed, the soft creak of the floorboards beneath my feet a reminder that this place, my sanctuary, was now a battleground. Every inch of it felt like it belonged to someone else, someone I wasn't sure I even knew anymore. I moved through the house in silence, the only sound the rhythmic tick of the clock in the kitchen. I had never understood the allure of clocks. They kept track of time, sure, but all they really did was remind you that it was slipping through your fingers. Slowly, steadily, it was gone, and nothing could bring it back.

A knock at the door jolted me from my thoughts. I hadn't expected anyone. I wasn't sure I wanted anyone. But I forced my feet to carry me toward the sound, my hand trembling just slightly as I reached for the doorknob.

It was Eliza. Of course. The last person I had expected, and yet somehow the first. Her smile was the same as it always was, bright and eager, but her eyes were darker. Shadowed, like she had something to hide. Or maybe it was just me. Maybe I was seeing things that weren't there. After all, I had been seeing a lot of things lately that didn't quite add up.

"Morning," she said, her voice light but with an edge I hadn't heard before. She stepped inside before I could invite her, brushing past me like she was already a part of the room. Her perfume was heavy—too heavy—and the cloying scent of it lingered long after she had moved away.

"Eliza..." I said, not sure where I was going with the words. "What's going on? You look like you've seen a ghost."

She laughed, but there was no humor in it. "Maybe I have." Her eyes flitted around the room as if they were searching for something. I tried not to stare at her too hard, but it was hard to ignore the way she seemed almost... off. Like she was wearing a mask, one that was beginning to crack.

I folded my arms across my chest, feeling the tension in the room mount with every passing second. "What's really going on, Eliza?"

She hesitated, her fingers fidgeting with the hem of her blouse, a nervous habit I'd never seen from her before. "I... I found something," she said, her voice low. Too low. "Something that doesn't make sense."

My heart skipped a beat, and I suddenly felt the weight of the room closing in. "What kind of something?"

She took a deep breath, her lips pressing into a tight line before she spoke again. "Something about Aiden."

Aiden. His name hung between us, thick and heavy, like an unspoken accusation. My pulse quickened, and I fought to keep my face neutral, to hide the surge of panic threatening to rise in my chest. "What about Aiden?"

Eliza shifted uncomfortably, her eyes darting away from mine as if the truth was too much to bear. "I found a letter," she said quietly. "A letter addressed to him, but not from anyone you know."

I blinked, trying to process her words. "A letter? Who's it from?"

She chewed on her bottom lip, looking torn. "I'm not sure. I couldn't tell from the handwriting, and there was no return address. But it's clear that whoever wrote it... they know him. They know things about him that no one else does."

My stomach dropped. "What kind of things?"

Eliza hesitated, then pulled a folded piece of paper from her purse and handed it to me. I took it gingerly, unfolding it with trembling hands. The words were scrawled in a hurried, jagged script, as if the person had been desperate to get them out. The message was simple, but chilling:

You're not the only one with secrets, Aiden. And if you don't make the right choice, they'll all come crashing down.

I read the words twice, then three times, each time the meaning sinking deeper into my chest, settling there like a cold stone. I handed the letter back to Eliza, my hands shaking now. "What does this mean? What are they talking about?"

"I don't know," she said, her voice barely above a whisper. "But it's not good. Aiden's been hiding something. Something big. And I think it's about to catch up with him."

I felt the floor tilt beneath me, the edges of my vision blurring as the world seemed to tilt on its axis. "I don't understand. Aiden wouldn't—"

"Aiden wouldn't what?" Eliza interrupted, her voice sharp. "He wouldn't keep things from you? You know better than that, don't you?"

I didn't know what to say. I wanted to defend him, to tell her that she was wrong, that she had to be wrong. But a nagging doubt began to claw at the back of my mind, a feeling I couldn't shake. I had always trusted Aiden, but now... now I wasn't sure who he was anymore. And I wasn't sure I knew who I was, either.

"I need to talk to him," I said, my voice a mix of resolve and fear. I needed answers, even if they tore everything apart. Especially if they did.

Eliza nodded, her face unreadable. "Just be careful," she warned, her eyes narrowing. "Some truths are better left buried."

I barely slept that night, each tick of the clock louder than the last, the shadows stretching across the room as if they were alive, searching for something. I kept replaying Eliza's words in my head, the weight of them pressing down like an unseen hand. I wanted to push them away, to pretend none of it was real, but the image of that letter—the ink smeared in places as if written in haste—clung to me like a bad dream. What was Aiden hiding? And more importantly, what would it cost me to find out?

The morning found me at the kitchen table, staring at the half-empty cup of coffee in front of me, its steam long since dissipated. I couldn't make sense of any of it. The life I thought I understood was unraveling before me, thread by thread, and I had no idea how to stitch it back together.

A knock on the door, sharp and urgent, snapped me from my spiraling thoughts. My heart jolted, knowing exactly who it was before I even opened it.

Aiden stood in the doorway, his expression unreadable, his eyes too still. I had seen him like this before, a man on the edge of something he couldn't control, but it was different now. The tension between us crackled in the air, suffocating and thick, as though every word we had ever exchanged had led to this moment.

"Hey," he said, his voice low, the way it always was when something was wrong, when he didn't know how to fix it.

I stepped aside to let him in, my pulse quickening as he crossed the threshold. There was something about him today, something almost foreign in his usual confidence. I couldn't put my finger on it, but the way he looked at me—like he was searching for something—made me want to look away.

I closed the door behind him and leaned against it, arms crossed tightly. "What's going on, Aiden?" I asked, the words coming out more brittle than I'd intended.

His jaw tightened, and for a moment, he seemed to struggle with his answer. "I didn't want you to find out like this," he said, his gaze dropping to the floor. "But I guess it's time you knew."

Time I knew what? I wanted to scream it, but instead, I bit my tongue. I had to know what he was hiding. Whatever it was, it had been eating away at both of us, a slow, insidious thing, until the truth could no longer stay buried.

"Aiden," I whispered, my voice hoarse, "what are you involved in?"

He lifted his eyes to mine, and in that moment, I saw the man I loved—the man I thought I knew—shatter like glass. "There's so much I should have told you," he said, his voice strained. "I wanted to keep you safe, but it wasn't just about me anymore. I made a choice—a terrible one—and now it's all catching up to me."

The words hung between us, heavy with implications I wasn't ready to face. I took a step toward him, my heart in my throat. "What kind of choice, Aiden?"

He swallowed hard, his hand running through his hair in frustration. "I've done things... things I'm not proud of. People are looking for me. They know about us. They'll come for you if I don't make it right."

I felt the room tilt, a strange, hollow sensation crawling up my spine. "People? Aiden, you're talking in riddles. What are you saying?"

He met my eyes again, his gaze raw with a mixture of regret and fear. "There's no easy way to explain this, but you need to understand that everything I've done, I did to protect you. To protect us."

I searched his face, trying to find any trace of the man I had fallen in love with, but the more I looked, the less I recognized him. It was like a mask had slipped off, and underneath it was someone I couldn't quite reach.

"I need to know everything," I said, my voice trembling. "Everything, Aiden. Now."

He nodded, his shoulders slumping as if he had already been carrying too much weight. "I'll tell you, but not here. Not now. We need to leave. We're not safe."

His words sent a chill down my spine. Leave? What did that even mean? I glanced around the room as if it would somehow hold the answers, but there was only the oppressive silence that had settled between us.

"I'm not going anywhere until you tell me exactly what's happening," I said, my voice more forceful than I felt. "I don't care where we go, but I need to know why."

Aiden's expression hardened. "It's too dangerous. Please, trust me."

I shook my head, a sharp laugh escaping me, though there was no humor in it. "Trust you? You've been lying to me, Aiden. Keeping secrets. How am I supposed to trust you now?"

His face fell, and I saw the flicker of guilt cross his features, but it was quickly replaced by something else—something darker. "You're right. I've kept things from you, but not because I wanted to. Because I had to. I'm not the man you think I am. I've made choices, choices I regret. But I'm trying to fix them. Please, just come with me."

I could feel the tug of him, the gravity of his words pulling me closer to him despite myself. I wanted to believe him. I wanted to so badly. But there was something in my gut telling me that no matter how much I wanted this to end neatly, with us in each other's arms, it wouldn't. There was a price to pay for every lie, and every secret came with a cost.

I took a breath, trying to steady my racing thoughts. "Where do we go?"

Aiden's eyes softened, the briefest flicker of relief washing over his face. But it didn't last. "We leave now," he said, the urgency clear in his voice. "Before it's too late."

And I knew, without a doubt, that when I stepped out that door with him, I would be leaving behind everything I had ever known. There would be no going back.

I stepped out into the cool morning air, the crispness of it biting at my skin as if the world itself was waking up, trying to remind me that life was still moving, still demanding something of me. The soft thud of the door closing behind us was drowned by the rush of blood in my ears. Every step I took felt like an echo, a warning, reverberating in the pit of my stomach. The weight of Aiden's words hung over me like a dark cloud, following me as we moved farther from the safety of our home. A home that suddenly felt more like a cage.

Aiden's presence beside me was both grounding and unnerving, the quiet between us now thicker than it had ever been. He kept glancing at me, as if expecting me to break the silence, to ask questions that had already formed in my mind a thousand times over. But I couldn't bring myself to speak. What could I say? What words were there to bridge the chasm that had opened between us in the past twenty-four hours?

We made our way to the car, parked haphazardly at the curb, and the metallic click of the lock seemed too loud in the stillness of the morning. Aiden slid into the driver's seat without a word, the engine's hum a low vibration that felt strangely comforting. The world outside continued to turn, indifferent to the storm that raged within me.

The city stretched out before us as we drove, the streets blurring by in a sea of gray concrete and rusting metal. I watched the world go by, but my mind was elsewhere. There were so many questions, too many to ask, but I had to start somewhere. My fingers tightened around the strap of my bag, the only thing that seemed to anchor me in this whirlwind of uncertainty.

"Aiden," I began, my voice barely more than a whisper. "What happened? What did you do?"

His jaw tightened, and he gave me a quick glance before focusing back on the road. "I made a mistake," he said, his voice strained. "But I never wanted it to go this far."

That was it. That was all I got. I pressed my lips together to hold back the flood of questions threatening to spill over. "You've been keeping something from me," I said, trying to keep my voice steady. "What aren't you telling me?"

He didn't answer right away, but the way his hands gripped the wheel made me think he was fighting something—whether it was guilt, anger, or the sheer weight of whatever secret he was carrying, I couldn't tell. The silence between us stretched thin, and I realized I was holding my breath, waiting for him to crack.

"I didn't want to involve you in this," he said finally, his voice low, almost apologetic. "But now there's no way out. You're in this whether you like it or not."

I turned to face him, my heart thudding in my chest. "In what, Aiden? What is this?"

He clenched his fists around the wheel, his knuckles going white. "I got mixed up with the wrong people. People who don't care about anything but their own gain. I tried to get out. I thought I could just walk away, but they don't let you go that easy."

My mind raced, trying to piece it all together. "Who are these people? What do they want from you?"

He shot me a look, the intensity in his eyes almost burning. "It's not just about me. It's about us now. They know about you, Emma. They know everything."

The words hit me like a slap. I had known something was wrong, but hearing him say it aloud, hearing him acknowledge that we were both in danger, made the weight of it unbearable.

"Why didn't you tell me this sooner?" I demanded, my voice rising despite my best efforts. "Why wait until we were already tangled up in this mess?"

He exhaled sharply, and for the first time since we'd left, he seemed to soften, just a little. "Because I was trying to protect you," he said, almost defensively. "You don't get to walk away from people like this. They don't just disappear."

I shook my head, the frustration bubbling up. "And now what? What do we do now, Aiden? Where do we go from here?"

He didn't answer immediately. Instead, he kept driving, the hum of the engine the only sound between us. It felt like the calm before the storm, the air too still, too heavy. I could see the tightness in his posture, the way his body seemed to brace for something—something I wasn't sure I was ready for.

The car slowed to a stop at a red light, and for a brief moment, everything felt frozen. The world around us was static, suspended in time, and I could feel my pulse quicken, the weight of the decision before me pressing down, suffocating. Whatever was coming, whatever choice I had to make, it was about to hit, and there was no way to prepare for it.

I turned toward Aiden, my voice trembling despite my attempts to stay calm. "I need you to tell me everything. I need to know what we're up against."

He met my gaze, his eyes dark with something I couldn't place. It wasn't just guilt anymore—it was something deeper, something far more dangerous. "I'll tell you," he said, his voice tight. "But you need to understand. Once you know, there's no going back. You won't be able to unsee this. Unknow this."

The light turned green, and he pressed the accelerator, the car lurching forward as if it too was being pulled into something we couldn't outrun.

"Whatever it is, Aiden," I said, my voice steadier than I felt, "I'm already in it. I'm already with you."

For a second, his gaze softened, a flash of something like gratitude flickering in his eyes. But it was gone as quickly as it came, replaced by a tension that seemed to suffocate the air between us. We sped through the streets, the world outside rushing past us in a blur, and I realized, with a sickening twist in my gut, that we weren't just driving toward something—we were driving away from something, from everything we had ever known.

And whatever waited for us at the end of this road, I wasn't sure we would survive it.

Chapter 27: Love and Lies

I stood in the dim light of the living room, the curtains drawn tight against the late afternoon sun, casting long shadows on the hardwood floor. The air was heavy with the scent of the coffee that had gone cold on the kitchen counter, a reminder of how long we had been standing here, circling the truth like two wary animals. Aiden's face was as pale as the empty mug, his jaw clenched so tight I wondered if it hurt. I could feel the pulse of my own heartbeat pounding in my ears, a symphony of uncertainty and anger that I couldn't quiet.

His eyes, normally so bright with warmth, were dark now, an ocean of regret I wasn't sure I could swim through. The words he had spoken had done more damage than any argument, any fight. The lies he'd told, the truths he'd hidden, they were now woven into the very fabric of who we were. I had always known that things were never as simple as they appeared with Aiden, but I hadn't expected this. Not this.

"I never meant for it to get this far," Aiden's voice broke the silence, soft and hesitant. He took a step toward me, but I didn't move. I couldn't. "I just wanted to protect you."

"Protect me?" I laughed, but the sound was hollow. It felt like I was watching someone else in this moment, someone who hadn't been lied to, deceived. Someone who wasn't standing on the precipice of losing everything she thought she knew about the person she loved. "By lying to me? By keeping things from me? How does that protect me, Aiden?"

His eyes flickered with something—guilt, I guessed—but there was something else there too. Something darker. He opened his mouth to speak, then closed it again, as if he were searching for the right words.

"I never wanted to hurt you," he said finally, his voice more strained. "It just... it just all spiraled out of control. And then—then I didn't know how to stop it."

I shook my head, pushing my fingers through my hair in frustration. "Spiraled? Aiden, you don't just accidentally lie about your entire past. You don't 'spiral' into withholding the truth about your family, your life. You choose to do that." The words tumbled out in a rush, all the hurt and disbelief clawing their way to the surface.

His eyes softened, and I felt the battle between wanting to trust him again and needing to be angry for the lies grow fiercer inside me. Aiden had always had this way of looking at me, like I was the only person in the world, but now, in the quiet aftermath of his confession, I didn't know if I could trust that gaze. I didn't know if I could trust him.

"I know," he said quietly, his voice thick. "I know I should've told you. From the start. But I didn't know how you would react. I didn't know how to tell you the truth without losing you. I couldn't risk it."

"And what about me?" The words came out before I could stop them, sharp and accusing. "What about how I would've reacted if I'd known the truth? You never gave me that choice, Aiden. You kept me in the dark, made me think you were someone you weren't, and now... now I don't know who you are anymore."

The silence that followed hung between us, heavy and suffocating. I could hear the sound of my own breathing, ragged and uneven, and yet I felt like I was waiting for something—something I wasn't sure I was ready for.

He took a step back, his hand running through his hair in frustration. His gaze never left me, though. His expression was a mixture of pain and confusion, as though he were trying to piece together the wreckage of everything we'd built.

"I didn't lie about how I feel," he said, his voice barely above a whisper. "About that, I swear. I never meant to hurt you, but I do love you. I always have."

I swallowed hard, the lump in my throat making it impossible to speak for a moment. Aiden's love, his words, they had always been a comfort, something I thought would never fail me. But now, they felt like a trap, like a promise I wasn't sure he could keep.

"But what if love isn't enough?" The question hung in the air, bitter and unfamiliar. "What if it's not enough to undo the damage? What if it's not enough to fix what's broken?"

Aiden's eyes searched mine, his expression shifting from guilt to something that looked a little like desperation. "I don't know. But I'm willing to try. I'm willing to do whatever it takes, if you'll let me."

The words hit me harder than I expected, knocking the wind out of me. I didn't know if I could forgive him—not yet, not after everything. But there was something in his eyes, something raw and vulnerable that made my heart ache. He was right about one thing, though—his love had always been real. Even now, in the face of everything that had happened, I could feel it. I could still feel the warmth of it, like a beacon in the dark.

But was that enough? Was love really enough to rebuild a foundation that had cracked under the weight of lies? I didn't know the answer, and that uncertainty gnawed at me, leaving a taste in my mouth I couldn't shake.

"I don't know what to believe anymore," I whispered, the words tasting like defeat.

Aiden's shoulders slumped, his gaze falling to the floor. "I don't expect you to. But I'll do whatever it takes to prove it to you. To prove that I'm not the man who lied to you. I'm the man who loves you."

His words hung in the air between us, an unspoken plea that I wasn't sure I could answer.

The room felt smaller now, as if the walls were leaning in, too heavy with the weight of unspoken truths. My mind was spinning—part of me wanted to scream, to let all the anger out, to demand that Aiden face the full force of his deceit. But there was another part of me, a quieter part, that just wanted to collapse into his arms and pretend none of this had ever happened. It was a dangerous thing, this pull between fury and forgiveness. But the truth was, I wasn't sure I knew how to navigate it. I had always prided myself on being able to see people clearly, on trusting my instincts, but now I was doubting everything.

Aiden shifted on his feet, his eyes still locked on mine, the weight of his unspoken words pressing down on both of us. I could see the storm raging inside him—the way his jaw worked and his fingers flexed, as though he was trying to hold himself together in the face of everything falling apart. The man who had been so steady, so certain of himself, was unraveling before my eyes. And it was a terrible thing to witness, to know that the one person I had trusted most had shattered that trust in ways I wasn't sure could be repaired.

"I know you're angry," he said finally, his voice a little too soft, as though he were afraid of what would come next. "I would be, too. I don't expect you to just forgive me. I don't even know if I can forgive myself." He paused, his gaze dropping to the floor, his shoulders sagging with the weight of his own shame.

"Then why should I?" The words escaped before I could stop them. There was no venom in them, just raw, unfiltered truth. "Why should I give you a second chance when you've been lying to me this whole time?"

Aiden took a deep breath, and for a moment, I thought he might just crumble. But instead, he straightened up, his eyes meeting mine once more. There was something in his gaze now—a quiet resolve, a silent plea. "Because despite everything, I love you. And I know that's not enough. I know it's not a good enough reason to ask you to forgive me. But it's the truth."

I wanted to argue. I wanted to throw his words back in his face and tell him that love didn't erase the lies, didn't fix the damage. But there was a quiet part of me, buried under the hurt, that knew he wasn't lying about that. I had felt it, every moment I had spent with him. The love was real. It was as real as the pain. As real as the disappointment that now twisted in my chest.

"I don't know if I can do this," I said, the words tasting like surrender. "I don't know if I can just pretend everything is okay."

Aiden flinched, and the flash of pain on his face made my heart twist. He took a step toward me, slow and hesitant, as though he were afraid of scaring me away completely. "I'm not asking you to pretend. I'm asking for a chance to make it right."

A bitter laugh bubbled up from my throat, and I couldn't stop it. "Make it right?" I shook my head, the incredulity in my voice so sharp it stung. "Aiden, you can't just fix this with a few heartfelt words. You can't just... undo all of this." I gestured between us, my hands trembling despite myself.

"I know," he admitted, his voice low and steady. "But I can try. I can prove to you that I'm not the man you think I am."

That was the crux of it, wasn't it? I didn't know who Aiden really was anymore. The man I had fallen for had been this carefully curated version of himself—charming, a little broken, but always there when I needed him. The man standing before me now, wracked with guilt and desperation, felt foreign in comparison. He wasn't the man I thought I knew, and that terrified me.

"I don't even know if I can trust you anymore," I whispered, my voice barely audible.

His expression faltered for a moment, but it wasn't the defeat I expected. There was a flicker of determination there, something fierce and unwavering. "I know. And I'm not asking you to trust me right now. I'm asking for a chance to earn it back. I won't ask for your forgiveness until I've done that."

The silence that followed was thick, suffocating almost. I stood there, my arms crossed tightly against my chest, unsure of what to say or how to move forward. My mind was a whirlwind of emotions—betrayal, hurt, love, and a strange sense of longing that I wasn't sure how to reconcile.

"I don't know if I can watch you destroy yourself over this," I said quietly. "I don't know if I can live with the idea of you constantly apologizing, constantly trying to prove yourself. I don't want you to keep feeling like you're not enough. I don't want to be the one who makes you feel like that."

Aiden's eyes softened, the pain on his face only deepening. "You're not the one doing that. I'm doing that to myself. I'm the one who messed up. I'm the one who lied." He stepped closer, his gaze unwavering. "But I'm not going to stop trying. And if you'll let me, I'll spend the rest of my life proving that I'm worthy of your trust again."

I could feel the weight of his words sinking in, settling like stones in my chest. I didn't know if I was ready to forgive him—not yet. But a part of me, the part that still loved him despite everything, wondered if maybe... just maybe, he was right. Maybe it wasn't about erasing the lies, but about building something new from the wreckage. Something stronger. Something real.

But was I strong enough to try again?

The silence between us stretched long and taut, the kind of silence that had the power to break something, to shatter it into pieces too small to ever put back together. I was standing there, still with my arms wrapped around myself as though I could hold all the anger and confusion inside, when Aiden took a small step forward. He looked so fragile in that moment, like a man who had built a house out of glass and was now afraid of the storm.

"I can't make you believe me," he said quietly, his voice rough, edged with desperation. "I can't undo what I've done. But if you'll give me a chance, I'll show you. I'll do everything I can to make it right."

There it was again—his love, woven through everything he said, even in the midst of the wreckage. I wanted to ignore it. I wanted to push it away, to deny that there was anything left of us after the lies, after the trust I had so willingly handed over to him had been shredded like paper. But that pull, that aching tug in my chest, told me something different.

"You don't get it, Aiden," I said, my voice tight. "It's not just about fixing things. It's about... everything. About who you are, who I thought you were, and who I am now that I've seen all of this. You've changed everything."

His eyes darkened, his hands balling into fists at his sides. "I know," he said, the words coming out in a near whisper, as though he was admitting to some unspeakable crime. "I've changed everything, and I hate myself for it. But I swear to you, the love I feel for you hasn't changed. Not for a second."

I closed my eyes, a bitter laugh escaping me. "You know, it's funny. Because the more you say it, the less I believe you."

Aiden didn't back away. Instead, his gaze softened, his voice lowering. "I can't fix this overnight. But I can try, every damn day, for as long as you'll let me."

The vulnerability in his tone caught me off guard. It wasn't something I'd ever expected to hear from him, not from the man who had always been so sure of himself, so certain of his place in my life. The cracks in his armor were visible now, and I wondered, with a twisted sort of fascination, if he'd ever truly been the man I thought he was—or if he was still figuring it out, just like the rest of us.

I took a step back, shaking my head. "I don't know if I can live in this... limbo. Not knowing whether I can trust you, whether you'll keep your promises. I don't know how to keep giving pieces of myself when I'm not even sure who you are anymore."

"I'm still the man who loves you," Aiden said, his voice raw with pain. "I might not be perfect. I might've messed up in ways I'll never be able to make up for. But I can't go back to pretending that I don't want to fix this. I can't pretend that I don't need you."

It was like a knife twisting in my chest, and I had no idea whether it was the anger or the love that hurt more. His words echoed in the hollow spaces of the room, bouncing off the walls and ricocheting back into my ears like something I couldn't escape.

The truth was, I wanted to believe him. I wanted to fall into his arms and pretend that the last few days hadn't happened, that nothing had changed, that love could still fix everything. But I wasn't sure that it could. I wasn't sure that he could fix what was broken between us.

The longer I stood there, staring at him, the more I realized something. My heart was still there, beating in rhythm with his, still tethered to him in ways I didn't want to acknowledge. But there was also a growing fear in my chest, a fear that maybe, just maybe, I wasn't strong enough to survive if I opened that door again.

"You don't understand," I said, voice shaking now. "I don't know if I can keep doing this. Keep loving you like this, in the shadow of all the lies. Every time you say you love me, it feels like a betrayal. Like you're telling me you love someone I don't even recognize anymore."

Aiden winced, as if I'd struck him physically. But he didn't retreat. He stood there, still, waiting. Waiting for something that I wasn't sure I had the strength to give.

"I'm not asking you to trust me right now," he said, his voice steady despite the rawness beneath it. "But I'm asking for a chance to prove myself, to show you that I'm worth the risk. That we're worth the risk."

IN THE DARK

The room felt impossibly small. The air was thick, my chest tight with conflicting emotions. I wanted to scream at him to leave, to leave me with my anger and hurt. But there was a part of me, a dangerous part, that wanted to reach out and forgive him—before I even understood if it was possible.

"I need space," I said, finally. The words felt like surrender, like a slow admission that I wasn't ready to let him go. But I needed time, needed to think. "I can't... I can't do this right now."

Aiden's face fell, the light in his eyes dimming with my words. He opened his mouth to say something, but I held up a hand to stop him.

"I just need some time," I repeated, voice firmer now. "Please."

He nodded, his expression tight with something I couldn't quite place. "I'll be here. I'll wait. But if you're sure this is what you need... I'll give you space."

I didn't watch him leave. I couldn't. Instead, I turned away, closing my eyes against the tears I refused to shed. The door closed softly behind him, and I was left standing in the silence, the echo of his words hanging in the air.

But as the minutes passed, a thought gnawed at me, one I hadn't wanted to face. What if the lies weren't the only thing between us anymore? What if the truth of who we were now—the versions of ourselves that had been shaped by everything we'd gone through—was something even more complicated? Something that couldn't be fixed by just love alone.

The question lingered, unanswered, as I stood there in the growing darkness, uncertain whether I was ready to face whatever truth came next. And then, just as I turned toward the window, I heard it—a knock at the door.

Chapter 28: An Oath in the Dark

I stood there, the moonlight slanting through the gaps in the curtains, casting a faint glow on the rough edges of the room. The air between us was heavy with the weight of unspoken words, yet in that silence, I felt a connection stronger than anything I had ever known. Aiden's fingers brushed mine, the touch tentative at first, as if testing the water before diving into a deeper pool of emotions. His hand, warm and sure, wrapped around mine, pulling me closer. The smell of his skin, familiar yet always intoxicating, seemed to wrap around me like a shield, making me forget for a moment everything that had led us here.

His eyes, dark and intense, flickered with something unreadable—hope, doubt, fear, or perhaps all of them combined. I couldn't tell, but I knew one thing for certain: this moment, as fragile as it felt, was ours. Nothing existed outside of it. The rest of the world—its chaos, its lies, its battles—couldn't touch us here, in this small corner of the universe, where it was just us and the promise we were about to make.

"You know, I've never been good with promises," Aiden murmured, his voice low and rough, as if it had been worn down by the weight of too many unsaid things. "Not like this. Not like... this."

I lifted my chin, meeting his gaze head-on, the corners of my lips lifting just slightly in a half-smile. "Who said we had to make perfect promises?" I replied, my voice a little breathless, the weight of his words settling in my chest. "You don't have to be perfect. You just have to be real."

He exhaled, the tension in his body easing slightly, though I could feel the battle still raging inside of him. There was always something torn in him—some jagged edge he couldn't smooth over. And I could never tell if it was the past that had left its scars, or if it was the present, this moment that we were carving out together, that made him feel so lost.

But I wasn't about to let him go. Not this time.

"I want this," I said quietly, the words rolling out before I could stop them, the raw honesty of them catching even me by surprise. "I want us. I don't care what comes next, Aiden. I just... I just need you to know that."

His lips twitched, an almost imperceptible smile, but it was there, flickering in the dark. Then he pulled me closer, his arms tightening around me, as if he were afraid I might slip away if he let go for even a second. I didn't mind. In this moment, I needed the closeness too—his heartbeat, steady and sure against mine, a reminder that we weren't completely alone in the world.

"I can't promise you the stars," he said, his breath hot against my ear, "but I can promise you this: I'll always be here. In whatever way I can."

The vulnerability in his voice made my chest tighten. Aiden wasn't someone who offered promises lightly. He didn't trust easily. And yet, here we were, tangled together in the quietest of ways, two souls seeking comfort in the storm we'd created around us. It wasn't perfect, and maybe it never would be, but somehow, the mess felt real—felt right.

I closed my eyes, letting myself feel the beat of his heart, the warmth of his touch, the reassurance that whatever happened, I wasn't walking this path alone anymore. There were still so many unanswered questions, so many shadows that lingered, but in that moment, I knew we were facing them together. And somehow, that made all the difference.

The sound of distant thunder rumbled through the night, like a warning, but I wasn't afraid. Not with him beside me. Not when I had finally allowed myself to believe in something more than the shadows lurking in the corners of my mind.

He pulled away just enough to look me in the eye, his expression softened by something deeper than mere affection. It was a look of resolve—of shared strength. "No more secrets," he promised again, his voice firm, as if staking his very soul on it.

"No more secrets," I echoed back, my voice steady and sure. And for the first time, I believed it. I believed in us.

Aiden leaned in, brushing his lips lightly against mine, the kiss soft but lingering, a silent vow carried in the touch. The kiss deepened, slow and sweet, a reminder that we still had something pure amid the chaos that surrounded us. And though the night still hung heavy with uncertainty, with danger waiting on the edge, there was a part of me that couldn't help but hope—that couldn't help but believe in the promise we had just made.

We were tangled together, not just in the physical sense, but in a way that made everything else feel distant, unimportant. The world could burn, and yet, as long as we held on to each other, it wouldn't matter.

The darkness outside our window seemed less oppressive now, as if it too was waiting, biding its time. But whatever storm was coming, I knew we would face it side by side. Together, we were stronger than the fear that threatened to consume us. Together, we could weather anything.

The days that followed felt like a delicate dance, an uncertain waltz between silence and words, between desire and fear. Aiden and I slipped into a rhythm that neither of us had expected, but somehow, it felt right. We spoke in half-sentences, knowing glances, and subtle touches, as if we were both too cautious to let go fully, to let the past settle into the present. But the trust between us had shifted. It was like standing on a precipice—both thrilling and terrifying—knowing that one step forward could either lead to freedom or fall.

The mornings were the worst. When the world outside was at its loudest, bustling with the energy of new beginnings, Aiden and I would sit in the quiet of the kitchen, our backs pressed against the old wooden chairs, the clink of coffee mugs the only sound between us. His eyes would linger on me, sometimes with a trace of something unspoken, and I'd catch myself holding my breath, wondering what was behind that look.

"I told you," he said one morning, as if speaking to the distance between us, his voice steady despite the undercurrent of tension, "I won't lie to you again. No matter what."

I didn't know if he meant it as reassurance or a warning, but I nodded, a soft exhale slipping through my lips. His promise was both a balm and a weight, pressing down in ways I hadn't yet fully processed. There was still a part of me that wondered if I was living in the calm before the storm. But in that moment, as sunlight filtered through the kitchen window, turning everything golden, I chose to believe him.

"You sure?" I asked, my voice teasing, though the question hung heavier than I intended. "You're not going to decide to start keeping secrets again? Like how you didn't tell me about your obsession with lemon bars?"

Aiden's lips quirked in a rare smile, the corner of his mouth lifting in a way that made my heart do a funny little flip. "That's not a secret. It's just... inconvenient knowledge."

"Right. Because knowing your weakness for baked goods is such an earth-shattering piece of information." I sipped my coffee, letting the cool bitterness of it ground me in the present. "But really, no more secrets? I'm going to hold you to that, you know."

He leaned forward, his eyes narrowing playfully, but there was something more intense underneath, like a storm waiting to break. "If you don't hold me to that," he said, his tone low and dangerous, "then I guess we're both in trouble."

I raised an eyebrow, unsure whether to laugh or brace myself. Aiden had a way of making everything feel like a dare, and yet there was a tenderness to his words, a vulnerability hidden beneath the bravado. It was those moments—those small, unguarded gestures—that made me feel like I was finally starting to see him, not just the man wrapped in mystery, but the person who was learning, just like me, how to trust again.

We didn't speak about the vow we'd made in the dark, but the promise hovered between us like a shadow, an invisible tether we were both afraid to break. I wondered if the silence was a blessing or a curse. There were times when I felt like it was all too much, like the weight of the world was pressing down on me. Yet, even in those moments, when my doubts threatened to take over, there was Aiden—his quiet presence a balm, his steadying hand a reminder that we weren't alone in this.

The evenings were different. As the sky darkened and the noise of the day faded, we found ourselves in the spaces where the unsaid lived, where every touch, every word, seemed to carry more weight. Our conversations were fragmented, incomplete, as though we were both waiting for something to break—waiting for the next chapter to unfold, one we weren't sure we were ready for. But in those moments, with Aiden beside me, the world outside felt irrelevant. It was just us, tangled up in our quiet understanding, our promises, and our fears.

One evening, we found ourselves walking through the streets of the city, the air cool against our skin, the scent of autumn leaves swirling around us. The world felt alive, buzzing with the energy of a thousand unseen lives, and yet we moved in sync, two people tethered to each other in ways we couldn't quite explain. I wanted to reach out and touch him, but something held me back. I could feel the undercurrent of uncertainty running between us, like an electric charge that neither of us was ready to acknowledge.

"Do you ever think about where this is all going?" I asked, my voice quiet, as though speaking louder might shatter the fragile peace we'd built. "About us, I mean?"

Aiden glanced at me, his gaze sharp, his expression unreadable for a moment before something softer flickered in his eyes. "Every day," he said simply, his words lingering in the air like a confession. "But sometimes, I think it's better to just... let it happen. See where it takes us."

I swallowed the knot in my throat, the fear of the unknown creeping back into my chest. "And what if it doesn't take us anywhere good? What if this... whatever this is... burns out like everything else?"

He stopped walking then, turning to face me fully, his hands sliding into his pockets as his eyes locked onto mine. The weight of his stare was palpable, but there was no judgment in it—only a quiet understanding. "Then we figure it out. Together."

I almost laughed, though it wasn't a laugh of amusement—it was more of a startled exhale, a soft, aching breath. Aiden's words hit me harder than I expected, the weight of them settling in my bones. It wasn't a promise, not really, but it felt like one, and that was enough. For now, it was enough.

And so we stood there, in the middle of the street, two people at the edge of something neither of us could define, and the world kept turning around us. The uncertainty, the fear—it would always be there, lurking just out of sight. But there was something else too. A glimmer of hope. A flicker of trust. And in that moment, as the wind whipped around us, I finally understood: maybe it wasn't the destination that mattered. Maybe it was the journey, the path we chose to walk together, no matter how uncertain or impossible it seemed.

The days blurred into one another, slipping away in the haze of promises we had yet to keep, but also the ones we were starting to live by. Aiden was present in a way that made my heart stutter with every glance, every touch, as though each moment we shared was a quiet rebellion against the storm we both knew was coming. It wasn't perfect, and we weren't perfect, but there was an undeniable magic in the way we found each other amid the mess of our lives.

I didn't ask about the secrets that still lingered in the corners of his past, and he didn't ask about the shadows I carried from mine. We let the quiet between us fill in the gaps, finding solace in the spaces where words weren't needed. Yet, even in the stillness, I could feel the tension pulling at the edges of our connection, a constant reminder that we couldn't outrun the truth forever. The unspoken pact we had made—no more secrets—hung over us like a fragile thread, ready to snap under the weight of whatever was yet to come.

It was on one of those rare afternoons when the sun shone through the dusty windows of the apartment, casting long shadows on the floor, that I found myself sitting on the couch, my legs tucked beneath me, absentmindedly flipping through a magazine. Aiden was at the window, his gaze fixed on the street below, his posture tense, as though waiting for something—or someone. I couldn't help but watch him, the way the light hit his features, softening the sharp edges of his jawline, making him appear less guarded, more... vulnerable.

"Hey," I called out, the casual tone belying the undercurrent of uncertainty I felt creeping into my chest. "What are you thinking about?"

He turned, his eyes flickering for a moment before his lips twitched upward, a faint smirk that didn't quite reach his eyes. "How much I'd love to throw someone out the window," he said, the wry humor in his voice failing to mask the tension in his shoulders.

I raised an eyebrow, setting the magazine down on the coffee table. "Who exactly? Or should I start worrying about my own safety?"

He chuckled, but there was an edge to it. "You know the answer to that. Don't worry, though. I'm not that desperate to make a point."

"Good," I replied, though my tone was more serious now. "But I can tell something's bothering you. So, what is it?"

He hesitated, then walked over to the couch, sitting down beside me with a careful distance between us. For a moment, neither of us spoke, the silence thick with things unspoken. I could feel the pulse of his thoughts, like they were vibrating through the air around us.

Finally, he let out a long breath and met my gaze. "It's not you. It's just... everything. There's something coming. I can feel it." His words were clipped, but the gravity behind them was unmistakable. "And it's not just about the past anymore."

I shifted on the couch, the weight of his words settling like stones in my stomach. "What do you mean?"

He turned his head slightly, his jaw working, as if chewing on a bitter thought. "I can't explain it. Not yet." His eyes softened, just a fraction, and for a moment, I saw a glimmer of something raw—something that made my chest tighten. "But I need you to trust me, even if I can't give you all the answers right now."

I swallowed hard, the uncertainty clinging to me like a second skin. "Trust is the only thing I've got left, Aiden. You know that, right?"

His hand reached out, resting lightly on my knee, the touch grounding, steady. "I know. And I'm not taking it lightly. I just... need you to hold on a little longer."

The words settled between us like a promise, but the unspoken weight of them was almost too much to bear. I wanted to ask more, to demand the answers that were dancing just beyond his reach, but something in me—something I didn't want to acknowledge—told me that pushing him wouldn't get me closer to the truth. Instead,

I nodded, hoping that the trust I was offering would be enough to carry us through whatever was coming.

The next few days passed in a tense sort of peace, a fragile balance we both tiptoed around. Aiden was more withdrawn, lost in thoughts I couldn't penetrate, and though he never shut me out completely, there was a subtle shift in the way we moved around each other. It wasn't that the love between us had faded—it was still there, simmering quietly beneath the surface. But there was something else now, an undeniable tension that gnawed at the edges of everything we did. We were both waiting for the other shoe to drop, and the anticipation of what would come next was almost unbearable.

And then it happened.

One evening, as we sat together in the dimly lit living room, the sound of a car pulling up outside broke the fragile stillness that had settled around us. Aiden's head jerked toward the window, his face draining of color.

Before I could ask what was wrong, he was on his feet, his movements quick and decisive, as if he had already known who would be arriving. His expression was hard, his jaw clenched, and the air around him seemed to vibrate with tension.

I stood up slowly, my pulse quickening as the doorbell rang, cutting through the thick silence. "Aiden?"

He didn't answer, just moved toward the door, his body rigid with something I couldn't place. I hesitated for a moment, my hand trembling slightly as I reached for the edge of the couch, wondering what was coming through that door. What part of his past was about to collide with our present?

The door swung open, and I froze.

A man stood in the doorway, tall, with a dangerous sort of elegance, his dark eyes scanning the room with an unsettling intensity. There was something about him—something familiar and yet completely foreign—that made my heart skip a beat.

Aiden's entire posture shifted. "I thought you were done with this," he said, his voice tight, controlled.

The man smiled, but it wasn't a smile meant for reassurance. "You know that's never the case."

Chapter 29: The Calm Before the Storm

There's a certain kind of magic in the quiet moments, the ones that slip by without making a sound, like a drop of water falling into a pool, sending ripples across everything without us even realizing. It's in the way the sunlight falls across the kitchen table, warming the edges of the chipped mugs as we sip our coffee in comfortable silence. I could've spent forever like that. Just us, nothing else in the world demanding our attention, no looming shadows casting doubt over the joy that seemed to radiate from every corner of our little world.

The first morning of the new routine was almost too perfect to be real. My toes barely brushed the cool tile of the kitchen floor before I felt his arms encircle me from behind. It was an ordinary embrace—except nothing about it felt ordinary. His breath, warm against my neck, was a promise I hadn't dared make to myself. I leaned back into him, letting his steady heartbeat sync with my own, the rhythm of it grounding me, reminding me of something I hadn't allowed myself to remember: that this, whatever it was, could be real.

The scent of coffee mixed with the earthy musk of his skin, and I couldn't help but close my eyes for a moment, drinking in the moment like it was a rare vintage wine. He always smelled like something indescribable. Something safe and wild all at once. A contradiction wrapped in warmth, and I wanted to keep it that way. No need to unpack it. No need to analyze it.

"I've got to run a few errands later," I said, breaking the silence as I reached for the sugar, stirring my coffee absentmindedly.

"Errands?" His voice was thick, still tangled in the last vestiges of sleep.

I could hear the smirk, even without looking at him. "I'm still a human being, you know. The world doesn't stop just because we're... occupied." I shot him a teasing look over my shoulder.

He snorted, half-laughing, half-disbelieving. "Occupied. You mean your idea of 'busy' is lying in bed with me and pretending we're not both running away from our responsibilities?"

I chuckled. "Hey, no judgment. This is your fault, remember? You're the one who decided to corrupt my perfectly balanced life."

He leaned down to place a kiss against the top of my head, his voice soft but serious. "I don't think I could have corrupted you if I tried. You were always this way—complicated, layered. Just… waiting for the right person to figure it out."

I scoffed, though I couldn't help the way my heart fluttered at the sentiment. "You're far too generous with your praise. I'm a mess."

He didn't argue, just pressed his lips to my ear in that way that made my pulse pick up, as though he were claiming me in the most subtle of ways. "Maybe, but you're my mess."

And just like that, the world outside the kitchen faded, the world where things went wrong and people broke apart. Here, in the quiet sanctuary of our tiny home, I allowed myself to believe that we might be one of the lucky ones, the ones who beat the odds.

But, of course, life is a relentless teacher. And as much as I wished to linger in the soft bubble of this moment, I knew I couldn't. No matter how much we tried to outrun the dark, it would always catch up. And even if we fought, even if we made this work somehow, the storm that was circling around us—too quiet, too steady—would eventually make its presence known.

The first sign was almost imperceptible, the way his brow furrowed slightly when his phone buzzed. I pretended not to notice. It wasn't the kind of thing I wanted to acknowledge, not now, when we were so carefully crafting this illusion of peace. But it was there, hanging in the air, like the low hum of an oncoming storm.

"I should get that," he said, his fingers brushing the back of my hand before he let go.

I turned my attention back to my coffee, willing my body to remain still, to not betray the churn of emotions inside. There was no reason to be jealous of a phone call, no reason to imagine the worst. But my instincts, those old, jagged things, didn't listen to reason.

He stepped into the next room, closing the door behind him with a soft click that resonated far too loudly in the otherwise silent house. And for a moment, I was alone with the thick tension in my chest, the one that had crept in like an uninvited guest, a warning. I didn't want to admit it, but I couldn't shake the feeling that something was coming. Something big.

The door to the kitchen swung open again, and he returned with a look I couldn't quite read, his expression a little too guarded, a little too careful. He didn't meet my eyes immediately, his focus trained on the coffee pot as he took the last of it, all the while avoiding my gaze.

"You okay?" I asked, unable to keep the concern from my voice, even as I wished I could bury it deep down where it couldn't reach me.

He hesitated, then nodded. "Yeah. Just a little business stuff. Nothing to worry about."

I didn't believe him, but I didn't push either. Instead, I chose to take his word for it—this time. It wasn't about trust. It was about preserving what little calm we had left.

We couldn't escape the storm forever, no matter how hard we tried. And as the silence stretched between us, I realized the truth: the storm wasn't waiting for us to be ready. It would come, with or without our permission.

The afternoon sun poured through the open window, its golden fingers tracing the curve of his jaw, casting him in a soft, haloed light. It made him look almost too perfect, like a piece of art I could never quite capture, no matter how many times I tried to memorize the lines of his face. The way his eyes crinkled when he laughed. The way the corners of his lips tilted up as if he knew something I didn't, and wasn't in a hurry to tell me.

"You know," I said, my voice a little too loud, a little too eager, "I think the day is officially perfect. I mean, it's not often I get to sit here on a Wednesday afternoon, doing nothing but enjoying the view and a good book."

He raised an eyebrow, casting me a sideways glance from across the room. "A good book? Are we still pretending that book is more interesting than my company?"

I put the novel down on the table, a playful glint in my eye. "Well, I have to admit, the plot has more twists than I'm used to. But you do make a compelling argument. Perhaps I should give you my full attention for a while."

His lips curved into that smile—the one that made everything else blur. "I'm a fan of full attention."

I laughed, but it felt a little strained. There was something in his tone, a slight undercurrent of tension that my mind couldn't quite place. It had become a familiar pattern. We'd fall into these stretches of lightheartedness, only for a crack in the facade to show itself—something unspoken, something waiting in the wings.

I glanced at him, watching as he leaned back in his chair, looking almost too at ease. There was no denying how much I'd come to rely on his presence, how much I'd let myself enjoy this false sense of normal. But what exactly was this? A lull? A detour from whatever it was we'd been running from? The calm before the storm, as I'd called it earlier.

I could feel it now, the shift. Like a breath held too long, the world holding its collective inhale, waiting.

"So, what's really on your mind?" I asked, my voice quiet but pointed.

His fingers drummed absently against the armrest. "Nothing. Just thinking."

"About?"

"About... everything." He didn't meet my eyes. Instead, his gaze traveled toward the window, as if something outside was going to offer an answer he hadn't found inside.

I leaned forward, my elbows on my knees, watching him closely. "It's not nothing, though, is it? You're not that good of an actor. What's bothering you?"

For a long moment, he said nothing. His jaw worked slightly, as if he were deciding whether to speak or to keep his thoughts locked away where I couldn't reach them. But I wasn't going to let him slide past me this time. Not when something was shifting between us, threatening to break.

"I don't want to drag you into this," he finally said, his voice low, almost apologetic.

That, right there, was a red flag. I knew it. I felt it in my bones. Whenever someone says they don't want to drag you into something, it's usually too late. They've already dragged you into it. And once it's said, that space between them and you, no matter how small, feels like a chasm.

"You're not dragging me into anything," I replied, trying to keep my voice steady, though I could feel the edges of panic creeping in. "You're just telling me what's going on."

His eyes flicked over to mine, and for a brief moment, I saw something there—something raw, something unguarded. But just as quickly, it was gone. Replaced by a mask of indifference.

"It's nothing that concerns you," he said, this time the words a little sharper, more final. "Just some... complications. Stuff from my past. It's better if you don't get involved."

Complications. Stuff from his past. My gut twisted. I had no idea what he was talking about, but the very fact that he was trying to keep it from me meant it wasn't something trivial. It was something serious. Something dangerous.

I stood up, the sudden shift in my body language not lost on him. "I don't believe you," I said quietly, my voice more confident than I felt. "You're not the only one with a past. But if there's something going on, something that could affect both of us... then we need to talk about it."

He shook his head, his fingers gripping the edge of the chair, knuckles going white. "Not yet. It's too soon. Let's just... stay here for a little longer. Pretend nothing's wrong."

I took a step toward him, my breath steady, though my heart was racing. "I don't want to pretend. I want the truth. I want to know what you're hiding."

He stood up suddenly, his chair scraping harshly against the floor. "I'm not hiding anything."

But his voice didn't sound convincing, and the way his eyes avoided mine told a different story. "Look," I said, my voice softening. "Whatever this is, we can handle it. But only if we face it together. I'm not going to sit back and watch you unravel without doing something."

He stared at me for a long time, the tension between us thick, and for a fleeting second, I thought he might let me in. Might let me help him shoulder whatever weight he was carrying.

But then he turned away, his face set in that familiar expression of resolve. "Not today, okay? Not today."

And just like that, the distance between us grew once more, leaving me standing there, feeling more alone than I had before. The calm had broken, and I knew, deep down, the storm was no longer a matter of if—it was a matter of when.

The night was quieter than usual, the kind of stillness that makes you wonder if something is about to happen. I lay in bed, staring at the shadows dancing on the ceiling, listening to the soft rhythm of his breathing beside me. It was comforting, the way we had settled into this routine, as though we had found a space carved out just for us, away from everything else. But even in the warmth of his arm around me, I couldn't shake the feeling that something wasn't quite right.

I shifted, trying to find a more comfortable position, my mind still racing, but my body heavy with the pull of sleep. The room was dark, save for the faint glow of moonlight spilling in from the window, casting a silver hue across the furniture. I could feel the weight of his presence beside me, the quiet pulse of his warmth, but I still couldn't get rid of the feeling that something was about to change.

"Can't sleep?" His voice broke the silence, low and sleepy, as he tightened his hold on me just a little.

I pressed my face into the pillow, trying to ignore the unease gnawing at me. "Just thinking."

"About?"

I hesitated, unsure of how to articulate what I was feeling. It was one of those moments when you know something's wrong but can't quite put your finger on it. It was the way the air felt too thick, too full of unspoken things. The way the calmness between us felt fragile, like it could break apart with a single wrong word.

"I don't know," I murmured, rolling onto my back to look at the ceiling. "It's just... there's this feeling. Like everything's too quiet."

He didn't respond right away, and I felt the tension in his body, his muscles stiffening beneath the sheets. It was subtle, but it was there. The silence between us grew, pressing in on me, and I felt the weight of it.

"I don't like it either," he finally said, his voice tight. "But we can't keep looking over our shoulders forever."

"I know," I said, my voice barely a whisper. "But I'm not looking over my shoulder. I'm just... waiting."

"For what?"

The question hung in the air, charged with something I couldn't name. His eyes locked onto mine, searching, as if waiting for me to give him the answer he needed, or perhaps the one he feared. I could feel his breath on my skin, steady but with an underlying tension that mirrored my own.

"I don't know," I said again, this time the words sounding hollow, like I was speaking them into a void. "But I feel like something is coming. I can't explain it, but it's like the calm is just a pause before… something else."

He sat up, running a hand through his hair in frustration. "We can't keep living like this, you know. Worrying about everything, about what's coming. It's not healthy."

I propped myself up on my elbows, meeting his gaze with a new resolve. "It's not about being healthy. It's about being prepared. You might be able to pretend it's all fine, but I can't. Not when I know there's something out there, something you're not telling me."

His face went cold. "You don't know anything."

My heart skipped a beat, the words like ice against my skin. The distance between us grew, the space that had once been filled with easy laughter and quiet intimacy now crackling with tension. "Don't do that," I said, my voice low but firm. "Don't shut me out."

He looked away, his jaw clenched. "It's not about shutting you out. It's about keeping you safe. From things you don't understand."

I took a deep breath, trying to steady myself. The air in the room felt suffocating, the weight of his secrets pressing down on me. I had been patient, I had waited, but I could feel my patience wearing thin. "I can handle it," I said, my voice almost pleading, though I hated the vulnerability that slipped through. "Whatever it is, we can face it together. But you have to tell me."

There was a long silence before he finally spoke, his voice tight and strained. "I wish I could. But some things aren't mine to tell."

"Whose are they?" I asked, my heart pounding in my chest. "If it affects both of us, then it's ours, isn't it?"

He shook his head, running a hand over his face in frustration. "I can't explain it right now. I just can't."

I sat up fully, the sheets falling away from my shoulders. "Then you'll have to live with this. With the fact that you're not being honest with me. And that's something I can't ignore."

His eyes flashed with something like anger, but it was gone as quickly as it appeared. He stood up from the bed, pacing across the room with quick, sharp steps. I watched him, feeling the distance between us growing with every movement, every unspoken word.

"This isn't easy for me either," he said after a moment, his voice rough. "But you don't understand. You don't know what you're asking of me."

I wanted to say something, to push him, to demand answers, but the words caught in my throat. Instead, I just sat there, watching him. Watching him struggle with something he wasn't ready to share, something that could tear us apart if I knew the truth.

The silence was thick between us, louder than any words could ever be. My breath came faster, and I could feel my pulse in my ears, pounding. Whatever was happening, whatever he wasn't telling me, it was breaking us. Slowly, surely, the storm was arriving, and no matter how hard we tried to ignore it, it was going to tear through everything we'd built.

I opened my mouth to speak, but before I could, there was a sudden knock at the door.

And just like that, everything we had been avoiding was standing on the other side.

Chapter 30: Shattered Promises

The rain pounded against the windows, a constant, furious drumbeat that matched the turmoil swirling inside me. I sat there, unmoving, as the air around me grew thick with tension. Aiden was standing by the door, his silhouette framed by the dim light spilling in from the hallway. His voice was the first thing I'd heard in what felt like hours, but the words he spoke were foreign to me. They didn't belong to the man I thought I knew. The man I thought I loved.

"Is this how you want it?" His voice cracked, just barely. It should have been the smallest of signs, the kind of thing that would have stopped me in my tracks if I wasn't so consumed by the wreckage of the moment. But I couldn't seem to find the part of myself that still cared enough to react.

I stared at him, the space between us stretching impossibly wide. His face, once so familiar, now seemed as alien as a stranger's. There was guilt there, yes, but also something else—something colder, sharper. Maybe it was the flicker of regret, or maybe it was just the weariness that comes from knowing you've done something unforgivable. Whatever it was, I couldn't bear it. I couldn't bear him.

I tried to speak, but the words clogged in my throat. The anger that had been simmering inside me, buried under layers of confusion, bubbled to the surface. My fists clenched at my sides, nails digging into my palms, and I could feel my heart pounding in my chest, not with the wild thrum of love, but with the cold, sharp sting of betrayal.

"You told me you would never hurt me like this," I finally managed, my voice low, but carrying a weight it had never known. "You said you would always protect me, that we were in this together. But now—now I find out you've been lying to me all along?"

His face twisted, the familiar expression of remorse now a stranger. He took a step toward me, but I instinctively backed away, as if his proximity was somehow a tangible thing that could smother me. I couldn't let him close, not now. Not after everything.

"I didn't want to hurt you," he said, his voice strained, like he was choking on the words, but I wasn't convinced. I wasn't sure I ever could be again. "This wasn't supposed to happen. You have to believe me, it was never meant to go this far."

"Go this far?" I repeated, incredulous. The words stung, and I wondered if he even realized how insulting they were. "It went too far the moment you made your choice. The moment you decided to lie to me." My breath caught as I said it out loud, the full weight of his betrayal settling like a stone in my gut.

I watched his hands clench at his sides, his jaw tightening as though he was trying to keep himself in check. But all I saw was a man who had lost control long before this moment, a man who had been playing a part for far too long. It was as if the Aiden I thought I knew had been an illusion, a carefully crafted story I had believed in with all my heart. But now the truth was unraveling, and there was no way to put it back together.

"I never wanted you to find out like this," he murmured, his eyes dropping to the floor. "I thought—god, I thought I could make it right. But I was wrong."

I shook my head, a bitter laugh escaping before I could stop it. "You thought you could make it right?" I repeated, disbelieving. "How? By continuing to lie to me? By making me believe that everything was fine while you were—while you were doing that?"

My voice faltered, the word 'that' hanging in the air like a poisoned arrow, but I didn't want to dignify it with any more specifics. The pain was too raw. The betrayal too vast.

"I never meant for you to find out this way," he repeated, his voice desperate now. "Please, just—please, listen to me."

But I couldn't. I couldn't listen anymore. The words were too much, too loaded with things I wasn't prepared to hear. Things I didn't want to understand. His guilt was suffocating, but it wasn't enough. It would never be enough to undo what he'd done.

I turned away from him, my gaze drawn to the rain streaking down the glass. I used to find comfort in storms—the wildness, the chaos—but now it felt like a mirror to the storm inside me.

"You should have told me the truth," I said, my voice tight with something raw and bitter. "Instead of dragging me through this, making me believe in a future that was never really ours to begin with."

I felt the weight of his stare on the back of my neck, but I didn't dare look back. Not yet. Not while everything I had believed in was crumbling to dust.

There was a long silence before he spoke again, his voice smaller, quieter, like a man who knew he had nothing left to fight with. "I'm sorry," he whispered. The words fell into the air like useless coins tossed at the feet of a beggar.

I didn't answer him. I didn't think I ever would again.

I couldn't escape the gnawing sensation that something inside me had been irrevocably broken, that no amount of time or apology would ever put it back together. I wanted to run, to escape this suffocating room, to breathe air that wasn't heavy with the bitterness of his betrayal. But my feet were glued to the floor, as though the storm outside had wrapped its furious tendrils around me, holding me captive just like Aiden had.

He moved closer, his voice desperate in a way that made me want to claw at my own skin. "Can we just talk about this?" The words came out ragged, like a man pleading for his life.

I didn't turn to face him. Instead, I kept my back to him, the cold edge of the window at my fingertips, as if it might offer some semblance of relief. But even the glass felt too hot, too tight with the weight of everything unsaid between us.

"You've talked enough," I muttered, my voice hardly more than a whisper. "I don't think anything you say will fix this. Not anymore."

I could hear him move, the sound of his footsteps tentative, as though testing the ground beneath him. As though if he approached carefully enough, he could somehow undo the damage. He could make me feel like the woman who had once curled up in his arms, safe in the promise of forever.

But I wasn't that woman anymore. I wasn't even sure who I was, standing here with my heart turned to stone and my trust shattered into a thousand jagged pieces.

"I never wanted to hurt you," he repeated, each word slicing through the silence between us like a blade.

His words hovered in the air, heavy with the weight of regret, but I was no longer interested in the sound of them. Regret didn't change what had happened. It didn't change the truth. I could feel my pulse throbbing in my neck, a sharp reminder that I was still alive, still breathing, despite the suffocating ache inside me.

"Do you think that's enough?" I asked, my voice growing sharper as the rawness inside me began to surface. "Do you really think you can just say 'sorry' and it makes everything okay? That we can just pretend like nothing's changed?"

He was close enough now that I could feel the warmth of his presence, and despite the way I tried to distance myself, something in me longed to close the gap. To forget what had happened, even just for a second. But I knew better. I knew that the cracks were already too deep to ignore.

Aiden's voice wavered, the usual confidence now completely stripped away. "I was stupid," he admitted, his tone barely audible. "I was selfish, and I messed everything up."

Selfish. The word burned its way into my mind, a constant reminder of how little he'd thought of me. I was left standing here, bruised by the selfishness of the man I had once believed would protect me from the world.

"Selfish doesn't even begin to cover it," I said, my words dripping with contempt. "You didn't just think about yourself. You thought about what you could get away with, about how far you could push me before I would catch on. You took my love, my trust, and you played with it like it was nothing."

I could see him flinch, the guilt flashing across his face, but I didn't feel satisfaction from it. Not anymore. His regret didn't heal the wound he had opened.

"You have no idea what it's like," I continued, my voice shaking with emotion, "to believe in someone, to think that they are everything you ever wanted—and then to find out they never truly cared. They were never really with you at all."

There was a long silence, and for a moment, I thought maybe he was going to speak again, try to make it right, try to convince me that it hadn't been intentional, that it wasn't as bad as it seemed. But the silence stretched on, thick and suffocating.

And then, just as the tension began to drown me, Aiden spoke, his voice softer now, the hardness gone. "I wish I could take it all back."

I closed my eyes, a bitter laugh escaping me before I could stop it. "You can't. No one can. And that's the problem, Aiden. You can't undo this. You can't change what you did."

I wanted him to understand. I needed him to. But part of me wondered if he ever could. How could he truly grasp the devastation he'd caused? The life we had built, the future we had shared, were now nothing more than smoke and mirrors, illusions shattered by his selfishness.

Aiden's footsteps came closer again, but I couldn't bring myself to turn around. Not when the world I had known was slipping through my fingers like sand.

"Please," he whispered, his voice now laced with desperation, "don't walk away from me."

I shook my head, a tear slipping down my cheek, a painful reminder that I was still human, still capable of feeling, despite how much I wanted to shut it all out. "You walked away from me a long time ago," I whispered back, more to myself than to him.

And for the first time in what felt like forever, I felt something stir deep inside me—a flicker of freedom, the first hint of space to breathe without the weight of his lies smothering me.

I didn't know where I would go from here, or if I could ever trust again, but I knew one thing for certain: Aiden was no longer the man I had once loved. And as much as it hurt, I had to let go.

The air was heavy with the weight of unsaid things, and I could feel the silence pressing in on me, the storm outside only amplifying the chaos inside. I didn't want to look at him anymore, didn't want to hear the pleading in his voice that only twisted the knife deeper. He had taken everything I thought I knew and shattered it with a few careless actions—actions that were now laid bare for me to see. And I couldn't unsee them.

I turned away, moving slowly, deliberately, as though each step took me further from the wreckage of the life I thought we'd built. Aiden's voice called after me, but I ignored it, focusing on the rhythm of my breathing, the pulse in my ears, anything to block him out.

"You're not the only one hurting," he called, a desperation creeping into his words. "I'm not the only one who's lost something here!"

I stopped, my fingers curling around the edge of the counter as if I could hold onto something solid, something real. But all I had now was this—this fractured version of a man I used to know. A man who had already broken me once and was now asking for my forgiveness, as if he hadn't done enough to destroy everything in his path.

"You think I don't know that?" I finally said, turning to face him, my voice low, edged with fury. "You think I don't feel the pieces of my heart splintering every time I think about what you did? You don't get to pull the 'we're both hurting' card, Aiden. Not when you're the one who set the whole thing on fire."

I saw the flash of guilt cross his face before it was quickly masked by something else—something colder, more guarded. "You're right. I hurt you. But I never wanted this. You've got to understand—"

"I don't need to understand!" My chest tightened as the words escaped, more forceful than I intended. "I don't need you to explain why you thought it was okay to lie to me. What I need, Aiden, is for you to stop pretending that I'm the only one who lost something here."

He took a step forward, and I instinctively took one back, not out of fear, but out of sheer exhaustion. "I'm sorry," he said, his eyes softer now, almost pleading. "I was stupid. I never thought—"

"You never thought," I repeated bitterly. "That's the problem, isn't it? You never thought about what we built, what we meant. And now you want me to just forget it all? Like it was nothing?"

I could see him struggling with something, trying to find the words that might fix everything, but the more he spoke, the more I realized there was nothing left to fix. I had already given him everything. Everything I had, I had handed over willingly, trusting him with pieces of myself I had never shared with anyone. And now, those pieces were scattered, torn, and irreparably damaged.

"I don't know how to fix this," he said finally, his voice barely more than a whisper. His words were raw, vulnerable, but they weren't enough. Not anymore. "But I will try. I will do anything. Just... please don't walk away."

I looked at him then, really looked at him, and saw not the man I had fallen in love with, but someone else—a stranger wrapped in guilt and regret. The sadness in his eyes, the frustration in his posture, it was all there, but it couldn't change the fact that he had already made his choice. And I was no longer sure that I was the person he even wanted in the first place.

"You don't get to decide if I walk away," I said, my voice steady now. "That's not your choice anymore."

For a long moment, neither of us moved. The storm outside still raged, its fury matched only by the turbulence between us. I felt a familiar pang of sadness deep in my chest—sadness for the person I had been before this moment, before all the lies had come crashing down. For the woman who had believed in love, who had been certain that trust was enough to keep everything intact. But that woman was gone, swept away like dust in the wind.

Aiden seemed to realize it too. His shoulders slumped, the fight draining out of him as the reality of my words settled in. "So that's it then?" he asked, his voice quiet. "You're just going to walk away, without even trying?"

"I've tried, Aiden," I whispered, shaking my head. "I've tried for so long, and now I'm just... done."

I turned, the weight of my decision pressing on me with the force of the storm itself. I didn't know where I was going, didn't know what came next, but for the first time in what felt like forever, I felt a small, fragile glimmer of freedom.

But before I could make my escape, there was a sharp knock at the door. Aiden froze, his eyes darting toward the sound, then back to me, confusion and fear flickering in his gaze.

I didn't want to answer it. I didn't want to deal with whatever it was, whoever it was, at this moment. But the knock came again, more insistent this time. Something about the urgency in it made me hesitate, made me wonder if maybe it was fate stepping in to interrupt this unbearable goodbye.

Aiden moved toward the door, his hand hovering just over the knob, but before he could open it, I stopped him.

"Aiden," I said, my voice trembling, "what if this is the end? What if there's nothing left for us to fix?"

He looked at me, his eyes dark with emotion, but the door was calling. And so was the future, even if it was one I hadn't yet begun to understand.

He glanced back at the door, then back to me, as if searching for something in my face. Finally, he gave a soft, almost resigned sigh, and opened it.

What I saw standing there, though, made everything else seem small in comparison.

Chapter 31: Unmasking the Enemy

The house smelled of pine and damp wood, the scent of old books mixing with the faint tang of tea leaves, but it did nothing to settle the storm raging inside me. The fire crackled in the hearth, the flames dancing wildly as though mocking my every thought. I stared into the flickering light, seeing nothing but the jagged shards of a life I once thought whole, the pieces now scattered beyond repair. Aiden had been my anchor—steady, strong, my constant in a world that seemed to teeter on the edge of chaos. But it wasn't the world that was tipping, it was everything I had believed in. The weight of the truth had settled over me, heavy and suffocating, and no matter how hard I tried to ignore it, I knew I couldn't walk away from the mess it had left behind.

The letter was the first clue, a tattered envelope slipped beneath the door late one night, its paper rough and old, as though it had been hidden for years. No return address. No name. Only a single sentence scrawled across the front in dark ink: "You've been looking in the wrong places." That was it. Just that. My heart had skipped a beat, the kind of skip that only comes when you've just uncovered something you weren't ready for. But I had no choice but to dive in.

I remember sitting at the kitchen table with the letter in front of me, staring at it until the edges of the paper blurred in my vision. I hadn't realized how much I needed this—needed something to make sense of everything that had crumbled around me. Every morning, I had woken up with the hollow ache of betrayal gnawing at my stomach, but I hadn't known where to direct that ache, hadn't known how to channel it into something that might offer me a sliver of clarity. Until now. Until this letter.

So I'd started with the letter, following its cryptic hint to the shadows I hadn't dared to peek into before. The next few days were a blur of sleepless nights, frantic calls, and trail after trail leading me further into the murky depths of my family's past. The more I uncovered, the worse it became. At first, it was just whispers—old rumors of affairs, questionable investments, and hidden debts—but it wasn't long before I found myself staring at names I hadn't heard in years. People I thought were long gone, buried in the past. But they weren't gone. They were still here, weaving a web around me, pulling the strings from places I never suspected.

I had learned the hard way that nothing—nothing at all—was ever as it seemed.

But the real blow came when I saw the name I had once trusted more than my own. My father's closest friend. The man who had always smiled just a little too wide, his voice just a little too smooth. I had never questioned him before. It had never crossed my mind. But when I found his signature on documents that linked him to every disaster my family had suffered, when I saw the thread of his influence woven through every bad decision, every shattered dream, the world shifted under my feet. My father had been blind, or perhaps just too kind. Too willing to believe in the goodness of people when, in truth, it had all been a lie.

I spent the next few days gathering evidence, running from one place to another, piecing together a portrait of deception I couldn't even begin to process. All the while, my thoughts kept returning to Aiden. I didn't know what to do with him. How could I explain to him that the very people who had promised to protect us had been the ones who brought us to the brink of ruin? The thought of losing him in this mess was almost more than I could bear. But if I didn't uncover the full extent of the damage, if I didn't find the last pieces of this twisted puzzle, how could I ever trust anyone again? How could I expect him to trust me?

One late afternoon, I sat on the edge of my bed, eyes scanning the latest batch of papers in front of me. The room was growing dark, the last of the sunlight retreating behind the mountains, casting long shadows across the floor. My head ached, the weight of the day's discoveries too much to bear. But I wasn't ready to stop. I couldn't stop. I had come too far.

That's when I found it. A ledger, tucked away in the back of an old drawer in my father's study, its pages yellowed with age. It was a financial record, an account of dealings that had been hidden for decades. As I flipped through the brittle pages, something caught my eye. A name. A single, familiar name.

Aiden's.

It was impossible. It didn't make sense. How could he be connected to this? But as I looked closer, the puzzle pieces clicked into place. The money transfers. The signatures. The shadowy meetings. My heart pounded in my chest as I realized the truth I had been avoiding: Aiden had known. He had been part of it. Not willingly, but still. He had been too close to the storm, too entangled in the lies. He hadn't told me. He hadn't trusted me with this. And that—more than anything else—was what stung the most.

I slammed the ledger shut, the sound sharp in the quiet room. My mind raced. There had to be a reason. I had to confront him, to ask him, to understand. But as I reached for the door, a voice stopped me.

"It's not what you think."

I turned, heart skipping again, as Aiden stood in the doorway, his face ashen, eyes wide with something—regret? Fear? Maybe both.

"Then explain it to me," I whispered, my voice breaking. "Please, explain it all."

The silence between us was thick, heavy with years of unspoken truths and the weight of everything I thought I knew. Aiden stood in the doorway, not entering, just watching me like I was some fragile thing that might break at any second. His face was pale, his lips set in a line that I hadn't seen in so long. It made me ache, deep in a place I didn't even know was still capable of hurting.

"You don't get to do this," I said, the words sharp despite the tremor in my voice. "Not after everything. Not after what you've kept from me."

His eyes flickered with something—guilt, fear, regret. Maybe all of it, rolled up together in a package I didn't want to open. But I had no choice. I wasn't going to let him hide behind silence any longer. I wasn't going to let him turn this into another mystery I had to solve alone.

"Aiden," I said again, more forceful this time. "Tell me the truth."

He took a step forward, his broad shoulders hunched as if the weight of his own secrets was too much to bear. But he didn't speak. Instead, he reached into his jacket pocket, pulling out a crumpled piece of paper. It was old, the edges curled, the ink faded in places. My stomach clenched. This was it. The moment I'd been dreading. The moment where everything I thought I knew about us—about him—would unravel.

"I should've told you," Aiden said, his voice low, almost strained. "But I thought I could protect you. I thought... I thought you didn't need to be part of this."

I stared at him, the pieces of the puzzle still clicking in my mind, the ledger still fresh in my thoughts. "Protect me?" I scoffed, the bitterness slipping out before I could stop it. "You've been keeping me in the dark this whole time, and you thought that was protecting me?"

He winced, and I hated that I had the power to hurt him, but right now, I couldn't bring myself to care. The truth was a living thing between us, and I wasn't about to let it slink back into the shadows.

He took another step closer, and I could see how his hands were shaking now. "It's not like you think. I never wanted this. I never wanted any of it. But I was already too deep. And when you found out, when you started looking... I knew there was no going back."

I was so tired. So damn tired of the lies, of the half-truths and the things left unsaid. "You don't get to pull me into your mess and then act like I'm the one who's wrong for asking questions."

The paper trembled in his hand as he slowly unfolded it, revealing a name I'd hoped I'd never see again—my father's name. My heart lurched, but I forced myself to focus. This wasn't about my father, not anymore. This was about Aiden. This was about us.

"What is this?" I demanded, but my voice had turned cold, detached, even as it shook.

Aiden exhaled slowly, running a hand through his hair as if he couldn't stand the weight of my gaze. "It's the last thing I could find. The last piece of the puzzle."

I grabbed the paper from his hand before he could stop me, my fingers trembling as I read the faded ink. The words blurred in front of my eyes, but I made myself focus, reading them again and again until they finally sank in.

There it was. The link between everything. The missing thread that had connected Aiden to the very people who had been destroying us from the inside. My father's investments. The shady dealings. The names on the ledger. Aiden's name was right there, buried under so many others, but it was there. It had always been there. I felt like I'd been punched in the gut.

"You were part of this? You were involved with them?" I whispered, not trusting myself to say it louder. Because the more I read, the more I understood—he had known. He had been tangled in all of it.

"No," Aiden said quickly, his hands raised in surrender, but the look on his face told me everything. "Not in the way you're thinking. Not in the way you want to believe. I didn't have a choice, okay? There's more to it than you realize."

I shook my head, my breath coming fast now. My pulse thrummed in my ears, a deafening roar. "How could you let this happen? How could you not tell me? How could you stand by and watch me—us—fall apart?"

His eyes softened with something like guilt, but it didn't ease the pain, didn't take away the betrayal that had settled so deeply in my chest. "I never wanted to hurt you. You have to believe that." His voice cracked, and I saw the boy I had fallen in love with—the one who had kissed me under the stars, the one who had made me laugh when I thought I would never stop crying. He was still there, but buried beneath the weight of secrets and lies. And the worst part was, I didn't know if I could forgive him. I didn't know if I could ever trust him again.

"I don't know what to believe anymore," I murmured, my heart heavy with the truth I didn't want to face. "I don't know what's real."

His face twisted in pain, and I saw the vulnerability in him I hadn't seen in years. "I'm not asking you to forgive me. I'm asking you to see the whole picture. To understand what I did, why I did it. I never meant to hurt you. Never."

I wanted to scream at him, to throw the paper in his face and demand he fix it, but instead, I stood there, paralyzed by the weight of it all. His presence in the room, so close, but so far away, was suffocating. Everything I thought I knew—everything I thought I understood about us—was slipping through my fingers like sand.

"I need time," I said finally, the words barely above a whisper. "I need time to figure this out."

Aiden nodded, his shoulders slumping in defeat, but he didn't fight me. He knew, just as I did, that there was no easy answer to this. And maybe, just maybe, there never would be again.

The days that followed were an exercise in holding my breath, in trying to live in a world where the floor could drop out from under me at any moment. I avoided Aiden. I didn't know how to look at him, let alone speak to him. I needed space. I needed to breathe without the weight of his secrets suffocating me. Every time he called, I let the phone ring until it stopped. His messages, his desperate pleas for me to talk to him, piled up in my inbox, but I ignored them all. The silence between us was deafening, but it was also the only thing I could rely on in that moment.

The only thing I trusted was the truth, and even that felt like it was slipping through my fingers. The more I looked into it, the darker it became. Every corner I turned, another layer of deceit. It wasn't just Aiden. It was everyone. My father, his associates—there were more people involved in this than I had ever known. People I had trusted. People who had smiled at me, told me everything was going to be fine, while hiding their knives just out of sight.

The world had been a stage, and I had been the naive, unsuspecting audience. The anger, the betrayal—everything felt like an open wound that refused to heal. And yet, as I stood in front of the mirror that morning, staring at the reflection of someone I barely recognized, I knew what I had to do.

The sound of the knock on the door was sharp, startling in the stillness of the room. My heart skipped, but I didn't jump. I didn't want to. I didn't want to feel anything for anyone right now, least of all Aiden. He had crossed a line, and no amount of apologizing or pleading was going to take that away. Not when I was still unraveling the knot of his betrayal, not when I was still trying to stitch together the remains of my family.

But when I opened the door, it wasn't Aiden standing there.

It was my father's old friend. The man whose name I had seen on the ledger. The one whose smile I had always found just a little too wide, a little too perfect.

"Can we talk?" he asked, his voice smooth, unsettling in its calmness.

I wanted to slam the door in his face. I wanted to scream. I wanted to pretend I didn't see the threads that connected him to everything that had been torn apart in my life. But something kept me from shutting him out. Maybe it was the sheer audacity of his appearance, showing up like nothing had changed. Maybe it was the tiny voice in my head that whispered that this was it—the final piece of the puzzle.

"What do you want?" I managed, my voice barely above a whisper, my stomach clenching as the familiar tension crept up my spine.

"I think you know why I'm here," he said, his eyes narrowing slightly. "You've uncovered the truth. But there's more to it than you realize. And I think you're going to want to hear it."

I stood there for a moment, my mind racing. There were a thousand questions I wanted to ask, a thousand things I wanted to scream at him, but I knew I had to be careful. This wasn't just about Aiden anymore. This was about something bigger. Something deeper. And I wasn't going to let him walk away without giving me the answers I needed.

I stepped aside, not saying a word, and motioned for him to come in. He entered, his polished shoes clicking against the hardwood floor, his sharp, tailored suit almost too perfect. He looked like a man who had never once had to worry about consequences. A man who thought he could get away with anything.

"Sit," I said, gesturing to the armchair in front of me. I didn't want to show him any respect, but I knew this conversation was inevitable. I needed to hear him out, no matter how much I hated it.

He sat down, smoothing his suit with practiced elegance. "You've been digging, I see," he said, his tone still that unsettlingly smooth one, like everything was a game. "And I suppose you're wondering why I didn't come to you sooner. Why I let all of this play out the way it did."

I didn't answer him. I didn't need to. I could feel the weight of his words like a cold hand on my chest, suffocating me.

"I thought I could keep you out of it," he continued, his eyes now fixed on me. "You're a smart girl. Too smart, really. But you weren't supposed to find out this way. It was supposed to be cleaner. I thought I could keep you protected, but the truth is—" He paused, a flicker of something like regret flashing across his face before it was gone. "You were always going to find out. And now that you have, there's no turning back."

My heart thudded in my chest. "What are you talking about?" I asked, my voice tight, barely a whisper.

"The people you trust... they weren't the ones pulling the strings. The ones who've been controlling everything? They've been right under your nose this whole time." His smile was tight, almost amused. "I suppose you thought Aiden was the problem. But no. No, the truth is far worse than that."

I stood, the room spinning as everything inside me froze. "What do you mean?"

He leaned forward, his voice dropping to a whisper. "Aiden... wasn't the one who sold you out."

I blinked, my breath catching in my throat as the words sank in. My mind raced, trying to make sense of what he was saying, but nothing made sense anymore.

Before I could respond, before I could process anything, the door behind me slammed open. My heart stopped in my chest as I turned.

Aiden stood there, his face pale, his eyes wide with something that looked like fear. "You don't know what you're dealing with," he said, his voice hoarse.

And that was when I knew, for certain, that everything had changed.

Chapter 32: Rising from the Ashes

The rain was a heavy curtain of silver as it fell in sheets, washing the dust from the pavement and turning the streets into rivers of murky water. It was as if the world itself was holding its breath, bracing for something monumental. I stepped out into the downpour, my boots sinking slightly into the soaked ground with each step. My jacket clung to my back, the damp fabric a constant reminder of how far I'd come to get here. The cold air stung my cheeks, but it wasn't the chill of the storm that made my skin prickle—it was the anticipation, the raw, unfiltered need to finally put everything into words.

Aiden's house stood like an island, looming ahead, the lights in the windows soft and inviting. But I knew better than to be lulled by its warmth. This place had been our battleground, our sanctuary, and now—what was it? A ruin, perhaps. A place where we'd once dreamed of forever but now stood as the backdrop to an inevitable confrontation. The door was slightly ajar when I reached it, as if fate itself had opened the way for me, or perhaps it was just Aiden's half-hearted attempt at waiting for me.

I pushed the door all the way open with a deliberate shove, the sound of it creaking as it swung against the wall. Inside, the silence was thick, heavy like the air before a storm breaks. The light in the hallway was dim, casting long shadows that twisted in strange shapes on the walls.

"Aiden?" My voice cracked, but I willed it to steady. This wasn't the time to falter.

His figure emerged from the shadows like a ghost, tall and lean, his posture stiff, as if bracing for impact. The hair that had once been so perfect now hung in wet strands over his forehead, and there was a weariness in his eyes that hadn't been there before. He looked older, maybe even defeated, but there was still a spark beneath it all. A glimmer of the man I had once loved.

"You found it, didn't you?" he asked, his voice hoarse, barely above a whisper. It wasn't a question, but a statement of truth. He knew. He had known all along.

I nodded once, my throat tight. "I found the truth."

His eyes closed for a brief moment, and I could see the flash of pain before he masked it with a brittle smile. "I figured you would."

I took a step forward, the distance between us closing like the gap between the past and the present, and suddenly, the years didn't feel like they had passed at all. The memories of us—our laughter, our late-night talks, our plans for the future—flooded my mind. They hit me with such force that I almost stumbled. But I couldn't let myself waver. Not now.

"You lied to me," I said, the words slipping from my mouth before I could stop them. I wanted to soften the blow, but the anger I had been holding in for so long bled through. It was raw, unfiltered, and perhaps a little unfair, but it was what I had been carrying for too long.

He winced, but he didn't back away. "I never meant to lie to you," he said, his voice barely audible now. "I was trying to protect you."

"Protect me?" I echoed, incredulous. "You thought keeping the truth from me was protecting me? You—" I paused, inhaling sharply. The rawness of my own pain was almost too much to bear. "You broke me, Aiden. You broke us."

His eyes searched mine, as if trying to find something—some flicker of the connection we once had. I couldn't give it to him. Not now.

"I thought I was doing the right thing," he said, a note of desperation creeping into his voice. "But I was wrong. God, I was so wrong."

The air between us crackled with tension, a thousand unspoken words hanging in the space like a thick fog. I could feel the heat of his gaze on me, the pull of the past, but I resisted.

"I know who did this to us," I said finally, my voice steady but filled with a kind of quiet resolve. "It wasn't just you. There's someone else behind all of this. Someone who wanted us to fall apart."

His face went ashen, his eyes widening with something between disbelief and fear. "Who?" he asked, his voice barely above a whisper.

I didn't answer right away. Instead, I stepped closer, closer than I had in weeks, feeling the tension between us like the frayed edges of a thread that could snap at any moment. The truth was like fire, burning in my chest, and I had no intention of letting it smolder any longer.

"It doesn't matter," I said finally, the words like a weight being lifted from my chest. "What matters is that we've both been played. We've been lied to, manipulated, and dragged through the mud for someone else's gain."

Aiden's hands clenched into fists at his sides, the veins standing out against his skin as if he were physically trying to hold himself together. "I don't care about them anymore," he said, his voice low and fierce. "I care about us."

I let out a short, humorless laugh. "You can't just pick up the pieces and expect it all to be the same. We're broken, Aiden. There's no 'us' anymore."

But as I said it, something shifted. A spark—barely noticeable but undeniable—flickered between us. It wasn't hope. Not exactly. But it was the possibility of something new. Of something different. And, for the first time in what felt like an eternity, I could feel a spark of something more than just bitterness and resentment. A flicker of the woman I had been before everything fell apart. The woman who was capable of more than just surviving—she was capable of rising. Rising from the ashes.

"I don't know if I can ever forgive you," I said, the words tasting bitter on my tongue. "But I won't let us die like this."

Aiden took a tentative step forward, the air around us crackling with the weight of the moment. "Then help me fix this," he pleaded, his voice rough, raw. "Help me make it right."

And for the first time, I didn't turn away.

He didn't reach for me—didn't try to touch me or pull me into the familiar comfort of his arms, though I could see the tension in his frame, the ache in his eyes. He was waiting. Waiting for me to decide what came next.

I didn't know what came next. How could I? A lifetime of trust had crumbled, swept away like sand in the tide, and now there was nothing but the raw, exposed truth between us. I wanted to believe him, wanted to pretend that the flicker of hope I saw in his eyes was enough to rebuild everything, but my heart wasn't ready to forgive him just yet. Still, I couldn't help but feel a pull. Maybe it wasn't love anymore—maybe it was just the remnants of what we'd once shared. But it was there, lingering like the scent of rain after a storm.

"I can't promise you that everything will go back to the way it was," I said, my voice quieter now, more vulnerable than I intended. "But I can't keep running either. We're in this together, whether we like it or not."

Aiden nodded, his lips pressed into a thin line. There were things I could say to him, so many words I had kept locked away, but I didn't know how to untangle the mess that was my heart. Instead, I asked the question that had been haunting me for days now, the one that had driven me to the edge of madness.

"Who is it, Aiden? Who's behind all this? Who wanted us destroyed?"

His eyes darted to the floor for a brief moment, as if the weight of the question might break him. And maybe it would. After everything, it was almost impossible to imagine the full scope of the betrayal. I had my suspicions, of course. A piece of me had always wondered if the truth had been hidden in plain sight, if the enemy had been closer to us than I'd ever imagined.

"I'm not sure," he said, the words tumbling out in a low, strained voice. "But I have a theory."

The air between us seemed to hold its breath as he hesitated. The theory? He had a theory? Was that all we had now? A possibility? But it wasn't just that, was it? Aiden wasn't the type to settle for half-truths, and if he was saying this, it meant he was onto something.

I crossed my arms over my chest, trying to contain the whirlwind of emotions threatening to rip me apart. "A theory? Aiden, we don't have time for theories. We need answers."

"I know," he replied, his voice rough, as though each word pained him. "But sometimes, the answers don't come all at once. They're like pieces of a broken puzzle. You have to find them, one by one, before you can see the bigger picture."

I wasn't sure if that was supposed to comfort me, but I nodded, silently agreeing. He was right. It was messy, uncertain, and terrifying. But we didn't have the luxury of waiting anymore. The clock was ticking, and I could feel the weight of everything pressing down on us, as if time itself were conspiring to unravel the fragile threads we were trying to rebuild.

"So what do we do now?" I asked, finally allowing myself to look at him fully, to meet his gaze without the veil of anger that had consumed me for so long.

Aiden's lips curved into a small, uncertain smile. There was no bravado in it, no attempt to convince me that everything was fine. It was real. Vulnerable. And, for the first time, it made me feel like we were on the same team again. "We do what we've always done, I guess," he said softly. "We fight."

My heart twisted at the simplicity of his words. The truth was, we had fought for so long. Fought for each other, fought for our love, fought against the forces that sought to tear us apart. But this time, it felt different. This time, the battle wasn't just about love—it was about survival.

"I don't know if I have the strength to keep fighting," I confessed, my voice barely a whisper. "Every time I think we've won, something else comes along to knock us down."

Aiden reached out then, his hand tentative, as if testing the waters. I didn't pull away. Instead, I let him take my hand, the touch grounding me in a way I hadn't expected.

"You're stronger than you think," he said, his voice steady. "And I'm not going anywhere. Not this time. Whatever happens, we face it together. No more lies. No more secrets."

I squeezed his hand, the gesture small but meaningful. There was a part of me that wanted to argue, wanted to tell him that it was too late for promises, that the damage had been done. But as I looked into his eyes, I saw something that made me hesitate. Maybe it was the flicker of the man I used to love, or maybe it was the simple, undeniable truth that we were both still here—still standing after everything that had torn us apart.

"I don't know what's going to happen, Aiden," I said, my voice thick with emotion. "But I do know this. I'm not giving up on us—not yet."

There was a quiet pause, and for a moment, I thought maybe we were just two people who had lost their way, who had been shattered by life's cruelty, trying to find something to hold onto. But in that brief silence, I could feel the shift. The spark that had remained dormant for so long was finally beginning to glow again, and despite everything that had come before, it felt like a promise—a new beginning.

"Then let's find those pieces," Aiden said, his voice low but filled with purpose. "Together."

And for the first time in a long while, I believed him.

The hours between us seemed to stretch out longer than the days we'd spent apart. Every minute, every second, pulsed with a strange urgency, like we were both caught between worlds—one foot in the past, another in some uncertain future. I could hear the rain outside, tapping against the windows in a steady rhythm, but inside, there was only silence, the kind that can either bring clarity or shatter what little remains.

Aiden's hand rested beside mine on the table, the warmth from his fingers pressing into my skin, grounding me. I didn't pull away. I didn't want to. I wasn't ready to, even if I wasn't sure where we were headed. The truth we'd uncovered had cracked something wide open, but it also felt like a door half-closed. We weren't fully free yet. Not by a long shot.

"Do you think it's really over?" I asked, breaking the silence. My voice was steadier than I felt, but I couldn't hide the uncertainty in my eyes.

Aiden let out a soft breath, a sound so heavy with everything we hadn't said that it hung in the air between us like a weight. "I don't know. But I'm tired of waiting for the other shoe to drop."

I nodded, feeling the exact same way. It seemed like we'd spent our entire relationship waiting for some disaster to hit, some bomb to explode. And when it finally did, it nearly obliterated everything.

"Then let's move forward," I said, surprising even myself with the words. "Whatever happens next, we face it together."

The promise felt fragile as it left my lips, but there was no going back now. Not for either of us. We had no choice but to go forward, even if the path ahead was paved with more uncertainties than I cared to admit.

Aiden's gaze softened, his thumb gently tracing circles on my hand, an absent gesture that somehow felt more intimate than any words he could've said. "I wish I could say I had all the answers. Hell, I wish I knew who to trust anymore." His lips twisted into a half-smile, but there was something desperate beneath it. "But I know this much. I want to fight for this—us."

The weight of those words settled deep in my chest, and for a moment, the ache of the past didn't feel so suffocating. Maybe it was the touch, maybe it was the sincerity behind his words, but something in me began to relax, just a little. I could still feel the sting of betrayal, but I also felt the faintest stir of something that had been buried under anger and confusion—hope.

"You think we can fix this?" I asked, my voice barely a whisper.

He squeezed my hand, his fingers firm and steady. "I think we can try."

I wanted to believe him. I did. But the reality of our situation was heavier than the promise of a future that was still just a vague outline in the distance. How could we possibly rebuild what had been destroyed? It wasn't just the lies or the manipulation that had done the damage—it was the erosion of trust, the constant fear that our love was always teetering on the edge of collapse. And now, after everything, I wasn't sure I even remembered how to trust him.

"We can't do this alone," I said, the thought more of a statement than a question. The enemy we'd uncovered was far from defeated. They were out there, watching, waiting for us to make a mistake. The web of lies they had spun was so tangled, so deep, that I couldn't see a way out without exposing every single thread, without risking everything. "We need help."

Aiden's expression grew serious. "You don't have to ask me twice. But who can we trust?"

The question hung in the air, suspended between us, unanswered. Every name I considered felt like a betrayal in itself, each person a potential threat lurking in the shadows. Even the allies we thought we had, the ones we believed we could lean on, seemed compromised. How do you move forward when the ground beneath you is nothing but shifting sand?

"I don't know," I muttered, staring down at our hands. "But we need to start somewhere."

Aiden nodded, his jaw tightening. "We'll figure it out. We always do."

I wanted to believe that too, but as I looked at him, I couldn't shake the feeling that the biggest challenge we were about to face wasn't just finding the enemy—it was deciding whether we could trust each other again. Could we really rebuild, or were we just playing at hope, pretending that the pieces of what we'd once had were still intact?

Before I could voice my doubts, the sound of a car engine revving outside shattered the quiet, followed by the unmistakable squeal of tires on wet pavement. Aiden's posture stiffened immediately, his hand leaving mine in an instant, as if some primal instinct had kicked in.

"That wasn't supposed to happen," he muttered under his breath, more to himself than to me. He stood up, moving toward the window, his eyes narrowing as he peered out. I followed him, my heart beating faster as I tried to make sense of what was going on.

A sleek black car was parked across the street, its engine still running, its headlights cutting through the rain. A shadow moved inside the car, the figure too far to make out, but it was enough to send a shiver of recognition down my spine.

"Aiden," I whispered, my voice tight with the sudden rush of fear, "who the hell is that?"

He didn't answer at first, his gaze locked on the car, his face pale. The blood drained from my face as realization hit like a slap to the chest. I wasn't the only one who had secrets. And if the person in that car had anything to do with the web of lies that had already torn us apart—then we were in far more trouble than I'd ever imagined.

Chapter 33: A Reckoning in Flames

The wind howled through the charred trees, their gnarled branches scraping the heavens like ancient fingers grasping at some distant, unreachable truth. Smoke billowed around us, thick and choking, twisting in the air like it had a mind of its own, curling and splintering in erratic shapes as if alive. Each breath I took was a battle—hot, acrid, filling my lungs with the stench of something long dead. It was fitting, I suppose. This was the end. The kind of end that should feel like the closing of a door, but instead, it felt more like the world holding its breath, waiting for me to make the first move.

Aiden stood beside me, a quiet strength radiating off him. His jaw was clenched, and his eyes burned with the kind of determination that came only after years of fighting. His hand brushed against mine—just enough to remind me that we were still here, still fighting, still breathing. The battlefield had been set in the most unlikely of places—what had once been a thriving town now lay in ruins, the remnants of homes reduced to little more than smoldering heaps of ash. And standing at the center of it all, like a god risen from the embers, was the one we had come for: Isolde.

Her silhouette cut through the smoke, tall and regal, her eyes glinting with an unnerving sense of superiority. She had always carried herself with that cold detachment, as though she were above the world she had played with, manipulated like a child with a broken doll. But tonight, there was no mistaking the reckoning. The final act of her twisted game. I could feel the heat in my veins, the rush of adrenaline that turned my thoughts into fire. She had taken so much from me, from all of us, but what she had never understood was that she had also given us something—something raw, something primal. She had given us the will to survive.

"Do you know what it feels like?" I asked, my voice cutting through the smoke, though it trembled more than I intended. "To be used? To be nothing but a pawn in someone else's twisted little game?"

Her lips curled into a smile that sent a shiver down my spine. "I didn't use you, dear. I created you. You were never meant to be more than an experiment, a fleeting shadow in my grand design."

My heart twisted at her words. How easy it had been for her to twist the truth, to make me feel like I was nothing more than a puppet, a plaything for her cruel amusement. But I wasn't that person anymore. The fire that had been kindled in me, the fire that had burned away my doubts and fears, would never be extinguished again. Aiden was right beside me, his hand close to mine but not quite touching. I could feel the way his presence steadied me, anchored me in a way I hadn't thought possible. We were here together, and no matter what came next, we had already won.

"You were never the one in control, Isolde," Aiden's voice rang out, low and steady, though it carried the weight of a thousand storms. "And you never will be."

Her eyes flickered for a moment—just a moment, but it was enough. There was a crack in the veneer of invincibility she had so carefully cultivated. She was no longer the powerful force she had once been, no longer the woman who had plotted our destruction from the shadows. She was just a woman now. And we were no longer her puppets.

"Do you think you can defeat me?" she sneered, taking a step forward, her boots crunching against the smoldering earth beneath her. "Do you think you can survive the fire that is about to consume you?"

The ground beneath us seemed to tremble in response to her words, as if the earth itself were unsure of who would come out on top. But I knew. The fire was ours now. It was the fire of all our lost years, of the pain we had endured, of the love we had fought for, and the promise of what would come next. It was a fire that would burn everything she had built to the ground.

With a single, sharp motion, I reached for the dagger hidden at my side. Aiden's hand was already on his weapon, his eyes sharp, never leaving her for a second. There was no more hesitation. No more uncertainty. Only the raw, unrelenting need to see this through.

Isolde raised her hand, a flicker of magic in her fingers. The air around us began to crackle with energy, the kind of dark power that I had once thought could destroy everything in its path. But now, it felt different. It wasn't a force that terrified me—it was a force I had learned to fight against.

"I've walked through fire," I said, stepping forward, my voice barely a whisper against the roar of the flames. "And I've come out the other side. You can burn me again, Isolde, but you will never break me."

Aiden moved with a fluidity that I had come to admire, the sharp edge of his sword cutting through the air with lethal precision. He was a force unto himself, no longer the man weighed down by his past, but the man who had fought and won against every shadow she had cast. Together, we surged forward, unstoppable.

Isolde's smile faltered, but only for a heartbeat. The fire around us intensified, but we were the storm now. We were the reckoning.

And the world would never be the same.

I could hear her breathing, steady and calculated, cutting through the crackling roar of the fire like the hiss of a snake poised to strike. Isolde hadn't moved, not yet. The magic she wielded was palpable, heavy in the air around us like a looming storm. The familiar weight of the dagger in my hand felt grounding—its cold hilt a reminder of everything that had led us to this moment. I had never thought I would be here, standing in front of the woman who had turned my life into a twisted labyrinth of lies, and yet, here I was.

"I never imagined it would end like this," I said, my voice steady, but the words somehow felt foreign to me. Isolde wasn't the monster I had once thought her to be. No, she was something worse—a reflection of what I could have become, had I not fought for my own redemption. She was the embodiment of everything cold and calculating, everything I had once feared I might be capable of.

She tilted her head, a mockery of curiosity in her eyes, like a cat toying with its prey before the kill. "Oh? And how did you imagine it would end, dear? With you and Aiden skipping off into the sunset? How quaint."

I felt Aiden's presence beside me, solid and unwavering, but it wasn't enough to stop the flicker of doubt that threatened to gnaw at my insides. I had always been a survivor, but there were still moments when fear clawed at my gut, when I wondered if I was truly strong enough to stand against someone like her. But I knew, deep down, there was no turning back now. We had come too far, endured too much. We were already more than what Isolde had ever imagined.

"You're wrong," I said, my voice rising, carrying the weight of every year of suffering, of every moment she had used us both like marionettes. "You see, you never understood us. You never understood me."

She raised a brow, as if my words were nothing more than a mild inconvenience to her. Her smile never faltered. "I didn't need to understand you, my dear. I only needed to control you."

And in that moment, I realized just how deeply I had underestimated the depths of her depravity. The control wasn't just physical, it was psychological. She had twisted my very sense of self, manipulated my thoughts until I no longer knew where the lines of truth and illusion blurred. That was the real cruelty of it—she had never needed to break me physically, because she had already cracked me from the inside out. But no more. I had rebuilt myself, piece by fragile piece, and I was no longer the woman she had created.

The fire around us seemed to crackle louder, as if it were a living thing, feeding on the tension in the air. It was as though the world itself was holding its breath, waiting for the inevitable. And still, she didn't move. She didn't flinch. For all her talk of control, I knew she was just as trapped as we were. She had created this world, yes, but she had also made herself its prisoner.

Aiden stepped forward, his hand steady on the hilt of his sword, his gaze never leaving Isolde. He had fought too many battles to let her provoke him now. "This ends tonight, Isolde. No more games, no more manipulation. You've lost."

She scoffed, the sound of it like nails on a chalkboard. "Lost? You think I've lost?" She laughed, a sharp, hollow sound that didn't reach her eyes. "You've lost already. Both of you."

It was then that the true weight of her words hit me. Not because they were true—no, because for a fleeting second, I thought she believed them. She was a woman so consumed by her own hubris that she couldn't fathom how completely she had been outplayed. She had been so certain that she controlled every aspect of our lives, but she hadn't counted on the simple, unstoppable force of human will.

"I never asked for any of this," I said, my voice growing firmer with each word. "I never wanted to be part of your game, but I'm done now. We're done." I looked at Aiden, and for a moment, everything fell silent. It was just us, standing there, the past and future collapsing together in a single, defining instant.

Then, as if we had synchronized without speaking, we both moved. The clash of steel rang out, a symphony of violence that echoed through the night. Isolde's magic shot toward us in a surge of dark energy, but Aiden was faster, deflecting her strikes with a swift precision that left her momentarily off balance. She hissed in frustration, her eyes glowing with that same terrible, unwavering belief that she was invincible. But the thing about invincibility was that it was built on the illusion of control. And she had never controlled us—not really.

I lunged forward, using the momentum of my own fury to close the distance between us. The blade of my dagger sang through the air as I aimed it at her heart, the place she had wound her lies so deeply into. But she was prepared, of course, a flash of her own dark magic sparking between us, forcing me back with a force that knocked the breath from my lungs. But she hadn't accounted for the one thing she had never understood—her greatest flaw.

I was unpredictable. And Aiden? He was my rock, the one person who knew how to anticipate my every move. Together, we were unstoppable.

She stumbled, her eyes narrowing, and I could see the moment her confidence shattered. The fire around us seemed to rise in response, the heat of it licking at my skin as though the world itself was burning with our resolve. We were no longer the victims in this game. Tonight, we were the reckoning.

The earth beneath our feet seemed to tremble, as if it were caught in a war of its own. Every step we took through the fire-scorched ground left a mark, a reminder of what had been and what was now being fought for. The flames curled around us, desperate to consume everything in sight, but we were unyielding. Isolde, standing tall in the midst of it all, was no longer the orchestrator she once was. The energy that had once flowed so freely from her now sputtered, as though the very air rejected her.

She swayed slightly, the sweat beading on her brow, and for the first time since we had met her, I saw a flicker of vulnerability. It was small, but it was there. I wasn't sure if it was fear or frustration, but it didn't matter. The world was no longer hers to control.

"You still don't get it, do you?" Isolde hissed, wiping the sweat from her temple, her fingers trembling ever so slightly. "You think that because you've faced a few trials, you understand what it means to truly rule. To bend the world to your will."

I laughed, the sound bitter. "Oh, trust me, I've learned a lot. But the one thing I've learned most is that no one is truly in control. Not you, not me, and certainly not the people who think they can make us into what they want us to be."

Aiden's gaze never wavered from her, but the silence between us thickened. He was waiting. Waiting for the right moment, just like me. We had learned, over time, to be patient with each other, to trust that the other would see the opening when it arrived. It was the trust that had kept us alive all these months, the unspoken understanding that, no matter how desperate the odds, we would always find a way through together.

But Isolde was unpredictable, and I couldn't help but wonder how long she would hold her ground before the inevitable collapse. Her power was slipping, I could feel it. The magic that once pulsed from her fingertips had grown erratic, like a candle flickering in a storm. Her face twisted in rage, and with a sharp gesture, she summoned a burst of power so violent, it sent a shockwave through the ground beneath us. I barely had time to react, but Aiden was faster, grabbing my arm and pulling me to the side, just as the air around us cracked and exploded. The force knocked the breath from my lungs, sending me crashing to the ground.

My heart raced as I scrambled to my feet, my vision swimming. The world spun around me, disorienting in its intensity, but I refused to let myself fall into the chaos. Not now, not when we were so close. When the haze cleared, I saw Aiden already back on his feet, eyes narrowed, lips set in a grim line. Isolde stood across from us, her hands trembling, her magic fizzling out in tendrils of smoke.

Her voice, sharp and ragged, cut through the air. "You think this is over? You think I will let you take everything from me?"

"You've already lost," I said, breathing heavily, my hand clutching the dagger like it was the only thing keeping me grounded. My own hands were slick with sweat, but there was no going back. There never had been. "The only thing left for you to do is accept it."

She sneered, her lips curling back in a flash of teeth. "You think I'm afraid of losing? I don't care about power anymore. This isn't about that." Her eyes flickered, as if a deeper truth was trying to claw its way to the surface. But then the moment passed, and she straightened, an eerie calm settling over her. "This is about survival. And I will do whatever it takes to survive."

Survival? The words rang hollow in the air. What was she really saying? Was she still playing the role of a victim? I couldn't tell if her words were the last vestiges of the woman who had orchestrated so much destruction or if she was simply trying to justify the crumbling empire she had built on the backs of others.

But I wasn't interested in her justification anymore. There was nothing left to say.

Without warning, she lunged forward, a flash of dark magic spilling from her palms, enveloping the space between us in an inky blackness. I staggered back, blinded, but Aiden was already moving, his sword raised high, cutting through the air with the precision of a seasoned fighter. His blade met the magic with a sharp, guttural sound—an explosion of light that threw us both backward. The force of it knocked me to the ground once again, but I barely noticed the pain. This time, something was different. Something had shifted.

I looked up to see Isolde stumbling back, gasping for air, her once-steady stance faltering. A sharp cry escaped her lips as she looked down at her hands, as though the power she had wielded for so long had turned against her. The ground beneath us cracked open, the earth itself seeming to rebel against her.

"This... this isn't over," she choked, her voice strained, wild with desperation. "You can't—"

Before she could finish, the ground beneath us gave way with a deafening crack. It was as though the very earth had decided it was time to take matters into its own hands, breaking open and swallowing her whole. I barely had time to grab Aiden's arm and pull him back as the earth crumbled beneath us.

But as the dust settled, there was no sign of Isolde. Just the remnants of the battle, the scorched earth, and the silence that followed in the wake of the storm. My heart pounded in my chest, a wild rhythm of uncertainty. Had she fallen into the abyss? Had she...?

Suddenly, a low growl echoed from the darkness.

And then, from the blackened ruins, something began to rise. Something that was not Isolde—but it was unmistakably her.

The world seemed to freeze as I realized—this was not the end.

Chapter 34: Hearts Forged in Fire

I stood there, my boots sinking into the charred earth, the remnants of what had once been a vibrant meadow now reduced to smoldering ash. The air still carried the acrid scent of burning wood and singed grass, mingling with the heavy, metallic tang of blood that clung to my skin. But beneath it all, there was the faintest trace of something else—a kind of stillness, like the quiet after a storm, when the world holds its breath and wonders if it's safe to breathe again.

Aiden stood beside me, his silhouette barely distinguishable against the smoky haze, but his presence was undeniable. His shoulder brushed mine, a silent promise that no matter how scorched the world around us had become, we would walk through the ruin together.

"Are you alright?" His voice, low and rough, reached me as though from a great distance, as if the very act of speaking required an effort, a war against the silence we had inherited in the aftermath of the battle.

I wanted to say something comforting, something that could offer the solace we both needed, but the words wouldn't come. The weight of what had happened hung between us, an unspoken knowledge that neither of us was willing to confront yet. Still, I managed a weak nod, hoping it would be enough.

Aiden's gaze met mine, his expression unreadable, but his eyes—the same eyes that had once held so much warmth and tenderness—were now clouded with a sorrow so deep it threatened to swallow him whole. His hand, when it reached out to me, was rough and calloused, his palm warm despite the chill that had settled in my bones.

"We'll rebuild," he said, his words a quiet vow. The promise lingered in the air, but the truth of it was uncertain, like the distant echo of thunder in the sky. I wanted to believe him, needed to, but the past few days had taught me that promises, no matter how deeply intended, could be shattered just as easily as glass.

"I don't know how," I whispered, my voice cracking under the strain of the raw emotions I had yet to fully process. How do you rebuild a life when everything you knew had turned to ash, when the very ground beneath your feet had been scorched by the fires of betrayal and loss?

He didn't respond immediately. Instead, he squeezed my hand, his fingers pressing into mine with a force that was almost painful, grounding me in that moment, in this broken world that we now shared. And in that silence, I realized something: Aiden hadn't just lost something in the battle. He had lost everything—his family, his place in the world, the very foundation of who he was.

And yet, here he was, standing beside me, offering me his strength when I had none left to give.

"Do you remember the first time we met?" His question was unexpected, pulling me from the depths of my thoughts. His voice was soft now, almost playful, as though he were testing the waters of a world that felt anything but safe.

"How could I forget?" I replied, unable to keep the ghost of a smile from tugging at my lips. The memory felt like another lifetime, a moment before all the chaos had come crashing into our lives. "You were so certain you knew everything, like you could charm the stars out of the sky if you tried hard enough."

He laughed, the sound strained but familiar, like a song that had been played too many times but still carried the power to move the soul. "And you were just as certain that I was a fool." He paused, his thumb brushing the back of my hand in slow, deliberate circles. "I think I've spent most of my life proving you right."

I tilted my head to look at him, surprise flashing in my chest. "That's not true."

"It is," he said, his voice dropping. "But I don't mind anymore. I'm not afraid to be a fool if it means I can have this. Have you."

I had no response to that, no clever retort to mask the raw emotion that bubbled up within me. It was terrifying, the way his words had pierced through the layers I had so carefully built around my heart. And yet, there was something in the way he said it, in the way his eyes held mine with a quiet intensity, that made me believe him.

"You don't have to prove anything," I said softly, my voice barely above a whisper.

For a long moment, neither of us spoke. The world around us was still, as though even the earth itself had paused to listen, to feel the gravity of what we had just shared. But it wasn't until Aiden's hand tightened around mine that I understood what he was trying to say.

I had been running from my own feelings, hiding behind walls I had constructed out of fear, of loss, of heartbreak. But Aiden had seen through it all. He had seen me, not just as the woman I was before the war, but as the woman I was becoming in its aftermath.

"You're not a fool, Aiden," I murmured, my voice barely audible against the wind. "You're the only thing in this world that makes sense right now."

He turned to face me, his expression unreadable for a split second, before the corners of his mouth lifted just slightly. "Then I suppose we're both fools, then. Because I can't imagine a life without you in it."

The words hung in the air between us, a fragile thread that bound us together, and for the first time since the battle had started, I let myself believe in them. Because despite the wreckage that surrounded us, despite the pain we both carried, there was a part of me that understood now—deep down—that love, true love, was never about perfection or timing. It was about surviving the worst of it together and finding a way to move forward, even when the path ahead was anything but clear.

Aiden's fingers laced through mine, grounding me as the smoke from the smoldering wreckage of our world drifted around us like a shroud. The sun, still hidden behind a wall of thick clouds, filtered through in thin, gray beams, casting the world in a muted light. It felt like the earth itself was waiting for permission to breathe again, as if we had all been holding our collective breath ever since the last blow had landed, ever since the first betrayal had struck.

I could feel the tension in his grip, like a taut string ready to snap, but there was also a steadiness to it that anchored me. A promise without words. In the midst of the chaos that swirled around us, in the face of everything we had lost, Aiden was still here. He was still ours, as much a part of this broken world as I was.

"Do you remember the way the sky looked before all of this?" I asked, the question slipping from my lips before I had time to second-guess it. It felt odd, talking about things that once seemed so simple, so far removed from the mess we now found ourselves tangled in.

Aiden's gaze drifted upwards, tracing the same broken clouds, and for a moment, his expression softened—his guard lowered just a fraction. "You mean the sky that wasn't on fire? Yeah, I remember." His lips quirked into a smile, but it didn't reach his eyes. "The kind of sky that made you believe everything was possible."

"And now?" I prompted gently, nudging him with my elbow, trying to coax a spark of that old light from him.

His smile deepened, though there was a wryness to it. "Now, I'm just waiting for the storm to pass. But it seems like we're caught in the middle of it."

"I think it already passed." The words left me with surprising certainty, as if my own voice had decided the matter for me. "What we're seeing now... this is just the aftermath. The sky will clear. Maybe not today. Maybe not tomorrow. But it will."

Aiden turned to face me fully now, his brow furrowed, eyes searching mine as though trying to decipher the puzzle I had become. I could feel the weight of his unspoken question pressing into me. How could I be so sure? How could I possibly believe the worst was behind us when the future felt so unpredictable, so fragile?

"You've always been good at pretending," he said softly, almost tenderly, his thumb brushing the back of my hand again. "You've always known just what to say, just when to say it."

The words, though gentle, stung. They were true. I had always hidden behind my words, carefully constructing my version of the world so that no one would see the cracks. But now, standing here with him, amidst the remnants of everything we'd once known, I realized something: there was no more need for pretense. Not with him. Not with anyone.

"I'm not pretending," I said quietly, meeting his gaze. "I'm just... choosing to see it differently. I've spent too long letting the darkness swallow me. I'm ready to move forward." I paused, swallowing the lump that had suddenly formed in my throat. "With you."

Aiden didn't speak immediately, and the silence between us stretched long enough that I could almost hear the weight of everything unsaid—everything still hanging in the air like the fog that clung to the ground. But then, just as I was about to pull away, he spoke.

"We don't know what's coming," he said, his voice low, but not unkind. "And sometimes, the waiting is worse than the storm itself."

"I know," I replied, my voice steady despite the tremor in my chest. "But if we face it together, maybe it won't be so bad."

His eyes softened, a flicker of something—trust, maybe—dancing behind the layers of pain. Aiden had always been a man of action, never one for soft words or promises that couldn't be kept. But in that moment, something between us shifted.

"We've both lost everything," he said, a slight rasp in his voice. "We've both been burned in ways we'll never recover from. But if you're telling me that there's a chance to find something after all of this, something worth fighting for, then I'm in. For you. For us."

It was strange, how much those words meant to me. How in the simplest of admissions, a shift in his tone, I could feel the truth of his resolve settle in my chest like the steady beat of a drum. Aiden wasn't just talking about survival anymore. He was talking about living, about finding something more than just the remnants of who we had been.

"You really believe that?" I asked, blinking back a tear that threatened to escape, embarrassed by its sudden appearance.

"I do," he said, squeezing my hand tighter, his grip unwavering. "I didn't think I had anything left to give. But then you showed up, and you were stubborn enough to make me believe in something again."

I laughed softly, the sound unexpected in the silence of the aftermath. "I'm stubborn?"

"An understatement," he muttered with a grin, the corners of his mouth lifting as he turned slightly toward me. "But it's a trait I've come to admire, I'll admit."

There was an edge to his words, but beneath it, I could hear the warmth, the affection that had always been there, even when we were at our worst. It was in the way he looked at me, the way his shoulders seemed to relax when we were together. And for the first time in what felt like forever, I let myself feel the glimmer of hope that we could rebuild—we, not just me, not just him, but the fragile pieces of us that had managed to survive the storm.

"Well, I'll take that as a compliment," I said with a teasing smile, though my heart was racing. I wasn't sure how we would do it. But I knew that whatever came next, we would face it together. There was no question about that anymore.

The stillness that surrounded us was deceiving. Though the world had paused, holding its breath in the wake of destruction, I could feel the electric tension between Aiden and me. It was as if the air itself was thick with all the things we hadn't said, all the questions we hadn't asked, and all the truths we hadn't yet confronted.

Aiden's fingers, still intertwined with mine, were a quiet comfort, but there was a tightness to his grip that betrayed the war waging silently within him. His body, once so easy to read, had become an enigma in the aftermath of everything. His jaw was clenched, the muscles there working in rhythmic waves as if he was trying to swallow back a truth he couldn't yet speak.

"You're thinking too much," I said, the words slipping out before I could stop them. It was a habit, one I had picked up from him long ago. We'd always been too good at thinking our way out of things, analyzing and overthinking every decision, every action. But the truth was, I didn't need him to think. I needed him to feel, and that was something Aiden had never been particularly skilled at.

He turned to look at me, his eyes catching mine for a brief, electric second. There was a flicker of surprise, but only for a moment. "I can't help it," he replied, his voice gravelly, as if he hadn't spoken in days. "Every time I let my guard down, something comes along to remind me that nothing lasts."

I laughed softly, though the sound was edged with something darker. "Aren't you a ray of sunshine?"

Aiden's lips twisted, not quite into a smile, but not a frown either. It was the closest thing to a grin I had seen from him in a while. It felt like a small victory.

"I'm just being realistic," he said, but there was an unfamiliar vulnerability in his eyes, one that took me off guard. "I don't know how to stop thinking, how to stop wondering what happens when this—" He gestured around us, at the wreckage, the smoke curling in the air, the scars that seemed to stretch out forever, "—is all over. What happens when there's nothing left to rebuild?"

The question hung between us, raw and impossible. The weight of it pressed on my chest like a thousand-pound stone. And yet, for all its heaviness, I didn't feel crushed by it. Not entirely. There was something in the way he asked, something in the way he looked at me, that made me believe there was still a chance. A chance for more than just survival.

"You're looking at it wrong," I said after a moment. "We aren't rebuilding. We're starting fresh. There's a difference."

He raised an eyebrow, clearly intrigued but also skeptical. "Starting fresh? After everything that's happened?"

"Yes," I said firmly, the words gaining strength the more I said them. "Because nothing will ever be the same. We've both changed. The world has changed. So why keep trying to patch up the old life? Why not create something new? Something that's ours."

Aiden stood there, silent, his brow furrowed, considering my words with a weight I couldn't quite place. The way he was looking at me made my heart beat a little faster, but not from fear, no. It was something else entirely. Hope. I could feel it—a spark that hadn't been there before.

"I didn't know you had that in you," he said quietly, a faint trace of admiration creeping into his voice.

I shot him a look, half-amused, half-impatient. "What, you thought I was just some delicate little thing to fix up? I'm tougher than I look, Aiden."

He chuckled, the sound rough but real. It was the first time in what felt like forever that I heard it, and I found myself wanting more. "I know that. Believe me, I know."

The space between us seemed to close, and for a moment, everything else faded into the background. The charred remains of the world, the rubble, the wreckage of what we had both once believed... it all melted away. There was only this—only him and me, standing in the ruins, and yet, there was something beautiful in it. Something unexpected.

But just as quickly as the moment had appeared, it was gone. A cold gust of wind stirred the smoke and pulled us both out of our reverie.

"We're not done yet," Aiden murmured, his expression darkening as he stepped back, scanning the horizon with a sharpness I hadn't seen in him before. The shift in his demeanor was so sudden, so stark, that I found myself blinking in confusion.

"What do you mean?" I asked, trying to read him, trying to understand why the warmth in his eyes had been replaced with something colder, more guarded.

"There's still a threat," he said, his jaw tightening once more. "We may have won the battle, but the war isn't over. Not by a long shot."

His words hit me like a slap, and for a moment, my mind spun as I processed them. The war? Of course, I knew that. We had both known that we were never truly safe, but hearing him say it out loud—hearing the weight of it in his voice—made the reality sink in. We had been living with the illusion of peace, as if the storm had passed. But it hadn't. It was still brewing, just waiting for the right moment to strike again.

I took a step toward him, my pulse quickening. "What are you saying?"

Aiden's eyes locked onto mine, hard and unyielding. "I'm saying that there's someone out there who won't rest until they finish what they started."

The words sent a chill down my spine, and I felt a cold sense of dread creeping up from my gut. I knew, in that moment, that everything had just shifted again. What we had—what I had—was no longer enough to protect us.

I opened my mouth to ask more, but before I could speak, a sudden noise broke the tension. The sharp, unmistakable sound of footsteps approaching from behind us. My heart skipped in my chest as I spun around, my senses on high alert.

And then I saw him—someone I never expected.

Chapter 35: A New Dawn

I stood at the window, watching the dawn light spill across the horizon, the first touch of warmth on my skin almost surreal. There was something about that early morning glow, something that made the world feel just a little bit safer, as if the darkness that had so often clung to my life had decided to retreat, leaving only this quiet, promising start. Aiden was still asleep in the next room, a steady rhythm of breath that somehow soothed me even from afar.

I should've been used to it by now, the sense that everything could change in an instant. But this time, I wasn't holding my breath, waiting for the other shoe to drop. It was different. I'd never really let myself believe that peace could last—could it? But now, as I stood in the stillness of our home, I realized I didn't need to wait for disaster to strike anymore. We had come this far. And it was enough.

I took a deep breath, inhaling the faint scent of coffee brewing downstairs. Aiden had already started the morning routine without so much as a word. The coffee pot clicked, the familiar sound grounding me in a way I hadn't thought possible just months ago. This place—this life—had been a distant dream, one I thought was too fragile to hold onto for long. Yet here we were, amidst the remnants of what we'd built together. A life that was more than just survival.

Downstairs, the kitchen had that soft, cozy feel to it, the kind that came with routine and comfort. The light filtered through the curtains, casting delicate patterns across the table where we'd shared so many conversations, so many decisions. Aiden was at the counter, his back to me, pouring two cups of coffee like he did every morning. The man was always predictable in the best of ways. His quiet presence, the way his hands moved so deliberately, made the world feel a little more like it was supposed to. As if this was exactly how things were meant to be.

I leaned against the doorframe, taking him in. He was never one for grand gestures, always the kind to show his care in the smallest, most unexpected ways. It had taken me so long to recognize it—maybe even longer to accept that someone could love me in a way that didn't come with strings or conditions. He looked up, catching my eye, and offered a smile that made my heart stumble in its usual rhythm. That smile, that quiet acknowledgment, was everything.

"You're up early," he said, his voice husky with sleep, though his eyes were already alert, as if he'd been waiting for me to wake up with him.

I smiled back, pushing myself off the doorframe and walking over to the counter, my fingers brushing against his as I reached for the cup. "I couldn't sleep," I lied, though it was true in a way. I hadn't slept because I couldn't stop thinking about everything we'd been through, everything we were still building. "The sun's coming up."

He raised an eyebrow, amusement flickering in his gaze, though there was a depth to it, too. "The sun has a way of doing that. It's always there, whether you see it or not."

"Is that supposed to be some kind of deep wisdom?" I teased, the words slipping out easily, like a rhythm I'd grown accustomed to. It felt good to laugh, to be this comfortable. With him. With myself.

"Maybe," he said, his smile turning wry. "You never know when the sun's just going to surprise you."

I took a slow sip of coffee, the bitter warmth flooding my senses and settling in my stomach. It was strange, but in that moment, I realized that the battle had never really been about fighting the darkness. It had always been about finding the courage to let the light in. To let go of the fears that kept me chained to a past I couldn't change. And, slowly, I was learning to trust that we were more than just a series of fortunate accidents. We were here. Together. And that mattered more than anything I'd ever known.

"You know," I said after a beat, turning the mug between my hands, "I used to think that I couldn't have both. A good life and peace. That it was one or the other."

Aiden nodded, his eyes dark with understanding. He hadn't had an easy life either, and I could see that he was searching for the right words, the right thing to say. But, as always, his silence spoke louder than any words could.

"Yeah," he said finally, "me too."

The silence that followed was not one of awkwardness, but of something deeper. Of knowing that we shared something more than just love. We shared a past, a future, and a commitment to both. The battles we'd fought individually had brought us to this point, but it was the way we fought for each other that had built this foundation, this home.

I set my mug down, suddenly aware of how much had shifted in me over the past few months. The person who had walked into this house, bruised and wary, was not the person standing here now. I was different. Stronger, yes, but gentler in ways that I hadn't expected. The fire that had once burned too hot had tempered, and in its place was something steadier, something more enduring.

"We're going to be okay, aren't we?" I asked softly, not needing an answer, but needing to hear it aloud, to make sure it wasn't just a dream.

Aiden didn't hesitate. He reached across the counter, his hand covering mine. "We are. And we'll keep being okay. Every day."

The truth of his words settled into my bones, and for the first time in as long as I could remember, I believed it.

Aiden didn't let go of my hand right away, and for a long moment, we stood there, simply being. As the early morning light grew brighter, spilling over the window sill and onto the floor, it filled the room with a kind of gentleness that made everything feel new, even the air. It was almost too quiet, the kind of stillness that begged for words, but neither of us were quite ready for that yet.

I pulled away first, needing to move, needing something to do. I had spent so many years running, always keeping busy to fill the spaces where the pain used to live. It wasn't that I feared the silence. It was that I had forgotten how to make peace with it. I grabbed the dish towel from the counter, wiping it across the already clean counter like it mattered. Like the small, domestic act of tidying up would somehow convince me that I was exactly where I needed to be.

But Aiden didn't need me to convince myself. He simply waited, watching me with a quiet knowing. His patience was both grounding and maddening—he was a master at letting me come to things in my own time, even when I wanted to scream at him to hurry me along. There was something about the way he stood there, arms crossed, head tilted just slightly, that made me feel like he could see the layers of me that I didn't always know existed.

Finally, I couldn't stand it anymore.

"So," I said, trying to sound casual, "how long do you think it'll take before we really get this whole thing figured out?"

He raised an eyebrow, amusement flickering in his gaze. "You mean the living-in-domestic-bliss thing? You think we're supposed to figure that out?"

I chuckled, and just like that, the weight of the moment lifted. "I don't know. I guess I thought there'd be a manual or something."

His grin was slow, like he was savoring the tease. "If there was a manual, I think we'd both be hopeless at following it. But it's more fun this way, right?"

I shot him a sidelong glance. "Fun? The way I see it, you're playing the long game here. Keeping things vague so you can get out of all the heavy lifting."

He laughed, the sound so rich and genuine that I couldn't help but smile along. "Maybe. But I have to admit, I'm starting to enjoy all this heavy lifting."

We fell into an easy silence after that, the kind that only came with knowing someone for long enough to understand how to be together without forcing conversation. It felt good, this quiet rhythm we had now, something comfortable and steady that didn't require constant validation. But, of course, being me, I couldn't leave well enough alone.

"I've been thinking," I said, my voice more tentative this time.

Aiden didn't look at me immediately, his focus still on the cup in his hand. "Uh-oh," he murmured, barely audible.

I leaned against the counter, folding my arms. "No, seriously. I've been thinking about what's next. For us, I mean."

At this, he finally looked up, his expression suddenly serious, the familiar warmth in his eyes giving way to something far more intense. "I thought we agreed to take it slow," he said, though it wasn't a question.

I nodded. "I know. But it's just—there's this part of me, this part that I've buried so deep for so long, that's starting to wonder if maybe... maybe it's time to think beyond just surviving."

He set his mug down slowly, like he understood the gravity of what I was saying, even though I wasn't entirely sure I did myself. The room felt smaller, the air thicker, but Aiden's presence didn't feel suffocating. It felt like a promise.

"I'm not going anywhere," he said softly, as if reassuring himself more than me. "But you have to decide what you want. I'm happy with whatever you need."

I let his words settle over me, heavy and sweet. I had spent so many years surviving—surviving the chaos, the heartbreak, the unpredictability of life. But here, with him, I wondered what it would feel like to just live. To allow myself to have the things I had always feared—things like happiness, or stability, or even just the simple joy of being with someone who didn't ask for anything in return.

The silence stretched between us, and for the first time in a long while, I didn't feel the need to fill it with words. I could just breathe, just be, and let the weight of all the "what nexts" drift to the back of my mind.

"So," I said finally, breaking the quiet, "what are we doing today?"

Aiden's smile was easy, but there was something in his eyes, something soft and sure, that made me think this wasn't just a casual question. He took a step toward me, his hands reaching out like he was considering something unspoken. "Whatever you want, but we have to get the garden in shape."

"Ah, the garden," I said, making a face, "the great source of domestic ambition. I swear, I'll have the greenest thumb in the county by the end of the month."

He chuckled, the sound rumbling deep in his chest. "I'm sure you will. You always get there, eventually."

And for the first time in a long while, I believed him.

We spent the rest of the morning in an easy, quiet rhythm—more than just surviving, as I'd told Aiden. We were thriving, in the most unassuming way. It was the small things: the way the dirt smelled rich and damp when we started pulling weeds from the garden, the soft murmur of his voice as he explained how to prune the roses (even though I suspected he didn't have a clue, either), the way his laughter wrapped around me as I dropped a shovel right into the compost bin. I was sure there were better, more elegant ways to handle gardening, but at that moment, it didn't matter. We were together, and that was all I really needed.

By noon, we had made a dent in the yard, and I was surprisingly proud of our progress. The sun had climbed higher in the sky, and I could feel the warmth of it soaking into my skin, the heat beginning to make everything shimmer. The world felt alive in ways I hadn't expected. I ran my hand across the rough bark of the old oak tree in the corner of the garden, the leaves rustling in the soft breeze. It had always been there, standing watch over the house, an ancient sentry that I'd never noticed before, but today it seemed to carry some deeper meaning.

"Think this tree will still be here in fifty years?" I asked, glancing over my shoulder to where Aiden was dragging the wheelbarrow full of weeds.

He stopped for a second, tilting his head, then wiped the sweat from his forehead with the back of his hand. "I think it's more likely we'll still be here in fifty years, don't you?" His voice was a mixture of teasing and something softer. I wasn't sure if he was joking, or if he was asking me to make a promise.

I met his gaze, trying to read his eyes. I could feel the pull, that thread between us that always seemed to tighten whenever I least expected it. And maybe he didn't realize it, but I knew what he was asking.

I didn't answer right away, because it wasn't just a simple question. It was one that carried weight—beyond the house, beyond the garden. Aiden was asking me to believe in forever. He was asking me to trust that we could make it through anything, together. A promise I wasn't sure I was ready to make.

"I don't know," I said, my voice low, my heart thudding harder than it had any right to. "But I'd like to think so. For once, I'd like to think that we could have something lasting."

He nodded, but there was a faint flicker in his eyes—something guarded, something that made me wonder if he was also standing at the edge of the same abyss. The thought of forever, after all we had both been through, felt impossible to grasp.

But for the first time, the impossibility didn't scare me. It was just... a thought. A hope. A possibility.

As if on cue, a car's engine roared down the street, breaking the quiet. Aiden and I both turned our heads, our peaceful bubble punctured by the noise. The car didn't slow down; it was speeding, almost recklessly. I couldn't help but notice the way Aiden tensed next to me, his gaze narrowing as the car barreled past. It wasn't just any car—it was the kind that didn't belong in our quiet neighborhood. I saw the dark, tinted windows and the faint outline of a figure in the front seat.

"Who the hell..." I began, but Aiden was already moving toward the fence.

"Stay here," he said, his voice low but sharp. There was an edge to it that I hadn't heard in weeks—something cold and distant that sent a ripple of unease through me.

"Why?" I asked, half-expecting him to say it was nothing, but already knowing the answer.

"I'll be right back," he muttered, his tone more commanding than I was used to. And without another word, he was across the yard, disappearing behind the hedge that bordered the property.

I stood there, staring after him, feeling that familiar knot in my stomach tighten. There were times when I hated how Aiden could shut me out, even for the briefest moments. It wasn't as if I didn't trust him—it was the secrecy, the way he'd always tried to protect me from the darkness that loomed over his past.

I paced, my fingers trailing over the rough stone of the garden wall, feeling more restless by the second. What the hell was going on? I couldn't hear anything over the rush of my thoughts, but something inside me told me that this wasn't just some random occurrence. I knew Aiden—knew him better than he probably wanted—and the way his shoulders had tensed, the quickness of his movement, told me everything I needed to know.

Then, as if to confirm every instinct I had, I heard the sharp crack of a voice, followed by a sound of something heavy hitting the ground.

I didn't hesitate. I pushed through the gate and hurried toward the sound, heart hammering in my chest. The last thing I wanted was to be caught in the middle of whatever this was, but I couldn't let Aiden face it alone. Not again.

I reached the corner just as Aiden appeared, his shirt half untucked, his jaw set in a way I knew meant trouble. His eyes met mine, and for just a moment, they softened.

"Go back inside, Ellie," he said, his voice grim.

"Not a chance," I snapped, stepping toward him. "What's going on?"

His gaze flickered past me, to the house, to the yard—like he was trying to decide whether or not to tell me. And then I saw it. The car from earlier had stopped a few houses down, and two men were now walking toward us. They didn't look like they belonged here, and the air between us thickened with tension.

"I'm not going anywhere," I repeated, my voice firmer than I felt.

Aiden's lips tightened. He stepped closer to me, lowering his voice to a near whisper. "They're not here for you."

But I wasn't so sure.

Chapter 36: The Forever Flame

The rain had started out as a gentle whisper against the windows, but by the time I found myself standing in the kitchen, it had turned into a full-on symphony, the kind of downpour that fills the silence of a room with the rhythm of its pounding beat. The warmth of the fire in the hearth flickered and danced in the reflection of the glass, casting shadows that seemed to move in time with the storm outside. I reached for the kettle, watching the steam curl and twist from the spout as it began to whistle, breaking through the soft murmur of the rain. It was a sound I'd come to crave—the promise of comfort, the small ritual of making tea that had always felt like a lifeline in moments when everything else seemed to be spiraling out of control.

Aiden, with his quiet strength and the sharpness of his blue eyes that never missed a thing, was sitting at the table, his hands wrapped around a cup of coffee. He looked so at home here, in the quiet spaces of this cottage that we'd turned into something ours. There were the familiar touches—his leather jacket draped over the back of the chair, the books scattered across the table, and the faint scent of wood and earth that seemed to follow him wherever he went.

I moved to the counter, carefully placing the kettle down before joining him, pulling out the chair across from him with a soft squeak. The dim light of the storm outside didn't quite reach into the corner of the room where we sat, but it didn't matter. His presence filled every inch of the space.

For a long moment, neither of us said anything. The storm did its thing—its relentless, soothing percussion filling the spaces between our words. It was like the world had pressed pause, giving us this brief moment of stillness to just be, and for once, neither of us seemed in any hurry to fill the silence with idle chatter.

I took a sip of my tea, the warmth seeping into me, and let out a sigh. Aiden's gaze was steady, watching me from over the rim of his cup. It wasn't the kind of gaze that demanded attention, but the kind that made you feel as though you were the only thing in the world worth seeing. And I couldn't help but feel a little caught off guard by how much that look still made my heart trip in my chest.

"You've been quiet," I finally said, breaking the silence.

He shrugged, his movements slow, deliberate, like he was still considering something, weighing it. "Just thinking."

I tilted my head, raising an eyebrow. "About what?"

He shifted in his chair, setting the coffee cup down, his fingers drumming lightly on the wood. "About how we got here, I guess."

I couldn't help but smile at that. "And where exactly is 'here'?"

His lips curved in a smile that was equal parts wistful and amused. "Here," he said, his voice soft, like he was savoring the word, "in this house, in this moment. With you."

It wasn't just the words, it was the way he said them, the weight they carried. There was something about the way he looked at me, like he had never imagined any other path, as though every turn had led him to this small kitchen, this worn table, this moment of contentment. It made my chest tight, but not with sadness—no, with something else. Something deeper. A fierce tenderness that I didn't know how to name, but I felt in every breath I took, every beat of my heart.

"I'm glad we're here," I said, my voice a little rougher than I'd intended. But it was true. So true.

Aiden's gaze softened, his fingers brushing over the edge of his coffee cup. "You know, I never thought I'd end up in a place like this. Not with you, not with anyone. I didn't think it was something I deserved."

The words hung in the air, heavy with truth. It wasn't something we talked about often—the past, the places we'd been, the things we'd survived. But I knew enough to understand the weight of what he was saying. I knew the scars that ran deeper than the skin, the memories that had left marks too stubborn to fade.

I leaned forward, setting my cup down, my eyes never leaving his. "You deserve all of this, Aiden," I said, my voice fierce now, as if I could will the truth of it into him, as though saying it out loud could erase all the doubts he'd carried for so long. "You deserve more than this house. You deserve every happiness I can give you."

A long breath escaped him, the kind of breath you take when you're holding in a storm, trying to keep it from spilling out. He looked at me, really looked at me, as though seeing me for the first time all over again, and in that look, I saw a question. One he didn't need to ask because I already knew the answer.

"I'm not going anywhere, you know." I smiled, my own heart stuttering a little at the thought. "We're in this. Together."

Aiden leaned back in his chair, his smile stretching into something that made my pulse race. "I know," he said, his voice steady. But the storm outside raged on, and as I watched the light flicker across his face, I realized something. It wasn't just the storm that had brought us here, not just the fire that had crackled between us over the past months. It was the quiet moments—the ones where the world slowed down, where it was just the two of us, and everything else could wait.

This wasn't the end of our story. It was just the beginning.

Aiden's fingers brushed lightly over the back of my hand, the touch so fleeting, so quiet, that I almost doubted it had happened at all. But I felt it. Felt the spark of something—a promise, maybe, or a question. It wasn't enough to say anything, but it was enough to make me hold my breath for a second longer, as though the air itself was charged, waiting for the next moment to unfold.

The storm outside was growing fiercer, the sound of rain slashing against the windows as though the heavens were pressing in. I found myself wondering if it always rained when we found each other in moments like these—when everything felt still, and the world seemed to hold its breath, as though afraid of disturbing something too precious. The fire in the hearth cracked and popped, but even that sound felt distant, like the warmth of it was all happening in some faraway world, and I was watching it from the edges, unsure of whether I was part of it or not.

I leaned forward, letting the warmth of the fire seep into my skin, and met Aiden's gaze. There was something different in the way he was looking at me, something raw, like he was seeing me for the first time all over again. It made my stomach tighten, not with fear, but with the recognition of how much we still had to discover about each other. Even now, after everything, I knew there were pieces of him I hadn't yet found.

"What's going on in that head of yours?" I asked, the smile tugging at my lips even though I was half-terrified of what might come next. He had a way of making me second-guess everything, of throwing me off balance with nothing more than a few words and a glance.

Aiden chuckled, low and steady. "You're asking me that? You should be the one telling me what's going on in yours."

"I'm not the one who's been distant," I teased, leaning back in my chair. "You've been quiet. You're never quiet."

He smiled then, but it was more of a smirk, the kind that made my heart race just a little faster. "Maybe I've learned to appreciate silence," he said, the words heavy with something I couldn't quite place.

I raised an eyebrow. "Or maybe you're plotting something."

He shrugged, but his gaze didn't leave mine. "Maybe. Maybe not."

I shifted in my chair, the warmth of the fire making my skin tingle, but the tension between us was palpable now, thick and suffocating, like we were standing on the edge of something—something we both knew we had to face. I couldn't help but wonder if this was the moment, if everything we had built was finally coming to a head.

It wasn't that I didn't trust him. No, that wasn't it at all. It was that I didn't trust me—didn't trust the impulse that I felt inside of me, the urge to walk away before things could get too real. Aiden had always been the one to dive in, the one to take risks and follow his instincts, while I was the one who second-guessed, who held back, who questioned every decision until it drove me crazy.

But maybe that was the beauty of us—his fire and my hesitation. It wasn't perfect, but it worked. I just wasn't sure how long it would work, not with everything else in the world trying to pull us apart.

"Are you going to tell me what's bothering you, or should I guess?" I said, leaning forward again, trying to push past the sudden weight that had settled between us. I didn't want to back down, didn't want to give him the satisfaction of knowing that whatever was in his eyes was enough to send me into a spiral of confusion.

"I think you already know," Aiden said, his voice suddenly low, quiet, like the storm outside had found its way into the room with us. "But you're not ready to hear it."

I swallowed, the words hanging in the air, and for a moment, I felt like I was choking on the truth of them. He was right. I did know. Deep down, I had always known. But knowing something and being ready to face it were two entirely different things.

"I don't think I'll ever be ready," I said, my voice softer than I intended, my hands trembling slightly as I folded them in my lap.

Aiden didn't speak for a long time, and I thought, just for a second, that he might not say anything at all. But then, his hand slid across the table, covering mine with the gentleness I had come to expect from him—slow, steady, as though he were trying to reassure me that everything was going to be okay, even though I wasn't so sure.

"I'm not asking you to be ready," he said, his thumb stroking the back of my hand in slow, soothing circles. "I'm asking you to trust me."

I met his gaze then, really met it, and something in the depth of his eyes told me that he was asking for more than just trust. He was asking for everything. And the terrifying part? I was ready to give it to him. All of it.

"I trust you," I said, my voice barely above a whisper. It was a promise, a vow, and it scared me more than anything else in the world.

But then, as I looked at him, the weight of his stare not just seeing me but understanding me, I realized that maybe, just maybe, I had been ready all along.

The room was quieter now, the tension simmering down to a steady hum as the last of the storm passed through, leaving behind a damp stillness in the air. It was the kind of silence that could swallow you whole if you let it. But Aiden's hand still lay over mine, his touch the only anchor to reality as the weight of everything hung between us like a promise we hadn't yet fully made.

I should've pulled away. Should've let go of his hand and taken a step back. But I didn't. It was the kind of touch that demanded attention, not because it was forceful, but because it had a quiet power. It was the kind of thing you didn't pull away from—not unless you were ready to walk away entirely. And I wasn't. Not anymore.

"I've been thinking," I said suddenly, the words slipping out before I could stop them.

Aiden's eyebrow quirked. "Uh-oh. That sounds dangerous."

I couldn't help but laugh, the sound feeling strange after the weight of our conversation. But there was something about the way he said it, that teasing edge to his voice, that made everything feel just a little bit lighter. Like maybe we hadn't fallen off the edge just yet.

"I've been thinking that we've been doing this wrong," I said, meeting his gaze.

"Doing what wrong?"

"This," I waved a hand between us, gesturing to the kitchen, the dimly lit room, the pile of dirty dishes by the sink, the fire crackling in the hearth. "We keep dancing around the truth. We keep saying we're fine, that everything is good, but we're not fine. And you know it. So I think we need to stop pretending."

There was a beat of silence, a long, drawn-out pause where I wondered if I had crossed some invisible line between honesty and madness. Aiden's face didn't change, not at first. He just stared at me, his gaze steady, the kind of gaze that made me feel like he could see every crack in my soul and still be willing to pick up the pieces.

"Maybe you're right," he said slowly. "But then again, maybe I've been waiting for you to figure that out."

I blinked, caught off guard by the simplicity of his response. There was no defensiveness in his tone, no accusation, just an observation, as though he had been waiting for the moment to come—not for my confession, but for my recognition.

"What do you mean?" I asked, my voice betraying me with a slight tremor.

"I mean, maybe we've been running around in circles because we've both been too scared to face the truth. And maybe the truth is that we're both terrified of what happens when we finally admit that this—" He gestured between us again, "—is everything. That we're not going anywhere, no matter how hard we try to convince ourselves we can."

His words were sharp, but there was no bitterness behind them. Only honesty, the kind of honesty that cut deeper than anything else we had shared. I swallowed, the tightness in my throat making it hard to speak.

"I'm not scared," I said, my voice barely above a whisper. "I'm not scared of us."

Aiden raised an eyebrow, a smirk tugging at the corner of his mouth. "Then why does it feel like we're teetering on the edge of something?"

"Because we are," I said, my breath catching. "But that doesn't mean I'm afraid. Not anymore."

There was a moment of stillness, the kind that made everything feel fragile, like a vase on the edge of a table just waiting for the wrong movement to send it crashing to the floor. Aiden's fingers twitched slightly, as though he was about to pull away, but he didn't. Instead, his gaze softened, and his voice dropped to a whisper.

"I never wanted to hurt you," he said, the words rough as if they were a confession he'd held in for far too long.

I shook my head. "You haven't hurt me. Not the way you think."

"You sure about that?" His eyes searched mine, searching for something—reassurance, maybe. Or the truth he thought he might not find in my words.

I nodded, though my insides twisted. "Yeah. I'm sure."

It was one of those moments where nothing could prepare you for what came next, where the ground beneath your feet shifted without warning. Aiden stood, his chair scraping against the floor, and for a split second, I wondered if he was leaving—if this moment was just the prelude to a final goodbye.

But then he reached out, his hand settling gently on my shoulder, the touch warm and grounding, and I saw something in his eyes that I hadn't seen before. It wasn't regret. It wasn't fear. It was something deeper, something that made my breath catch in my throat.

"I need to tell you something," he said, his voice low, the words coming out in a way that made the room feel smaller, more intimate, like the whole world had disappeared and it was just the two of us, standing on the edge of something impossible.

I felt a flicker of unease, that familiar knot forming in my stomach. "What is it?"

He hesitated for a moment, the air between us crackling with the weight of whatever he was about to say. And then, just as he opened his mouth to speak, the door behind us creaked, a soft sound that barely registered at first. But then came the unmistakable sound of footsteps—heavy, deliberate, like someone had entered without us noticing.

I turned toward the sound, my heart leaping into my throat.

Milton Keynes UK
Ingram Content Group UK Ltd.
UKHW030825181124
451360UK00001B/132